TRENCH 1915

THE DAWN OF
MODERN WAFARE

A NOVEL BY

JAKE BARRETT

ISBN 978-1-961093-10-2 (Softcover Book)
ISBN 978-1-961093-11-9 (eBook)

Published by Silversmith Press—Houston, Texas
www.silversmithpress.com

SILVERSMITH
PRESS

CONTENTS

PROLOGUE

Trench 1915: The Dawn of Modern Warfare is inspired by events that unfolded over a hundred years ago. Millions upon millions of soldiers would take part in this mighty struggle of this World War or the Great War.

This fictious adventure tale explores the possibilities of what a modern war would look like in various aspects and perceptions of fictitious characters. The characters and factions portrayed in this series are works of fiction, and any resemblance of our real historical figures and events are purely coincidental. The weapons, gear, and vehicles portrayed in this story are for educational purposes and no manufacturer had sponsored this book.

In June 1914, Archduke Franz Ferdinand, heir to the Austro-Hungarian throne, was assassinated by Gavrilo Princip, a Bosnian Serb nationalist who was then arrested. Austria-Hungary would send an ultimatum to the Kingdom of Serbia which eventually lead to the July crisis as a string of ultimatums, diplomatic communications, and threats that culminated in the outbreak of the First World War and would change the world forever. The events of late 1914 would end in a stalemate as the war of movement ceased and what followed would be hellish trench warfare.

Among the fires and embers of this developing war comes a secret elite military organization from the German Empire; a unit that performs clandestine operations or Black Ops, espionage, and other various forms as they conduct themselves to make attempt to change the course of the Great War. Most importantly, they must remain hidden from the public for they do not exist but, those in powerful positions such as the Kaiser, the Bundesrat (Federal council), and German high command are aware of their existence, for they are the ones who have given the approval to one intelligent yet ambitious officer for the creation before the war even started. This secret unit would be known as Kaiserliche Waffen Spezialisten Battalion or the K.W.S Battalion. This is their story.

Somewhere in the train station in Oppenheim a German officer holding files in his hand stands in wait for his train. He checks his watch to see the time.

"Hmm, train is running late," Jorgensen said to himself. Another Officer calmly walks up beside him. On his uniform was the rank of Major and he wore a monocle.

"Train is running late, huh captain...uh...apologies, I mean Commander Jorgensen."

"It's alright Reinhard, I know it takes some time to get usedtoit.It'sbafflingreally,"saidCommanderJorgensen.

"Too right, my friend. Two years ago, you were a Captain, then suddenly the unit you dreamed of creating gets the go ahead and you become a Commander. Certainly, interesting times we live in," Major Reinhard said.

"Came to see me off, Major?"

"As pleasant as it may sound but, no. I came here to ask why are you going? A Commander's place is away from the frontlines not close to it, especially in the Eastern Front."

"There is reason to why I'm going."

"And what's that?"

Commander Jorgensen handed the file to Major Reinhard. He took it and opened it and saw two small photos of two young soldiers and their description. The first one read:

Name: Friedrich Wilhelm Maxis
DOB: 11/20/96
Height: 6'0 Ft
Hair color: Brown
Eye color: Greenish blue
Build: Athletic
Language: German, English, and Russian.
National: German
Military unit: Kaiserliche Waffen Spezialisten Battalion
Rank: Sergeant
M.O.S: Classified

Siblings: One sister, Monika Maxis
In the photo Maxis is wearing his pickelhaube without the cover. Reinhard read the second file.

Name: Ludvig Hansel Lothar
DOB: 6/10/96
Height: 6'1
Hair color: Black
Eye color: Brown
Build: Strong
Language: German, English, French
National: German
Military unit: Kaiserliche Waffen Spezialisten Battalion
Rank: Corporal
M.O.S: Classified
Siblings: Two brothers

"Hmph, I remember these two. They blasted through the whole training and conditioning process in the span of three months. Sgt. Maxis was the very dedicated one, being able to figure things out quickly, and physically fit to the point of carrying a lot of gear with ease. Intelligent and strong, but I also heard he gained three nicknames during his fight in Belgium. Der Wolf, Black Wolf, and the Black Wolf of Mons. Then there's Cpl. Lothar. Strong, brave, and being right behind Maxis. Nothing here said anything in terms of titles or nicknames besides a heroic fighter in Tannenberg. I'm still curious on how they managed get through it and...oh, I see now. These two were trained by the legendary Sgt.

Kurtz before they even got recruited into the Battalion! God rest his soul." Major Reinhard finishes, with a look of surprise on his face and hands the files back.

"Correct Major. Our form of advance training was modeled by him and few other salty old, experienced sergeants."

"But that doesn't answer why you are going to the front, Sir?" Major Reinhard asked.

"Because I personally deployed those two to a quiet sector in the Eastern Front. Not to mention I am the Godfather to Maxis because of my friendship with his father."

"How so?"

"It's a long story, I'll tell it another time. Do not see it as form of favoritism, though I may be a hypocrite to that point but there have been strange reports regarding that area and so I'm giving them a real mission rather than the miscellaneous ones I've already bestowed upon them. They're ready and already skilled enough to get it done. Second, after the mission I intend to check on the construction of our other two bases in the east, Odin and Jotunheim."

Commander Jorgensen paused as the train finally arrived, screeching to a halt. Soldiers and officers disembark.

"It looks like your train is here, Commander. Atrociously slow if you ask me." Reinhard hands back the file.

"Indeed, I'll put in a request for our own train and probably our own rail system that can get us anywhere with better timing," Jorgensen said, as he stepped on the first step of train car. "Well, this is where we part ways my friend."

"True but, temporary. Though I strongly advise caution, Sir."

"Fear not, Reinhard. I'll be careful though. Who knows? Something might come out of this trip...shall we say a breakthrough on the Eastern Front? Then I would certainly be pleased since the Hapsburgs already have their backs against the Carpathians."

"If you were pleased then you would share that sentiment with nice bottle of wine." Major Reinhard smirks.

"Always the classic one, huh Major?"

"Always will be, even your wife would agree. Safe travels, Gott Mit Uns (God with us), Commander Jorgensen!" Major Reinhard bid, with a salute.

"Immer mit Präzision (Always with Precision), Major Reinhard." Jorgensen returned the salute, then boarded the train. The train leaves the station bound for the Eastern Front. Major Reinhard walks away and back to his private automobile.

With Jorgensen on his way to meet our two protagonists on the Eastern front, what lies within the frontlines is unknown, but what is known is that they will not be spending their time in war inside a...Trench.

CHAPTER 1

BEHEMOTH OF THE EAST

February 27th, 1915, Bochnia, near the Galician Front

"Being deployed to Austria-Hungary after joining and training with the Kaiserliche Waffen-spezialisten Battalion (Imperial Special Weapons Battalion) or the KWS battalion before being sent to Austria-Hungary under the orders by my godfather, Commander Jorgensen, was not how I wanted to spend my time during this war. We were stuck doing reconnaissance missions, support, and helping improve the Hapsburgs' lacking combat effectiveness. I guess that was the reward that Lothar and I earned for our bravery. My actions in Belgium during the Schlieffen Plan may have given me some recognition for my "strategic maneuvering," not always in the ways my commanding officer hoped, while leading my squad in taking vital key positions. As Lothar always said, "The actions of the few are more noticeable than the of actions of the many," Maxis entered in his journal.

During the Battle of Tannenberg, Lothar was part of a machine gun crew. Once, as he tells it, they were hit by an enemy shell during the Russian assault. After the shelling, two were dead, one was badly wounded, and Lothar received some shrapnel to parts of his left arm and leg. Lothar still got up and manned the machine gun. He managed to hold off an entire company of Imperial Russian infantry on his left flank.

It really takes two soldiers to man the machine gun, but Lothar can handle himself in situations like that. So, he loaded the gun, despite the pain he endured from his wounds, and he kept fighting. By the time the left flank was reinforced they found Lothar still clutching the machine gun and fifty meters in front of him lay two hundred fifty dead Russian soldiers, from the tree line to the open field. I'm quite curious what our first mission will entail. Though if I remember what Sgt. Kurtz told me, it is to be prepared for anything or anyone. Wish he was here now."
Maxis put his journal down and stood to attention with Lothar and saluted the Commander.

Commander Jorgensen walked into the tent. Both men held attention until the Commander returned their salute.

"I have a mission for you two, and a peculiar one at best. The scouts from the Austria-Hungarian 1st Army have reports of strange activities beyond the enemy lines. Reports state that large trees have been knocked down like dominos and the ground shakes at certain parts of the day besides the normal artillery hitting the battlefields," Commander Jorgensen finished.

"So, it's a Reconnaissance mission, Sir?" asked Maxis.

"No, this a search and destroy mission, Sergeant." Jorgensen continued, "The Austrian-Hungarian High command believes it to be nothing more than large troop movement and heavy equipment, but that's a load of exaggeration coming from Field Marshal Conrad von Hötzendorf himself. I believe there is more to this than meets the eye, that's why I'm going to send you two to investigate.

"The two of you are capable of infiltrating the Russian lines with or without the need of support from us or that of our allies. Once you get through their lines, gather as much enemy intelligence as you can and if possible, destroy whatever they are working on and come back to our lines safely. Any questions?"

The two responded with a crisp, "No Sir!"

"Report to Quartermaster Heinrich to receive your equipment and that is all. Dismissed!"

Lothar and Maxis salute again as the commander walked away.

"Search and destroy, huh?" Lothar asked. Maxis responded with a nod. "I guess we should go see what Heinrich has for us," says Lothar.

"You go ahead. I have to go survey the sector so we can make our approach." Maxis replied.

"Oh, so that's your excuse for not coming to get your equipment. Got it," Lothar nodded with a grin and walked away.

Lothar made his way to the tent where Heinrich was sitting. He walked in to be greeted by a man sitting at his desk and behind him are crates of weapons and ammo. Heinrich turned his head toward Lothar and asked with a smile, "To what do I owe the pleasure?"

"Heinrich, we're going to need the shipment that you received."

"Oh, what for?" he questioned.

"All I can say is that we need to infiltrate the Russian line."

"Well, that is the most insane mission I've ever heard, but alright," Heinrich rebutted.

"So, what do you have for us?" Lothar inquired.

"Hold on." Heinrich walked away then grabbed a large crate. "Here." Heinrich put the large crate on the table, then immediately used a crowbar to open it. "Alright, let's see what we have here," says Heinrich, as he reached into the hay-filled crate.

"Well, this is interesting. A well modified Madsen light machine gun," said Lothar as he focused his gaze on the gun. Heinrich continued to speak.

"Hmmm, this is an interesting design. Built-in wooden foregrip for increased control, painted reflex sight, and the barrel has been shortened by six inches."

"I like it already," Lothar responded, with a smile on his face.

"Well, she's all yours! Moving on." Heinrich reached in again to see what else was within the crate. "Well..." Heinrich paused just a moment as he pulled out a strange rifle with a large magazine.

"What is that?" Lothar asked.

"This is the Mauser M1913 Selbstlader (Self-loader)."

"How do you know that?" Lothar furrowed his brow questioningly.

"I didn't, just read the note that came with it.,'" Heinrich responded. "Here, take a look." He passed the note over.

The note read:

"Dear Sgt. Maxis,

I'm a representative of the Mauser company in Oberndorf. I've heard great things from Herr Jorgensen about your in accomplishments in Belgium and the special Battalion that you been enrolled in. My company is currently working on a couple of prototypes for the German Imperial Army. I've taken the liberty to let you have the privilege of trying out one of our new experimental rifles, the M1913 Selbstlader (self-loading) long rifle version. What makes this rifle unique is the detachable fifteen round magazine – not stripper clips, but a bona fide "magazine" and you can attach a bayonet lug at the end of the barrel as well. We do hope to hear some feedback about our rifle.

Respectfully,

Mayer Clausewitz

Representative, Mauser GMBH"

Lothar finished reading the letter and turned it to Heinrich and spoke. "That was interesting, and also why were you looking through his letter?"

"I was bored and there was nothing to read besides the shipment manifest," Heinrich responded with a smirk on his face. He shrugged his shoulders.

"Just be glad that we're not in Germany, otherwise this would be a federal crime," Lothar retorted.

"Anyway, here's the ammunition for the two of you, six magazines each, four new M1915 stick grenades. Which means the two of you get to use them first since there are delays that are preventing the rest of the Imperial German army from receiving them. Also, a prototype grenade discharger attachment, one magazine filled with blank munitions to help propel the grenade from inside the discharger, some dynamite, and 3 smoke grenades for the discharger!" Heinrich finished with a flourish of excitement.

"Alright, thanks." Lothar picked up the equipment and headed out of the tent.

Meanwhile, Maxis surveyed the area. He found the high ground and went as far as literally climbing a tree. He also studied battle plans and maps provided to him by Commander Jorgensen thoroughly for his operation. He memorized everything from troop movement to guard posting, to the highest concentration of troops and where they were located, and went so far as to stay up to date with Hapsburg scouts that had the latest intel from the field. Later he returned to the tent.

"This has to work," Maxis mumbled to himself and looked at the map on the table.

"We need to make this work, otherwise we'll end up dead for trying. Kurtz made it look easy, I just hope I can do the same," Maxis thought to himself.

"Delivery!" Lothar shouted as he walked into the tent carrying their equipment and gear.

"You're back already?" Maxis remarked sarcastically but with a smile.

"Of course, and I brought back many good gifts, courtesy of our friend Heinrich," Lothar says as he lays the bag down.

"Here's your gear and a special letter from the Mauser company."

"The Mauser Company?" questioned Maxis.

"It's better if you read the letter." Lothar handed him his letter. Maxis opened the envelope and began to read. Soon his expression changed from interest to surprise as he reached the end.

"An experimental rifle?" Maxis asked, as he picked the M1913 up with its sling. "Fascinating." He gripped the rifle and aimed it downward. "I've handled a self-loading rifle before, during my time in Belgium, though I sort of had to make a switch while the quartermaster wasn't looking. And I had to load it with stripper clips, but this is better," he remarks as he detached the magazine from the rifle.

"Well, at least you have some experience using these things in combat...As for me I'll stick with bolt-action rifles and machine guns," Lothar replied.

"So, when will this operation begin, Maxis?"

"We'll move at dusk," Maxis responded.

"Dusk? Why dusk?" He glanced up as he awaited the reply.

"From what I've gathered, there will be less activity on the Russian line, and ours too."

"Ok then, what happens if it gets too dark? There won't be a full moon tonight," Lothar questioned.

"We can't light our lanterns after we pass through their defensive line, so we have to memorize the sectors before dusk turn to night, Lothar."

"Alright, one more question if I may?"

"Shoot." Maxis shrugged.

"What happens if we run into the enemy?" Lothar asked.

"Our objective is to infiltrate their least defended line without attracting the attention of the entire Russian Army, but, if things get out of hand, then we'll have no choice but to go out guns blazing."

"Fine by me," Lothar said confidently.

"Good, let's get moving." The two walked out of the tent with their gear and equipment in hand to a safe vantage point overlooking the battlefield. There they waited till dusk.

"Are you ready?" Maxis asked, as he readied his rifle and placed the black fabric on his pickelhaube.

Lothar loaded a fresh magazine in his machine gun and cocked it, then replied, "Lead the way, Maxis."

"Alright, let's move," instructed Maxis.

As darkness drew near, they quickly made their way to the 1st Hapsburg trench line, passing Hapsburg troops as they sat and watched the Germans walk pass them. They heard the crushing of dirt beneath their boots along with that of gravel. Among the whispering pines and the sound of battle beyond the trench, the two find a nice spot in the forward observation trench. Maxis peered over the parapet carefully before ducking back down.

"Lothar, let our first infiltration begin," Maxis whispered.

"Understood, let's go," Lothar whispered back.

Maxis and Lothar began their approach as they climbed out of the observation trench. They crouched, moving quickly through the darkened field all the while avoiding the artillery. The explosions created by the bombardment light the way. As they kept moving, from time to time they stumbled over the fallen bodies of both Hapsburgs and Ruskies. Lothar raises a short prayer before he moved on.

"We're almost there, we just...quick, get down!" Maxis immediately dropped to the ground. Lothar followed suit as a ray of light shone over them. "Spotlights. Crawl slowly, move only on my mark..." Maxis whispered to Lothar.

"Alright," Lothar answered, his response barely audible. The spotlight passed over them again. Maxis snapped his fingers to give the signal after the spotlight passed. They continued a low crawl carefully through the dirt and paused when the spotlight came around again. Eventually, they made it to the blind spot where the spotlight could not shine on them.

In the Eastern front trench warfare was not entirely common. Both sides would still need to entrench themselves, though, temporarily. The trenches would span from five to ten feet wide depending on the situation. Maxis got up on one knee slowly and pulled up his binoculars.

"What do you see?" Lothar whispered.

"I can see the trench, but there's one problem."

"A problem?"

"It seems that we're either too late, or the damn Hapsburg scouts delivered outdated intel," Maxis said angrily. "There is a large concentration of Russian troops in that trench line."

"So, what do we do, Maxis?"

"The night is still young, and we've come too far to back out now...Lothar, get ready to run." Maxis reaches down for his satchel to grab the grenade discharger and fixes it on the rifle's muzzle. Then he reached down to his satchel again and grabbed a magazine with a painted white mark and three smoke grenades.

"I guess we still have a plan, Ja?" Lothar asked with confidence as he readied himself.

"Yes, we still have plan," Maxis answered, loading the magazine full of blanks.

"I'm going to fire three smoke grenades into their trench. We have a limited time before the smoke dissipates, so we'll run like hell. We must make a beeline to the heavily forested area," Maxis finishes.

"Ok, I'll follow your lead, just say when." Lothar replied.

Maxis took aim and fired the smoke grenade into the dimly lit trench, then follows it with the other two. A cloud of smoke appeared and the sound of panic and confusion from the Russian soldiers in the trench. Maxis quickly removed the grenade discharger and stuffed it back into his satchel.

"Los! Los! Los! (Go! Go! Go!)" Maxis ordered. Maxis and Lothar leapt up and ran straight to the trench. They built

22

momentum from sprinting and as they reached the trench while the Russians were distracted. They approached the front-line trench as the smoke cloud starts to clear.

"The smoke is clearing up!" observed Lothar.

"Then double time it!" Maxis yelled back. When they reached the trench Maxis ordered "JUMP!" and they leapt across the trench and landed heavily on the other side. and made a mad dash to the tree line. When the smoke cleared, a Russian soldier caught Maxis and Lothar running to the tree line and began yelling to his comrades as he pointed at the two Germans. They immediately opened fire.

"Maxis, one of them saw us!" cried Lothar, as bullets whistled pass them.

"Just keep moving, we'll be out of their sight soon enough!" Maxis responded as a bullet hit the tree next to him.

They reached the tree line and gained some cover from the foliage. Taking cover behind a tree, they paused to catch their breath and hide. Suddenly they heard chatter and leaves crunching, the soldiers fast approaching.

"Hold your fire. Let them pass," stated Maxis with a low tone.

The sound came from a group of Russian soldiers scouring the area for two German soldiers that gave them the slip. One soldier was armed only with a lantern flashlight, while the rest had their rifles. One of the men began speaking German in an attempt to draw them out.

Maxis and Lothar slowly and stealthily moved to get away from them as they drew near to their position.

Maxis found a large tree root and they hid behind it. A Russian soldier walked right by them. Maxis and Lothar held their breath and waited for him to pass. As the soldier leaned against the tree and lit a cigarette, Maxis heard the soldier muttering to himself.

"I don't understand why we're searching for two damn krauts or Hapsburg scum in the forest at night," muttered the Russian soldier. "We'll end up food for the wolves if we don't get out of here!" he continued and threw the cigarette to the ground, smashing it with his boot.

They heard a howl from afar, and the Russian soldier, spooked, quickly rejoined the group he left. Finally, others in the search party heard the howl and retreated to the line as well. After they left, Maxis and Lothar emerged from behind the tree root with a sigh of relief.

"That was too close. I think it is time we pause and collect our thoughts, Maxis."

CHAPTER 2

EYES OF WOLVES

"Agreed," Maxis responded, detaching the magazine full of blanks, cocking the rifle back ejecting the blank cartridge out of the rifle. He loaded the rifle with a new magazine with live ammunition.

Lothar set his tornister down and reached inside. He pulled out a flashlight first and handed it to Maxis, then an oil lantern with mirrors inside that project light for himself.

"Alright, we're all set," said Lothar, as he lit the lantern and attached it to his webbing.

"Ok, it's 0200 hours and our objective is 5 kilometers north of here. If my estimations are correct, we should be able to reach our destination in two hours at best," Maxis said, looking at his pocket watch. "Also keep your guard up, because that Ruskie said something about wolves roaming at this time of night."

"Understood," Lothar replied.

They began to walk to their destination with Maxis taking the lead and Lothar watching their backs. As they moved through the forest, the sounds of the night could be heard all around, including the sound of war far behind them. Another howl echoed through the forest and Lothar clenched his LMG tightly as he scanned their surroundings for any sign of trouble.

Two hours pass later Maxis and Lothar have yet to reach their destination.

"Something is not right here. The forest has gone completely silent and the only thing that can be heard are our own footsteps and the crunching of leaves. Suddenly I can feel a chill down my spine." Maxis thinks.

"Hold position," Maxis said, raising his hand. "Do you feel something wrong?" he asked and attached his bayonet to his rifle.

"Which one? The part about the forest going completely silent or do you think we're being hunted by someone or something?" Lothar responds.

"Both," Maxis replied and shone the flashlight around them and revealing the reflecting eyes of wolves surrounding them. The wolves gave off a vicious growl and slowly revealed themselves from the bushes. Their eyes were nothing short of an absolute predator looking for its next meal.

"I count five," Lothar said.

"Same," Maxis agreed.

The two readied themselves for the fight of their lives. Maxis fired the first shot, killing the wolf closest to him. Lothar fired his light machine gun into the pack, wounding several that were behind them. The rest of the pack immediately scattered into the darkness.

"I guess we drove them off," Lothar stated with confidence.

"No...It's not over. They're regrouping and are going to try again. This time without holding back," Maxis responded firmly. "We need to go now!" The two proceeded to move through the forest as quickly as possible.

Maxis and Lothar moved through the darkened forest with haste, then Maxis heard something moving toward him from his left. Out of nowhere, a wolf jumped from the shadows and attacked. Maxis managed to swing his rifle around in time, stabbing the wolf in the chest with his bayonet and firing a shot to get it off the blade.

A second wolf came out from the darkness and pounced on Maxis, catching him by complete surprise. Maxis hit the ground, losing his grip on his rifle, and barely kept the wolf's head away from his neck. He struggled to hold the wolf at bay as he tried to reach for his second knife hidden in his boot. The predator wildly gnashed its teeth in front of Maxis, its motivation for the kill insatiable.

Lothar fired a burst from his LMG, killing the wolf instantly. The wolf gave a yelp as it hit the ground dead. Quickly Lothar moved to Maxis to help him get up.

"I owe you one," said Maxis, getting up.

"You can buy me a beer later. For now, we have company," remarked Lothar, as he hands him his rifle.

The two stood back-to-back, readying their weapons, and Maxis shone his light into the darkness to reveal more glowing eyes. The wolf pack had returned. They began circling Maxis and Lothar with haste but

Lothar quickly reloaded his LMG with a fresh magazine and cocked it.

"Ready?" Maxis asked Lothar, while taking aim at one of the wolves.

"Ready when you are!" Lothar responded.

Maxis shouts out "Fire!" and the two unleashed a hail of bullets into the pack. Lothar killed the first three in the pack, then Maxis picked them off one by one and bayonets any wolves that get too close.

By the break of dawn, the small battle is over. The two German soldiers have almost exhausted their ammunition. Around them are spent cases of ammo, magazines, and the carcasses of the entire wolf pack, all twenty of them. Maxis and Lothar sat on the ground in exhaustion from the ferocious attack they endured from the wild animals.

"I had six mags, and now I have two left," said Maxis, as he looks through his bag.

"Same here."

"Hopefully, we don't run into any more trouble, because we won't be able hold off anything with this little ammo," Maxis says, as he removed his bayonet from the rifle and sheathed it.

"Well, we weren't expecting to fight an entire pack of wolves. Welcome to the Eastern Front," said Lothar.

"Either way, we still have a job to do. Let's make it count."

"Lead the way."

The two readied themselves and moved out. With the sun rising, their flashlights are no longer needed. It's

0600 hours, two hours past the estimated time of arrival. Maxis and Lothar stop to rest a little, knowing they were past harm's way for now. Lothar pulled out a blanket to rest on and Maxis sat against a tree, arms crossed. Their ten-minute rest now interrupted by low rumblings in the ground.

Maxis and Lothar got up quickly in response to the disturbance. The sound of falling trees can be heard in the distance and they watched a flock of birds fly away from the noise. While Lothar packed up, Maxis pinpointed the location of their objective.

"Judging by the direction the birds came from, our objective is north of our position," decided Maxis.

"Whatever our objective is, it's going to take lot more than some dynamite to destroy it," Lothar observed.

"Alright, let's get a move on." The two moved through the forest, north. As they went, they stumbled upon a lot of tracks.

"*Strange. It looks like a large Russian wagon convoy must have gone through here, but that doesn't explain how the trees got torn down in such a weird way nor any hoof prints to be seen,*" Lothar thought.

"Well, this is an unusual sight," pondered Maxis, as though it weren't obvious.

"You can say that again," Lothar agreed.

"Let's keep moving, we are getting close." They pressed on until they reached their destination. Maxis gave the signal to go prone and they slowly crawled to a big bush in front of them. As they move to the bush, they start to hear Russian voices chattering and shouting beyond it.

Maxis whispered, "Stop," as they entered the bush the leaves covered the two them. They are shocked by what they see. In front of them was an entire Russian military camp, set up with multiple tents, an ammo dump, and a large tent that Maxis assumed was a command post. He grabbed his binoculars to get a closer look.

"My God, they must have an entire Battalion out here," Lothar gasped in disbelief.

"Yeah, but why?" Maxis wondered, looking through the binoculars. Then the ground rumbled and shook again. "Where the hell is that coming from?" Maxis asked in frustration.

Lothar looked to the right and his jaw dropped in horror when he saw a gigantic machine 30 feet from their position roll right past them. He tugged Maxis' shoulder vigorously.

"What is it?" Maxis paused when he saw what Lothar was pointing at: a machine that looked like a tricycle with two giant wheels in the front and a tiny one in the back, armed with four machine guns around the top, two cannons on both sides of the wheels and at least four more machine guns around the under carriage.

"That is the biggest tricycle I've ever seen in my life," said Maxis.

"So, how are we going to do this, Max?" Lothar questioned.

"I already came up with a plan."

"Alright, let's hear it."

"This is what we're going to do. I'll make my way to the command post to steal any documents relating to the giant tricycle and hopefully not set off any alarms. Lothar, you take the explosives with you and start planting them at the ammunition dump; that way if we get caught, we'll have a diversion ready just in case," Maxis instructed.

"What about that hulking behemoth that's running around in the woods?"

"I'll think of something when I get inside the command tent; hopefully, it has a weakness so we can expose," Maxis replied.

"Okay, let's do this," Lothar responded eagerly.

Maxis nodded and slung his rifle to his back, then broke left into the enemy camp while Lothar went right. Moving very carefully, Maxis picked his way through the enemy encampment. He took cover behind supply boxes and barrels to avoid detection. At one point, a guard on his cigarette break blocked his way. Maxis had to find a way to get past without alerting him. Then, he spotted a half full vodka bottle and had an idea. He sneaked up on the guard and choked hold until he passed out. Then he placed the unconscious soldier on a chair behind a tent with the bottle in his hand.

Maxis thought to himself, *"so far so good. What else can they throw at me?"* Then the ground started to rumble, and the sound of trees being uprooted in the distance broke through his thoughts. Taking cover under a wagon, Maxis watched the mechanical monstrosity coming out of the forest.

The machine made a complete stop near the command post. Maxis saw ten men come out of the machine and form a line. A Russian officer exited his tent with his entourage of support staff and inspected the vehicle and the crew. Maxis took the chance and crawled out of the wagon, sneaking past them while they are chatting. He headed to the back of the tent, since the front entrance was still guarded, pulled out his bayonet and slowly cut a slit to crawl through.

Meanwhile, Lothar made his own way to the camp. He got to the ammo dump tent with ease and set up the charges. While he placed the charges, he noticed a crate labeled "Madsen Machine gun ammo 7.62x57" from the corner of his eye. Knowing that he exhausted his ammo dealing with the wolf pack earlier, he helped himself to some free ammo. He also picked up some smoke grenades for the return trip, and a new type of grenade. On the side of it he reads "incendiary." A big grin appeared on his face and he grabbed four of them.

"Nice, but I better save one for Commander Jorgensen to see when we get back from this mission," Lothar thought to himself as he saved one grenade in his tornister. Before Lothar leaves, he noticed a small green velvet chest on top of several boxes of ammunition. He walked toward it and opened it. A look of surprise crossed his face, but suddenly he saw five Russian soldiers moving slowly to the command post tent. "Scheiße (shit), Maxis," Lothar whispered quietly.

CHAPTER 3

THE ENEMY UNVEILED

Maxis had already entered the command tent. Checking his surroundings, he was astonished. The command tent had a lavish interior fit for an officer, complete with a nice carpet, a globe with a hidden mini-bar, and a war room with a table map that showed the area of operation. Maxis moved toward the war room and saw files and paperwork on the table.

"Nothing useful regarding the giant behemoth we saw, troop movement, or any form of intel. There must be something here,." Maxis thought.

Maxis noticed a desk with its drawer slightly open, right beside a bed. He rushed toward it and yanked it open. He is shocked to find a letter and a folder marked with the Russian Imperial seal, that says "konfidentsial'nyy (Confidential)" stamped in red. Maxis opened the letter first. It read:

"Colonel Vorshevsky,

We are glad to hear of the ongoing success of Lebedenko's creation on the field and hope to hear more. There is a bit of concern about your choice of the "testing ground" for Lebedenko's design or the 'Tsar tank'. It's not unknown that you chose to field test the armed version so close to the front. Please note we are still testing the unarmed version back at Moscow through various terrain trial runs to find any weaknesses. So far, we have discovered the obvious, that the machine is prone to getting stuck in mud if driven through it. We nearly got it stuck during one trial run. Second, the vehicle itself can be vulnerable to artillery fire from the enemy. The only flaw in design is the rear wheel being too heavy, which can create the problems mentioned previously. We hope you have returned with good results regarding newfound tactics with the second prototype, as well as the armament fitted with it.

Respectfully,

Major Makarov,

Imperial Russian High Command"

Next, Maxis opened the folder. He sees schematics regarding Lebedenko's creation. It's armed with four Maxim M1910 machine guns at the top and at the bottom. The bottom can provide covering fire for advancing troops. It's also armed with two British ten-ponder guns on flanks.

"*Finally!*" Maxis said to himself, putting the documents and schematics in his bread bag. "*Now I need to get back to Lothar so we can try to destroy this tank before they can unleash it, .*" he thought. Almost immediately, Maxis felt the cold steel of a rifle barrel on the back of his neck.

"Don't even move. Put your hands where I can see them," said a soft but serious female voice. Maxis froze with his hands in the air. Then, he heard the sound of someone slowly clapping behind the mysterious woman, along with boot steps.

"Well done, Sergeant. I might say your skills are impressive. Not only did you pass through our lines, but here you are standing in my personal tent stealing from me. I must say I am utterly impressed; however, my little scout says otherwise. Oh, but where are my manners? I'm Colonel Vorshevsky, the commander of the Imperskiy Tayna Brigada, or the Imperial Secret Brigade."

Maxis remained silent. More guards entered the tent with rifles drawn on Maxis.

"Turn around slowly, Sergeant." Colonel Vorshevsky commanded.

Maxis turned slowly and looked at Colonel Vorshevsky and the scout. Colonel Vorshevsky towered Maxis. He was tall fellow with a well-groomed beard, brown eyes, and brown hair and appeared to be in his forties. Maxis takes a good long look at the scout. She is wearing a dark green gymnasterka (military tunic) with brass buttons, black trousers with a red stripe on the side, black military boots, and a small shako cap that looks Prussian except this one has the Russian double head eagle. Her crimson red hair is tied in a bun and she has violet eyes that Maxis never has seen before, The two stared at each other for a moment before quickly looking away.

"*Such a beauty, yet so deadly. I'll have to think of something fast,*" Maxis thought to himself. "You knew I was coming. May I ask how?" Maxis asked.

"Well, I will allow her to answer that question," Colonel Vorshevsky replied, looking at his scout. She nodded at the Colonel, then turned to Maxis and began to speak.

"Some Austrian deserters informed our officers about a special German detachment sent here to assist. When the Colonel got wind of this, he sent me to investigate. I stayed behind the line, out of sight of my own brothers and your sentries, so I could observe. When dusk came, I climbed a tree and rested a bit, ignoring the explosions, gun fire, and shouts from the battlefield. That is, until I started hearing bullets whistling below. I saw two dark figures run right past the tree I was in, accompanied by a group of soldiers with flashlights chasing after them. So, I followed, staying out of sight, and waiting until the squad left. Finally, you emerged from the shadows, igniting your flashlight and lantern. I stayed on your trail until the wolves caught your scent and surrounded you. I thought my job was done, but I was wrong. When I saw you and your comrade had fought off the wolves and proceeded to advance. I was somewhat impressed," she concluded.

"So, you had been following us up until a certain point and retreated just so you could strike at the right moment? That explains why we felt like someone was watching us before the wolf attack."

"That's right, Sergeant. Now I have a question for you. Where is your other comrade?" she asked. Before he could answer, he sees a small glimmer through the entrance of the tent out to the tree line.

"It's Lothar, and he's signaling me with a small mirror reflecting the sun in Morse code. He is trying to say something...Get...Ready...To...Run."

Suddenly came the sound of a huge explosion, followed by smaller ones. Everyone in the tent turned toward the noise, including the scout for a moment. Maxis seized his chance and sprinted past the scout and everyone in their tent. Outside, he quickly readied his rifle.

Making his shots count, he rushed to Lothar's position. Maxis killed several Imperial Russian soldiers. He stabbed an officer with his bayonet then held him as a shield. Several soldiers fired at Maxis, missing him but killing the officer. Using the officer's Nagant revolver Maxis returned fire.

Lothar provided covering fire from his position on the hill. He fired in short bursts and suppressed the on-coming Russian forces. Maxis made it to Lothar's position and the two ducked behind the hill for cover and reloaded their weapons.

Lothar spoke first. "What do you think of my fireworks display, Maxis?"

"A work of art, my friend," Maxis responded.

"I assume you have an escape plan?" Lothar inquired.

Maxis looked over the hill and saw the entire camp in chaos with the majority of the tents on fire. The commanding officers struggled to maintain order. Maxis spied a couple of horses tied to a hitching post. Maxis ducked down, then turned to Lothar.

"We will use those horses to get out of here. That is our exit strategy."

"I like it. Always wanted to ride a horse." Lothar admitted with a bit of joy.

"Well, here is our chance. We move on three." There was a short pause until they both yelled "Three!"

They made a mad dash to the horses, past burning tents. They unhitched the horses from their posts in a hurry but calmed them down a bit before mounting. The two mounted up and Lothar shouted "YA!" to get the horses moving. They rode to the tree line with haste and kept riding until the sound of chaos was far behind them.

Standing outside of the command tent, the scout looked through her binoculars. "We will meet again soon enough, Maxis," she said to herself. Colonel Vorshevsky walked up beside her.

"They have escaped, Sir," the scout complained.

"No matter. They will meet their end soon enough. I believe the time has come that we unleash the Tsar's greatest weapon yet. Not only are we at war with the Central Powers, but we are at war with another military organization just like ourselves. The will of the Russian Empire and her people depend on us. We will not fail."

"Well said, Father," answered the scout.

"Junior Sergeant Arina Vorshevsky, I am placing you in charge of the upcoming shock operation that we will launch very soon. You will provide support with the Tsar tank during the assault. You know where Maxis and his Lapdog came from, and I am sure you'll be able to track them down. I shall send a telegram to the division commander in this sector so he can be notified of our activities. Any questions?" Colonel Vorshevsky asked.

"When do we begin?" Arina responded with a smirk.

"In two days. Any more questions?" Colonel Vorshevsky paused only briefly before finishing, "Then dismissed, Sergeant." Arina stood to attention and saluted. Colonel Vorshevsky returned her salute and walked back inside the command tent. Arina headed back to her own private tent to gear up and get ready for the shock operation.

Meanwhile, Maxis and Lothar slowed down a bit after they made some distance between them and the Tayna Brigade camp. They stopped to let their horses rest and dismounted. Lothar sat on the ground, and Maxis leaned against a tree then reached down to his bread bag to pull out the files he stole from the Colonel.

"Maxis, I must ask, what the hell happened in there? First, I saw you sneak inside the tent with no problem. Then five minutes later, after I set the charges, I saw multiple guards moving toward the tent. I thought you were a goner; that is, when I didn't hear any gunshots," said Lothar.

Maxis explained as he put the files and documents aside, "I thought my small infiltration would not bring any attention. I was wrong. Somehow a female Russian scout managed get the drop on me."

"A female scout?" Lothar interrupted.

"Yes, I can hardly believe it, either. She is also the one that stalked us before the wolves attacked. If she can sneak up on me that easily, who knows what else she is capable of. Also, we are not the only special unit operating in this war. I had a nice chat with Colonel Vorshevsky while I was at gun point by the scout and the guards. We are dealing with The Imperskiy Tayna Brigada, with Vorshevsky as its commander. Before I was caught, I managed to grab these documents regarding that Behemoth we saw," Maxis finished.

"Well, that is interesting indeed," Lothar remarked, as he sipped from his canteen.

"Oh, before I forget, I got something courtesy of the Tayna Brigade." Lothar put down his tornister, opened it, and reaches down to grab two unique pistols along with some ammunition.

"I recognize these models! I am quite surprised that they got their hands on them. Here I have a Borchardt C-93 semi-automatic pistol and the other is Bergmann-Bayard M1910," Lothar explained.

Maxis grabbed the C-93 and the ammo for it. He put the Nagant revolver he had held on to from his encounter with the Russian officer into his rucksack, then placed the new pistol in his holster.

"I have one more thing to give you," Lothar says, reaching down into his tornister one more time.

"Goodness, Lothar, since when did you become Saint Nick?" Maxis joked. Lothar hands him three smoke grenades and one incendiary grenade, explaining to Maxis about the special grenade.

Maxis thanked Lothar for the new tools. He picked up the files and documents that he set aside so he can go over them again to understand the Tsar tank a bit more. After looking through the documents, two letters fell out.

"Huh?" Maxis wondered, as he picked them up.

"What is it?" Lothar asked.

Maxis did not answer but opens one of the letters and begins to read. "This one is a requisition order for those two pistols," Maxis began, "One of them is supposed to belong to the good Colonel and the other one..." Maxis paused for a moment.

"What of the other one?" Lothar prompted.

"The other one belongs to Junior Sergeant Arina Vorshevsky. So, the scout is the daughter of the Colonel. Well, this is not all that bad, at least we know the identity of the mysterious woman. The second letter is addressed to the scout as well. Though this one must be a personal one, because this says, 'From Mama,'" Maxis stated.

"This is interesting, but may I suggest that we get a move on. The last thing I want is to get surrounded by a pack of wolves again," Lothar said, Maxis nodding in agreement.

The two packed up their things and mounted up. They proceeded down the path they came from last night, until they stumbled upon a noticeable landmark. Lying before them are the decaying corpses of the wolf pack they fought last night. The foul smell of dried blood and death is in the air as they pass through. Then, suddenly, Maxis hears the whimpering cry of a wolf pup.

"Hold on, Lothar." Maxis stops and dismounts. Lothar held his position to see what he is doing. Maxis moved carefully through the corpses and found a little wolf pup next to what appears to be its deceased mother. Maxis knelt slowly so as not to scare the little pup.

"Lothar, pass me the meat rations," he softly asked. Lothar handed them to him.

Maxis took a piece and held it out to the pup. The wolf pup takes notice and slowly approaches Maxis with curiosity. The pup sniffed the meat rations and immediately began to consume it. After it finished eating, it wagged its tail and panted with excitement.

"I hope you know what you are doing, Maxis. That's no ordinary dog, that's literally a wolf's pup. Do you think you can tame it?" Lothar questioned.

"What? Do you suggest we just leave him here? Commander Jorgensen used to train guard dogs in his early years in the Imperial army, so I am sure he can train this one. Plus, he might make a fine addition to K.W.S. or the two of us," Maxis responded, as he picked up the little pup.

"I like the idea of having our own attack dog, but a wolf?" admits Lothar.

"Sure, why not?" Maxis responded, smiling as the little wolf pup licked his nose.

"Alright, Maxis if you're ok with this then so am I," said Lothar.

"Ok, playtime is over. I know where to put you so you will be safe," Maxis said, as he put the pup into his rucksack. After putting the pup in, its little head popped out of the top. Maxis mounted up and the three continued the path, until they make it to a point where they can hear gunfire and explosions in the distance.

"So, how do we get past them this time, Max?" Lothar asked.

"We could rush right pass them with the horses." Maxis responded back.

"I see. We use the smoke bombs and the new stick grenades, throw them into their trenches and then ride like the wind back to our lines," Lothar finished.

"That sounds like it can work perfectly, Lothar," Maxis agreed.

"Really? I thought that would be something you would come up with. I guess your influence is making me think for once," joked Lothar.

"Well, thank you. I am not one for role modeling, but it has its perks," Maxis replied. They continued their ride until the sound of battle can be heard.

Maxis immediately raised his hand in a fist form, telling Lothar to stop. Then he grabbed his binoculars from his bread bag. He looked through them and can see the battlefield, along with a small trench network, with the Russians already garrisoned there. There is also a rear guard posted behind the trench network.

"Ok, here's how we are going to do this. Lothar, you will be the one tossing those grenades while I cover you. I only have one magazine left so let's make it count. Are you ready?" Maxis asked.

"Let's do this!" Lothar replied with excitement as he prepped the stick grenades.

Maxis yells "ADVANCE" and the two gallop their horses toward the Russian trench. Maxis quickly dispatches the rear guards with his Mauser M1913 while

Lothar pulls the pin on the smoke bombs and then the stick grenades. The smoke bombs created a large fog of smoke from the trenches along with the sound of explosions and flashes from the stick grenades. The screams and shouts of Russian soldiers can be heard as the fragmentation grenades go off and the smoke bombs cover the trenches.

As their horses jumped over the trenches, Maxis provided covering fire until he ran out of ammo then switches to his pistol. After getting past the trench network, they were now entering no-man's land. The sight of dead bodies, scattered equipment, and shell holes is an unpleasant sight for Maxis and Lothar, but they press on to avoid artillery from both sides. Maxis felt a little jolt on his shoulder and taps on his lower leg but ignored it as he rides away.

Meanwhile, back at the Austro-Hungarian lines, Commander Jorgensen is with the troops watching through his binoculars.

"Are you sure they are coming back, Commander?" asked an Austro-Hungarian officer.

"They are coming. Have faith, Major," Jorgensen responded.

"How can I have faith in group of soldiers from a Battalion I have never heard of going up against The Great Russian Bear and expect them to return? Why should I take orders from you? Just because you are under the thumb of the German Kaiser does not mean you have full jurisdiction over my unit, Commander Jorgensen!" the Major retorted.

"I'll ignore your lack of self-control, Major. We were sent here to assist in your current operations because of your military leader's severe incompetency. I made the decision to send a small detachment of the battalion's best to assist you. Now we are dealing with a threat that the Russians might do something that can change the war. So yes, Major, I am entitled to command the soldiers in this area under my jurisdiction because of the continued military failures your Empire seems to display. There is my reason, and if you so much as step out of line again, I will have you court martialed for insubordination. Now, be ready to order your men to cease fire once they are in sight," Commander Jorgensen finished.

"Yes, Sir," said the Major begrudgingly.

Five minutes later, a soldier shouts out saying he sees someone on horseback approaching their lines. Commander Jorgensen rushed over and looks with binoculars and saw Maxis and Lothar approaching. He turned to the Major and told him to order his men to cease fire. The officer does so with haste. The men lowered their weapons and waited until the hooves can be heard. Then two horses come into sight, jumping over the trench line and putting the soldiers in a bit of shock.

"Whoa!" shouted Maxis, as the horse grinds to a halt. Lothar follows suit, making his horse stop in its tracks. The two dismounted only to hear the cheers of some soldiers for their return. Commander Jorgensen walks to them quickly.

"Do you have the Intel?" Commander Jorgensen asked firmly, as he approaches Maxis.

"We got it, Sir," Maxis reported, and handed him the documents.

"Good. Then we are making great progress, Sergeant," Commander Jorgensen replied.

Two soldiers appear behind them to take the horses away. Lothar handed the commander the incendiary grenade he took from the camp and explained. Jorgensen nodded and stated they will be sent to R&D when this mission is over.

Maxis started to feel a bit of pain in his left shoulder and lower leg, but again he ignores it. Then he pulled out the wolf pup from his rucksack. The little pup began to run around and yelp with joy. When Jorgensen began to speak, Maxis and Lothar stood to attention.

"What you did today would be considered insane in the eyes of military officials. This is a great feat that the two of you have performed. I also see you brought back a new friend from your operation, though I'm sure you'll have an explanation for this 'pup' after the debrief. You will have to fill out a report of your findings to the High Command. Is there anything you wish to say before I dismiss you?" Commander Jorgensen inquired..

"Sir, we may be dealing with a special unit from the Russian Empire and...and..." Maxis couldn't finish his sentence before he appeared to lose focus.

"Is there something wrong, Sergeant?" Commander Jorgensen asked.

"Maxis, are you alright?" Lothar repeated with concern. The sound of Lothar shouting his name becomes distorted as Maxis blacks out and collapsed to the ground.

Maxis are on alright?" contain reported with concern
The sound of Lothar shouting his name becomes
distorted as Maxis blacks out and collapsed to
the ground

CHAPTER 4

RECOVERY BEFORE COMBAT

Two Days Later...

Maxis woke up in the medical tent with his left shoulder and lower leg bandaged. He saw the pup sleeping beside him and the medic writing on his clipboard.

"Oh, you're awake. Don't worry, you're in a safe place now," reassured the medic.

"What happened?" Maxis asked.

"You had a couple gunshot wounds on your left shoulder and lower leg. From the look of it, you were bleeding badly before I could patch you up. Combined that with a little bit of exhaustion and that's what led to you passing out. I'm glad that you didn't die on my watch," replied the medic.

"I didn't even feel the bullet hit me but did feel a bit of pain when I got back."

"That was probably the adrenaline rush that managed to conceal the pain of the bullet wound during your return trip from no-man's land." The medic finished his diagnostics.

"How long am I stuck here?" Maxis inquired.

"It's already been two days. A wound like that takes a day or two so the wound can heal up. Other than that, you should be good to go," the medic responded.

"I'll go inform the Commander that you are awake and..." the medic is interrupted as Commander Jorgensen enters the room.

"Good, you're awake, thank God," said Jorgensen. "Gave us quite the scare you did, even made your corporal worry to death, but you're alive and that's what counts. Let's cut to the chase. You said earlier we have a rival special unit in the Russian Empire. Who are they?" Commander Jorgensen asked.

Maxis explained the existence of the Tayna Brigade and their purpose in the war, which would help Jorgensen understand why Tsar tank was being tested so close to the battlefield. Maxis gave more details on the leadership of the Tayna Brigade, especially details of a father-daughter connection between a colonel and a scout. This intrigued Jorgensen and concerned him knowing that the Tsar had deployed his own special weapons unit.

"I'll be sure to let High Command know of this and send a coded message to the rest of the battalion to be wary when operating on the eastern front. I will inform them to not engage in combat with this particular purple-eyed redheaded femme fatale striking a green tunic, and a shako cap. I'll put in a capture order as well since she is likely to have more intel on this Tayna Brigade. There is one matter you need to attend to," Commander Jorgensen says and points to the yawning pup.

"Lothar already told me how you acquired the little bastard. My question is what are you planning to do with it?" Commander Jorgensen asked.

"Didn't you once train guard dogs in your earlier years in the military, Sir?"

The Commander sighed. ""Sigh Sometimes I wish I didn't tell your parents of my early occupations. Yes, I did," Commander Jorgensen responded as he lit his wooden pipe. "If you want me to train him, I'm afraid I won't be able to. As you can see, I'm managing an entire Battalion, but I know someone who can," Commander Jorgensen explained as he smokes. "There are Militarpolizei (military police) who can help train your little monster. His name is Pvt. Bartek. I'll make a transfer request so he can be a part of the K.W.S. Battalion. There is just one more thing. Have you given your pet a name?" Commander Jorgensen took another tug on his pipe.

"Ulf. His name is Ulf," Maxis replied, holding the pup.

"Ulf is a good name for him. I'm sure he'll turn out to be very helpful." said Commander Jorgensen.

Suddenly, several explosions can be heard outside of the medical tent. Maxis, still holding Ulf, takes cover. Commander Jorgensen and the medic follow suit quickly. The artillery barrage lasts for ten minutes, then it stops. The three get back on their feet.

Maxis and Commander Jorgensen quickly realized that the barrage was a warmup for a big offensive. Maxis handed the medic the little wolf pup and went to the trunk at the end of his bed where his tunic and gear are stored. Opening it, he put on his Feldgrau (Fieldgrey) M1907 tunic, a pistol holster he wears across his chest, his military webbing, and the rest of his gear, pocket watch, C-93 pistol, and pickelhelm.

"Can you keep an eye on Ulf for me while I deal with the Russians?" Maxis asked the medic while he gears up. The medic nodded in response.

"I'll go to the Command tent to try to correspond with the other units. Hopefully we can get a grasp on the situation. As for you, Sgt. Maxis, link back with Cpl. Lothar at the trench line to assist the Austro-Hungarian soldiers in defense of this sector," Commander Jorgensen ordered.

"Yes Sir!" Maxis responded affirmatively.

The two bolted out of the medical tent and headed in separate directions. Maxis, without a rifle, sprinted to trenches as the Hapsburg soldiers shouted commands as they got to their battle stations. Maxis can see Quartermaster Heinrich handing out rifles and ammunition to the troops lined up with such speed, like handing candy to children except with high caliber bullets.

Maxis sees Lothar waving him down. He quickly moves to his position and jumps into the trench. He turns to Lothar and asks, "Lothar, what's going on here?"

"Oh, thank God you're up and going! I was just sitting here cleaning my gun until I started hearing the sound of artillery, then the whistle of a shells about to make impact," Lothar responded. "Where is the Commander?"

"He went to the command post tent to find out if other friendly sectors are experiencing the same attack," Maxis responded while readying his pistol.

"Oh, that reminds me, here's your rifle," Lothar said, as he handed Maxis his custom Mauser M1913 along with sixteen magazines.

"I took the liberty of trying to clean the damn thing while you were out and boy, this thing is complicated. I had to ask Heinrich to assist me," explained Lothar. Maxis thanked Lothar as they got into battle position. Several Hapsburg soldiers join them with their rifles at the ready. Suddenly, everything is quiet.

Then comes sound of Russian soldiers yelling out "URA" several times, before the trench whistle blew, and the infantry started going over the top while screaming out their war cry and charging toward Maxis and Lothar's position. Maxis fixes his bayonet quickly while they approach.

"Get to ready to fire on my mark, Soldaten(soldiers)!" Maxis shouts to the troops. Some of them understood while others had to make gestures to others who can't understand or did not speak the speak the same language.

"They are getting too close Max...just say when..." Lothar says as he aims down the sight of his machine gun.

"Steady, steady...OFFENES FEUER MÄNNER (OPEN FIRE MEN)!" As Maxis shouts, they start to receive rifle fire from the oncoming Russian troops.

Everyone in the trench to opened fire. Maxis and Lothar lay down a hurricane of gunfire. The two's kill rate is significantly higher than the rest that are with them in the trench. The Hapsburgs were suffering heavy casualties, but Maxis and Lothar made up those losses by making the Russians pay for it in blood every step of the way. Lothar does most of the damage with his modified Madsen Machine gun. He fires in controlled bursts, taking down rows of enemy troops. Maxis uses his impeccable marksmanship, scoring multiple kill shots on infantry and officers alike, especially on the officers, which causes bit of confusion among ranks, making them easier targets.

Before they know it, thirty minutes have passed, and the Russians have had enough and begin to fall back after suffering severe casualties. The surviving defenders cheer in joy, as they have just held the line. All except for Maxis and Lothar.

The barrel on Lothar's Madsen is glowing orange, and he is surrounded by spent shell casings strewn about their position. Maxis has empty magazines, and his bayonet is covered in blood. In front of them lay dozens of now deceased Russian soldiers, some of them in the trench itself.

"Lothar, you have seen this before. Is it over?" Maxis asked, as he loaded another magazine into his rifle.

"Nein...this was just the first wave; more will come. Though we fared better than the Hapsburgs,"

Lothar responded, as he poured water on his LMG to cool down.

"MAXIS! LOTHAR!" Commander Jorgensen shouted as he passes a trail of wounded soldiers falling back from the trench line.

"Sir!" responded Maxis, as he stood to attention. Lothar does the same.

"I got some good news and some bad news," Jorgensen continued. "The good news is the other sectors on this front are not experiencing any type of large-scale offensive. The bad news is that I have a clear idea who's leading this attack. I believe the Tayna Brigade is spear heading this assault. There is no doubt they will try to break this line. Even worse, they might try to unleash that experimental weapon they have on us," Commander Jorgensen finished.

"Hey. There's something in the tree line!" A soldier shouts out just before his head jerks back as he falls to the ground dead.

Commander Jorgensen, Maxis, and Lothar duck down into the trench. Maxis slowly pops his head out with his binoculars. He sees the outline come out of the tree line, then the ground starts to tremble.

The Tsar tank makes its appearance with its engines roaring and the sound of trees crashing. Accompanying the Tsar tank is a platoon's worth of the Tayna Brigade's soldiers, armed with their standard issued M1891 Mosin Nagant rifles, some armed with double barrel shotguns, and the last few armed with some Chauchat LMGs. Maxis sees a strange figure standing on the top center of the tank.

"Arina Vorshevsky," Maxis whispered to himself.

Arina can see Maxis from where she stands on the Tsar tank and immediately takes aim with her imported Winchester M1895 lever action rifle, but he takes cover quickly when they both make eye contact through their scopes. The Tsar tank stops and opens fire on the entire Austro-Hungarian trench with its sponson cannons and machine guns, inflicting large amount of damage.

"I hope you have a plan for dealing with that behemoth before it runs right through us," Commander Jorgensen asks, in bit of concern.

"We can try to lure them away from our base of operations and lead them to where the artillery positions are at. That way it will be in the open for the artillery to disable the Tsar tank and we can go in with the dynamite to finish it off." Maxis thought up that plan in the nick of time. He relayed his plan to Commander Jorgensen and Lothar.

"That's insane, but give it your best shot, Maxis. I'll inform the rear artillery line and tell them to hold position until you arrive. Good luck!" said Commander Jorgensen as he walked away to the command tent, ignoring the explosions all around.

"Lothar, let's gather the remaining Habsburgs. I know perfect spot in the tall grass where we can draw that thing's attention," Maxis said to Lothar.

Maxis and Lothar went regroup what's left of the decimated Austro-Hungarian defenders and lead them away from the trenches to a spot. They all get into position and wait. The ground starts to tremble once more as a clear sign the tank is on the move. They ready themselves and await Maxis' signal.

The Tayna Brigade moves through no-man's land unopposed. Arina disembarks from the tank to move ahead. She is surprised to find the trench line is deserted and still littered with bodies of dead Habsburg and Russian soldiers. The rest of her platoon joins her, along with the Tsar tank tower over them.

"Tch, now where have you gone?" she muttered.

A fellow soldier walked up to her and gave her a report. "We checked all over this line there is no one left except for a few..." He doesn't finish his sentence as a bullet rips right through his chest. He falls flat on the ground. Arina wipes the speckles of blood from her face and looks to the direction where that shot came from. She sees Maxis waving with a grin on his face before clenching his fist.

Immediately Lothar and a group of Austro-Hungarian soldiers appear out from the tall grass. The soldiers shout, "For the Daul Monarchy!" as they begin to open fire. Arina goes prone and returns fire. Soon, the rest of platoon does the same and the Tsar tank repositions itself and unleashes its side guns and machine guns.

Immediately Maxis' group started to take heavy fire from the oncoming barrage as bullets whistle past them and tank shells explode beside them. The group consists of fifteen men, including Maxis and Lothar, but one by one they begin to fall, until there are only five of them left.

"Retreat to the Artillery line, let's go!" Maxis orders.

They immediately go to a full retreat to the artillery positions. The small platoon detachment of Tayna Brigade also suffered casualties. The last remaining soldiers of the platoon fall back behind the Tsar tank as it charges forward. Arina disappears from the battle.

The remaining five soldiers make a mad dash to the fallback position with the Tsar tank not too far behind. It continues to rain down fire from its two ten pounder guns. The group keeps running as fast as they can until they lose sight of the behemoth. Finally, they make it to the artillery.

"We're here but where the hell is everybody?" Lothar asked as he looks at the deserted guns.

Maxis notices a field artillery officer waving at them and surrounding him are bodies of deceased Austro-Hungarian artillerymen. They move quickly to the field officer before anything happens to him. They introduce themselves.

"What's your name and what happened here?" Maxis asked, as he looks at the dead.

"I'm Second-lieutenant Andris. We suffered a surprise attack from the enemy," the officer responded. "We heard the barrage and began getting ready to provide artillery support. We waited for command to give us coordinates, until one of my men fell while he was carrying one of our shells. I thought he just tripped until I saw a bullet hole in his head. Then I heard gunshots and more of my men started going down. Instead of defending the guns, the rest panicked and hightailed it out of here, leaving me with the guns. I waited for the

Russians to come out but all I saw was a strange Russian soldier in a green tunic sprinting away."

"Verdammt (Damn it), she beat us to the artillery," Maxis thought to himself. He then turned to Lothar and the others. He simply asked, "How do you guys feel about operating the big guns?"

One of the soldiers stepped forward and spoke, "We will give it our best shot, if it means killing that monstrosity."

"Wait, what monstrosity?" the officer asked.

"I'll brief you on the way Second Lieutenant. I'll keep these guys safe while they operate the gun, Maxis," Lothar said.

"But what are you going to do Sergeant?" another soldier asked.

"I'm going to wait for them to come out and deal with any remaining foot soldiers left. The four of you need to get that artillery piece ready before they get here," Maxis directed, and the soldier nodded his response.

Maxis moved out. Lothar and the rest moved to the artillery. When Lothar's group was in position, they readied the 12 cm Kanone M80 siege gun.

The field artillery officer gave instructions to the group on what to do. Lothar grabbed the crate filled with armor piercing shells and high explosives rounds while the others prep the siege gun. Maxis slowly walked to the center of the field and crouched down. He waited for a bit with his rifle on his right and his left hand to the ground, trying to feel for the tank's presence. He took a deep breath and readied himself as the ground began to shake.

"This is it..." Maxis thought to himself. He took aim with his rifle and waited. The shaking stops. Suddenly he sees the first Russian soldiers wearing dark brown khaki appear through the bushes. There is a squad of ten. Maxis aims for the soldier in the front and fires the first shot.

The Tayna soldier jerked back and fell down dead. The other soldiers took notice. One shouts in Russian, points at Maxis, and opens fire. But Maxis kept his cool and continued firing until the entire scouting party is dead. When it is over, he checked himself to see if he is hit, then reloaded his rifle and readies for a full-on assault.

He waited again until a bullet flew right over his head. The shot came from his right flank. Maxis repositioned himself and got ready. The Russians burst out of the tree line screaming and shouting "URA!" Maxis took aim and fired. There were twenty of them charging at Maxis, with bayonets affixed to their rifles. Maxis managed to take down the first five, before slowly moving back, continuing fire. He lies prone to avoid one of the Russians' LMGs firing on his position. Six of them are closing in on him. Suddenly an explosion blasts out of nowhere, taking out three of the enemy soldiers and knocking the rest off their feet. The explosion comes from Lothar's group, firing the artillery with success.

Maxis gets back up and fires on the three remaining Russians in front of him. After finishing them off, he hears a small chuckle behind him. He turns to it's one of the machine gunners with his Chauchat, pointing directly at Maxis. The machine gunner grunts, "Umri, suka (Die, you bitch)!" and pulls the trigger. But he hears a click. His weapon is jammed with dirt. He switches to his side arm but Maxis takes the opportunity to fire one shot right between his eyes.

"That was close," Maxis mumbled, taking a moment to breathe.

The remaining eight Russians gathered themselves up for one more attack, this time with the Tsar tank approaching. A trench whistle can be heard, and the ground began to shake. The Tsar tank broke through the trees with great force. It advanced with the remaining squad on to Maxis' position. Maxis made an immediate tactical withdrawal back to Lothar's position.

Meanwhile at back, the artillery officer is looking through his binoculars. He could see Maxis running back to them. "I can see the Sergeant coming back, boys," said the artillery officer. He checked again and his jaw dropped as he sees a massive structure on wheels appearing out of the tree line.

"We got company and it's a big one!" yelled the artillery officer.

"Quickly, lower the gun to right angle so we can fire at that thing. Load the AP shells," Lothar commanded. Lothar and another soldier quickly rotated the siege gun while the other two lowered the barrel to aim center mass at the tank before loading the gun. Maxis makes it to their position.

"Sergeant, we got the gun ready. Just say the word and we will rain down hell," declared the artillery officer.

"I'll let you know when to fire. Lothar, I need you on security as we have Russian troops escorting the tank," said Maxis, pulling out his binoculars.

"I'm on it!" Lothar reassured, as he picked up his Madsen from the ground and got into position.

Maxis looked through his binoculars and said, "Standby to fire on my mark!"

As the behemoth comes within range, Maxis shouts out, "Feuer (Fire)!" and the crew fires a shot. It ricochets off the left side gun. The artillery officer yells at the crew to reload quickly and wait for the order to fire. The tank commander and crew inside the Tsar tank felt that ricochet and immediately returned fire. Lothar laid out suppressing fire on the Tayna soldiers slowly approaching.

"Gun ready!" shouted the artillery officer.

"Feuer (Fire)!" Maxis shouts.

The crew fires and it makes its mark on the left side gun. The gun blows up and spews out smoke and fire, but the Tsar tank is still moving toward them. They quickly load another shell and wait for the signal.

"Feuer (Fire)!" Maxis shouts again.

The crew fires another round. This time the shell hit the wheel. It pierces right through the axle that is holding the two wheels and hurtles into the right-side gun. This causes an explosion that also rips the right wheel off, leaving the Tsar tank completely disabled as it falls on its side. The remaining Russians and Tayna soldiers that have been moving with the tank flee after seeing it get knocked out of action. The crew inside of it opened the back metal door and managed to escape.

"We did it! I can't believe it!" gasped one of Hapsburg soldiers.

"I wouldn't celebrate just yet, Soldat (Soldier). Lothar, did you manage to grab some dynamite before we came here?" Maxis asked.

"As of matter of fact, I did." Lothar takes off his tornister and reaches down to grab a rollup pack of dynamite and its wire connected to the detonator. He hands it to Maxis.

"Thanks, this should do the trick," declared Maxis. He moved quickly to the disabled tricycle tank and set up the dynamite, trailing the wire back.

Once he was at a safe distance, he detonated the dynamite, and a huge explosion can be seen and a thunderous sound fills the air. Maxis and Lothar have successfully destroyed the Tsar tank. Lothar and the rest of the group walk over from the cannon to congratulate Maxis on his success.

"The tank is destroyed, but something is off. I can sense someone is watching me and...the chill feeling running down my spine..." Maxis' thoughts were interrupted suddenly as five shots were heard, all of them whistling past him, hitting everyone but him.

One hit the artillery officer in the chest, another hit a soldier in the shoulder, the third soldier took the bullet in the neck, and the fourth was killed with a headshot. The last bullet grazed the left side of Lothar's face, causing a painful wound.

Maxis turned around quickly to see Arina charging at him with her bayonet. He immediately countered by blocking it with his own rifle. He jumped back and took aim at her leg. Maxis pulled the trigger, but he heard the dreadful sound of a click. The rifle jammed. Then he heard Arina chuckle a little.

"Ha, not very sporty of you, Sergeant. You don't have the stones to even consider continuing our little dance," Arina jeered in a mocking tone.

Maxis grinned after hearing Arina. "I believe in resolving conflicts quite quickly, but if you're offering a challenge, I'll be much obliged to accept," Maxis answered.

Arina dropped her rifle and pistol, then brandished a double-edge Cossack dagger from her sheath and pointed it at Maxis.

"You humiliated the commander and decimated our camp. Not to mention destroying the Tsar's new toy. You have been quite a headache today. I'm also impressed that you are still alive. So here is the deal, if you win, I'll simply be your POW, but if I win, that is if you survive, I'm taking you back to base as a POW and you will suffer the wrath of the Colonel. Does that sound fair to you, Sergeant Maxis?" Arina finished with confidence.

Maxis responded by taking the bayonet off his rifle and putting the rifle down, along with his pistol. He also dropped his rucksack and satchel and moved into a defensive stance.

"Shall we begin, miledi (milady in Russian)?" Maxis challenges with a smirk.

She charged at him and struck first with her blade. Maxis blocked it with his bayonet and pushed her back. He then held it in reverse and goes on the attack. He swung his blade at her, but she dodged to the right quickly. Arina tried to nail Maxis from his exposed side. He quickly countered it and his wounded comrades heard their blades clashing. The duel continued for several minutes, with no one gaining the upper hand. Arina and Maxis both exposed their strengths and weaknesses during the battle. They seemed equally matched in skills and techniques. Several times their blades locked together, and one must push, punch, or grip the other's wrist to break the stalemate or get the upper hand. Both sustained cuts and damage though not serious.

The duel was taking its toll on Maxis, as the pain from his shoulder and leg wounds grow, and exhaustion is showing. Arina was also showing signs of fatigue. Their blades lock one more time, but the result is different this time. Arina spit in Maxis' eyes, blinding him for a moment. She then kicked him down to the ground. Maxis tried to recover, but he saw her coming. He swung his bayonet and hit her dagger, but his bayonet snapped in half. Both were stunned for a second, but Maxis quickly kicked both of her legs at the same time. Arina fell flat on her face.

"Verdammt (Damn it), my bayonet snapped. I can't continue with a broken blade even if it has a sharp tip. I need some form of a plan without getting killed or captured. There must be something...Her letter...that's my plan. Hope

it works." Maxis crawls to his bread bag but hears Arina getting up.

"Oh, you do not feel like admitting defeat? Going for your equipment isn't going to save you, you cheat!" says Arina, springing on to Maxis.

She jumped on to Maxis' back. He turned around just in time and grabbed her forearm preventing her from plunging the dagger into his shoulder. Still a foot away from reaching his bread bag, now he must worry about Arina trying to stab him. Maxis had a flash back to when the wolf tried to rip his throat out. The problem is, he is not dealing with a wolf, but a woman. As Maxis tried to reach for the letter, he can see the seriousness and determination on her face. He has seen very few people with that type of spirit.

Time was running out for Maxis as the blade was getting closer than ever. The end seemed almost certain, until he feels the letter in his hand; quickly he grabbed it and showed it to Arina. She held her attack and paused for a moment to look at the letter. A look of surprise appeared on her face. She got up, sheathed her dagger, and snatched the letter from his hands. She turned her back to Maxis and walked a few feet before growling at Maxis.

"Where did you get this?" Arina demanded.

Maxis shifted into a sitting position and explained. "It was among the documents I took while at your camp. I had no idea it was there until it fell out. I had every intention of returning it to you. My question was how? That is, until now," Maxis finished.

Communication with loved ones during the Great War was not easy since telephones were not entirely common yet. A letter is considered personal to a soldier being so far away from home. This letter was highly valued. Arina says nothing. Her back is still turned to Maxis. She walks over to pick up her rifle and pistol. Then, she puts the letter in her pocket and sprints into the brush, disappearing from sight.

Maxis got up and took a deep breath. He heard Lothar grunting as he appeared beside him.

"How are the others?" Maxis inquired.

"One wounded, three dead," Lothar replied, holding a piece of cloth to the side of his face. "That was quite the show you put on."

"Indeed," Maxis agreed.

"I've got one important question to ask," Lothar said with a serious tone.

"What is it?"

"How's my face?"

Maxis turned to Lothar with a stern look. Lothar stared back. Maxis began to crack a smile, and then a laugh. Lothar does the same. After they are done, they go to tend to the wounded and head back to base for debriefing.

Meanwhile, Arina and her battered platoon returned to the base camp of the Tayna Brigade. Colonel Vorshevsky waited for their arrival. He was disappointed that the assault failed, along with the Tsar tank, but glad to see his daughter make it back.

Arina is fatigued and tired. Whatever is left of her platoon is severely decimated, with its best soldiers either dead or captured. She pulled out the letter that Maxis returned and looked at it.

The Tayna Brigade was packing up its base camp to relocate to a new sector after the disaster that the two K.W.S. soldiers caused them. During packing up, the Colonel approached the group. A few medics rushed past the Colonel, tending to the remnants of the platoon. Arina immediately dropped to her knees, as the exhaustion has taken its toll on her. Colonel Vorshevsky moved hastily to his daughter's aid.

"I was afraid the Sergeant would certainly have bested you. For a moment I was fearful you would suffer the same fate as your platoon did. Tell me what happened," said Colonel Vorshevsky as he holds Arina.

Arina explained the details of the Shock Operation, until she got to the one-on-one duel with Maxis.

"He and I fought so ferociously and with vigor. Neither of us was gaining the advantage. Until I broke his blade, then I was certain of victory, that is until he revealed this to me," Arina said as she holds up the letter that says "Ot: Mama (From: Mama)." Colonel Vorshevsky is surprised to see the letter in her hand.

"Alana, my dear Alana. It looks like your letter saved our little girl," he thought to himself.

"I meant to hand that to you when you returned from your scouting mission, but it ended up missing after those two Germans came," her father explained.

"While we dueled he said he meant to return this. I was furious at first and was ready to kill him, but I didn't. For that I listened to his explanation and have... forgiven him," confessed Arina in a low tone.

"Well, it seems Sergeant Maxis has some respect and honor for his rivals. That is certainly lacking in the world. But you must know that the world is changing now and doing such things will not end well for you. You were lucky that the German accepted your challenge but hear me when I say this...Never do that again. We've chatted long enough. Shall we read the letter together?" suggested Colonel Vorshevsky.

Arina nodded and stood up. The two opened the letter and read it together. As they read, Arina had a feeling that this won't be the last time she'll being seeing the young Sergeant.

With the attack halted, the threats of the frontlines being breach are put to rest with Austro-Hungarians still fighting the Russians in Carpathians. It was a success for the K.W.S., but the world will never know of such a feat. Little do they know this was just the beginning of what they will encounter in this Great War, in this modern war.

CHAPTER 5

OLD FRIENDS, NEW ENEMY, AND A NEW TYPE OF WAR

Three weeks after the events in Bochnia. Commander Jorgensen was back in his office in the K.W.S. main HQ building. The events regarding the Tayna Brigades attack was still fresh in his mind as he shuffled photos and documents in a neat order. A knock on the door broke his focus and he quickly gathered his documents and placed them into his desk drawer.

"Enter," Commander Jorgensen replied. The door opened and in came Major Reinhard. He walked a few steps before stopping and giving a salute. The commander rose and returned his salute before taking his seat again.

"Major Reinhard, it's good to see you."

"Like wise, Sir. I came to report that our western field base, Ragnarök, is almost fully operational. Just needs the finishing touches."

"Excellent! Now we have a permanent area of influence than a run of the mill military camp we had before. I'm sure our troops will be glad to hear the news. Anything else, Major?"

"The request you put for our own train and rail system has gone through. We should have construction crews begin work in a couple of weeks. I'll also inform R&D to start making some plans for the attachments needed for your new train. That is my report, Sir."

"This was good news indeed. Better than what I received three weeks ago," Commander Jorgensen said, as he stands up and faces the window. Reinhard takes a seat on the chair facing Jorgensen's desk.

"Sir, I been meaning to ask. Do the Russians really have their own elite unit that is similar to ours?"

"Similar but, not the same, Major. I doubt the commanding officer went to the Tsar's palace while carrying everything from the omnibus with plans, documents, and so on, to present to him. Not like how I did it," Commander Jorgensen said firmly, peeping through the blinds.

"Ah yes, I remember that moment. You skipped the chain of command to present your idea to His Majesty himself in Potsdam. I was Second Lieutenant back then and I was also the one helping you carry all that stuff," Reinhard recalled and took out a cigarette and lit it.

"I did what was necessary since those old fools didn't even take the time of day to even read my suggestions. I took the biggest risk in my career, and even yours, to get what I wanted."

"Hence, here we are with me as Major and you as a Commander. I'll never forget the look the Kaiser gave when he read everything you wrote. He was enthralled by your ideas being properly set up. He then spread it to others thus birthing the Battalion." Major Reinhard takes a drag from his cigarette before continuing. "Now, about this commanding officer of the Russian unit. It sounds like you know a little about him, Commander. His name is Colonel Vorshevsky from the reports."

"That I do. From the mouth of Sergeant Maxis and his report. I wasn't even the slightest surprised when I heard that Vladimir Sasha Vorshevsky was in charge of it."

"So, there is history? What's the short version?" Reinhard asks, as he takes a seat.

"Let's just say we both fought together during the insurrection in China," Commander Jorgensen said, as he takes a seat once again and pulls out an old photo from his desk. The photo contains an image of himself with Vorshevsky's arm on his shoulder, and two other officers.

"Insurrection in China...you mean the Boxer Rebellion?"

"Is that what they called it? Goodness, I haven't been up to date. Anyway, at that time I was recently promoted to Captain, while Vorshevsky was a Major. He would punch my shoulder while I would punch his harder, like brothers in way. We would get into lengthy debates of whose Emperor is better or whose army was more superior before we would break into laughter and have a drink."

"Sounds to me this was the creation of a beautiful friendship."

"Yes, but now all my friends are now my enemies in this war. What a world," Jorgensen lamented, as he put the photo away in the desk drawer.

"As unfortunate as that is. What about his daughter?"

"I do not know much besides seeing her once when she was a little girl. The Geist Platoon dug into it and put together what they could find on her. Here's her file, though sadly there is no photograph of her." Commander Jorgensen pulled out a file from his desk and handed it to the Major.

"The Geist Platoon, your new secret police/spy unit. I still don't like the idea of them existing," Major Reinhard commented as he opened the file.

"Whether you like them or is not a great concern since it's a necessary evil to ensure our presence in the world remains a secret and to keep our troops from running their mouths or writing something top secret in their letters to home. I am making sure they are kept on tight leash. We recruited spies and other sorts whose skills are best not wasted in a prison cell," Jorgensen firmly stated.

"Hmph," Reinhard reacts as he investigates the file, and it reads.

Name: Arina Svetlana Vorshevsky
DOB: 10/30/95
Height: 5'10
Hair color: Red (Crimson)

Eye color: Violet
Build: Athletic
Language: Russian, German, English
M.O.S: Unknown
National: Russian
Military unit: Imperskiy Tayna Brigada

"Hmm, a typical Russian redhead with...violet eyes? I don't believe it, Sir!" Reinhard spoke as he placed the files on the desk.

"Believe it, Reinhard. It coincides with Sergeant Maxis' report. She's just another representation of the mysteriousness that is Russia."

"I understand that, but I find it baffling that a woman like her managed join the Tsar's Army. I cannot safely assume how." The Major takes another drag before putting out his cigarette in the ash tray.

"If you're assuming her father got her in, then that is most likely, though I have feelings of a doubt. Another woman who joined the Russian military had petitioned the Tsar. There is still a third one, though a Serb, who fought in both Balkan wars and the Serbians made big deal out of it."

"I see. Then we have our hands full in the Eastern Front though I pray we don't encounter something like this in the West."

"Tsk, Tsk, you shouldn't have said that Reinhard. In this new war, anything could happen. We may be the first of our nation's military to conduct a new type of warfare, one that favors a highly trained squadron of troops using our country's best weapons, prototypes, and vehicles on a grand level. Not just our own but even our allies as well. It won't be long before someone takes notice and tries to copy us. The question is when, Major. Now, may I ask a favor of you?"

"Yes, Sir?"

"Can you go and retrieve Sgt. Maxis and Cpl. Lothar from the Hildegard Biergarten. I have a special assignment for them regarding two prime locations I need them to go and investigate. I would get them myself but, I have a lot of things to do here around base."

"Of course, Sir! I'll go fetch them," Reinhard responded proudly.

"Good man," Jorgensen said, as he got back to his work. Reinhard leaves at once.

CHAPTER 6

SABOTEUR OF PRZEMYŚL FORTRESS

March 16, 1915, Dexheim, Germany

"The weeks went by after our battle with the Tsar tank in Bochnia. Though half that time was spent cleaning up the wreckage and rounding up any Hapsburg soldiers that survived the battle to make them swear and sign a secrecy agreement to the Bochnia incident. This was the only way to keep our activities secret from the world. Eventually we were relieved from our support role by another K.W.S. squad and were sent back to our HQ in Dexheim for some rest and relaxation. I did, however, take extra time training to improve my hand-to-hand combat just to be prepared during our long-awaited down time. There is one thing that left me wondering...if it's certain that weapons of war like the Tsar Tank can be built and used for combat, then what else will the Triple Entente throw at us and how long

will it be until we start doing the same thing in outclassing them in whatever insane creations of war. Only time will tell, but one thing is certain...The Kaiserliche Waffen Spezialisten Battalion has their work cut out for this. Though the question is how?"

"Hey, Maxis, are you still among the living?" Lothar asked as he tapped Maxis' shoulder.

"Yeah, I'm fine. I was just writing in my journal about recent events."

"Well, you can write about it another time, besides here comes Hannah with our drinks."

"Alright," Maxis replied, as he put his journal away.

Hannah approached the two with their beer in hand.

"Here we go, one specially brewed Kolsch for the Sergeant and one Dunkel for the Mighty Lothar," says Hannah as she hands them their drinks with a smile.

"Danke (Thanks), Miss. Hildegard," said Maxis.

"Yeah, thanks. Hannah always know how treat customers like royalty," said Lothar.

"Oh, stop it! You two are the ones who treat me with more respect than anyone else in the Biergarten. Like my father always said, treat others how you would like to be treated."

"Now that you mention it how is your father doing?" Lothar asked.

"He's doing fine though I try my best to help him out running this place," Hannah replied, as she started cleaning the mugs.

"Why don't you take the reins and run this place yourself? You know the bar well and you can even deal with any rowdy patrons yourself without calling the bouncer."

"Don't think I didn't try to ask him to pass it over, Lothar. He is a stubborn man, but he thinks I'm not ready despite that I learned so much from him on how to run the business. Even I could handle a massive crowd during Oktoberfest. But in the end in his eyes, I'm still his little girl," Hannah commented, as her demeanor changed from cheerful to slightly depressed.

"He will come around someday. Give him some time. But hey, I know something that may cheer you up and help take your mind off the that sore spot," said Lothar.

"What would that be?"

"How about another one of my bizarre adventures this time with my friend Maxis?"

"All your stories are bizarre since we were kids. What's so different this time?" Hannah asked as a small smirk began to appear.

"Oh, this one is more recent. It was during our deployment in Russia and..."

"Lothar!" Maxis growled his name as he interrupts.

"Remember what Commander Jorgensen told us about telling civilians about our activities?"

"Ja, I remember. But don't worry Maxis, trust me I know what I'm doing." Lothar winked and gave the ok sign as assurance.

"So, there we were, me, the Mighty Lothar, and Maxis, the Black Wolf of Mons, against an army of a million Russian soldiers."

"*sigh The Black Wolf of Mons...that's a nickname I haven't heard for a while and for good reason too...*" Maxis in his thoughts as he drinks.

"A million Russian soldiers?" Hannah queried.

"Oh, it was not just us, we had the Hapsburg army there with us to face them together."

"Then what happen next?"

"We were in our trench until a sudden barrage of shells hit our position. Luckily, we took cover, but the Hapsburgs were severely decimated by the bombardment. When the artillery ceased, then came the Russians. Wave upon wave of their infantry were unleashed, though our numbers were small we unleashed a hurricane of bullets that halted their advance."

"Is that how you got that dreadful scar on your cheek?" Hannah inquired.

"Uh...I'm getting to that part," Lothar continues after taking another drink. "As we tore into the Russians, our allies began to fall back as the battle rages on. By the time the battle was over, there were six of us left. Then came a fog and everything suddenly got quite."

"Oooh, how eerie!" Maxis said jokingly.

"Then came a silhouette of a person coming through the fog walking at a slow pace. We approached with weapons at the ready, then suddenly five bullets were fired, but the shots didn't come from us. The five of us were hit, the bullet only grazed me, but I was hurt pretty bad. The only one that was still standing was Maxis. We then realize who the figure was...it was the Huntress of the East."

"The Huntress!?" Hannah reacted.

"She is one of the Tsar's best soldiers and her mission was to assist her fellow Ruskies during the attack."

"Oh, I see. How exciting!" Hannah exclaimed.

"Very," Maxis commented.

Lothar continues the over-exaggerated story of the ensuing battle between "The Black Wolf of Mons" and "The Huntress" while taking sips from his Dunkel drink. Maxis begins to think back. From his first meeting Arina to the inevitable confrontation between the two.

"When I think back to that day, I can still feel the adrenaline, my heart pounding in my ear, and every fiber of my being screaming for action. Then again, I came too close to death's door during the mission. I also came too close to being captured at the hands of Colonel Vorshevsky or his daughter. I wonder about Arina though, the only woman out there that can match my skills, even though her radiant beauty may have...distracted me. But I cannot think such things, we are at war...but still. " Maxis thought to himself as he finished his drink, his reflection staring back at him from the glass.

While Maxis pondered his thoughts, Lothar was about to reach the climax of his story with an ending that would come as a surprise to Hannah who was already invested into hearing the end.

"There they were, both sides exhausted and bloody up from their battle as the Wolf and the Huntress grip their blades tightly. They stare each other down waiting to see who will make the next move. Then, suddenly, the huntress sheathes her blade and begins to thank her opponent. She then disappears into the fog with her last words were 'till we meet again.' Leaving Maxis standing while I tended to the wounded." Lothar finished as he stood up on the chair in a heroic pose before hitting his head on the ceiling light.

"So, you mean to tell me that all the trouble she caused and she...just runs away?" Hannah asked with a bit of confusion in her voice.

"Pretty much," Lothar responded.

"Well, I must say that was an interesting story. By the way Maxis, did you really stand your ground while defending Lothar from the Huntress?"

"I really am not at liberty to say. It just happened."

"On the contrary, I believe soldiers of the Battalion are trained to stand their ground no matter the situation," said a nearby person with a soft soothing voice without stress.

Maxis and Lothar turned to the person who spoke and it was none other than Major Reinhard at the door. An officer sporting a handlebar mustache and a monocle was on his left.

Maxis immediately stands at attention and shouts "Achtung!" Every soldier in the Biergarten, including Lothar, stood at attention, and saluted Major Reinhard.

"As you were men. Pay no mind to me. I'm just here get a drink," says the Major.

Everyone returned to what they were doing after the Major gave the order. Then a man in a dapper suit got up from his table and approached Major Reinhard. The

Major noticed the man, the two shake hands then the man begins to whisper to Major, and then points at Maxis and Lothar, who were still chatting with Hannah. Major Reinhard nodded and the man heads toward the door. Major Reinhard approached the bar where Maxis and Lothar are sitting.

"So how are you boys doing today?" Major Reinhard asked, as he sits down.

"We're doing fine, Sir." Maxis responded with an affirmative tone.

"That's good to hear. Uh, barmaid may I have a lager bitte(please)?"

"Certainly, I'll get right on it," Hannah responded as she walks away.

"Well, she's a hard-working mädchen (girl), isn't she?" Major Reinhard observed.

"I've known Hannah since we were kids. Hard work is one way to best describe her, Sir." Lothar responded.

"Sounds to me you already got yourself a girl. I mean look at her." The Major points to the tall thin fish-tail-braided brunette preparing the Major's drink.

"Now, the question is where's the ring?" Major cajoled with a grin.

"It's not liked that Sir...I mean ...we simply care for each other's well-being."

"Oh, I beg to differ, Ludvig," Maxis interjected.

"Not you too, Maxis," as Lothar puts his hand to his face.

"I say, weren't you paying attention the way she was looking at you while you were telling your story," he said with a smirk.

"I was in the zone, Maxis. You know that."

"How about the part where she jumped when she saw your scar the moment, we walked in here?" He points at the scar on Lothar's face.

"Girls will jump at anything they see, like mice."

"Do I need to mention how she keeps calling you the Mighty Lothar instead of your first name or rank?"

"We call each with nicknames all the time, like that time I...um...well...you know what I mean." Lothar scratched his head with a confused look.

"Ok Lothar, you win, now if you excuse me, I'm going to ask Hannah if she'd like to take a stroll under the stars."

"Yeah, don't even think about it, Verdammt (Damn it)!"

"Ha, caught ya!" Maxis chuckled, as he jumped off his seat with a bit of laughter.

"Are you done, boys?" said the Major with annoyance in his tone as he takes a sip of his drink.

"Yes Sir, I think we're done." Maxis responds back as he sits back down.

"Good, now on to other matters."

After the brief child's play, Hannah came by to deliver the Major's drink. Hannah called it her "special brew" that her family had been making since long before they opened the Biergarten. The Major thanked her and began to drink his lager. When he was done, he turned to the two men and spoke.

"I didn't come here just to take a load off. Actually I'm sent here by the Commander to take you two back to base for a new assignment."

"Wait a minute Sir, our down time has not ended yet. We just started," Lothar protested.

"I understand your frustration, but if HQ sent me here that means its important. Do you understand that Corporal?"

"Yes, Sir. Sorry, Sir."

"And one more thing I should mention to you two before we get moving. You violated Protocol Three." Reinhard puts his hands on both their shoulders very firmly.

"Sir, we haven't broken any of the rules we swore by, certainly you don't mean..."

The Major raised his hand in the air, silencing Maxis. He spoke in a calm but serious tone. "Don't try to act innocent Sergeant, I know what happened here. Corporal Lothar, you violated Protocol Three by talking about a recent mission with a civilian, whether its factual or fiction. And, before you pull the 'where's the proof card' the man in the suit told me. He is also part of the Battalion."

"Him? I've never seen him before around base, Sir," Maxis said.

"Exactly. He's part of a new unit within K.W.S. called Geist Platoon. His job was simple, to maintain observation and provide details to a potential intel leak. That's why he was here at the Biergarten, and he is already on his way to inform Commander Jorgensen about you two and what you did."

"Well, Scheisse (Shit)," Maxis muttered, putting his hand to his face again.

"Now come along. We'll take my staff car to get back to Valhalla Base." Major Reinhard gets up from his chair and gestures to them to follow. Maxis and Lothar followed suit but before they left Maxis made sure to leave the amount owed on the bar for Hannah to pick up.

The three walk outside of the biergarten to be met with a Mercedes 37\95 automobile. An enlisted man stepped out of the vehicle to open the door for the Major at the front. The other two climb in the back of the automobile.

"Driver, take us back to base, on the *double*!" Major Reinhard ordered.

"Yes Sir," The driver responded as he shifted gears.

CHAPTER 7

VISITING VALHALLA BASE

They were on their way speedily and drove out of Dexheim into the countryside in matter of minutes. It would be an hour before they would reach their destination. During the drive there was absolute silence except for the sound of the engine and the wind.

"I did hear a bit of your story and I must ask. Who was the Black Wolf of Mons?" Major Reinhard asked.

"Sergeant Maxis, Sir." Lothar responded.

"Really? Sergeant how did you acquire such a nickname?"

"During the Schlieffen Plan, Major," Maxis answered.

"I see. I remember reading reports that the Belgians put up some stiff resistance."

Immediately the car hit a bump in the road and everyone bounced a little in their seats.

"They did Major, but nothing we couldn't handle."

Lothar noticed the bothered look Maxis was given after answering.

"Did something else happen in Belgium, Maxis?" Lothar wanted to know.

"Nope, nothing of the sorts, we can just move to different topic." Maxis' tone immediately changed, now annoyed.

"Hey, it's alright Maxis, we're all friends here. It doesn't hurt to shed a little light. Is it about Kurtz or..." Lothar was cut off as the driver announced, "Arriving at base, gents!"

As they drove over the hill, they could see the huge base and all its military glory. The automobile slowed down, then came to a complete stop. At the gate were three Feldgendarmerie (Military police) donning their metal gorgets around their necks. One of them approached the automobile and spoke.

"Guten nachmittag, Herr (Good afternoon, Sir). Identification, please," the guard asked.

Everyone in the vehicle pulled out their identification papers and handed them over to the guard. The guard looked at each ID carefully. During the process he can be heard mumbling to himself as he reads.

"Alright, everything seems to be in order, here you go." Returns everyone's IDs, the guard immediately walked over to where Major Reinhard is sitting.

"Sir, I need to ask for the password of today," he whispered.

"Well of course. Teutoburg," the Major responds softly.

"Alright they're clear, let them through! Welcome back to Valhalla Base, Major, have pleasant day." The guard salutes and Major Reinhard returns a salute back.

The two Feldgendarmerie began to open the large wooden gate and the automobile proceeded through.

The automobile zipped right through the base without pause, reaching HQ that was at the top of a large hill. The building was large, nearly two stories tall. The driver pulled over in front of the building and shifted gears to park the car. He immediately got out of the vehicle to open the door for the Major.

"Quickly now, let's get inside," said Major Reinhard, as he steps out of the vehicle.

The three enter the building through its large doors. They meet the receptionist at the desk. A civilian wearing the imperial uniform was working as a clerk typist. She looked up at the Major, gave a small smile and said in soft tone. "Is there something I can help you with Major?"

"Yes, is Commander Jorgensen in his office right now?"

"Why, yes he is."

"Danke (Thank you). Come on men, let's not keep him waiting," said Major Reinhard, and motioned the two behind to follow him.

The three proceeded through the hallways of the headquarters building. There were K.W.S. soldiers and officers moving about through the hallways, some carrying folders and others carrying stacks of paper. The rooms they passed in were interesting at best. One was a communication room where the telegraph was located and where there were soldiers wearing special headphones listening to messages and sending them via morse code. They were writing down the translated transcript, and then giving the piece of paper to another soldier so he can deliver the message or orders to someone higher up. There was also a telephone room that utilized the telephone for military purposes. Like in the telegraph room, the telephone operators performed similar tasks, but they speak in code to all K.W.S. bases across Europe and some parts of the middle east.

The HQ is very active on the first floor and it seems to be endless until the trio went to the second floor via the stairs. The sound of constant chatter, the telegraph keys snapping, and the typewriters tapping all ceased.

"Here we go, second floor," said Major Reinhard. They continued to the commander's office. Along the way they passed a couple more doors. One was the title logistics branch, another was internal affairs, and further down was the door they were heading to, titled "Commander of K.W.S. Captain Jorgensen."

The Major knocked on the door and they heard "Enter" coming from the office. They entered the office one by one and stood side by side at attention. In front of them was Commander Jorgensen reviewing some war maps on his large desk. Behind him was the banner of the K.W.S. Battalion.

The flag's design had an eagle with its wings above the head, it wore pickelhaube, in one of its talons held Stielhandgranate (Stick grenade) and on the other held a Gewehr 98 rifle, and finally an initial written in cursive on the eagle's chest was "KWS" in yellow. The design was inspired by the old Prussian flag from the Napoleonic wars. At the bottom is the motto "Immer Mit Präzision (Always with precision)"

Major Reinhard stepped forward and spoke. "I brought these two as requested, Sir!"

"Very good, you two take a seat," Commander Jorgensen ordered. Maxis and Lothar both took a seat in the chairs in front of the commander's desks, ready to hear what the commander had to say.

"Alright, good news first. Sgt. Maxis, the little wolf pup you retrieved last month is performing well as Pvt. Bartek reported, though he has a long way to go. When he has matured and is trained, he'll be fighting by your side in no time. Next on the list, the new feldgrau uniforms will be coming in next week with our unit emblem sewn on the sleeve. Also, I approved your request and forwarded it for your M1910 feldgrau uniforms to include red piping, as well as add red piping to the bottom of the tunic as well, for the two of you. Any comments?"

"Sir, I'm glad to hear that Ulf is doing well. He'll be a great asset to Battalion, Sir!" said Maxis with pride in his tone.

"No doubt about it, the little beast shows promise. Now on to the bad news. An agent of the Geist Platoon came in to report that one of you had violated Protocol Three. This disappoints me, the fact you two took the oath in secrecy to uphold our ten protocols like everyone else in the Battalion. For that, you must be punished, the both of you!" Commander Jorgensen crossed his arms as his facial expression turns to slightly disappointed.

"Both of us?" Maxis questioned.

"Yes, the both of you. Corporal Lothar. You are the one who violated Protocol Three and Sergeant Maxis, you let him run his mouth when you were supposed to stop him, since you're his NCO in charge. It's only reasonable the that the two of you should receive an equal punishment."

"A disciplinary action would be recommended, Commander," Major Reinhard spoke.

"Indeed, I know just the thing that would do the trick. Sergeant Maxis, I'll be sending you on a special assignment to Przemyśl Fortress which is currently under siege. Your job is simply to deliver mail sent by German high command, the Austrian high command, and from me. You'll have minimal armament to use on your way to the fortress because I don't expect you to do much besides being the mailman, so no heroics. Here's your ticket, your train leaves in two hours for Budapest so you better get going. There's a car waiting for you outside. Oh, one more thing, you'll be meeting one of our pilots there,1Lt. Hoffmann. That is all, you are dismissed!"

"Yes, Sir! I'll be on way," Maxis responded as he got up from the chair and headed toward the door. Lothar remained.

As Maxis moved down the hallway, he could hear Lothar shouting "WHAT?!" from behind the door. A small smirk crossed Maxis' face.

"It's a bit odd that the Commander gave me this assignment as a form of punishment. Sending me to a hot zone with few armaments. Has he gone mad or is this some sort of test? Another thing I wonder was what was Major Reinhard doing here in the first place? Last I checked he was leading the Battalion's base on the western front.

Hmm...I guess it's a need-to-know bases," Maxis thought to himself. Outside he approached the automobile with the driver waiting for him.

He instructed the driver to take him to the armory before proceeding to the train station. The driver took him to the armory quickly and Maxis hurriedly exited the vehicle and ran inside. A few minutes later, he returned with his gear, along with one new bayonet with a sawtooth back and a Bergmann No.5 automatic pistol in his holster. He reentered the automobile and off they went to the train station. They arrived at the train station with minutes to spare, Maxis boarding the train car just before the final call to board.

The train blew its whistle as it began to move, now heading to Budapest. The trip would take ten hours before they reached their destination, but for Maxis it felt like an eternity. Though it was a long ride, this gave him time to think and ponder his thoughts about the ongoing situation over at Przemyśl Fortress.

"Let's see, the fortress has been under siege since '14. Though the defenders showed resilience in the siege, I doubt it'll be their saving grace. The last I heard, von Hotzendorf tried to send a relief force and even launch three winter offensives, but all of them failed miserably. Now I'm going in alone. Hopefully the Russians don't breakthrough before I get there otherwise this mission would fail from the start. I'm more concerned about Lothar; what assignment will he be getting?"

The day turned to night and the sound of the rumbling from the train cars wheels over the track continued. Maxis closed his eyes to rest a little as he gets lost in his thoughts. It was enough for him to fall asleep. It felt like mere seconds when he heard the train whistle blow indicating they had arrived at their destination.

It was six in the morning as the dawn's light began to shine over the horizon. Maxis begrudgingly got up from his seat, feeling a slight pain in his neck. The rest of the passengers got up and started heading toward the exit of the train car. Maxis followed behind the crowd and was met with sight to behold.

The city of Budapest, one of the capitals of Austria-Hungary that never ceases to amaze. Even in the early morning it was busy, especially in times of war. The trolley can be seen moving through the center of the street, automobiles going past it on either side and the occasional horse drawn carriage.

"Hey, you! Are you Sergeant Maxis?" called an unknown voice with a firm tone. Maxis turned around to see a man in uniform approach him. The sun reflected off his black hair and he drew on a cigarette before tossing it to the ground. He walked up to the German sergeant.

"I said, are you Sergeant Maxis?"

"Why, yes, I am, and to whom am I acknowledging this?"

"1Lt. Hoffmann of the Prussian Blue Tails, that's who! Pleased to make your acquaintance," 1Lt. Hoffmann said affirmatively, putting his hand out for a handshake. The two shook hands.

"Well, I assume you'll be flying me to the fortress?"

"You mean flying you to hell? That's right," Hoffmann said sarcastically with a smirk.

"Hell? What do you mean?"

"In case you were uninformed, the fortress has been under siege for over a hundred days now. The condition is not so favorable for the Hapsburgs, supplies are running short, the Russians are getting bolder with their attacks, and morale is at an all-time low. Is that good enough for you, Sergeant?" Hoffmann said with his eyebrow raised.

"Quite so Sir, more than enough."

"Good. Now come on. It will take an hour to reach the air base from here." Said 1Lt. Hoffmann.

The duo walked down the sidewalk and around the corner was Hoffmann's vehicle, a Henderson 1915 motorcycle with a side car. He mounted the bike and started it. The Henderson's engine roared to life and a little smoke coughed out of the tail pipe. Maxis climbed in the side car and the Lieutenant handed him a pair of goggles to wear. He revved the motorcycle and off they went.

They were on the outskirts of the city and were headed to the countryside. The wind hit their faces along with several insects, and the smell of nature dominated their surroundings..

"So, what can you tell me about the Prussian Blue Tails?" Maxis asked loudly.

"That depends, can you keep a secret?" Hoffmann answered back.

"Better than my best friend could."

"Good answer! The Prussian Blue Tails are a work in progress, an air unit in K.W.S. Battalion!"

"So, it's a squadron?"

"It's more than a squadron and its bigger than a wing. That is all I can say about it. Does that meet your satisfaction, Sergeant?" Hoffmann asked as he shifted gears before making a slight right turn at the fork in the road.

Before Maxis could give a response, they arrived at the entrance of the air base. From there, they disembarked from the motorcycle. 1Lt. Hoffmann told Maxis to meet him at hangar number nine then left to retrieve his flight gear. Maxis made it to the hangar and saw their plane with a paint job on the tail in Prussian Blue. A minute later 1Lt. Hoffmann arrived in his pilots' outfit, carrying a spare aviator hat and leather coat.

"Here put these on. It'll keep you warm during the flight to the fortress. You can put your uniform top and pickelhaube in your seat for safe storage. Once you're done, help me get the plane onto the runway so the rest of the crew can get the plane ready to go. Oh, before I forget, the mail bag is in a separate compartment of the plane," 1Lt. Hoffmann concluded.

Maxis took off his pickelhaube to put on the aviator hat then put on the leather coat over his uniform. Then he helped Hoffmann move the plane onto the dirt runway. After they finished doing that several ground crewmembers came to get the plane prepped for takeoff. Maxis felt a sense of nervousness since this was his first-time riding in a plane.

1Lt. Hoffmann hopped inside the pilot's seat and signaled Maxis to get on board. The crewmembers finished up their check list and gave the thumbs up to the First Lieutenant. One of the crewmembers walked beside the propeller and started pulling it to get several revolutions in until the oil becomes rich for the plane's engine. After several pulls Hoffmann shouts "CONTACT!" and starts up the plane.

The plane's engines roared to life. It began to move, slowly picking up speed. Maxis was clenching the walls of the plane, bracing himself. The plane began to lift from the ground gaining altitude and then into the clouds. Maxis had his eyes closed trying to relax and not panic, taking deep breaths and finally opened his eyes to see the beauty of the skies.

The experience was calm, they were soaring high as the eagle. Maxis was amazed by the scenery around him. When he looked down below everything looks so tiny it was as if he had become a giant. He took in the gushing cool breeze, the sun shining, and clouds looking like fields of snow that stretches on endlessly. The view was priceless.

"Yesterday you were hooting with the owls, but today you're soaring with the eagles. Congratulations!" Hoffmann proudly exclaimed.

"Thanks," Maxis responded.

"I was expecting you to soil yourself, but so far you did okay, except the part where you were scared to death, ha. Don't even try to deny it I saw how you were clawing my plane!"

Three hours later their destination was in sight. Through the clouds the Fortress of Przemyśl could be sighted with the string of forts surrounding the outskirts of the city. The Fortress housed 120,000 troops as her garrison, but that number was dwarfed by the Russian Empire's 3rd and 11th Armies with a combined strength of 300,000. The situation is grave for the defenders, and artillery from the Russian lines constantly hammered the Fortress with a barrage of shells. Even outside the fort's walls the sight of death and destruction from both the attackers and defenders was astounding. What will Maxis encounter within the walls of this isolated fortress?

CHAPTER 8

ARRIVAL AT THE FORTRESS

March 17, 1915, 10:00 a.m. at Przemyśl Fortress

The plane made its approach toward Fortress, flying over the Russian lines. Maxis could see the Russians below looking at them as they point at the plane. The sight of the plane surprised some of them, but rest were disgusted.

"Taking in the sights, I see. Don't stick your head out for too long, you don't want to let those vodka drinkers get a lucky shot. Then again, they couldn't hit the side of a barn," said 1Lt. Hoffmann. He mocked the Russians with hand gestures until the sound of the bullet snap changed his mind.

"Ok, that's enough fun for now, preparing our descent into the Fortress."

Hoffmann slowed the plane on their descent toward the dirt runway at a makeshift camp. The plane's landing was rough as the wheels made contact to the ground, but successful. Immediately a group of Austrian-Hungarian soldiers double-timed it toward the plane before Maxis and 1Lt. Hoffmann could get out. The group arrived, standing in formation, then their Captain stepped forward.

"Which one of you is the courier?" demanded the soldier in a firm voice.

"This one right here, fellas," Hoffmann replied and pointed at Maxis.

"What is your rank and name, Soldat?"

"Sgt. Frederich Maxis of the Imperial German Army. I'm here to deliver messages to the Garrison commander," Maxis voiced affirmatively.

"Come with us. We'll take you to the command center." Maxis quickly took off the leather coat and aviator hat. He grabbed his pickelhaube, uniform top, and went to the special compartment of the plane to grab the bag full of letters essential to his mission. Once he was done, he moved along with the group on their way to the command center.

It was a long walk down the dirt road, then through the city streets. The place was quiet with little activity going on. There were some civilians walking, but their heads droop low as if they knew what's going to happen to them. Some children were playing around, smiles on their faces, blissfully ignorant of the current situation their entire home was in. The tension was present here and sorrow was all too strong from living in constant fear from this siege.

"I hope you got some good news from the high command, Sergeant," said the soldier.

"Yeah, I hope so too," Maxis replied as he looked at his surroundings.

Eventually they made it to central command in the middle of town. There the rest of the group stayed outside while Maxis and the soldier moved inside. The headquarters interior looked much like the one in Dexheim, but the activity here is quiet.

"The Garrison commander isn't present at the moment, but you can deliver the mail to his executive officer, Col. Otto Josef," said the soldier, pointing down hall.

Maxis followed the corridor to the Colonel's door. He knocked on the door, and immediately heard someone say "Enter," with a firm tone from inside. Maxis opened the door and saw a man in Austrian officer's uniform sitting behind the desk with a smoking pipe in one hand and some paperwork on the other. The man looked up to see Maxis standing in front of his desk. He chuckled a little and put down the items he was holding, then stood up.

"Now this is interesting. What is a German soldier doing all the way out here?"

"Sir, Sgt. Maxis of the German Imperial Army, Sir!" answered Maxis, as he salutes the Colonel.

The Colonel returned the salute and spoke. "Alright, state your business or intentions here soldat (soldier)."

"Sir, I have been tasked to deliver important messages from the Austro-Hungarian and German High Command and my superior, Sir."

"Well, then let's have it, Sergeant." Maxis handed the small bag to Col. Josef.

The Colonel immediately opened the bag and pulled out a small stack of letters. He opened the letter from German and Austrian High command and began to read. After a few seconds of reading, his demeanor changed from calm to anger. He gripped the paper tightly and quickly slams it on the desk.

"Those damn fools! First the siege, then Hotzendorf's pathetic winter offensive, and now they expect us to 'break out of this siege'! Ridiculous! It's downright delusion of the highest form, so much they disconnected themselves from reality. They are out of touch."

"Like the French or Russians, Sir?"

"Heh, quite right, Sergeant. Now let's see what your superior has sent."

Colonel Josef opened the next letter sent from Commander Jorgensen. As he began to read, the sound of him muttering to himself could be heard. When he was done, he put letter down with a "hmph."

"If there is nothing else Sir, I'll take my leave and head back to..."

"Not so fast, Sergeant, I may have a use for you. Take a seat."

The Colonel moved toward the windows and closed the blinds and did the same on the door's window. The room was dim, and the colonel sat down at his desk with his smoking pipe in hand.

"During the siege we held out for significant amount of time until the Austro-Hungarian Third army gave us some relief. Then the second siege began putting us in a precarious situation, and now things have gotten worse before you arrived. Our supplies are going missing, ammo dumps blown up despite being far away from the battlefield. I fear we may have a traitor in our midst. The reason I'm telling you this is that you're not from here, nor with the garrison, and getting a fresh pair of eyes might help us. So, I'm volunteering you to assist me to solve an internal problem we currently have."

"But Sir I need to report back to HQ or..."

"I understand your concern, Sergeant, that's why I'm willing provide a handwritten excuse with the garrison commander's signature stating that we inducted your services in our time of need. Does that sound like a reasonable proposition?"

"Yes, Sir. It will suffice. So, when do I start?"

"Now."

The Colonel pulled out a map of Przemyśl Fortress. On it were drawn Xs at certain parts of the map. He explained that the traitor has been targeting specific locations in the city.

"The bastard hit the ammo and supply depots, even guard houses were common targets. Officers were also targeted and killed except for one at the hospital here. This has been causing fear among the ranks in the fortress, except for myself and the garrison commander since we're closely guarded. These sabotages have caused a significant drop in morale and if not handled immediately, the only thing we'll have to worry about is mutiny. Alright, that about does it. Just remember, be discreet in your investigation. Report back to me if you find anything. When the Garrison Commander returns, I'll inform him of the current situation. You're dismissed."

Maxis got up from the chair, gave a salute, and headed out the door. When he got out of the building, he made his way back to the makeshift airfield. He wondered would if he could solve this before the unthinkable happens or worse, the Russians break this siege.

By the time he arrived at the airfield he saw 1Lt. Hoffmann sitting on a small chair reading a newspaper and smoking a cigarette. The plane was parked behind him, primed and ready to be flown again, only this time it'll have one passenger in its seat.

" 1Lt. Hoffmann..."

"Ah, Sgt. Maxis. You took your sweet time I see. The plane is fueled up and ready to go. Ready to get out of this depressing place?" he asked, as he put the newspaper down.

"There's been a slight change of plans."

"Oh, how so?"

Maxis explained the situation that he was currently in. when he was finished, the pilot took one smoke from his cigarette pack and then he got up and spoke.

"Well, this puts a damper on things. I have my current orders to return to base with or without you. Especially with this prototype we just flew in."

"Wait, this plane is a prototype?" Maxis asked.

"Yes, it is. Now I'll ask, do recognize this plane?"

"Can't say that I do."

"This is the Lloyd C.II but it's an improved model. Most planes from the Austro-Hungarians are used for recon but this one is for something else. I've been ordered by Commander Jorgensen and the Prussian Blue Tails Lieutenant Colonel Mückenberger, my boss, to test out this new variant. All I can say is that they are developing new air doctrine regarding planes like these. That's it," Hoffmann finished, taking another smoke.

"That's interesting," said Maxis, as he scratched his chin.

"It is, but I still need to return to give my report. I can't stick around should something happen."

"I understand, Hoffmann."

"But hey, I will return. Last thing I'd rather do is leave one our own in this place, even if you are playing the hero. When I get back, I'll put a request in to see if I will be the one to make a return trip since I know the place well. By my estimation it will probably be three days, but I'll be ready by then. You better work fast 'cause you're on the clock, bub." Hoffmann gestures as he points at his watch.

"I like working under a timetable. Makes things rather interesting," Maxis said with confidence.

"Hey, I like your spirit. Well, off I go."

"Hold on Hoffmann, one more thing. I may need to borrow the coat if you don't mind."

"Oh yeah, sure. Here you go." The lieutenant hands the leather jacket to Maxis.

Hoffmann and Maxis shook hands as he got in his plane and started it up. The roar of the engines coming to life never gets old. As the plane started to move 1 Lt. Hoffmann waves and shouts out, "Remember, three days!" before the plane took flight. Maxis waved back and the plane disappeared in the clouds. Maxis then thinks to himself.

"Hmm, three days, huh? That is, if I can resolve this in the allotted time I have. Though, I should look at the bright side, at least I would get to be like Sherlock Holmes in the books except he didn't have to go to war or dodge bullets and bombs. What fascinating times we live in. Now then, where should I start?"

Day 1, March 17

"As memory would serve me, there were three possible locations to consider. One was the army storehouse that is near the market, the guard houses, and the army field hospital where one of the targeted officers may have survived. I remember what the Colonel said about being discreet, so it was fortunate that I managed to get the coat from 1 Lt. Hoffmann before he left. I'll have to be careful whom I'm speaking to, otherwise I might arouse suspicion and alert the traitor. Incognito is key to my success!" After the thought Maxis put on the jacket and left his pickelhaube and uniform top in a secure location.

Maxis decided to go to the army field hospital on the outskirts of the city. As he went he grabbed a large white robe, a long white scarf, and a little cross from laundry line without the owner noticing. He took a moment to put on the get-up from the items he took before go-ing in.

When he arrived, he observed that the building is av-erage in size and white paint covers its walls. On the door was a sign that said Armee Krankenhaus (Army hospital). Maxis proceeded through the doors and no-ticed the receptionist at the desk was paying no atten-tion to whomever enters the building. He walked past the receptionist and headed down the hall where he ran into a nurse.

"Excuse me, Nurse. Is there an officer here who was recently wounded?" Maxis asked in a soft and gen-tle tone.

"There is one who survived a recent attack in city, though may I ask why?" The nurse had a suspicious look.

"I'm a Chaplain's assistant and I want to check on him and give the Lord's Prayer for his recovery."

"What unit or fort are you from?" the nurse asked.

"From the northern forts, uh...fort number ten," he offered hesitantly.

"Oh, dear. I heard things are rough there. Well, okay, I'll take you to Cpt. Mannfred."

"I don't enjoy lying, but it's necessary," thought Maxis, as he held the cross on his chest.

They headed to the patient's room. The nurse opened the door and announced to the wounded officer that he has a visitor. After introducing the chaplain's assistant to him, she left the two alone and then the officer spoke.

"You don't look like you're from the chaplain," Cpt. Mannfred said, with his eyebrow raised.

"An astute observation, Sir," Maxis responded calmly, as he took his notebook out.

"Figures as much. Then, why are you here?"

"Well, if you must know, I have been sent by Col. Josef to investigate the recent sabotages and uncover who the traitor might be."

"Hmph, a traitor. Surely, you're not serious. But then again, morale hasn't been high lately. There could be someone that might turncoat and run to the Russians. But sabotage? No," the patient mused.

"That's what I'm trying to figure out, who's been targeting the officers and destroying supplies. Now, can you tell me what happen before you ended up in the Krankenhaus(hospital)?" Maxis asked.

"Ok, if this helps resolves this. I was reassigned from the southern forts to assist the commanding troops at fort number seven. It was just me and four of my men who were escorting me at night. The sound of artillery and gunfire was all around, but you get used to it. That's when one of my men fell to the ground and the sound of rifle fire came after. In less than a minute, I found myself on the ground, shot in the abdomen, and three of my troops dead. Only one ran off to get help. None of us could see the sharpshooter. After that, I blacked out. Nothing but total darkness until I woke up here. I was the thirteenth officer that was attacked in the city, but I managed to survive. The other officers that perished before me were shot, most of them shot in the chest, killing them instantly," the captain finished and started to stretch, revealing his bandages.

Maxis jotted down everything he needed to know in his small notebook then asked, "Have you ever treated your men poorly? Possibly someone has it out for you."

"No, other officers might have, but I've tried to treat my men fairly despite the circumstances we're in. That's all I can give you. I hope everything I just elaborated will help in your investigation."

"It will. Thank you for cooperation, Sir."

"Gladly, Mr. Chaplain's assistant," the captain said with a grin as he lay back down in bed.

Maxis exited the room and the building. He started walking down the road toward the market where the Army storehouse was located. As he walked, he reviewed his notes. He ditched the chaplain's attire along the way and grabbed a newsboy's cap off a drunk who was passed out on the side of road and put it on.

- Expert Sharpshooter
- Possible range a mile or two
- Disgruntle marksman?
- Left alive?

Maxis arrived near the city center at the market or what used to be a market. Some of the businesses were boarded and marked 'closed' but others had stayed open, selling whatever was left to sell. Near the flower shop was the army storehouse. Though damaged, parts of the storehouse looked intact aside from a giant hole in the roof.

"Hmm, explosion from what may have been a freak accident or someone might have planted a bomb inside. The hole in the roof is at the center and where the fire had

spread and ended. There are soldiers still guarding the place even though it's partially destroyed, which means they're still using it. I'll have to ask them,." Maxis thinks to himself as he observed the place. He approached the soldier posted in front of the building.

"Guten tag (Good day), soldat! I wanted to ask a few questions for the military papers back home. Especially regarding to the depot behind you." He introduced himself as a reporter from back home while putting on his best Austrian accent. The soldier was hesitant at first as he gave a very stern look.

"Don't worry, most of what I write will most likely go through the Army censor board," he spoke. Immediately the guard let out a sigh and relaxed his shoulders a bit.

"Okay then, ask your questions," the guard said.

"So where were you before the incident?" Maxis asked.

"I was at my post before the storehouse blew up and caught on fire. It was at night, and all was quiet during my shift. Well, sort of, aside from the sound of battle happening far away. Around midnight things started get a bit odd," the soldier said, as he gripped his rifle firmly.

"How so?" Maxis asked as he kept writing.

"I don't know. I felt like I was being watched from somewhere, even with the dimly lit lights on the city streets. It was not enough to illuminate the darkness around corners and alley ways. At one point I swore I saw an outline of person in the darkness before disappearing. Next thing I knew, a peasant child came up from nowhere asking for help. So, I asked what the problem was, but he said that someone was hurt and needed assistance. I told two of my men to keep watch while I went with three others to investigate. Turned out to be nothing. That is until we heard massive explosion and rushed back. Only the storehouse was on fire," the soldier concluded as he let the butt of the rifle rest on the ground.

"So, you doused the flames before it got worse?"

"Yeah, but things got worse even though I prevented the fire from spreading. thank God the rain came that night. The two guards I left behind were found dead. One had his throat slit while the other was stabbed in the chest. After I examined their bodies, the stabs looked to me like something a Russian dagger would make, at least from my experience. It still bothers me that they were there and died alone." The soldier looked down as his expression changed and his fist clenched.

"That's terrible. You have my condolences."

"Yeah, well tell that to their families," the soldier retorted.

"What about the storehouse? Were there explosive ordnances?"

"Not that I know of. The only things in there were our rations in one room and the ammo in the other since our armories are non-functional."

"Well, that's all I can write down, thank you for your time," Maxis said, writing it all down.

"Hope your story turns out well but, wait a moment. How are you going to get out of here?" The soldier shakes his hand.

"By plane, Soldat (soldier)."

"Lucky you," muttered the soldier, rolling his eyes as he faces forward with his rifle to his side.

Maxis wrote down what he needed for his notes for the matter at hand. Then he went to a secluded spot to review his notes and reflect on his thoughts.

- Using civilians to distract the guards in resourceful manner
- Skilled and trained in stealth and hand–to-hand combat
- Using explosives unknown if its stolen or provided.
- Prefer blade type a dagger

"It seems our traitor is a little too well-trained to be an Austro-Hungarian soldier that would be willing to be a turncoat. Though it's possible this could be the work of a group of soldiers, but then what would they have to gain? All they would be doing is quickening the inevitable and they would end up in a POW camp where the treatment is even worse. This sounds foolish, but it's all I have for the moment. I'll continue this tomorrow. Hoping tomorrow may bear fruit, that is if the Russians don't breakthrough by then."

Maxis wrapped it up for now since it was getting late. He would go to the spot where he left his pickelhaube and uniform top then go check in at an Inn for the night.

As he lay in bed, he looked at his pocket watch to see the time, it was nine o'clock. He closed the pocket watch and stared at it for a little longer. The gold pocket watch was engraved with an "M" and showed Maxis' reflection. He then said to himself...

"I'm not sure whether you're proud of me, disappointed, or horrified at what I've become. An elite soldier going to faraway lands meeting new people or ending them. My only prayer is that I survive this war, as well as everyone I carry on my shoulder; and home by Christmas, though that's a bit of a stretch. I hope you can accept the new me, Mutter, Vater, und Schwester (Mother, Father, and Sister)." Maxis said a small prayer and went to sleep. Tomorrow would begin a new day.

CHAPTER 9

FIND THE SABOTEUR

Day 2, March 18

Maxis woke up early before the first light. He got his disguise ready and headed out the door. He still needed to visit a few guard houses in the city. Most of them were hit hard, so in his best interest he decided go to each one and "interview" them for more clues. After a couple of hours and longs walks to the three locations, Maxis was now leaning against a brick wall, contemplating in his thoughts.

"Bah, these Hapsburg don't even know what day it is! Nothing but vague information besides the small tidbit of info I managed to get out of them. The three guard houses I visited had little to give in terms of information. All I got from them was that the attacks happened at night though by morning there were no survivors and no witnesses, not even a soul. Unfortunately, most of them were new replacements dragged in from the front."

"I need something ease off this frustration," Maxis mumbled to himself.

It was midday and he headed to a nearby local tavern. To his surprise the tavern was empty even though the sign said open. He sat in the bar, going over his notes over and over trying to make the connections. The old barkeep walked over and he asked, "Are you here for drink, Sir?"

"Yes, I'll have beer, if that's available," said Maxis as he looked over his notes.

"Excellent choice. We have plenty since the army didn't destroy my secret stash."

"Oh right, the garrison commander gave the order to destroy everything that might be of use to the Russians."

"Spot on, Sir. Only a few soldiers and officers know about the stash. I kept it safe just in case someone still needs to loosen up and forget about the situation we are in. Now, let me get your get drink." The old barkeep walked away and disappeared around the corner of the bar where a small passageway was located.

Maxis looked over his notes again and thought to himself, "*The attacks seem to occur at night, that much is understood. It seems that assaulting the guard houses means to strain manpower from the frontlines and cause chaos in the urban areas. The attempt to destroy the storehouse where all their ammunition is stored partially failed due to the rain and Habsburgs intervening, ultimately preventing an entire block from being leveled. Lastly, there is one thing I still can't figure out...What was the purpose for leaving that one officer alive? Records show most everyone being shot dead. Something tells me that is not a traitor at all.*" His thoughts were abruptly interrupted when the bar keep returned with a mug in hand.

"Sorry for the wait, I had to go through a couple of my fine collections to get what you ordered. Anyway, enjoy," said the old barkeep as he placed the brimming beer mug on the bar.

"Thanks. A question, if I may ask? This may sound a bit ridiculous," Maxis asked as he gripped the mug.

"Ask away."

"Has there been anything out of the ordinary, here?"

"I can't say there has, other than soldiers and officers coming in to drown their sorrows away and...actually there is one thing that comes to mind."

"What?" Maxis eyes lit up and he leaned in to listen closely.

"There was someone here a few days ago who made a strange request for a drink. The customer in question was all covered up with a cloak and hood. Even his lower face was wrapped, obscuring all features, especially the eyes. There was only darkness," the barkeep finished as he started wiping the bar.

"What was the request this person made?"

"Didn't say anything, just wrote it out on piece of paper for a "Kvass." It's a particularly popular drink in some parts of Europe. I told the hooded stranger that a drink like that would take few days to ferment and then it will be ready."

"Then, why is this order strange to you?" Maxis asked as he put on a curious look.

"Because it's a Russian drink. Most the beverages I sell are beer and straight alcohol. Don't get me wrong, there are some families here that are Russian in origin, but that's overrun by the Polish and Jews that live here or used to before everyone was forced to evacuate. Except for small number, of course," the old barkeep said as he starts wiping the bar with a wet rag.

"When will the stranger be returning?"

"Tonight the fermenting is finished. After you leave, I'll close and have the special beverage ready then. If you're planning on some type of meet and greet don't bother, you'll just waste your time with some mute with strange taste."

"Fear not, I won't. Thank you for the beer," Maxis said as he finished the mug in one gulp. Maxis got up from the bar stool, paid for the beer and walked out of the tavern with a purpose.

After leaving the tavern he pressed his back against the wall in the alleyway and began to brainstorm. *"Finally, an actual lead. Now I must prepare a stakeout, somewhere so I can keep an eye on the tavern. Hmm...I guess the alleyway might work I just need keep myself concealed for the time being."*

Maxis waited patiently for the hooded stranger to appear at the tavern. Waiting for so long, he started daydreaming while maintaining watch at the tavern.

When dusk finally arrived, he could see soldiers acting as lamplighters illuminating the lamps. After the lamplighters cleared the streets there was no one else around; nothing but the emptiness of the streets and the constant sound of battle in the far distance.

The night grew darker but there was no sign of a hooded stranger. Maxis was about to give up when the hooded figure finally appeared from the shadows. He walked silently past the alleyway where Maxis was hiding and approached the door of the tavern whose lights were still on but with a sign that said closed. He entered the tavern.

Maxis waited outside for the hooded stranger to come out. Hours went by. He checked the time on his pocket watch; it was ten o'clock.

"Geez, how long does it take for one drink?!" Maxis said impatiently. Another thirty minutes pass and at last the hooded stranger came out of the tavern.

Once he passed by, Maxis emerged from the dark alleyway, moving silently. Maxis followed the mysterious figure through the city streets and many times he had to quickly hide or blend into his surroundings when the stranger would pause to check his surroundings.

This went on until they were on the outskirts of the city and out onto the dirt road. That's when the hooded stranger turned on his flashlight and continued walking. This was a bit of a challenge for Maxis since now the only place he could hide was the ditch on the side of the road.

After a while the stranger made a turn off the road and into a field. He immediately turned off his flashlight and disappeared into the darkness of the night. Maxis gave a small sigh of relief that he wasn't discovered and grateful that he now knows where the stranger's hideout might be.

"Hmm...in order to apprehend the bastard, I'm going to need back up because I do not know if there's more than

one out there. I'll have to make a landmark so I know where I stopped. I may have to wait until morning so that I can inform Colonel Josef about this."

Maxis pulled out his bayonet and inserted the blade into the ground leaving it as a marker. The way back to town is far, but the dimly lit lampposts made it easier for his return trip. He got back to the city and headed to the Inn to get some rest. It was one o'clock in the morning when he retired.

Day 3, March 19

The morning light shone through the room's window blinding Maxis as he wakes. Without a second to waste he put on his uniform and pickelhaube and ran straight for the door.

He arrived at the HQ building and proceeded through the door, down the hall and into the Colonel's office. The Colonel was sitting in his chair and smoking his pipe. He looks up and asks.

"It's been three days Sergeant, what's the current development?"

"Sir, I've come to a conclusion that we are dealing with an enemy saboteur, and I have evidence to back this up."

"Impossible! There is no way one of the Ruskies managed to slip through our defenses and could cause so much damage! Elaborate your findings, now!" Col. Josef demanded.

"Well, from what I've gathered, the saboteur strikes at night, targeting certain areas around the city. That much we already know. From wiping out guard posts, destroying your supplies, and even targeting your officers to disrupt the chain of command, if it's really a traitor, what would he gain from this? Nothing! For he is only trading in one hell hole for another in a Russian POW camp."

"Hmm...I see, but that doesn't answer my question on how the saboteur is an enemy infiltrator and not a traitor," the Colonel said, the sound of his foot tapping repeatedly echoing in the room.

"I'm getting to that part, Sir. First, he attacks and kills your officers from afar so that would make him a crack shot especially at night. Second, he uses civilians to get to his objective such as your ammo dumps and supplies. Third, the infiltrator wiped out some of your guards by utilizing stealth and a blade likely a Russian dagger or a sharpened Bebout blade to silence the soldiers. The reason is not just to cause a disruption but to also drain your manpower."

"So far, I'm having a hard time believing this, but get to the point, Sergeant."

"I was at the tavern last night going over my notes and I asked the owner about anything strange that was going. He explained about someone ordering a drink that was strictly Russian. I know it sounds ridiculous, but here's the twist. I tailed the guy who ordered it all the way to the outskirts of the city. I lost sight of him when he went into the field under the cover of darkness," Maxis calmly finished.

"So, does this mean you know where the bastard is hiding or not?!" The colonel slammed his fist on the desk.

"Yes, Sir I do. I need a small squad to search the area," said Maxis as he pointed on the map on the table.

"Done. I'll send three troops assist you, but that's all I can lend. I'll send the word. As we speak, the garrison commander is preparing to break out of this siege. The quicker we find this saboteur, the better. Now get going!"

Maxis left the Colonel's office without a second to waste and headed to the location where he would meet the three soldiers at the end of the city. He greeted the Austro-Hungarian soldiers. The three soldiers stood to attention and introduced themselves.

"Cpl. Zell, here to assist, Feldwebel (Sergeant)!"

"Pvt. Peterson, here!"

"Pvt. Dieter, reporting for duty!"

"Well met! Alright Männer (men), we'll need to double time it to landmark I placed on this road. Time is of the essence soldaten (soldiers), move out!" says Maxis in an commanding tone.

The small squad responded with "Ja, Feldwebel (Yes, Sergeant)!" and the group set out on the dirt road with haste. They arrived at their destination when Maxis spotted the grip of his bayonet sticking from the ground and some parts of the blade reflecting from the sun.

"Hold position," Maxis ordered as he approached the half-buried blade and pulled it from the ground. He put it back in the sheath and turned to the soldiers and spoke.

"Alright, we'll be searching on this side of the field. Keep your guard up, we don't know what we might find. I want a three-meter spread."

"Sergeant, what is it that we are looking for?" Cpl. Zell asks.

"Something a bit out of place like a camp or something, Corporal Zell."

"Understood. We'll begin our search. You heard him, men. Start looking!" the corporal ordered the rest of the troops.

The squad moved out into the field with their weapons at the ready. They searched the field for any signs of an encampment, but nothing. For half a day they kept looking.

"Sergeant, some of the boys are getting tired of this. We've been searching for hours but turned up nothing. How much longer should we keep doing this?" Corporal Zell asks.

"*Low groan* "Do one last sweep of the area and we'll call it a day," Maxis said in disappointment.

"Right. HEY! Peterson and Dieter, one more sweep and we're done!" The two men he was addressing groaned in disbelief and spoke.

"Are you serious?!" Said Pvt. Peterson.

"Yeah, there is nothing here but grass, dirt, and AHHHHHHH!" Dieter was cut short from his complaining as he descended through the ground, disappearing from sight.

Maxis quickly rushed over with his pistol drawn out expecting the worst but was relieved to see the private was all right. What lay in front of Maxis was a large hole in the ground with a rope ladder.

"Private, are you okay?" He asks while looking down at the hole.

"Yeah, guess I should watch where I step, huh," Dieter responded as he slowly got up and brushed the dirt from his uniform.

"Hold on. The two of you hold here," Maxis orders as he climbs down the small rope ladder.

"Well congratulations, Private. You found it. Now let's see where it leads." Maxis pulled out a lighter and ignited it.

In front of them was a dark tunnel. The two crouched down to move through the tunnel with Maxis taking the lead. The air was filled with dust and the particles could be seen even in the lighter's light. The tunnel was no better, the spacing was confined, giving a claustrophobic condition.

"How much further, Sergeant?" Pvt. Dieter whispered.

"Hold up, there's a drop off. Keep your weapon readied, I'm going in." Maxis slowly moved ahead and gently slipped out of the tunnel. Luckily the drop off wasn't deep, just a foot or two. He checked his surroundings for any sign of contact.

"Alles klar (All clear), get over here," Maxis said.

"Still can't see a thing, how can this person see through and live in this dump?"

"With lanterns, Private," replied Maxis as he lit a lantern nearby.

The lantern emitted a small light which revealed several other glass lanterns in the vicinity. Maxis quickly ignited the other lanterns until there was enough light to make their surroundings more visible.

"Well, quite roomy in here...perfect hideout for an enemy saboteur," said Maxis.

"I bet, or it could just be lowly scum hiding away from the public," said Pvt. Dieter suddenly, eyeing a gold necklace with diamonds sitting on a small table.

"Private, try not to touch anything! We need to make sure this place isn't booby trapped. So, don't even think about taking that necklace!"

"Come on, it could be worth a fortune."

"Nein! Show some integrity, Private! Plus, it could be the only thing that might be a trap, so leave it alone," Maxis snapped at the Private.

Maxis turned away from the Private and began checking the area for traps. After five minutes of searching there was no sign of any strings or pressure plates.

"The area is clear. Now we can begin without any worries," said Maxis.

They looked around the room for anything of intrigue. The surroundings of the place were nothing short of basic. The walls, ceiling, and floors were made of dirt just like the tunnel, though less dusty and claustrophobic. On the right side of the room was a makeshift desk of sorts and next to it was an entrance that leads to somewhere. To the left of the room was another table with some items on it and a chair leaning against the wall. Finally, in the far corner of the room was a bed made of hay with a blanket on top. Maxis went to the left to examine the table and could feel his pickelhaube drag across the dirt ceiling.

"Hmm...what do we have here?" says Maxis, as he picked up a rifle stock from the table.

"What did you find?" Dieter asked.

"Looks like a disassembled rifle by the look of the bolt on the table. An M91 Mosin Nagant with an attached scope. Seems he didn't finish cleaning it. I doubt you have many of these in storage."

"It's more of a luxury to have a rifle like that. It uses smokeless powder while ours is the exact opposite. Most of our equipment is outdated but it is all we got."

"Well, congrats Private. Here's your replacement! That is if you feel like putting it back together," Maxis said sarcastically as he hands the half-finished rifle to him.

"I'll pass."

Maxis put the rifle down and looked at the next item on the table. He picks up what seems to be a piece of wood with 13 notches on it.

"So, you're keeping track of your recent kills, eh. Too bad the thirteenth survive, Maxis thought ,"

as he put the wood down on the table and looked at the last item, somewhat confused.

"What the...a vase with flowers in it? Strange," he said picking it up carefully.

"What's so strange about that? So, what if Ruskie likes a little decency? This place is already uncomfortable enough, I mean..." He sniffs the air. "What's that smell it? It's sweet, like perfume," observed Pvt. Dieter.

"Probably just to throw anyone off by masking his scent."

"So, he wants to pass off as some harlot of the night?"

"Just keep looking, Private."

The search continued inside the saboteur's hideout. After going through what was on the table Maxis made his way toward the bed to have a look. He grabbed the lantern to make his analysis a little easier.

"Hmm...upon further inspection, the blanket's design is Slavic in origin but from what territory, culture, or country one can only guess? One thing is certain, this blanket is nice and soft like any ordinary blanket besides the hidden knife beneath the sheets. When in doubt carry a backup, there's also a something knitted at the corner...the letter V?" Maxis put the blanket back and moved on to the table at the left side of the room.

"Jackpot! Now this is what I was looking for!" said Maxis with a small amount of excitement in his tone.

When he shone his light over the table it revealed books, maps, paperwork and even files with profiles of certain individuals in them. This was certainly a treasure trove of enemy intelligence. Pvt. Dieter's jaw dropped when he saw what Maxis was looking at but could not begin to comprehend.

Maxis pus the lantern on the table and began looking through the items. The findings were incredible, the maps showed detailed drawings of the Fortress. It even showed the location of all Austro-Hungarian military positions in and out of the city as well as a detailed report of the number in strength of each fort from most active to the least. There was also a list of names of officers crossed off ...all except Cpt. Mannfred. But there was one thing that stood out from the rest, a folder.

Maxis picked up the folder to see the front. Written in Russian was the word "konfidentsial'nyy (confidential) in red and on the bottom right was a stamp of sorts, Maxis took a closer look.

The stamp had a bear's head with a crown floating above it with streamers and at the bottom were two Cossack daggers crossed blade. There was a description below "Official stamp of the Imperskiy Tayna Brigada (Imperial Secret Brigade)" and their motto was there too, "Tsar' i Bog (For Emperor and God)."

"*sigh*...It had to be them, huh. I should have known they were involved," said Maxis as he opened the file to read the documents.

"Soldier, this mission you have been given is vital for the brigade. The list of objectives has been set for you on the next page after you read this. Assuming that Colonel Vorshevsky has made it personally clear to you that this operation requires the upmost of stealth, so it's important that you do not get caught."

Maxis continued reading to the next page and found the list of objectives and explanations of why they were targeted. At the bottom of the page was this statement. "Our main goal is to drain the Hapsburgs of their resources, morale, and even deny them ever feeling safe. The Fortress itself could be vital in our future operations in the region, so the quicker you are to finish your mission the better. We do have contingency plan in case you have been compromised at the next page. See to it that you read it."

He flipeds to next page titled "Contingency Plan" in Russian. The page itself had set of guidelines of what to do.

"Tovarishch (Comrade), should you find yourself compromised in your mission, here is a set of guidelines for you to follow.

If the enemy has discovered your hideout be sure to set charges and destroy all evidence of your presence and relocate to a new hideout to continue the mission.

Should the enemy discover you...fear not, just lay low until their attention is averted elsewhere. Remain in your hideout until the coast is clear...if not refer to number 1.

If your hideout and you have been discovered and possibly unable to locate to a new hideout. Then you must abandon your mission and fall back to friendly lines. Do whatever is necessary to ensure your retreat is successful, the map of the evacuation point should guide you be sure always keep it on your person, at all times. Fret not soldier, we will be there to get you out.

After reading the files, the map was nowhere to be seen on the document. Maxis put the maps, files, and paperwork into the folder. Then he noticed a couple of books stacked on top of each other. He grabbed one of them to have a closer look.

"The Bronze Horseman by Alexander Pushkin...seems this saboteur has some good taste in literature." Maxis put the book down and picked up another one.

"Heh, now this is a classic, The Nutcracker by E.T.A Hoffman."

"What? You mean the play?" asked Pvt. Dieter.

"Nein, this is before they turned it into a play. Anyway, we're done here, let's get out of here."

"Sergeant, what was in that document that you were so fixated on?"

"Nothing you need to be worrying about, Private. Now let's go!"

Maxis went through the tunnel first with a lantern in one hand and the folder in the other. Pvt. Dieter did not follow instead stayed behind without a word. Maxis made it out of the tunnel and climbed up the rope ladder where Corporal and Pvt. Peterson reached down to pull him out. The light of day blinded Maxis.

"Sergeant, I'll assume you found something important in there since you came out of there in such a hurry," said Corporal Zell.

"Indeed, I did."

"If that's the case where's Dieter?"

"What?! I thought he was behind me unless... Oh no."

Meanwhile back in the hideout Pvt. Dieter was looking at the piece of jewelry with greed in his eyes.

"A trap he says, what does he know. This would surely fetch a nice price when this war is over. I'm not stealing, I'm confiscating it in the name of me and not that old coot in the throne. I'll just put it in my pocket and make sure to keep it safe." Dieter muttered to himself.

He grabbed the necklace but felt some resistance from it.

"What nonsense is this...a string? Probably a ploy to prevent someone from taking this. Now if I can just..." Dieter managed to get the necklace after a few pulls.

"There. Now to get out of here and...*click*." Before he finished his sentence, the whole hideout exploded unleashing a thunderous boom.

Outside the hideout, Maxis and the others were immediately flung off their feet by the explosion, hitting the ground hard. The dirt and dust were falling from the aftermath. There was no trace of Pvt. Dieters remains or the hideout now, just a giant crater. The Corporal and Pvt. Peterson got back on their feet and quickly helped Maxis up, then the Corporal asked, "What's the plan, Sergeant? We lost a man and whole place just blew up in our faces."

"First things first, we need to get back to central command and inform the Colonel of the situation before he leaves. I'll try to formulate a plan when we get there. Move out!" Maxis ordered.

The group double-timed it back to the city as fast they could. As they passed through, the city buzzed with activity in preparation for the oncoming breakout. Time was running out for Maxis. They made it to the central command building where they ran past the receptionist without him saying a word. Maxis headed down the hall and through the Colonel's door. He is standing in front of the window and turns to Maxis, seeing the file in his hand.

"Sgt. Maxis, I hope you have an update on the ongoing investigation," Colonel Josef prompts firmly.

"I have. More than you can imagine, Sir." Maxis raised the file for the colonel to see.

"That is good Sergeant, very good. But before we get this underway, I should inform you that a messenger pigeon came by. It's from your Commander. It stated that your pickup was delayed due to an unforeseen situation in Champagne, France. You're stuck here for a day and that is all.

"Now, show me what you have uncovered. Is it evidence of your theory that we may

have an enemy saboteur or my belief that there is traitor among us?"

Maxis placed the folder on the desk and opened it to show the Colonel the contents. The Colonel turned around, walked over to take a look, he put on his glasses and was shocked by what he saw. When he was finished, he sat down in his chair still surprised and feeling defeated.

"I guess you are right Sergeant. There I said it," admitted Colonel Josef with disgust.

"Gloating isn't my forte Colonel Josef. I only did what I was ordered."

"And that you did my boy, well done," said the Colonel, his demeanor changing quickly before he continued.

"Now with the information you provided we now know the saboteurs next move that means we can take it from here. For now, you can stay put and wait for your plane to arrive, but by time he gets here we'll be marching our way to Krakow," the Colonel said with cockiness in his tone.

"With all due respect Sir, I'm not staying put. In case you didn't see the symbol on the front of the folder, you're dealing with a military faction within the Russian Empire that is well equipped and well trained to elite status. They can send a small platoon who can tear your men asunder. If one of them is here in this Fortress, then it's no wonder he is causing so much damage. That's only half the truth I just told. The unit I come from is specially trained to deal with this type of enemy. So, here is my recommendation, Sir...let me continue my work here as I have already produced a plan to neutralize this threat." Maxis finished.

The Colonel was silent for a moment. It was uncertain how he would respond.

"Hmph, I see your point Sergeant. Therefore, I will take you up on your recommendation. However, we are low on time and manpower so elaborate on what you are planning to do, and I'll see in what capacity I'm able to assist you."

"Fear not, this will not require much, Sir." As Maxis prepared to explain his plan on dealing with the saboteur, he pulled one of the maps from the folder and began to speak.

"The saboteur will mostly like find his hideout destroyed and which will trigger one his fallback plans. He might find a new spot to keep operating in this area, so the plan is simple. We will have to make the city square a fake supply area using empty crates and boxes since we can assume he might know something about your current plans of breaking out of this siege. This will happen at night because of his preferred way of commencing his operations. Whatever manpower you can spare will help a lot to ensure the trap will work. Stopping him will not only foil Russians plans but guarantee your breakout can proceed without any interference."

"Impressive, even for a low-ranking soldier like yourself. You can come up with a plan that quickly, but what do you intend to do if it backfires?" the Colonel questioned.

"I wouldn't worry about it, Sir. Let's just say I have back up plan," Maxis said with confidence.

"Hmph, that's reassuring. All right, I'll see what I can do. In the meantime use the men I lent you to get your plan started. More will join you in time, just lead them in the right direction."

"Thank you, Sir," said Maxis as he walked out of his office and out of the building to inform Corporal Zell and Pvt. Peterson of the situation. After the briefing they went to the city square to begin the preparations. Eventually more arrived to help as they moved large crates and barrels in place to make the supply area look legitimate. With Maxis on the scene giving directions about what needed to be done, the group managed to finish setting up quickly. After everything was said and done Maxis gathered everyone to explain the next phase of the plan.

"Alright listen up Männer (men), next part of the plan will be simple. You are to stand guard here and protect the supplies. That is all, don't bother asking questions, just perform your duties as usual. Understood?"

Everybody responded with "Yes Sergeant!" and immediately took position. Maxis walked to an alleyway that had a clear view of the city square. He checked his pocket watch for the time. It was seven-thirty p.m., and all was well. Now it was time to wait and see.

"Well...this might take a while, but patience is a virtue they say. Let's see how true that proverb will hold. I should have told the men what to expect while on guard but then again, I need them act natural as if it's another assignment from the higher ups. Besides, since the Tayna Brigade is involved, I must make it a priority to capture him alive for interrogation that is if the Habsburgs don't get in my way."

CHAPTER 10

CONFRONTING THE SABOTEUR

Time went by painfully slow for Maxis as he waited in the alleyway for his target, but there was nothing. By the time the sun set there was huge barrage of artillery followed by machine gun fire in the distance; the breakout had begun. The men guarding the area breathed a sigh of relief realizing they didn't have to go back to the meat-grinder that was the frontlines, although this night shift would indeed be something out of the ordinary.

It was ten minutes till eleven and still nothing had happened; the saboteur had yet to appear. It was almost certain the plan had failed, realizing this Maxis waited a little longer. Then, something appeared around the corner. Maxis held his position to observe and think to himself.

"Children at this time of night? Better see what happens."

The group of children approached the group of soldiers guarding the bait. The kids were giggling and laughing as they made their way. At first, the soldiers had their guard up before realizing what had appeared; some blew it off as nothing while others were curious. The kids stopped right in front of the guards and one of them walked up and spoke.

"Down with dual monarchy and your folly war!" Then the boy and the rest of the children tossed mud and rocks at the soldiers and ran away in a hurry. This infuriated the men who immediately gave chase leaving their post empty.

"Not surprising but it worked. Now when are you going to show, huh?" muttered Maxis, still concealed in the alleyway.

Out of the shadows came a cloaked hooded figure walking toward the crates. The way he moved was subtle and very silent like a cat was moving through the space. The figure made his way to the stockpile and squatted down. Maxis pulled out his pistol and switched off the safety. He gingerly moved toward the cloaked figure, very carefully like a wolf ready to ambush his prey. He got close enough to see the explosives already on the ground waiting to be hooked up to the detonator, but the saboteur could not do that as Maxis was already right behind him. The barrel of the pistol made contact on the back of hooded figure's head and immediately he froze.

"Don't move. Get up slowly," Maxis orders. The figure slowly rises with his hands in the air, his back toward Maxis.

"Good. You and I are going to have a long chat before I hand you off to the troops."

The guards that left their post earlier appeared around the corner to see Maxis pointing his weapon at the cloaked figure. Immediately one shouted out, "What's going on here?"

Maxis shifted his eyes off the target for one moment. In that split second the hooded figure quickly grabbed Maxis' arm and threw him over his shoulder. He hit the ground hard and before he could act, Maxis heard a familiar "click" and saw a grenade falling to the ground. Without even blinking Maxis quickly moved out of the way shouting "Grenade!" and the soldiers hastily took cover. The grenade went off but instead of an explosion there was a large plume of smoke, and the hooded figure made his escape.

During the confusion, Maxis could hear what direction of the saboteur's steps, but at same time could hear Cpl. Zell calling out for him.

"Sergeant! What's happening? I can't see a damned thing."

"Corporal, raise the alarm! Alert everyone you see! I'll signal you with a flare on my current whereabouts, Okay. Now go!" Maxis jumped up, picked up his pistol and pursued the saboteur.

Maxis runs around the corner and sees the hooded figure making a break for it. He fires his pistol without hesitation. The noise of gunfire and the sound of bullets ricocheting off the lamppost filled the street. One of the bullets struck the glass of the lamppost forcing the hooded saboteur to shield himself from the falling glass. But still he pressed on.

"Verdammt (damn it), I didn't concentrate on my shots." Without a moment to waste, Maxis holstered his weapon and rushed over to where he last sighted the saboteur. As he arrived at the spot he caught a glimpse of the tail end of the cloak as it disappeared down the alleyway. Maxis raced over and saw him speeding down the alley, knocking things over in an attempt to break the pursuit. That didn't stop Maxis; he dashed right through the alleyway jumping over any obstacle that lay before him. He made it to the other end and saw the saboteur heading toward a three-story building that is under construction. He climbs up one of the ladders but by the time Maxis arrived at the location, the saboteur had already kicked the large ladder to the ground.

Maxis tried to figure out a way to get up there, and the answer was right in front of him. There was a bench with a rope attached to it and at the top was a counterweight.

"I've only seen this once at a play...here we go!"

Maxis drew out his bayonet and with one swing, he cut the rope. The rope jerked upward and the counterweight falls, flinging Maxis toward the top of the roof. He quickly lunged forward before the rope ran out and landed on the rooftop.

From there he has a clear view of the city of Przemyśl. It was a magnificent sight to behold, in the far distance of the city there were constant flashes on the horizon. The sight of muzzle flashes from machine guns and artillery could be seen as far as the eye can see, Russians and Austro-Hungarians duking it out.

Maxis snaps out of it and concentrates on what he was doing. He put his bayonet back inside its sheath, and scans the rooftops for any sign of the saboteur. Lo and behold, he sees him walking subtly at the other end of the rooftop!

"He didn't notice me...good, now's my chance to get the drop on the bastard and..."

Before he could finish his thoughts, a flare appeared behind him illuminating the sky and revealing the two to the soldiers down below. The saboteur turned around only to be blinded by the light for a moment and afterwards was met with surprise, shocked to see a soldier with a pickelhaube standing on the other end of the building. From Maxis' view point he saw the look of surprise in the only part that wasn't covered by the cloak; his eyes, now lit from the flare.

"There! He's right there, men!" shouted an Austro-Hungarian soldier.

The saboteur made a break for it and jumped over the short gap to the next building. Maxis did the same and pressed on with the pursuit. While they were crossing rooftops, the soldiers below followed. From time to time they would try to take a shot at the saboteur but ended up missing every shot, once even almost hitting Maxis, bullets whistling by. The interference from the soldiers, the sound and explosion going on elsewhere, and crossing the rooftops of Przemyśl only made the hunt more intense and dangerous.

"Watch your fire, you idiots!" Maxis warned while in pursuit.

They hopped from building to building during the chase so often that the soldiers lost track of them. Maxis soon realized that they were running out of roof and eventually would reach a dead end. He almost felt relief but that was about to change.

Suddenly the saboteur picked up speed and when he gained enough momentum executed the most daring act right in front of Maxis. The saboteur jumped off the ledge of the building across the street, managing to grab onto the edge of a windowsill, then climbed up the two-story building.

"Huh, so we're doing that, eh? Last time I did something like this was with my friends and I nearly broke my leg. Well, all or nothing. Immer Mit Präzision (Always with precision)!"

Maxis muttered and took a deep breath, and sprinting to gain momentum. Without hesitation he jumped off the building, catapulted through the air and grabbed onto the windowsill. He knocked over a couple of potted plants, his pistol falling with potted plants to the ground. And the pain from grabbing the sill was immense.

He climbed up the from the windowsill to a nearby drainpipe and from there managed to climb up to rooftop quickly. Maxis slowly peeked up and saw the saboteur walking away at slow pace. The saboteur stopped to look down at the skylight in front of him. Without a second to waste Maxis pulled himself up and moved quickly and quietly toward the saboteur. This time he was right where he wanted him to be. Suddenly a spotlight appeared on him from below...the soldiers below had spotted him.

"Verdammt (Damn it)!" Maxis cursed and without thinking twice ran and tackled the saboteur causing the two of them to fall through the skylight. Time seemed to slow down during the fall for Maxis.

"Strange...I apprehended the Ruskie but his body feels abnormal ...as if this saboteur is a..."

Before he finished his thoughts the two crashed onto the table on which broke their fall. There was a sudden scream and panic from the family who were enjoying their dinner. They evacuated the scene as two Austro-Hungarian soldiers kicked open the door and rushed toward Maxis who was trying to get up. The saboteur got up slowly, trying to regain his composure while feeling the pain from the fall.

"Sergeant, Cpl. Zell told us about the situation! We are here to assist," said one of the soldiers. The other soldier had his rifle trained on the saboteur.

"What do want me to do with this one?" the soldier asks while pointing his rifle.

Before Maxis could answer, he heard a sudden click and saw a grenade rolling on its side toward the soldiers. He quicky pushed the soldier next to him away and grabbed the other one by the collar and threw him to the next room. The grenade didn't explode but made a hissing sound and Maxis felt his nose burning.

"Tear gas!" he yelled. He immediately held his breath and covered his nose while signaling to other soldiers to get out. Suddenly the saboteur jumped through the window to escape the gas, shattering it.

Maxis jumped through and ran right after him, resuming the chase. He pursued the saboteur through the city constantly running without stopping to take slight breather or show signs of slowing down. Determined as Maxis was on acquiring his target, the saboteur was as persistent trying to lose him. The pursuit lead them outside the city to the dirt road where few lampposts continued. Far in the distance the Austro-Hungarians waged battle against the Russians, only this time through the darkness it could be seen more clearly.

The sound of gunfire, artillery, grenades, could be heard along with the sound of men yelling and screaming as they died.. The flashes from artillery shells hitting their target appeared every five to ten seconds and lit up the sky, then a pause and the pattern would repeat again. Maxis tracked the saboteur so far from the city that all that was visible was the dim light coming through the buildings and houses.

Then he saw the saboteur enter a three-story building which was partially destroyed. There was a large hole on one side of the third floor and a medium hole on the other side indicating the point of entry of the shell. The cloaked hooded figure disappeared at the entrance that was dimly lit by a lantern, the only source of light.

Maxis walked slowly toward the building breathing heavily, realizing he ran more than a mile. His legs felt sore and the sound of the heart beating pounded in his ear from the constant running and sprinting. Before went in, he pulled out the flare gun from the inside pocket of his uniform then fired it in the air, illuminating the sky before it slowly went out and turned into a small red dot of light.

"I hope they can see it from here, for once I actually need their help not before...sigh...into belly of the beast I go."

Day 4, March 20

As Maxis walked through the entrance, the first thing he saw was total darkness around every corner except for a lantern on the staircase that was faintly lighting the way. He needed more light, so he reached into the interior pocket of his uniform and pulled out a lighter. He ignited the lighter on the third try and though not bright, it was enough to see. As he walked up the steps, Maxis began to think over everything that occurred before setting up the trap and the whole chase escapade.

"Surprising how this all sort of turned out, but there is one thing that bugs me...that my conscience won't let go. The smell of perfume and that odd decoration of that plant, dead silence when the saboteur walks, deadly sharpshooting skills, clean stab wounds from a Cossack dagger, but most damning of all was the feel of the body when we were falling before slamming on the table. I think I came to a conclusion with whom I'm dealing with now...the deadliest of them all."

He proceeded to third floor and the windows started to give off light though it was faint. Finally, the full moon appeared from behind the clouds. There was some light at the end of the staircase and the weak sound of someone breathing heavily. As Maxis reached the top, he sees before him what was once an observation post. There was a pair of binoculars and periscope version on tripod alongside small fireplace still burning. Then he saw the saboteur slouched over, appearing exhausted and he could hear heavy breathing.

"You know how the old saying goes, 'I like it when they play hard to get.' Wouldn't you agree...Junior Sergeant Arina Vorshevsky?" Maxis said firmly.

The faint sound of the heavy breathing ceased, the figure stood up straight and slowly took the hood off. The moon's light reveals her crimson-colored hair in a fishtail braid, as it gently falls out. The figure then turned around and removed the covering to reveal a woman's face. Violet-colored eyes now shone in the lantern's light as she faced Maxis.

"You actually remember me, how sweet," Arina said in a light sarcastic tone before continuing. "But, if I re-call we never had a proper introduction when we first met, so how do you know my name and rank?"

"Simple, the pistols you and your father so gra-ciously donated to us back at your camp a month ago," Maxis responded.

"Oh, so you're the one who took them...figures. They told me my shipment was destroyed in the explosion your lacky set up. Speaking of which, where is he? Surely you two are attached at the hip, are you not?" Arina looked around before looking back at Maxis.

"Lothar is somewhere else giving your Entente bud-dies a hard time."

"Pfft, the Triple Entente is hardly an alliance. They use us for our numbers to keep you and the Hapsburgs busy while they struggle to make a breakthrough on their end. Giving us weapons hardly make us allies as our views and ideas differ with theirs," Arina scoffed as she crossed her arms.

"That's it, keep her talking Maxis until backup arrives, but then again...this may be the only time we might actually get to talk to her," Maxis thinks to himself.

"Anyway, you seem to know me well enough. Do you want to guess how I know you?" she asks softly with a grin. Arina begins to walk while keeping her distance from Maxis.

"I'll assume you have people inside that already told you," he too started to mimic her as they circled around like wolves.

"Mm, yes and no. My 'people' could barely get anything since the coded messages were certainly very difficult to crack. We only got names and nothing more but it's all thanks to the Hapsburg deserters who squealed everything about you and your friend. I must say, some of it I could hardly believe...a German soldier who is proficient with a rifle and a giant who could hold a machine gun and even fire it while moving, I had to see it for myself. That's not all. You see, when I decided to find out more details about you, I realized I had a chance at fighting the famous or infamous Black Wolf of Mons. And that's not all...fighting a legend was certainly a thrill since the soldiers I faced never lasted long," Arina finished, walking and facing Maxis.

Maxis didn't say a word after hearing this but he was silent and clenched his fist. However, while they were circling each other, he caught a glimpse of a shimmering light in the distance.

"Now the burning question is...how did you figure out it was me under the cloak?" she asked.

"The way you operate, your skills, and the hideout. Using nighttime raids and the most damning of all, how swiftly you killed the guards at their posts without making a noise! The way you walk so quietly like a wolf invading another pack's territory and assassinating officers from extremely far in one shot. Your hideout gave me some ideas. The smell of perfume, the women's necklace, and the knitted blanket. When I looked at it there was a signature V knitted at the corner," Maxis explained in a sincere tone.

"Is that all? Because honestly it could have been anybody besides me," she countered, with sincerity as well.

"That's not all. During the chase your movements mirrored the same way you rode on the top of and then departed from the Tsar tank. The last thing was when I, uhm...tackled...you and felt..." Maxis finished feeling a bit shy and embarrassed as he looked down for a second.

Arina, flustered by this, tried not to blush and went so far as to cover her mouth to hide her grin.

"Moy, moy (My, my). I did not take you for an intimate type, Maxis. Where did your Prussian discipline go?" she said, trying to sound serious, but failing after a slight crack in her voice.

"Well, as much I have enjoyed our chat together... hopefully not the last, I should really get going and..." she stopped as she turned toward the hole in the wall.

"Not so fast Vorshevsky, you're not going anywhere. I intend to take you in since you are someone of importance due to your connections and the intel about Tayna and the Russian Empire's military operations. Just come with me quietly. I'll be sure not to let anyone lay a finger on you," Maxis said with such firmness in his voice.

"And what happens if I refuse? You don't have a gun and I can easily just waltz through and escape, though you would probably keep on chasing me like any other boy would," she said as she twirled her crimson fishtail braid.

"Verdammt (damn it), she's getting ready to bolt. sigh There is one last hand I can play but, this might be the second dumbest thing I'll be doing today after losing my pistol. Well, here goes. Hopefully I'll buy enough time for them to get here. Let's see if the Trench Trooper training along with the extra CQC training paid off."

Maxis pulled out his sawback bayonet and pointed it at Arina.

"I have something else in mind," he declared confidently.

"What showing off your new bayonet? As much as I like the design, you'd better not get caught with it. I heard the Brits and Frenchies execute those harboring such a tool. Besides, you must do better than that to impress this girl."

"I'm not showing off, I am challenging you."

"Kakiye (What)?" she reacts as she turned back to Maxis with her eyes lit up.

"You heard what I said. If I recount our last dance, I was at a bit of a disadvantage. My shoulder and leg were still injured and I also forfeited by returning your personal belongings," Maxis said with a shrug.

Arina looked away for a moment when he referred to the personal letter from her mother.

"But now I'm all ready to go. The only thing is I won't be holding back. I want to see for myself ....me...The Black Wolf of Mons taking on you the 'Huntress'...to see if your skills are greater or lesser than mine. The rules are same as last time," Maxis says proudly and with a lot of boasting as he pulled out his nahkampf-messer (close combat knife) from the hidden sheath in his boot.

"Oh Gott (God), now I sound like Lothar and his ridiculous fantasied stories. Even saying that dreaded title!"

Arina froze for a moment after hearing Maxis and his interesting request. She remembered what her father had told her when she returned from her failed mission in Bochnia after fighting Maxis for the first time. "Never do that again," were the last words that echoed inside her head afterward.

"What should I do? The way he said it so vigorously and exciting, how can I say nyet (no) to a challenge like that? But my father's orders are to not engage in open combat with the enemy, but...its him who's asking...me," her thoughts ran rampant even though her composure was sincere, and her stance was calm.

The thrill of the chase, running over rooftops and crashing through the skylight and into the table. After all that, her adrenaline was still pumping and the fire in her still screamed for a challenge...a challenge like no other, and she offered her response.

"Da (Yes)!" She took off her cloak and tossed it aside. The light in the room revealed her uniform, a standard issued leather belt and suspenders of Russian design with a belt buckle that has the Russian double eagle, her iconic dark green Gymnasterka (military tunic) with brass buttons, black pants with a red strip, and surprisingly a furazhka (field cap with a visor) in the same color as her tunic hanging off her belt. The belt buckle bore the Tayna brigade symbol. Arina took notice of Maxis looking at her.

"I hope you were looking at the military emblem Sergeant, and nothing else. This is the symbol for the Imperskiy Tayna Brigada and soon it will be this that will fly over this fortress along with the double headed eagle of Russia," she said as she showed off, slowly grasping the Cossack dagger on her belt.

"I beg to differ. You already heard the sounds of battle in the distance which means the Hapsburgs are already breaking out of this siege, probably leaving your army decimated," Maxis retorted.

"Oh, so that was the commotion they were creating all night? I thought they were putting on nice fireworks display for my comrades, but I guess it would be destructive had I not told them about the breakout. Otherwise, they would definitely have been unprepared for it," she smirked as she spoke

"Was (What)?" Maxis reacted.

"I mean, if I hadn't wounded that thirteenth officer then I couldn't have procured the code book that helped my men crack the Hapsburg communications. If it wasn't on him then a little interrogation would have been in order but thankfully, I did find it," said Arina as she looked through the hole in wall to see the battle rage on.

"Those poor souls. But what can I do? Now then. Shall we begin, devushka (young lady)?" Maxis asked with a smirk.

"I'm going to enjoy fighting a living legend," Arina said.

"Osobenno krasivyy (Especially a handsome one)," declared her thoughts as she pulled out her Cossack dagger from the sheath.

The two stood facing each other in their combat poses, waiting for one of them to make the first move. The moon light shone down through hole in the rooftop when suddenly the sound of an incoming shell is heard and immediately explodes somewhere nearby.

Maxis and Arina leapt toward each other with their blades clashing. Though Maxis had the advantage due to his dual wielding, it was nothing compared to Arina's sharp reflexes. Maxis struck with his bayonet, but Arina blocked it with her dagger, then suddenly blocked the other attack from his left by grabbing his wrist and throwing him to the wall.

He quickly recovered just to encounter Arina jumping off some furniture to commence an attack from above. She is countered by Maxis as he dropped his bayonet to perform the same technique that she performed on him. He threw her over his shoulder and across the room. She recovered quickly and stood up fast, adjusting her neck which made a cracking sound.

"Is that all you got Sgt. Maxis?!" she spat in a sarcastic tone.

Maxis responded first with a neck crack of his own, then spoke.

"I've only just begun."

Arina charged forward shouting "URA!" and Maxis charged as well shouting "HURRA!" The fight continued. The moon shone brightly and with the view of the battle outside still raging, there was something quite poetic in their dance of death.

During their battle against each other, their strengths and weaknesses were once again demonstrated. Maxis tried utilizing his skills carefully, when he attempted to overpower Arina with his strength. She hastily used her heighten mobility to counter and escaped a hold or slash.

When Arina tried to attack Maxis' blindside she is quickly met with his second blade blocking her attempt of incapacitating him. Then he palm struck her to push her back, anticipating her movement. Unlike their last encounter they certainly have improved their combos and skills, but just like their last battle neither side was gaining the upper hand. Instead they wounded each other though not severely as they slashed their uniforms.

Time passed. Both are still standing but now exhausted and hurt. The two stared at each other intensely waiting to see who would make the first move again.

"I can't believe I lasted this long against her; she has improved since the last time but, I'm not done yet not by long shot. I already lost track on how much time has passed but I'm willing to keep this up as long as I can. I just wonder how much longer until they get here," Maxis pondered in his thoughts.

Arina's thoughts were different on the matter.

"Bog (God), he knows how to keep up with me. I was certain I had the advantage regardless. That will teach me to underestimate someone, even with additional training on close quarter he still won't go down. I see why he was called the Black Wolf...and I'm loving every moment of it," thinking, as she tried to control her breathing.

Maxis saw light reflecting in the shattered mirror, revealing three to five lights appearing close to the building. Suddenly he heard Arina shouting as she approached for one last attack.

"Hey Maxis, don't you know its rude to ignore a woman when she talking to you?" As she spoke, she held her Cossack dagger in reverse.

Maxis realized the time had come to end it, so he readied himself for one last encounter as she swung her dagger toward him. For a moment it was over. Then suddenly Maxis dropped his weapons and thrusted forward as fast as possible. He grabbed her wrist and arm, disarming her, then threw her against the wall. Her back hit the wall hard and before she could react Maxis had her dagger in his hand and threw it at her, landing it right next to her head.

"It's over Arina...you've lost," Maxis said, as blood slowly trickles down his left hand.

"It appears so..." Arina retorts as a small cut appeared on her cheek, dripping blood.

They recognized sound of footsteps stomping up the staircase and men shouting. The first to appear was Cpl. Zell who approaches Maxis with haste.

"Sergeant, are you alright? We saw your flare and came as quickly as we could."

"I'm still breathing am I not? But I'm glad you and your squad made it," Maxis responded as he picked up his blades.

"Oh, before I forget, I think this belongs to you," Cpl. Zell handed him his Bergmann No.5 pistol.

"Danke (Thank you)."

The soldiers had their rifles aimed at Arina who was already up...and wearing her cloak and her furazhka cap squarely placed on her head. She was barely intimidated by the soldiers around her as they were weary of her. Maxis walks past the troops with his pistol in one hand, but something changes as he approaches her, everything outside went silent.

"Hmph, I won the duel, but the Russians won the battle. " He thinks as he looks outside to see the flashes of MGs, rifles, and Artillery ceased.

"Pvt. Peterson, restrain her. I'll keep a close eye on her," Maxis ordered. The private pulled out shackles and slowly approached her, but showed hesitation. Arina takes one step back.

"How exactly do plan to keep me safe from these savages, Sgt. Maxis?" she inquired, putting on an innocent look.

"Vorshevsky, if you do as I say I will guarantee your safety...personally," he reassured in a low tone.

For a moment Arina felt touched by his words in his sentence but takes another step back slowly approaching the large hole in the wall.

"I wish I could believe you...I would...but we live in troubled times where people like me would surely suffer. I might as well take a different approach." She takes another step closer to the edge.

"Vorshevsky, I know what you are about to do. Don't do it!" Maxis slowly approaches. "Peterson, restrain her now! You've been given an order!" shouted Cpl. Zell.

"Tsar' I Bog (For Emperor and God). Dos vidaniya (Farewell), Maxis. You certainly changed my perception of you, and I enjoyed our time together," she said with a wink and a smile before she jumped through the hole in the wall with her arms crossed.

"NEIN!" Maxis reached out to grab her, but it was too late, as she disappeared within the darkness of the night enveloping her. The sound of a thud could be heard shortly after. Maxis froze for a moment then shifted into a sitting position trying to comprehend what had just happened.

"Men, listen up. Me and the Sergeant will check the third floor. The rest of you sweep the building," Cpl.

Zell spoke with an affirmative tone. The men moved downstairs leaving the two alone.

"Hey, are you sure you're going to be alright? I'm no detective but I did figure what was going on... somewhat."

"I just found out that I do have a heart," Maxis responded as he sat there watching the sun rise over the horizon.

Then suddenly one of the soldiers outside called out to them. They moved toward the edge to see what was going on. It was Pvt. Peterson.

"HEY! There's is no sign of her body here, just a smashed pumpkin and a sledgehammer!"

"WHAT!" both said at the same time.

The sound of an engine revving up is heard in the distance, then suddenly a motorcycle with a sidecar bursts from behind a large bush. Maxis uses the binoculars to take a closer look at the motorcycle driving away. He sees two soldiers on the motorcycle and cloaked figure in the sidecar. The figure stands up in the sidecar to reveal Arina Vorshevsky is alive and well. She blows a kiss goodbye toward Maxis and waves her field cap while riding away.

"You cheeky Mädchen (Girl)," he muttered.

"Come, let's not keep Colonel waiting," said Cpl. Zell with a smirk.

CHAPTER 11

KUDOS FOR THE SERGEANT

The two of them headed out with the squad following behind. Halfway through their walk they saw a plane flying overhead bearing blue pattern on the wings and tail along with the German crosses. Maxis and group headed toward the airfield to see 1Lt. Hoffmann chatting with Col. Josef. The Colonel notices Maxis and the group, he walks toward them. Everyone immediately stands at attention as he approaches Maxis.

"Sgt. Maxis, how are you, Soldat (Soldier)?"

"Good, Sir. But what are you doing here, Sir? I thought you were assisting with the breakthrough?"

"That's the thing Sergeant, it failed. I fear your efforts to stop the saboteur may be in vain because the Garrison Commander has called for a cease fire. I'm fearful we may end up as prisoners, everyone, except you of course. By the look of it I assume the enemy saboteur has been taken care of?" said as he looked at Maxis' blood stained and tattered uniform.

"Nein Kommandant, they escaped but I did foil their plans in the process," Maxis said very sternly as he faced the colonel.

"Hmph, pity. But you did your job. Sergeant. I may come across as stubborn and difficult to work with, but I do it for a good reason, if I do say so myself. For the record, I was aware of the existence of the Tsar's Secret Brigade for months, but Commander Jorgensen insisted I keep the information discreet from anyone else. I wasn't expecting them to be here though. It was fortunate that he was kind enough to send me a special soldier from K.W.S. to help, but I wanted to see how skilled you are. Now I have my answer. Ashamed really, I would have liked to join your organization, though Austrian High Command would probably reject it. Then again, Jorgensen would have found a way. You should get going, son. No doubt they saw the plane."

"Sir, it was honor working with you." Maxis salutes.

"The same to you, Sergeant. You should know your Commander thinks highly of you. That's no easy task to earn that high of praise." Josef salutes back at Maxis and gives a firm handshake.

"Hey, Sergeant, longtime no see. Sorry I was late. Some knuckle heads encountered trouble in Champagne so I was sent to assist. Now come on, we don't have all day," Hoffmann called out.

Before Maxis gets on the plane a soldier walked up holding his leather coat. He thanked him with a nod and put it on. He notices the plane was different and so he asks, "Is this new prototype?"

155

"You have a keen eye, Sergeant. This is the AGO C.I. It's a pusher-based plane. They have yet to officially fly it but since our Battalion is so special, I get to fly it first. Plus, I was being thoughtful since enjoy flying. I picked this plane just so you can sit at the front seat and be king of the world!"

"You are selfless and yet a jerk," Maxis said, laughing. He got in the plane and strapped in.

The small crew begins to perform several revolutions for the oil to become rich, then 1Lt.Hoffmann shouts "CONTACT" and flips the ignition switch. The engine roars to life and the plane begins to move.

Colonel Josef ordered all to stand in formation and face the plane with their rifle butts on the ground then gave the command "Present Arms." The whole squad saluted as the plane taxied, their final goodbye. Hoffmann and Maxis saluted back until they were out of sight. Now in the skies, everything began to shrink. They flew over the city and over the forts, then viewed the destruction from last night. It was horrid sight.

The Austro-Hungarian infantry lay scattered outside the fort's wall, their light blue uniforms still visible. On the other side of the battlefield were those who fared better but still, they suffered much.

They made it over the Russian lines where small Russian columns of troops were seen marching toward the fortress in parade formation, celebrating their greatest victory- – conquering the Fortress of Przemyśl. There were also more soldiers behind the lines resting, but still alert.

Maxis saw one soldier getting his rifle ready and taking aim. Then he saw Arina step beside him and gently lower his weapon. She looked up staring at the plane as it flew by. Maxis felt their eyes locked on to each one last time, even at a thousand feet.

"I hope Lothar doesn't get wind of what happened here between me and her, but then again, he always finds a way to make fun of me, heh," Maxis thought.

"So, I assume you have an interesting story to tell. It is a long trip back," 1 Lt. Hoffmann shouted out.

"Actually, I do. Let me tell you about the time I spent my nights at Przemyśl."

Meanwhile, behind the Russian lines at the small Tayna Brigade camp, Arina stood and watched the plane fly away into the clouds.

"We'll meet again...Sergeant Friedrich Maxis, The Black Wolf of Mons. You sure know how to show a girl an enjoyable time...not exactly a normal date. For the first time ever, someone actually bested me in a fight and I'm kind of glad you're the one and...Why am I obsessed over this? He is the enemy and yet I still get flustered back there and even back at Bochina when we were. Nyet (No), we are at war and there is no time for such feelings and emotions. In the name of the Tsar, I will do my duty for Motherland ...but still. Hold on, did he call me the Huntress?"

She continued staring into clouds as the plane disappeared, then she heard the sound of footsteps approaching from behind and felt a hand on her shoulder.

"You did fine work at the Fortress, Junior Sergeant Vorshevsky. I'm proud of you," said Colonel Vorshevsky, standing right beside her.

"Thank you, Sir."

"There are however a few questions I have based on your reports during your mission. In your report you said the Germans were involved?"

"Da, K.W.S. sent one of their best to the fortress."

"Hmm, Jorgensen is one step ahead as always. Now, were you able to identify the K.W.S. soldier?"

Arina hesitates for a second.

"It wouldn't happen to be that infamous Sergeant Maxis, was it?"

"Nyet (No)..."

"*Sigh.* Then explain to me why your uniform is in tatters? Please don't tell me you engaged in combat with the Sergeant like last time...and if you did so help me God..." the colonel said, as anger built up in his voice.

"Nyet (No), it wasn't like that! Maxis managed to coordinate with the Hapsburgs and got the drop on me by destroying my hideout! I manage to get to the second hideout after I lost them and sent the signal," Arina denied.

"He cannot know what happened on that wonderful night," she thought to herself.

"It was smart of you to bring the messenger pigeon with you, but Pvt. Fedorov and Cpl. Petrenko tell a different story."

"Oh, now I'm going to kill them with extra training in the snow! When I see them! "

158

"Those two told me how you took down a squad of Hapsburgs before Sgt. Maxis could intervene. When those two arrived to pick you up, they provided covering fire for you while you ran to their motorcycle."

"On second thought I'll buy them drinks...a lot of drinks."

"Well, that's all I need to know. Now follow me. We need to prepare for the Tsar's arrival at the fortress. He'll be impressed that we have taken a great prize that the army struggled for so long to accomplish," said the Colonel, as he walked with his daughter by his side.

By the end March 1915, the Fortress of Przemyśl had fallen to the Russian Empire. It was complete blow to Austrian-Hungarian Empire, not only losing the fortress but also losing 120,000 troops garrisoned there. It was a great humiliation for the Dual Monarchy and a subsequent victory for the Russians. It wouldn't be until May of that same year when Przemyśl would be recaptured by the Germans and Austrians in combined offensive. This was the bloodiest siege on the Eastern Front of World War 1

CHAPTER 12

FARMERS YESTERDAY, SOLDIERS TODAY

March 16, 1915, Valhalla Base, Germany

After Maxis left the office of Commander Jorgensen, the sound of Lothar shouting "WHAT!" could be heard from behind the door, then a loud slap followed. Lothar, still sitting in his chair, was rubbing his head after getting smacked by Major Reinhard.

"Show the commander some respect, Junge (Boy)!" said Major in furious tone.

"Stay your hand Major. We're not here to beat up our troops, verstanden (understood)?" Commander Jorgensen said calmly.

"Of course, Commander. As you wish," said Reinhard as he crossed his arms, still keeping an eye on Lothar.

"Okay, I'll repeat myself one last time and you'd better be listening well, Corporal."

"Yes, Sir, sorry Sir." Lothar responded.

"I try to be fair with my punishments depending on how bad it is, but in your case it's a mix of bad and worse. So, I'm assigning you a new charge. He is a private and you are now his mentor. I won't tell you how long you'll be doing this, all I can say is perhaps when you learn to take responsibility for your actions. Try to take an example from Sergeant Maxis as well, try to copy him. Show your new charge how we operate."

"I hate it when they compare me to Friedrich. It gets annoying sometimes. Even Kurtz did it too before he died," Lothar thinks to himself.

"Should you refuse to do your mission Cpl. Lothar, Major Reinhard already has an alternative for you," as he signals, Major Reinhards turns to speak.

"That I do. Reinhard's hardcore physical training camp. I shall give the very definition of pain through endless amount of P.T. (Physical Training). Even strong men like you will not survive what I have in store. For example, I will make you do a hundred pushups in full gear weapon included, make you run ten miles nonstop in full gear, make you go under and over the armored car fifty times, and for the finale you will march up the hill while carrying our unit flag. If you stop even once, then you will start all over again," Reinhard finished with a devilish smile.

"When do I begin my mission, Sir?" Lothar asks in a hurried tone.

"Your mission details are in this file including a profile of your new charge. Head to the armory to receive your equipment then go straight to the station. A train will be leaving for the Western Front soon. Your new charge will also be waiting for you so don't be late! Its destination will be Champagne. That is all, dismissed!" Jorgensen placed the file on the table.

Lothar got up, saluted Commander Jorgensen, and left the office with the file in hand. After he left, Major Reinhard turned to Jorgensen and asked.

"Commander, if I recall..."

"No need for formalities, Gunther. You can talk freely. No one is here but us," Jorgensen interrupted.

"Alright Augustus, didn't you already plan for them to take on these assignments and not as form of punishment?"

"Originally, I was, before the Geist platoon reported their slip up. One of them would have reacted the same under different circumstances."

"Then why send them separately? Their combat records show they're a deadly combination when working together."

"I know it's foolish to split up the pair, but Lothar eventually needs to learn that being a careless brute won't get him anywhere but an early grave, and as for Maxis well...his case is different," Jorgensen said, lighting his wooden pipe.

"I see. But why send one to Przemyśl which is under siege and the other to Champagne where the French are about to finish up their ill-fated offensive?"

"I sent Maxis to Przemyśl to investigate a possible Tayna Brigade presence in that area. I expect him to be resourceful until he returns, then we'll know for certain. As for Lothar, Champagne should be less active, but I have a feeling that one my old friends besides Vladimir Vorshevsky might play his next hand."

"You seem to think highly of the young Sergeant. Is there motive, Augustus?"

"Not exactly Gunther, I knew his parents, especially his father Albert who served under me with Sgt. Kurtz a decade ago. He and Kurtz saved my life during the Seymour expedition. His performance was admirable, so I expect his young son to do the same or beyond expectation."

"A fine answer, Augustus."

"Indeed, Gunther, indeed."

Lothar arrived at the armory with the help from the Commanders private driver. He walked in to see the quartermaster sitting as he looked at his clip board until he saw Lothar walk in. He slowly got up to find out why he was here.

"Something I can help you with soldat (soldier)?" he said gruffly.

"Yeah, I'm here to receive my equipment."

"Name and rank, bitte (please)."

"Cpl. Lothar."

"Hmmm...Cpl. Lothar, ah yes, they informed me that you were coming. Wait one moment." The quartermaster walked away to retrieve his gear and returned with large box in hand.

"Ok, here is your standard infantry gear along with the necessities, a Roth-Theodorovic pistol with a holster, your tornister, and an entrenching tool with sharpened edge. That should be it."

"Wait, that's it? What about a rifle or machine gun?"

"I'm sorry, Corporal. I've been ordered by the higher-ups to give you this. One of our own will provide the remainder at whatever destination you're going to."

"Damn you, Jorgensen." Lothar murmured under his breath.

Lothar headed out of the armory and back into the car, and off they went to the train station. They arrived at the station early and yet there was no sign of the new guy. He exited out of the vehicle and walked over by the train car to wait.

"Great, I guess I must wait for him. In the meantime, I should read his profile to learn a bit about him and his combat record." After the thought, he looked at the file at hand and began to read.

"**Name:** Noah Richter

Rank: Private

Age: 17

Combat Records: Siege of Liege, Battle of Ypres and the Marne."

"Hmph. He should already be battle hardened. Then why are they assigning him as my new charge?"

Before he could read the description, heard a low voice coming from behind him.

"A-Are-you Cpl. Lothar?" said a mysterious skittish voice.

Lothar turned around to see a soldier wearing the new M1915 Feldbluse with the K.W.S unit patch on the side. He was wearing a pickelhaube with the fabric on it but without the spike. On his person was standard issued equipment however, one thing that stood out: his weapon, a shotgun along with two bandoliers of shotgun shells one across chest and the other around his waist.

"Huh, so that's what the new unit patch looks like," said Lothar.

"U-uh, say again?"

"Nothing. You must be my new charge. Pleased to meet you, Pvt. Richter. I'm Cpl. Lothar." Lothar held out his hand for a handshake.

Richter looked at him for a moment before realizing what he was doing.

"Oh, sorry uh...yeah. Pleased meet you, too, Corporal Lothar."

"Ok...we can chat inside the train car...come on."

"Yeah...right behind you," remarked Pvt. Richter in uneasy tone.

Why does he sound so stressed...maybe I should read what his description says. He opened the file again to see the part that says conditions and it states.

"Condition: Despite showing signs of being unease, he was very adamant to join the Battalion regardless of what the medics had said to him. The best advice is to keep an eye on him if he shows signs of any problems. He might shake it off, but, if his condition gets worse, we'll have to send him home with full honors, for he might prove to be a liability."

"Heh, of course," Lothar muttered to himself.

They boarded the train car where there were a few other soldiers sitting. Lothar finds a seat and Richter sits across from him. There was silence between the two until Lothar began to speak.

"I would like us to get to know each other alittle better before we reach our destination. I do have your file here. Let's view your record first. It says you fought in Liege, Ypres, and Marne. I have to say, you have seen your fair share of action," Lothar said in his calm but serious tone.

"More like a fair share of nightmares and horrors," Richter responded sounding depressed.

"Why? What happened? I wouldn't know since I was deployed to the eastern front at the start of the war. I didn't exactly know what went on in Belgium besides the siege of Liege, but I might have an idea about the other two."

"Well, it didn't start at Liege, that much I can say. It happened at Ypres. And it was a bloodbath."

The train's whistle can be heard as the final "All aboard!" can be heard before the train begins to move.

"What do you mean a bloodbath?" Lothar asked.

"I mean everyone I knew got killed. Then I get a transfer to the Marne, and it was even worse." Richter looks down.

"Geez, this took a dark turn...I've seen my fair share of what he's talking about, but I don't let it get to me. I guess some people aren't as strong minded as others."

"How did you end up in K.W.S.?" Lothar asked.

"A squad found me when I was hiding among the dead. They knew me from Liege and were surprised to see me having survived from a failed assault. After that, I was sent back to Germany for evaluation. They were questioning my stability, but I convinced them I could carry on because I wanted to do my duty and at least to carry on for the memories of my fallen friends. I apologize Corporal, I didn't mean to sound so depressing."

"Nein, I should be sorry for bringing it up. The one thing you can do is just keep your head up high and don't let the bad times destroy you. All you can do is march forward."

"I think that was my best one yet. I'll have to become the flame of inspiration to a dimly lit candle." Lothar thought.

"Yeah, I-I will try, I'm just bit nervous about going back to the Western Front. I only recently finished E.I.T.C. (Elite Infantry Training Course). Getting sent back to front so soon is a nerve racking."

"Well, never fear chum because The Lothar will be ready face the enemy head on and keep his friends safe!" Lothar slams his fist to his hand while boasting. Richter gave off a small chuckle and a smile appeared across his face.

"Let's switch to something more positive like where are you from?" Lothar inquired.

"I come from the Rhineland in a small farming community. My parents are potato farmers along with my younger siblings. Two brothers and one sister."

"That's funny though, my mother owns a small vineyard, and my father runs the lumber mill along with my two brothers. It may not be much, but my mother makes the finest wine across Germany. I always helped around after school either at the vineyard or cut and move some logs. Hence, my epic strength!" Lothar said as he flexes.

"Seems like a very successful business on both ends," Richter leans back.

"Quite, but they weren't exactly happy with me leaving to join the army with my best friend. He and I wanted to go on an adventure since we were kids, so we joined the army hoping to see the world, but dodging bullets and bombs isn't exactly on our list of experiences, heh." Lothar laughs a little as he looks out the window.

"Or Kurtz taking us in and trained us the necessity to survive this new kind of war..."

"I think it wasn't the plan at all, I say," Richter laughs as he starts to get relaxed on the chair.

"Too right. My second reason for joining was to find something out there like knowledge, experience, or something that I can bring back...I haven't found it, but I'll keep looking, right? Richter?" Lothar looks to see that Pvt. Richter has fallen asleep in the booth.

"The built-up stress in him has finally have been alleviated by being around good company. Heh, it seems he hardly slept before he got here. It is going to be a long trip so I better review the mission while I have the chance."

Lothar opens the file turns to the mission details, and they are:

"By the time you are reading this you would have already been informed by the Commander, but if not, here it is.

The Champagne Offensive will be ending soon as of the information provided by our intelligence gatherer "The Geist Platoon". Our mission is to provide support to the 3rd Army in the sector. Our forces held the line against the French during their offensive, but reports came in that they need an additional reinforcement for they sustained heavy casualties. Four squads have been deployed to the area one squad of the K.W.S. Trench Surgeon Korp (Panacea squad), two squads of Advance Riflemen (Perseus and Ares Squad), and one Machine gun specialist along with his Trench Trooper who is trained in close quarter combat."

"Trench trooper? Oh, so that's what the shotgun is for, it makes sense now." He continues reading as He looks at Richter's shotgun.

"Remain in the mission area until the main army can reinforce themselves. We have a special telephone line wired all the way back to base in the HQ dugout. The commanding officer of the dugout will be expecting you. The mission details given to the current holder of this document will have a name to stay anonymous when communicating with the phone operator or Valhalla base. You are being deployed to Sector D (Duff). Transportation will be provided.

Your squad's name is Titan

Phone operator Name: Hermes

Valhalla base: Wotan

Memorize this file then destroy it. Preferred method: burn it."

"Pfft. Titan squad. How ironic of them, using Greek and Norse mythology as form of nicknames. The memorizing part is something Maxis would do, but I have no choice. If I need back up this might be the very thing that could save my life. Wotan must be Commander Jorgensen; I figure as much."

Day turns to dusk on the ride to Champagne and Lothar studies and memorizes the mission. They arrive at their destination at nine pm at the train station, as the train comes to screeching halt where a jolt can be felt in which wakes Richter up.

"Wha – are we already here?" Richter says, checking his surroundings.

"Ja, come on let's go get a ride." Lothar got up and walked to the exit of the train car. Richter followed along.

They walked outside of the train car and were met with a cool breeze from the wind and greeted with stars in the night sky. They see the rest of the soldiers from the train car heading toward a Daimler Marenfelde truck, quickly boarding it until it was filled. The truck started up, and the driver honked the small horn on the side of the truck then drove off.

"Well, that is just great. How are we going to get there now?" Richter complained.

"The old fashion way Private...the old fashion way." Lothar points toward a horse drawn wagon.

They approach the wagon and see the driver feeding his horse while smoking a cigarette. He turns to Lothar and Richter, takes in one more drag and blows out a plume of smoke.

"How may I help you two on this lovely night?" The wagon driver asks as he pets the horse.

"Are you the driver of this wagon?" Lothar asks.

"That I am, are you the special unit deployed to this area?"

"That we are, can you get us to sector duff with haste?"

"Why of course I can. I'll get you there in no time. Climb aboard and we'll be on our way," he said calmly as he throws his cigarette to the ground then stomps on it.

The two climb onto the back of the wagon as the driver gets to the front. First the sound of driver yelling, "Ya!" then hooves begin clattering, and the wagon moves quickly on the dirt road.

"So...What's with the shotgun? The mission file stated that you were a Trench Trooper?" Lothar asked.

"Yeah...Commander Jorgensen and other officers including military theorists wanted a new type of soldier that specializes in close quarter engagements. This includes advanced hand-to-hand combat, extra conditioning in strength and speed, and expertly utilizing an already existing weapon, the shotgun. They said, 'The war is changing by the day, so we need to stay ahead even it means breaking few rules to be effective,'" Richter said as he glanced at the shotgun.

"So, that's why Maxis spent all that time training, not only to acquire a new skill but to increase his knowledge of close quarter combat. Probably to be prepare for his encounter with that woman in green, Vorshevsky. If he ever

faces her again. I should do the same when I can,." Lothar thought as Richter continues.

"The shotgun however wasn't issued to me; my family gave it to me. This is a Drilling(triple) shotgun made by J.P Saurer & Son. It has third barrel that fires a rifle round while other two fires twelve gauge, and it's still new. I also carry an array of shotgun shells like slug, buckshot, and even birdshot." Richter explained.

"That might come in handy where we're going, but one thing is bugging me. Where is your pistol?" Lothar asks.

"What? I thought officers were only ones allowed to carry them?"

"Not in this Battalion. Jorgensen's doctrine states that every soldier regardless of their rank carry a side arm before deploying on a mission," Lothar shows him his Roth-Theodorovic pistol.

"Oh, I guess I miss that part during orientation," Richter, embarrassed.

"Fear not, my friend. Once we arrive, we'll head straight to the quartermaster to get you one, not to mention get my weapon as well."

"Say, why don't you have your..."

"Don't even ask," Lothar interrupts, his tone sounding annoyed.

There was silence once more as the ride continued. Eventually the sound of rifles popping in the distance and the noise of impact artillery can be heard. The wagon slowed to a halt.

"We have arrived at our destination. Welcome to Champagne, men. The quartermaster's tent should be around here somewhere," the driver informed, and pointed to a low-lit military camp.

"Thanks for the lift. Come on Richter, let's go," said Lothar, as he hopped off the wagon.

They walked around looking for the quartermaster's tent but instead came to a collection of tents in one big group almost like a small village, with soldiers performing their normal tasks and some leaving before entering the trench network. The two moved toward the middle of the encampment until they spotted a large tent with crates and a sign that said "Quartiermeister (Quartermaster)".

"That must be it," said Richter, as he moved ahead of Lothar.

He was the first to enter the tent and was met a man whose back was turned to him. They could hear him humming as he looked at the clipboard, checking things off. Lothar finally spoke.

"Uh, hey quartermaster! I'm here to make requisition request for me and my friend here."

"Mein Gott (My God), I thought you would be dead by now," the quartermaster said in a surprised yet oddly cheerful tone. Then turned around.

"Heinrich?? What the hell are you doing here? I thought you would be with Austrians on the Eastern Front?" Lothar asked.

"Ahh, but that's the thing. Due to my deep connections, I was able to join K.W.S. and so the Battalion gets a charming quartermaster!" Heinrich said with an eccentric tone.

"You mean you used your political connections to land you a job and sent you to the worst place of the war?"

"Nein, my brutish Lothar. I used my connections with different arms companys and contacts to can get the battalion more prototype weapons, most of which are in the unique category. My contacts may vary from a lovely lady whose husband runs the largest arms manufacturing plant to the Merchant of Death himself. Just one call or letter and he'll be here with the best weapons for the right price," Heinrich said with an extravagant manner.

"So, you have access to the secret market or something?" Lothar asked.

"Black Market my boy, Black Market. So, who's the new kid? Did you drop the Sergeant or did the Sergeant drop you?"

"Sgt. Maxis is on an assignment. This is Pvt. Richter my, er, new charge." Lothar slowed down at last bit.

"Oh dear, listen kid. The Mighty Lothar is great and all but if there is one thing, I can assume is that teaching is not his forte, more likely his brawn is. You are better off with Sergeant Maxis. He is more a role model type."

"Okay, Heinrich! I'm sure the Commander would have said otherwise," Lothar interrupted.

"Sigh. I feel like I'll never leave Maxis' shadow at this rate," Lothar thought, feeling annoyed and defeated.

"On the contrary, Cpl. Lothar and Sgt. Maxis were the two most recommended soldiers back during

E.I.T.C. Examples of teamwork and bravery. When they showed us a photograph of them taking down that Russian giant tricycle, we knew we must live up to our battalions' expectation, though that is going to be hard in my case." Richter's proud tone quickly diminishes.

"Wait, there were photographs of us fighting that thing?" Lothar asked, puzzled.

"Well, most of the photographs showed the wreckage of the behemoth in the aftermath, however, there was only one that came from a team of war correspondents who took the pictures of the action. That photo was quickly confiscated, of course," Richter finished.

"Well, you seem to be in good hands then. Anyway, enough with the catching up, you said something about getting a weapon? Well, I'm here to provide all your killing needs, Hà!" Heinrich said with style.

"Yeah, do you have anything available, preferably of the machine gun category?" Lothar asked.

"Sadly, I do not have any in storage at the moment. My apologies, Lothar."

"Not even that custom-made Madsen that I used before?"

"The custom variant is back in Valhalla base, and the other normal LMG's are already deployed with the regular army and the three other squads that came before."

"Verdammt (Damn it)! What about that Selbstlader (self-loader) that Maxis had?" Lothar responded with frustration.

"If I recall, Sgt. Maxis returned that to me after that incident in Bochnia, with a letter that he was sending to Mauser company along with a comment about the rifle. And I quote 'Send this jamming schiss (crap) back for major improvements,' end quote."

"Yeah, that definitely sounds like Maxis," said Lothar.

"Also, do you even know how to work with a self-loader? Of course, you did try to clean it but not the best at it. When I joined up, they instructed me to assign certain weapons to soldiers who have acquired training, so you're out of luck. Actually,I do have something special I've recently just finished. Wait one moment, please," Heinrich left to retrieve the item in question. He returned hauling an unusual weapon and placed it on to the table in front of them.

"Gentlemen, I present to you my best work yet," Heinrich offered proudly

"What's this? Looks to be a Hotchkiss Benét-Mercié machine gun," Richter commented.

"Good eye, private, but its more than just that. This is a specially modified Benét-Mercié M1909 LMG now converted to use our ammo. It has a bipod fitted at barrel, an idea inspired by the American variant, an added metal foregrip, created by yours truly, and zeroed-in optic sights," Heinrich finished.

"You really out did yourself this time. Truly remarkable," Lothar complimented and picked it up, checking the sights.

"You can actually pick that thing up?" Richter asked.

"I can pick it up, aim down the sight while holding it or moving. Basically, I perform normal with machine guns like any other." Lothar held it with one hand.

"But don't you need loader/ammo bearer and isn't that S.O.P. (standard operating procedure)?"

"I can carry the ammo myself when it comes to LMG's and load it myself so to hell with S.O.P." Lothar responded.

"He is what you call 'unique' in the Battalion, everyone is...even you, Private. It can be your greatest asset, weapon, and weakness," Heinrich intervenes.

"Well, Heinrich, this is fine weapon. I'll take it in the meantime. Oh, do you have spare side arm for him? He forgot to pick one up,"said Lothar, after analyzing the LMG.

"Of course. Here we have a Reichsrevolver M1883 and a holster, but that's all I got. Before you go, here is one more thing; your ammo box with a strap that is already loaded with strips, just begging to be used. How many bullets I don't know, I lost count at two hundred-forty-five," Heinrich remarked, placing the items on the table.

The pair took the items from the table and thanked the kind quartermaster. They walked out of the tent armed and fully prepared for action. They made their way to the fire trench (first trench) but had to guide themselves through the trench lines. Fortunately, the trenches had electricity and light bulbs spread out along the way. They noticed the sound of their boots making contact with a wooden floor instead of dirt as they entered the trench. It was evident that the whole trench network was like this, adding some luxury and lowering the risk of getting trench foot. They passed a group of soldiers sitting around campfire in the reserve trench which made Lothar remember something.

"Hold here for second, there something I must do."

"I'll be here then," Richter responded calmly.

Lothar walked over to the campfire and greeted the soldiers.

"Lovely night we're having. If I may ask, can I add something keep the flames going?" Lothar asked.

"Certainly, soldat (soldier), just make sure it's not laced with something that might blow up, verstehen (understand)?" warned one the soldiers.

"Verstanden (understood)," he responded as he pulled out the file and tossed it into the fire. The men glanced around with confused looks on their faces, then one of them then questioned, "What was that you just threw in?"

"Nothing you need concern yourself with. Have good night, jungs (boys)." Lothar walked away and rejoined Richter.

The two continued their way through the support trench then to the fire trench. The trench had less activity going on as there were very few troops stationed here. There were few men maintaining watch behind rifle shields, looking for any sign of enemy troops, while others sat resting. The sound the artillery firing from behind friendly lines and the enemy firing across no-man's-land, the noise of it was a regular event for the soldiers of the trenches. Lothar and Richter entered the cross-section of the trench and sat down with their backs against the wall.

"Corporal, why are we in the first trench line? Shouldn't we being doing something out of the ordinary to help these guys out?" Richter asked in a low tone.

"We are doing something, Richter. We are providing support to them. It may not seem much, but our presence here makes a difference should they face heavy resistance. We'll be here to help as much as we can. We are their first and last line of defense."

"I can sort of understand, it's just I don't feel safe here."

"Well, get used to it. Danger will always be around the corner. We all knew what we signed up for and..." Lothar couldn't finish his sentence as the sound of several grenades hitting the floor made a metallic sound.

"HIT THE DECK!" Lothar shouted as he and Richter took cover.

The grenades exploded throwing shrapnel all over the trench. Some of the soldiers managed take cover in the dug outs, but the unfortunate souls that did not get out of the blast radius were torn to shreds, their bodies on floor, some missing limbs, and some left as a bloody mess.

"Grabenangriff (Trench Raid)!" screamed a German soldier.

Lothar gets up to see the silhouettes appearing over the parapet with one of them shouting "Attaque (Attack)!" and what followed was men shouting, "Pour la France!" It was an attack conducted by a French trench raiding team. Some had portable shields and were armed with either a club, pistol, or rifles, but mostly carbines. The soldiers immediately came out of the dugout with their rifles ready and their bayonets mounted while some had only their knives or shovels. Lothar quickly got his machine gun ready and opened fire at the silhouettes before they could jump into the trench. The soldiers fired few shots before engaging in bloody close quarter combat with the French.

"Richter, watch my back! I'm pressing forward into fray! Richter, did you hear me?" Lothar ordered as he put a new strip into the machine gun.

No response came from Richter causing Lothar to turn around. He saw Richter still on the ground plugging his ears in a fetal position, sobbing. Suddenly a French trench raider appeared behind the private with a portable shield and a trench club, ready to attack. Without hesitating Lothar aimed the down sight and opened fire at the trench raider who hastily blocked a barrage of bullets with his shield. Lothar hurriedly switched to his pistol and fired a shot in the raider's leg which caused the raider to scream in agony, leaving himself exposed for Lothar to finish him off.

"Richter, get back on your feet! Help me out, NOW! THATS AN ORDER, KID!" Lothar shouts affirmatively with a hint of anger. Richter still showed no response, and Lothar turned his attention back to the fighting at hand.

"I need to end this raid quickly now, but how...Okay, I have an idea but it's risky," he thought.

Lothar loaded another strip into it and cocked it then shouted out.

"Men, take cover! Firing machine gun!"

The men heard what Lothar said and rushed back into the dugouts and some went prone as Lothar unleashed a hail of bullets into the trench clearing out every French soldier in the trench line. In the end there was nothing but corpses of soldiers in their horizon blue colored uniforms, now riddled with bullet holes and blood stains.

Lothar, still standing, held his weapon firm with the barrel still smoking waiting for any more of them to appear. Suddenly a bullet grazed his right arm which forced him to drop his machine gun. He quickly turned to see a French soldier charging at him with his Label rifle mounted with a bayonet. Slightly irritated by this, Lothar readied himself for the Frenchmen's attack. The soldier thrust his bayonet forward only to miss as Lothar dodged then grabbed his arm and flung him across the cross-section with force.

The soldier quickly recovered only to see Lothar standing tall and now armed with his shovel. He beckoned him. The Frenchmen raised his rifle and charged him; and as he did gave out his loudest war cry. Prepared for his bayonet charge , Lothar left blocked the Frenchmen's attack with his shovel on the left and in one swing dug his shovel into the Frenchmen's neck. A gurgle-like sound could be heard as the attacker collapsed to the ground. Lothar pulled the shovel out from his neck and sheathed it. The trench raid was over as the last enemy soldier was killed.

Lothar walked over to Richter who is still whimpering on the ground. He pulled him up on his feet and spoke.

"Richter, Richter! Snap out of it, come on!"

Richter was still whimpering until Lothar delivered a slap to face. Then Richter began to slowly come back.

"Lo-thar?" Richter stammers his words.

"What the hell happened back there, Private? Why did you freeze up like that and break?"

"I-I saw them Lothar, my friends back at Ypres and the Marne! Their faces, I saw them...when the bombs went off, I was back in those places, reliving the horrible moments of my life...I'm...sorry. That's why I called myself a coward because I hid among their corpses during the battle...I didn't want to share the same fate." A tear fell from his eye and his face turned red.

"Listen to me. Apologies are not going to bring them back. You can't freeze up like that during combat otherwise you'll be the reason why I'll die or anyone else for that matter," he sighed. "Here's a little technique I learned a long time ago. Repeat after me."

"Okay." Richter replied.

"Count to three, then inhale. Count to three and exhale. Keep it up until your mind is at ease. While you're at it, think of something that makes you happy," Lothar said slowly, demonstrating. Richter repeated the technique until he was at ease.

"Now come on, let's report to the commanding officer of this sector."

CHAPTER 13

OVERCOMING FEAR

The two headed to the support trench and followed the cross-section until they found the company HQ dugout. Lothar opened the door and walked right in with Richter following behind him. There they spotted the table with a map on it along with some wired telephones. On the left side sat a telegraph operator and on the right were some bunk beds in the corner. An officer walked behind the table facing the pair.

"There something you need soldaten (soldiers)?" he asked.

"We're looking for the acting CO of this sector," said Lothar.

"Well congratulations, he's right in front of you. I'm Cpt. Schmitz, acting CO of this corner of the frontlines. State your name and rank and tell me why you are here?"

"Sir, I'm Cpl. Lothar." Lothar stood to attention while saying it.

"Sir, I'm Pvt. Richter of the special units Battalion."

"Special unit...oh that's right they informed me of your arrival. As you were men, now tell me what you must report," said Capt. Schmitz.

"Sir, we repelled an enemy trench raid, and the fire trench is secured," said Lothar.

"How many enemy trench raiders were killed?"

"Fifteen, Sir."

"Well, you didn't repel the enemy, you wiped out an entire trench raiding team. Nice job, but what were our casualties like?"

"They surprised us with grenades, five killed and ten wounded, Sir," Lothar said firmly.

"Hmm, this is the fifth time this week they raided us. If you hadn't shown up, myself and few others would have been killed or taken prisoner. We are seriously low on manpower right now and we're still awaiting additional reinforcement. I fear they might launch one more attack, but I don't know for certain. For now, they're probing for attacking this sector."

"Sir, that's why we are here, to provide support in any way possible." said Richter.

The captain was silent for a minute then spoke.

"Indeed...Soldaten (soldiers), I'm giving you a new assignment. I'm placing you two to keep eye on the enemy's trench for any sign of preparation for an attack. You can use the observation balloon as a start but do so in the morning. Now then go get some rest because there is a lot of work to do at dawn. Dismissed," Captain Schmitz finished.

Lothar and Richter responded with "Yes Sir!" and saluted the captain. Before leaving Lothar walked toward the telephone that was labeled "Special unit communication line". He told Richter to go on ahead to the underground barracks.

He picked up the receiver of the phone and was greeted by the operator on the other line.

"Number or code, Bitte (Please)," said the phone operator.

"Titan squad. I request an audience with Hermes."

"Standby...Connecting now." The sound of a click could be heard indicating the call had been transferred.

"This is Hermes, identify yourself."

"Cpl. Lothar of Titan squad, reporting in. I have at arrived at my destination."

"Very good Titan squad. Squads Perseus, Ares, and Panacea are already checked in, I'll send the report to Wotan. Is there something you need assistance with, if not the call shall end," said Hermes.

"I do have some concerns about Pvt. Richter. The mission file stated the 'conditions' that he has from his previous deployment before joining the Battalion. He froze up during a trench raid from the enemy and almost got me and himself killed. Any advice?"

"I'm not an expert on health, but it's usually common for soldiers to freeze up in combat, but if Pvt. Richter is going to be a liability and jeopardize the mission then you have full authorization to send him back to Wotan. We'll decide what to do with him. Is there anything else I can help you with?"

"Nein, that is all. Danke (thank you)."

"Do not hesitate to contact us if there's a development. We are always on the line. End Communication." Hermes ended the call as the line goes click.

Lothar put the receiver down and walked out of the HQ dugout. He made his way to the underground bunker where the barracks are located. After walking down the steps he saw Richter sitting on the bunks analyzing his equipment. Lothar walked over to him.

"How are you holding up?"

"Um...a little better. Lothar, about what happen during the raid I ..."

"Save it, I just got off the horn with command. Usually if a soldier is underperforming, they get transferred to the rear echelon and no longer have to worry about frontline combat. But in your case, you get a one-way ticket out of the army with full honors in other words you get a discharge. However, I believe in second chances here. You can buckle up and be a man or you can use this opportunity to get out of the Battalion and go home where its safe and peaceful. I'll be honest with you, the way you acted during the French attack on our trench is unacceptable. The last thing I need is deadweight, both figuratively and literally. That will get me, you, or anyone killed, do you understand? Even though I showed you a simple trick, that won't help if we engage in combat with the enemy," Lothar finished firmly.

Richter stayed silent and listened to what Lothar had to say, then responded with "Ich verstehe (I understand)."

"Good. Now get some rest then come find me at the trench line when you've made your decision. That is all."

"Wait, you're not going rest?" Richter asked.

"Nein, I'm going to help the first trench line clean the mess I made and stand watch for any sign for another surprise assault. Until then rest up, you already know where to find me," Lothar finishes and walks away leaving Richter alone.

Richter put his hands to face in embarrassment and let out deep breathe. He then said to himself.

"What am I going to do, what am I going to do? I can't believe I cracked and did nothing to help. I shouldn't stress over this. I – I need to lay my head down. Hopefully I can have clear mind once I wake up. Yeah, I'll do that."

Richter slowly climbed into bed and closed his eyes. He fell fast asleep and began to dream. The first thing he heard was voices...voices of the past, then started seeing images, memories from Liege, Ypres, and the Marne. The dream continued.

Come on Richter, don't want to be late before our train leaves everyone from our class is waiting! Can't believe we are going to war but I'm optimistic we'll win this one no sweat. We'll come back as heroes to our families and to the Vaterland (Fatherland). The sound train of the whistle is heard as it begins to move from the train station with every soldier's family there to see them off.

"We were naïve...thinking this would be a grand adventure that would get us fame and glory. Oh how wrong we were...our entire class was in same unit, all my friends..."

An image of the battle of Liege and its aftermath begins to form. With smoke on the horizon and German troops marching along a road.

They really don't want to make this easy for us do they, huh Ric...They may have given us a beating, but we won't break that easy...We did it Richter! We took Liege...

"Our first victory, Gotha was so happy, and the others were already bringing out the kegs...We thought we would find more success in future battles but instead the only thing we found was death..."

Another image of the first battle of Ypres begins to show.

Men listen up, high command wants this area taken...our artillery is already firing on the British as I speak. We must secure another victory for our empire, for our country...Now move all of you! The sound of a trench whistle could be heard and the raging screams of soldiers charging into battle is heard then the sound of machine guns.

"This is where the slaughter began...our own slaughter...oh Mein Gott...I don't, I don't want to go through this again...Please...No..."

Richter coughs up blood. *No-ah, you're the only one left...please don't forget us...continue the fight...continue the fight...*

His comrades can be seen strewn about in no man's land, bleeding and slowly dying. All except for him. Richter survived by hiding among the dead, watching his friends die.

"*Nein, Nein, Nein...this can't be happening, this can't be happening...Gotha, Bernhard, Schmidtz, and Engel...in a blink an eye...gone. I'm so sorry...I didn't want to die; I don't want to die..."*

He sees himself in the Dugout HQ at Ypres.

I'm sorry Pvt. Richter, but...you're the only survivor from your platoon. The battle turned into a stalemate, there is nothing else we can do. So, I'm transferring you to the 5th army that will be preparing for an attack on the Marne. Hopefully we can breach the Entente lines and bring end to this bloody war. Dismissed.

"*The battle of Ypres ended, along with my friend's lives...I thought I could put it behind me, but by the time I arrived at the Marne I was still having nightmares ...until I made new friends...then it stopped for a while at least...*"

*Once we take this sector, we'll march all the way to Paris and end this war! ADVANCE...*The whistle was blown once again, and the men went over the top and began their charge into enemy lines.

"*What followed next was a total massacre...*"

*Keep going men, just few more...*The NCO is cut off as bullets rip through him.

This is madness! We're getting torn apart and,, .(explosion)...

AHHHH...Helfen Sie mir! Bitte (Help me! Please)!

RICHTER...GET OUT OF HERE! Before we... (gargling noises)

The machine guns are firing, bombs exploding, bullets whistling, and soldiers screaming in agony from getting shot. Others die from a single shot to the head or the chest before they even hit the ground. Many barely make it to the enemy trench while many didn't make it at all. Among the dead was Richter, still alive with his rifle that hadn't even been fired. Fast forward to him holding a dear friend in his arms with his hands soaked from blood...their blood.

"I don't want to do this anymore...I don't want to do this anymore...Please for God's sake make it stop!!! I CAN'T DO THIS ANYMORE ...please make the pain stop..."

Richter...here's a little technique I learned a long time ago...Keep it up until your mind is at ease...think of something that makes you happy...

Count to three, then inhale...count to three, then exhale... think of something that makes you happy...somewhere I feel safe...

Suddenly he finds himself back home, back at the farm in the countryside. The sun is slowly rising and standing beside him is his father and out by the barn where his brothers and sister move sacks of potatoes. The birds were chirping, and the wind was blowing, the sense of peace was all around.

Noah, mein sohn (my son) ...life will never be easy for anyone, not even us. When your mother died after giving birth to your sister Mary...I feared the worst would come. Ursula, your mother was everything to me when she passed, however, she left me the greatest gift of all...her children... mein kinder (my kids). When my time comes, you will be man of this house, and you always have a home...you always have a happy place, never forget that...

Think of something that makes you happy...

"I understand now...NEIN! I do understand, I thought I was fighting for myself and my friends...but I'm fighting

*for them...my family...my happy place. I see now, I'll con-
tinue the fight for their sake, for their memories. I'll keep
serving under Cpl. Lothar for I am not giving up, NEVER!"*

Day 2, March 17

"Wake up soldat (soldier)! I said WAKE UP!" said a
soldier, shaking Richter back and forth trying to wake
him up.

"Wha-, what...where am I?" mumbled Richter.

"You're in the underground barracks in Champagne,
France. That's where you are," the soldier
said sarcastically.

"Oh, I – forgot. Entschuldigung (apologies)."

"It's alright, I just came back from my night watch.
Surprisingly, there was another soldier who was really tall and kept me and the others company, though he
never said a word, he just stood there watching in the
observation trench. Anyway, my twelve hours are up
so I'm here to hit the hay although you were thrashing
about in your bunk. That must be one hell of a nightmare, are you going to be alright?"

"Yeah, I just found the light at the end of a dark tunnel."

"That's good to hear, now if you'll excuse me there is
a bunk with my name on it." The soldier walked away
and immediately collapsed onto the bed facing down.

Richter looked at the clock, it was six-thirty in the
morning. He quickly grabbed his kit and readied himself
then rushed out the door up the steps, and outside. He
walked with purpose to the observation trench, where

he saw Cpl. Lothar observing through the periscope. He noticed Richter and turned toward him and spoke.

"Back among the living I see."

"You can say that again," Richter responded.

"Have you made your decision, Private?"

"I have and I'm not walking away. I built up the courage to get over the mental obstacle's that I must deal with. If I give up now, I'll be failing my country, my family, my fallen friends and...myself. So, I'm ready to give it my all, Corporal," Richter said with courage and confidence in his voice.

"It seems you got over your problems. That's good, Richter. I'm going to need that courage for an important job I have for you," said Lothar in a cheerful yet serious tone.

"What would that be?"

Lothar gets up from his chair and stood beside Richter. He put his hand on his shoulder and points forward with a smirk on his face.

"You are going on a ride in the observation balloon." Lothar points toward the balloon slowly taking form at the rear lines.

"We'd best get on our way, Ja," said Richter.

The pair began walking through the trench lines once again until they made it to the reserve trench then went out through the exit. They saw rear encampment, and on the right of it was the observation balloon. The balloon has taken form with the German cross on the side and the balloon operators were making the final adjustments before take-off.

"Is the balloon ready for use, Private?" Lothar asked.

"Yes, Corporal. It is almost ready, just a few more adjustments to the basket. The weather perfectly clear," the balloon operator responded.

They make one final adjustment by making sure the basket is secure. The balloon operators give each other the ok symbol and step away. One of them said, "We are all set."

"Alright Richter, climb inside the basket and I will explain what your task is. Now get going."

Richter moved to observation balloon and climbed inside the basket. What he found was a pair of binoculars, a notepad, pencil, and an A-2 camera. He stood up and saw Lothar right beside the balloon.

"Okay Richter, your task is simple. You need to get eyes on the Frenches trench and spot anything unusual. If there is nothing, then jot down any useful intel from troop movement to artillery and machine gun emplacement. Is that understood?"

"Jawohl (Yes Sir)," Richter said with an affirmative voice.

"Excellent! Alright ,send him up!" Lothar shouts at the balloon operators.

They slowly let the balloon rise off the ground, keeping a tight grip. Richter, looking nervous, held on to the edges just to be safe. When the observation balloon reaches a certain altitude, it stops. The cool wind blew past Richter as he takes in the view.

"This is certainly a sight to behold," Richter said, reading his binoculars.

He looked through the binoculars and saw the enemy trench line. The activity in the area was low for the most part. There were some sitting down looking relaxed while others walked by fully alert. Many of them now were wearing their horizon blue uniforms.

"Geez, why on God's green earth would they wear such brightly colored uniform? They stand out like a sore thumb."

Richter writes down everything he sees and keeps scanning the trench line until he comes across the observation trench. There he sees two Frenchmen occupying it. One was looking right at Richter with his own binoculars.

"Heh, I wonder if he can see me," Richter said as he starts waving at them.

To his surprise the French soldier gave smile and wave back before getting smacked in the head by soldier next to him with an aggravated look.

"Even in war, some still show a sliver of friendliness," admonished. Richter in his thoughts.

Richter shifted his sight away from the observation trench and continued his scouting.

"Hmm, so far there is barely much activity going on. Seems they really exhausted themselves during their offensive in terms of resources and morale. I almost pity them, almost. I guess there nothing much to report beside them doing absolutely nothing and..." Richter thoughts were immediately interrupted at sight of something odd.

He zoomed in for a closer look and a large buildup of French troops and some type of vehicles that Richter had no words to describe. Upon closer inspection of the troops, they seemed to be wearing blue uniforms and armed with some peculiar weapons and rifles that Richter couldn't recognize. He immediately grabbed the A-2 camera and took photographs of the small army. After he took the photographs, a bullet went by, followed by a snap. At first he thought nothing of it until another, then another started flying by. He quickly took cover then carefully peered up to see where the shots were coming from. There was a line of French soldiers firing at the balloon; an attempt to shoot him down.

"Verdammt (Damn it), they must be trying to stop me from looking at their buildup. I have to let the operator know to start bringing me down, " Richter thought quickly.

When there was a break from the suppression of fire, he stood up and looked down below at Lothar and the operators.

"HEY! GET ME DOWN FROM HERE!! THAY ARE SHOOTING!" Richter shouted.

Meanwhile, on the ground Lothar could only faintly hear what Richter was saying as he looked up. One of the operators walked up to him and says:

"Do you know what he is saying?"

"Not a clue. Do you have some way that I can hear?" Lothar replied.

"Now that I think of it, we might. Hold one second." The operator rushed over to the equipment trunk and starts rummaging through it until he pulls out something and runs back to Lothar.

"Here, use this hearing horn," says the operator and hands it to Lothar.

Lothar quickly put it to his ear and was able hear Richter.

"I SAID, LET ME DOWN! VERDAMMT (DAMN IT)!!" Richter yells, with tracers now flying by.

"Mein Gott (My God), they are firing at him! Quickly now, pull him down, do it now!" Lothar ordered the balloon operators. A group immediately assembled at the rope line and began pulling but the situation was about to get worse.

"Oh, finally you're pulling! I can stop worrying now and..." Immediately a stray bullet hit one of the ropes holding the basket. The basket tilted while Richter held on tight to the edges. Then another bullet hit another support rope causing the basket tilted even more to one side with Richter holding for dear life now. He saw the camera fall from the basket hit the ground hard getting destroyed in the process.

Lothar jumped in front of the line and started pulling even more rope down than the rest of the operators as he continued to watch his new charge struggling not to fall.

"Keep going men, we are halfway there!" Lothar shouts.

They kept pulling until the balloon's basket was on the ground. Operators quickly moved in to secure the balloon from rising again. Lothar went over as well to check on Richter who was still in the basket. At first glance he was completely terrified and his arms and legs trembling even after he landed. Richter slowly crawled out of the basket still shaken from the experience, but after taking a few deep breaths, he calms again.

"What the hell happen up there, Richter?" Lothar asked.

"There is a large buildup of French forces on the other side. They have vehicles that I have never seen before and their weapons are also something peculiar, indeed," Richter described as he slowly got up.

"Unidentified vehicles? Strange weapons? You're not making any sense, but a buildup that I can believe if they are making one final attempt. Anything else Richter?"

"The camera...I took photographs of it all. That is was why they started firing at me. They didn't want me seeing what they were doing. Where is the camera?"

"Right there." Lothar points at the broken remains of the camera.

Richter rushed over to see if the film survived. Luckily it did, as he gently salvaged it from the camera. He then showed it to Lothar.

"We're going to have to get this film developed first, Richter. However I'm somewhat convinced that there is something unusual going on over there."

"How long is that going to take? What's our strategy or our plan?" Richter asked.

"I need moment to think hold on."

Lothar stands there for a moment then begins to pace back and forth still thinking about what to do. He finally sat down on a crate, conveying his thoughts.

"Why did this assignment get complicated all of a sudden? What's our next strategy, really? That's one thing I

am seriously bad at. Maxis was always the one that comes with a plan and strategizes. I'm just the brawn. Verdammt (damn it) think Ludvig, think! What would he do, how would he handle this? How?! The last time tried to make plan I almost got him killed back at Bochnia. Even with me as a Corporal, I only received the rank when I joined the Battalion!"

Lothar struggled in thoughts and a look of frustration appeared on his face. For the first time in his life doesn't know what to do. Suddenly there was a sound of footsteps coming from behind him then he felt a hand on his shoulder.

"Still having the same old problems with thinking games, eh lumber head?" said an unknown voice.

"Wait minute, I recognize that snark tone. Stefan?" Lothar turned to look and recognized a soldier with a smirk on his face.

"That's right, Pfc. Felix Stefan at your service."

"Stefan, I haven't seen since graduation from school! What happened to you?"

"Allow me to give the answer. After you went to join the army back in '13, I wandered off a bit and may have gotten into some trouble with the authorities after I 'liberated' some fine jewelry. After getting thrown in jail, I thought for certain I was done for until the war began, and that is when the Commander came for a visit."

"Wait, what do you mean?" Lothar questioned.

"He was recruiting, Ludvig. I'm now part of the Geist Platoon. I have a set of skills to acquire things without anyone noticing which makes me a fine candidate for this unit. Along with additional training of course," said Stefan as points at the K.W.S. symbol with a small ghost at the bottom.

"Huh, acquiring things without anyone noticing. I guess I do have an idea after all," Lothar thought.

"So, what are you doing here Stefan?" Lothar asked.

"I was sent here by Wotan to check up on the squads here in Champagne. Even though you gave your reports to Hermes, we still needed to see if you are doing alright and if you need any support from us."

"What kind of support?" Richter questioned.

"Oh, the usuals like intelligence gathering, advance reconnaissance, espionage and so on so forth," Stefan explained.

"As matter of fact, I am in need of your services," admitted Lothar.

"Oh, and what would you require me to do, old friend?"

"Is it possible that you can infiltrate the French trench line and obtain documents regarding the large build up?"

"Hmm...Geist isn't exactly a combat unit. What you are asking is very risky and dangerous. I can, but it might be difficult, I'll assume you have some sort of plan," Stefan continued, sounding unsure.

"That's right. It won't be difficult for you because me and Richter will create a distraction. That way you can slip right through undetected, find the officers quarter, retrieve their intel, and escape without anyone noticing," Lothar finished.

"You have certainly changed since our school days, Lothar. No longer a brute but a thinker. Better yet, a strategist; my, times have changed. I do know the best way to get into their trench. I'll disguise myself as one of their own. I just have to find a uniform that isn't tampered with bullets or blood stains. It can blow my cover if they see something like that. So, when do we start?"

"Me and Richter will go to the quartermaster and load up while you find a French uniform. Let's synchronize our watches, right now it's nine o'clock Our operation begins at nine thirty,. Stefan, you will have thirty minutes to get this done. If we need to abort, use a flare gun to signal whether you were successful; blue for completion and red for failure. Got it?"

"Understood, see you when the deed is done," reassured Stefan as he walks away.

Lothar and Richter move out toward the quartermaster's tent to see what Heinrich might have in store for them. They walk right in to see Heinrich with his feet kicked up while writing something down on his clip board. He looks up and says:

"Back again I see. What do you need this time?"

"Heinrich, we are going to need some heavy ordnance to stir up a hornet's nest," Lothar said.

"Golly, first crossing Russian trenches and now you're trying to see how you can agitate the French into attacking?"

"It sounds crazy, but it is the part of plan, Quartermaster," replied Richter.

"Oh please! The things Lothar the brute and his hazard hungry friend Maxis do! Things that are beyond the definition of crazy. That's why I admire them since I'm the one that gives them the tools of destruction."

"Anyway, I just need a few grenades if you have any, and give the kid something nice as well, bitte (please)," Lothar requested nicely.

"Alright let's see what I have," he replied, rummaging through his supply. "Ok, I have five kugel grenades and two discushandgranaten (disk grenades). These are the defensive models so once you pull the pin and toss it, it will explode on impact."

"Perfect! That should do it," Lothar exclaimed, as he grabbed the kugel grenades and hands the disc grenades to Richter.

"Wait one moment I have one last thing, though it's for the Private," said Heinrich as reached down the crate and pulled out a unique weapon.

"Wow! Uh...what is it?" Richter asked.

"This is the Mauser Handgranaten M1915 bolt action grenade launcher, a converted Gewehr 98 for line throwing but also for offensive use. It fires experimental 40mm grenades that are already primed and uses blank rounds to launch the projectiles. If you ask me, this is the perfect weapon for a dedicated grenadier. Here is the ammo for it," Heinrich finished, handing over an ammo bag full of blanks, ten 40mm grenades, and the launcher itself.

"Yikes, you expect me to carry this much weight?"

"Expect it. My friend carried a lot more than you have now. In this Battalion you are expected to haul a hundred pounds or more, and march fourteen miles.

Does that answer your question? Come on, we're on the clock."

"Hold it right there! I noticed the film hanging out of your pocket. Do you need that developed? I have the tools to get it developed if you would like? It will only take twenty minutes give or take," offered Heinrich.

"Done! Here you go. Now let's move, Richter." Lothar quickly takes the film out and hands it to Heinrich. Richter nodded and grabbed the equipment. The two leave the tent as Heinrich waves goodbye to them and speaks.

"Have fun, good luck, and don't die! I need those back when you're done!"

Soon they arrived at the first trench line and Lothar went over the top first. Richter hesitated for a moment and asked.

"Wait what are you doing?"

"Heading to our new position, that's what we're doing."

"Into no man's land?" Richter said nervously.

"Yes. Now come on and stop wasting time. I know good spot and the fog will cover our advance."

"Oh-okay," said Richter as he climbed over the parapet.

They crouch sprinted across past the barb wire and into no man's land trying their best not to get spotted by the French. The sight of it all was haunting. Everything was devoid of life, as if hell had just moved in. Trees dead, the ground blackened, small fires still burning, and the chaos of war still raging with no end in sight. It doesn't matter because this is now a modern war! They would come across remains of German and French soldiers who had perished in this great struggle; ranging from skeletal remains to grotesque scenes of corpses still rotting and covered in flies with the fowl stench. The scenery would spark a memory for Richter as he flashes back to Ypres and Marne, images of his dead friends or what's left of them haunting him before snapping back to reality.

"Hold position. We're here," Lothar said softly, as he moved up slowly and pulled out his binoculars.

CHAPTER 14

DIVERSION FOR A GHOST

"I have visual on the French. Cover me. We'll make this shell hole our temporary holdout.

"Heard you, providing cover." said Richter as he surveys the area.

Lothar takes out his shovel and starts digging small mounds around the shell hole. After ten minutes he was done, and he signaled Richter to get in. From where they are located, they're in the middle of no man's land at some twenty feet away from the French trench line.

"Richter, time check."

"Yeah, its nine-twenty and fifteen seconds. We are officially ahead of schedule."

"Good, let's double check our gear just to be safe," said Lothar.

They sat in their makeshift fox hole getting ready for the distraction. Richter pulled the shotguns in his weapon supply and switched them out with two slug rounds from his bandolier and loaded them in. He then readied the grenade launcher by loading the blank round in the chamber and a grenade at the end of the barrel.

"Out of curiosity, how did you and Stefan meet?" Richter asked, as he shifted on the dirt.

"He and I used to go to school together; he was a troublemaker. Always getting into fights and giving the teachers a headache. Me, on the other hand, would just go along with it even though I ended getting into few scraps, put in the corner or hit with the ruler. That all changed when I met Maxis."

"If I'm not mistaken, you mentioned him before. He wouldn't happen to be the Pvt. Maxis, the one most my friends at the time called the 'Der Wolf' or 'Black Wolf of Mon'?"

"That's the one, though he is not a Private anymore. And he never liked that nickname, though I don't know why or how he obtained it. Whenever the topic comes up, he goes silent and gets annoyed if asked twice. Sometimes gets mad," Lothar said as he slowly peeps over the foxhole.

"Huh, interesting. So, continue your story. We still have time." Richter checks his watch again.

"Okay, so basically Maxis was the good kid and disciplined type or 'Goody-Goody' which Stefan calls him all the time. Maxis kind of made me see things differently. Instead of getting in trouble so much, he showed that doing the right thing would be beneficial for me in the long run...if I would follow his lead. Much to the dismay of Stefan of course, because those two never got along. Even when we played games or sports, Maxis played fair while Stefan did just the opposite."

"So, you mean Maxis was the angel and Stefan the devil?" Richter asked.

"Well, less glamorous than that. I mean he would get into some trouble as well, but he did so smartly by coming up with a plan while Stefan would outright do it without thinking. Like stealing some candy while the shopkeeper is distracted. That kind of thing. Eventually me and Stefan began to drift as years went by. I didn't think he would end up in the Imperial army, much less with the Geist platoon." Lothar said in disbelief.

"Even criminals have their uses. I wonder though, if he was recruited out of jail then he must be loyal to Commander Jorgensen since he gave him a second chance. Could that be the same for rest of the Geist Platoon?" Richter wondered.

"Beats me. Time check."

"Three minutes," Richter responded.

Lothar got up and moved to the edge of the foxhole, his LMG at the ready.

"What are you doing?"

"Starting our diversion early, so get ready." Lothar stood on the edge.

"Okay...ready."

"Good. Here we go! Hey you, blue baguette eating bastards!"

Richter was completely caught by surprise by what Lothar was doing.

"What are you doing?"

"Viens à moi (Come at me)! I'm taunting them that's what I'm doing," Lothar continues to insult the French troops in French. After five minutes Richter finally spoke.

"Mein Gott (My God), I doubt you're going to get them to respond and..." Richter was quickly interrupted by sudden furious loud "Raahhhhh!" coming from the French trench line. The two spot a French soldier and an officer rise from the top of their trench then the officer shouted.

"I may somewhat agree to everything except that last part, that's crossing the line. German scum!" said the French officer in total anger.

"Oh Scheisse (shit), you got their attention what did you say?" Richter asked frantically as the officer rambled on.

"I insulted their country, made fun of their manhood, their women, and said their food sucks."

"You did not just insult their food!" Richter gasped with a horrified expression.

"I just did!" Lothar said, with a devious smile as he turns to face the French officer.

"We fight not only for France but also for her honor too. Fix bayonets!" ordered the French officer as he pulled out his saber along with Modèle 1892 revolver.

They recognized the sound of the French fixing their bayonets onto their rifles, along with the metal clattering and shouts of the soldiers repeating the officer's order.

"Charge les hommes (Charge men)!" screamed the officer as he blew the trench whistle.

The French troops climbed out of the trenches giving out their loudest war cry yet and charging into the fog.

"I count ten...no, fifteen...twenty...screw it we have a whole platoon coming right at us," observed Richter as he angled his grenade launcher.

"More the merrier, Private!" Lothar responded, as he positioned his LMG.

The French ran into no man's land not knowing what they would encounter until it was too late. A hailstorm of bullets rained down out of nowhere and explosions cutting them down. Everyone dropped to prone and returned fire. The Officer that accompanied the troops shouts out to the men to press forward. Lothar kept laying suppressing fire while Richter fired the grenades at the pinned down French soldiers. Lothar or Richter lobbed grenades at them, and when they got too close, Richter took care of them with one blast from his drilling shotgun.

More soldiers from French trench line joined in the fray as their losses increased. Ten minutes passed, and Lothar was down to his last three strip magazines. Richter had used up all the hand grenades, slug rounds for shotgun, bird round, and rifle rounds. All he had left was buckshot which was not very effective at long range.

The scenery was as chaotic as ever. In front of the two were dozens of dead French soldiers in blue colored uniforms, a small number of them around their fox holes. There were shell casings and shotgun shells strewn about in their foxholes as well. The burning question was, "When will it end?:

"Verdammt (Damn it), last strip," Lothar said, as he loaded his strip magazine.

"What's taking Stefan so long? We're burning through our ammo fast!" Richter said franticly.

"I don't know, but at this rate we seemed to grab the attention of the whole French 4th Army."

Lothar continued firing his machine gun then heard the flare go up from behind. The two look up to see a blue flare illuminating through the fog.

"There's the signal! Get ready to run like hell.," ordered Lothar.

"We're already in hell by the looks of things," Richter replied.

"Ha, good one. Okay, I'll provide suppressing fire while we move, got it?"

"Loud and clear."

"ALRIGHT, SUPPRESSING!"

Lothar moves, firing his machine gun and Richter runs past him. After shooting a full magazine, Lothar begins to run like hell as bullets fly by. The two make a mad dash to their trench line with the French right behind them. They make it to their trench, jumping inside. They immediately shout at the machine gunners, warning them what's coming, and surely enough the sound of the MG08 firing at the incoming French was somewhat a sign of relief, safe in friendly lines.

They could hear one of Frenchmen shout "Se retirer (Fallback)!" and machine guns continued for another second, then ceased. Lothar and Richter got up from the ground, dusted themselves off and checked each other for any wounds.

"Well, I must admit that went better than expected, if I do say so myself," Lothar remarked, sounding confident.

"You call that a plan? We nearly called the entire French army down on us! How's that a job well done?"

"If you have forgotten Private, we needed to buy Stefan time to get in and get out. Even if we drew the attention of the 4th Army. Now come on, let's go find Stefan," Lothar finished as he walked away.

They walked around trench line for thirty minutes looking for the Geist Platoon member. Eventually their search led them to ask questions regarding the whereabouts of Stefan, though they were careful with their questions.

"Just great. The one thing I forgot is where to meet up. We literally asked five of the sentries if they saw anyone besides us making a ruckus with the French. I should have been more thorough with the plan. If Maxis was here, he probably would have told me do better but he's not here, so I must figure this out," Lothar contemplated in his thoughts.

"Hey soldat, have you by chance seen anybody returning back to trench line?" Lothar asked the soldier.

"Actually yes. An individual has returned and immediately had to be treated for wounds. You'll find him in the infirmary."

"Danke (Thanks)."

Lothar and Richter headed to the trench infirmary. They found the entrance of the infirmary and walked right in. The infirmary staff was triaging soldiers and treating the severely injured to the lesser. At last, they spotted Stefan sitting on a table getting bandages on his right arm. Lothar rushed over to Stefan.

"What happened to you?" Lothar asked.

"I got a little flesh wound. It's no big deal," Stefan deferred, trying to act cool.

"Yeah, I call nonsense on that statement by the look of the bandage. I can still see the blood."

"Alright, you got me. There was a minor complication during my infiltration. While you and the kid were dealing with the wrath of France, I managed to get through with no problem as I wore a disguise. One part of their trench had fewer troops in it, so no one batted an eye that a French soldier came out of nowhere from no man's land. After searching high and low I found their HQ and it was completely empty. I guess your distraction was working so well that even the officers had go check out what was happening. The place was filled to the brim with paperwork and maps and I thought I'd be stuck there forever looking for the specific documents regarding the large buildup of troops. That is until I saw a file under a lamp light that said 'confidentiel (confidential)' on the front in red. Just when I was about take it a French officer walks in. He started demanding to know what was I doing there before he put two and two together and realized I was an infiltrator. Shot me in the arm but I shot him in the head and made a hasty retreat and here we are," Stefan concluded.

"Geez, what a tale. Glad you managed to survive at least. Do you have the file with you right now?" Lothar wanted to know.

"Yeah, here it is. Apologies for the blood stains. Most of it will be in French." Stefan hands over the files.

"That's not a problem for me since I studied and learned the language."

"No doubt. I could barely contain myself when I heard you made fun of their entire existence."

Lothar grabbed the file and opened it. He began to read the file and translated what the contents said.

"Operation: Miracle spear

Leader of this operation: Cpt. Dubois

The government was kind enough to give us these new armored vehicles or "landships" to aid in this operation. None the less, Lieutenant-Colonel Molitor's orders are clear, we are to breach the German frontlines at this sector where their defenses are least defended. Our teams of trench raiders should have already probed and if possible, weakened the Boche before our assault. The equipment will be listed for logistical reasons.

Furthermore our reports stated that has been no reported sightings of the Elite German unit in this area, but that could change, so be prepared. The operation will begin with a wielding the fist of steel being thrown at cowardly defenders. This will be the last for the failing Champagne Offensive. If we succeed on taking Champagne back from the Germans then this war will be as good as ours. For glory of the Third Republic and la Division Spéciale Hasardeux (the Special Hazard Division or S.H.D.). Toujours prêt (Always ready).

Objectives:

Use the Boirault machines No.1 and our specially armored Breton-Pretot to breach and clear out the barbed wire. Escort will be provided by 1st platoon.

The second wave will come shortly, with more Boirualt machine No.1s along with our men moving behind them. Support will be provided by Gallus Company.

If successful in taking their trenches, we will press our advance further securing a launching point for the rest of the 4th Army, for their advance.

Lastly, we must secure the railways in Champagne to prevent any reinforcements or supplies coming through."

"Cpl. Lothar and Pvt. Richter, finally I have found you two. I finished developing the film!" Heinrich barges in, interrupting Lothar while he was reading.

"Well, let's have a look then," said Lothar.

Heinrich shows developed photos that reveal nine skeleton vehicles with a single overhead track, ten of what appears to be an armored car of some sorts, and lastly, four armored tractors with large wire cutters.

"Ok, first image shows the Boirualt No.1s. There is also the Breton-Pretot tractor with a vertically stacked cannon, and last is set of vehicles I don't recognize," Lothar finished.

"Wow, you figured out what those things are from the file alone? Amazing," remarked Richter, sounding surprise.

"To be honest, Kameraden, I thought I was looking at a military art show when I first saw them," admitted Heinrich.

"Alright, let me finish reading this. We need to know how many we are going to be dealing with," Lothar continued, then reads aloud.

"Logistics:

Nine Boirault Model No.1

Four Breton-Pretot armored tractors

Ten Filtz armor tractors

Five Chauchat LMGs squads

Twenty Rossignol ENT B-1 rifles squads

Ten Rossignol B-2 Machine rifles squads

Rest of our men will have the standard issued rifles and couple dozen portable shields."

"Looks like we're going have major battle here. Better get on the horn with Hermes about this. But what's worse is that there is another military organization operating in this area, Commander Jorgensen is not going to like this at all. It's safe to assume that they are specially trained or dare I say elite...yet to be determine," Lothar thinks while reading.

"Wait, did they mention 'Rossignol rifle' in the file?" Heinrich asks Lothar.

"Yeah?"

"How wonderful! I heard rumors that the French were working on something like that at some military college before the war. If you were to...I don't know 'obtain' one of these rifles, then I can send them back to R&D in Valhalla base to better improve our own designs."

"I'll think about it. In the meantime I'll inform Hermes on the situation. Come on, Private." Lothar puts the file in his tornister and walks out of the infirmary with Richter right behind him.

"Okay, see you later and thanks for visiting your wounded friend and...he's gone. Sheesh, I still can't believe that's the same Ludvig from my childhood. Guess Maxis was a better influence than I was," said Stefan.

"The young Sergeant Maxis has that effect. It's the development of his character at work. The kid is evidence of that and though the Corporal is two years older, he has the experience." Heinrich finished.

Lothar and Richter moved quickly to the HQ dugout to get on the line with Hermes. They arrived at the dugout and entered, passing everyone by. Lothar grabbed the phone and directed the operator to connect him to Hermes with haste.

"Connecting now," said the operator as a *click* can be heard. Lothar begins to speak on the line.

"Hermes, Hermes. This is Titan. We have a situation that is developing right now."

"This is Hermes. Elaborate on the situation."

"A member of Geist Platoon and I have obtained enemy intelligence regarding buildup in sector Duff and uncovering a French military organization."

"Interesting, what else do you know?" Hermes asked.

"There's more in the file along with a photograph of the enemy strength. Have any of the other squads encountered any like this on their end?"

"I'll have to check in to see. Do think you can handle this or require support?"

"At this rate we are going to need support. What's the ETA for the other squads to arrive at sector Duff?"

"At least a day on foot or twelve hours by truck."

"Send them my way and tell them to double time it," Lothar demanded.

"I'll send a request to Wotan and see what I can do. Is there anything else to report?"

"Nein. Do you have any helpful tips?'

"The tips were in the mission details, Corporal. If you need one now, here it is. Use what you've got and be resourceful until help arrives."

"Danke, I know what to do now."

"Good. Terminating call *click*."

"Be resourceful, huh? Now I'm starting to understand how Maxis feels about being forced to think of something during desperate times. Well, let's see how I can do this, shall we?" Lothar scans the room to see what he can use. A phone rings and a soldier answers it, which gives Lothar an idea.

"Cpt. Schmitz, Sir, you wouldn't have any spare telephone wires do you?"

"We have plenty of it in storage. Is this in regards to your getting prepped for the attack Corporal?" Cpt. Schmitz asks.

"Yes, Sir. This is part of the plan I mustered up that requires our artillery."

"Then by all means use them Corporal, if it helps get the job. If you get on the line with the artillery their nickname is Thunder."

Lothar walked out of HQ dugout and moved toward the reserve trench to find the storage area. There he found not only a telephone wire but also a box telephone. Richter was by his side, but a bit puzzled. He went along with it, then Lothar told him to find some engineers who could connect the wires to the telephone and lead the long line to the artillery position. Richter went to fetch the engineers while Lothar walked over to quartermaster's tent. He walked right in and spoke.

"Heinrich, I need something that can punch a hole into to those armored things. Do you have anything that can do that?"

"Give me a moment. I think I have just the thing." Heinrich said, walking around the crates and sounding excited. He pulled out a crowbar and began to open a large crate with word 'Ladera' on the side. After removing the top, Heinrich reached in and pulled out a strange large weapon. Heinrich brought the weapon over and placed it on the table.

"This is the Mauser Ladera M1913 anti-fortification gun. It's a self-loading weapon with enough armor piercing power to crack the walls of any fort or fortress you may come across. With the addition of a bipod, you can get yourself set up and ruin anyone's day if they are driving an armored car. Ten round magazines included. Mauser abandoned this weapon right before the war began, a few of my contacts in the company managed to acquire the schematics for it so now the battalion has armor piercing based weapons. Don't worry about what I said about being trained on this weapon. Right now, you need this, and I know you can figure out how to work this piece of machinery," Heinrich declared.

"Perfect," Lothar said, as he picked up the rifle and ammo box. He walked out of the tent with Heinrich waving goodbye. Lothar spotted Richter sitting on some crates with the box telephone by his side and a pile of wires that lead to somewhere.

"Alright Richter, I managed produce a plan, so listen up. The enemy will hit this place soon, so we need to be prepared for them. I'm going to run the wire all the way to our old foxhole and set up the telephone; that way we can communicate with our artillery back at our lines. I also have in my possession a special rifle that will give us an edge. Get resupplied and grab a few ammo boxes for me while you're at it. We'll meet up at the first trench line. Ten minutes, do not be late."

"Understood," said Richter.

The pair split up both heading in different directions. Lothar ran the wire across the cross-section of the trenches and over the top toward their old foxhole located on a small hill. The landscape seemed different without the fog covering and that also meant Lothar would have to lay low, crawling to the foxhole. He made it safely and crawled in.

He set up the telephone and placed the fortress gun aside, checking his surroundings. When he was finished, he put a cover over the telephone box and another over the Ladera rifle. He crawled his way back to the first trench line where he would meet Richter. After what seemed like forever, he arrived at the trench line where the private was waiting, wearing an assault pack. Richter looked up and spoke.

"I've got what you asked for including the extra ammo, but do you think it's going to be enough to stop them?"

"Let me tell you something, Private. Sure it's a matter who has the biggest stick but what matters a lot more who's swinging it. For now, either today or tomorrow, we're going up against Frenchie's best. So yes, Private, it'll be enough."

"So, we just sit here and wait?"

"That's the plan. I've set up the box telephone where our foxhole was. All we have follow the line to get there when fighting begins."

"How will we know it has started?"

"Well, their file mentioned something about "Wield the fist of steel" which probably means an artillery barrage, so when the shells start coming that's when we run like hell to foxhole."

"Alright then. Let waiting begin."

THEIR FINEST HOUR

Day 3, March 18

They sat in their trench, waiting for hours. Throughout the night more German troops started to arrive little by little, taking positions along the cross-section of the trench, fresh-faced recruits now a part of this region's war. Lothar passed the time by polishing his weapon while Richter counted how many shells he has for his 'drilling shotgun'.

They took turns performing lookout duties in case the French sends a trench raiding team. The only thing they had to worry about was the tiredness and exhaustion they felt from getting hardly any sleep. The only time they rested was only five, ten, and if lucky, thirty minutes, all the while keeping an eye out on the frontlines.

Suddenly, just before seven in the morning, a barrage of artillery was heard. Then came the all too familiar sound of incoming shells as they whistled their way down from the skies. Everyone took cover as the shells made impact. The men shouted orders and questions alike.

"In Deckung gehen! Eingehend (Take cover! Incoming)!" yelled one German soldier.

"Are they launching another offensive?!"

"Who cares keep your head down!"

The troops were confused and in a panic, while the more experienced veterans tried to maintain their composure and keep everyone calm. As for Lothar and Richter, this was their cue to go over the top and on their way to face the enemy in no-man's land.

"Come, Pvt. Richter, into the storm of steel we go! Follow the wire!" Lothar said in an affirmative voice.

"Right behind you, Corporal!"

A sergeant noticed the pair leaving the trench and going into no-man's land. He began to shout at them.

"HEY! Where the hell are you going? Deserters will be shot..."

"Leave them be Feldwebel (Sergeant), they have different mission to attend to," directed Cpt. Schmitz, as he slowly lowered the soldier's rifle.

Lothar and Richter followed the wire and checked it to make sure it wasn't cut. They moved quickly through the decimated land, all while avoiding the artillery. At one point an artillery shell exploded ten feet away from them causing them to pause as their ears started ringing, and their bodies vibrated from the sound of the explosion, their vision shaking. They still pressed onward to their makeshift cover. At one moment the impact sparked memory in the two, remembering almost getting killed by artillery. As for Richter, he almost back at Ypres and the Marne again.

"Count to three, inhale. Count to three, exhale," Richter repeated to himself.

They finally arrived at the foxhole and dove right in. Lothar uncovered the Ladera rifle and the telephone box. He immediately grabbed the phone. For a moment there was silence on the other end, then he heard a voice.

"Thunder here."

"Thunder, this Titan squad, priority control ordnance at my command. I authenticate on reign on fire missions, Thunder," Lothar screamed into the phone as the barrage continues.

"I hear you, Titan squad. Lend the coordinates and we'll bring down the hurt. Thunder standing by."

"Thunder, load HE shells and AP shells. Wait for my command to fire."

"Understood Titan, doing so now," the artillery officer shouts, ordering the men to load the requested shells.

Ten minutes later the bombardment ceased and there was nothing but an eerie silence in the air. Certainly unnerving. A line of smoke appeared thirty feet north of their position, then the sound of engines turning on, and a French soldier begins to speak.

"Remember men, what we succeed today could change the war tomorrow. For France and the Republic!" shouted Cpt. Dubois, as the trench whistle was heard along with a loud war cry.

Lothar handed the phone to Richter. He pulled out a small map of the area that was in a grid.

"I'll call out coordinates, you repeat it to Thunder. Understood?" Lothar ordered as he took position on the Ladera rifle.

"I got it," Richter replied as he readied the grenade launcher.

Through the smoke odd shapes appeared, moving at erratic pace. Something breaks through the smoke that leaves Richter in shock but would make Lothar more ready than ever.

Moving across the field were four Boirault Machine Model 1s. Along with them were four Breton-Pretot Tractors fully armored in the front with a cannon sticking out, and a platoon size unit following behind. The Boirualt Machines were in a spearhead formation that trampled over everything in its path, including left over barbed wire, abandoned wagons, dead trees, and logs. The skeleton bodies of the Model 1's revealed no drivers, as if engines were running by themselves. The tractors lined up, side by side behind the Model 1's and moved at a steady pace, their wire cutters at the front of the vehicles. The French infantry at the back of the formation were armed with label M1886 rifles, followed by small squads armed with Rossignol ENT B-1 self-loading rifles and three squads of Chauchat light machine guns.

Lothar took aim at the Boirault Machine at the front and fired, letting off a loud bang that jerked him back. The shot hit the machine and left a spark, but it was still moving.

"Woah, this has a kick," Lothar said, as he felt the shock from it.

He aimed at the same machine at the front of the line and fired. This time he hit something vital which caused the machine to burst into flames. Immediately one of the Breton-Pretot tractors shifted and aimed its cannon toward Lothar. It fired a round at the pair but missed which caused Lothar to react quickly. He returned fire at the Breton. He fired a shot at it but ricocheted off the front of the armor.

"Verdammt, time to put my marksmanship to the test."

Lothar took aim at what appeared to be gas canisters in the tractor. He fired and the thunderous sound erupted out of his rifle again, the bullet hitting its mark as a huge explosion is seen. The driver and gun operator were flung out of the fiery vehicle.

"Richter, fire mission coming up! Grid 3-2-7!"

"Thunder, this is Titan. Fire mission follows grid 3-2-7!" Richter yelled into the phone.

"Affirmative Titan, firing for effect."

Not a second too soon the sound of artillery could be heard and twenty seconds later shells rained down on the Model 1's and the Breton tractors on the left side. One Model 1 blew up completely while another was dislodged from its frame. As for the Bretons, some blew up and others were disabled, leaving some of the crew alive.

Lothar could now reposition himself to the right where the Breton-Pretot broke off formation and headed toward them with the 1st platoon following. Lothar fired a shot at the first Breton-Pretot he sees and immediately it stopped. Two people scrambled out of the vehicle and ran away, leaving the driver dead at his seat. Two others stopped and fired their cannons as 1st platoon sent two squads up the small hill and began to open fire to suppress Lothar. The squads were armed with Rossignol ENT B-1 self-loading rifles and continued firing on Lothar's position.

"Verdammt (Damn it), they got me suppressed and they are getting close!"

"How many are coming up?!" Richter asked.

"About ten at least, why?"

"Keep me covered, I'm about to clear them out."

"WHAT?! Are you crazy?"

"Just trust me!"

"Fine, covering fire," Lothar shouted as he began firing his modified Benet Mercie at the incoming French.

Richter threw three smoke grenades and just as the large plume engulfed them, he jumps out the foxhole and sprinted into the smoke that the French squad was about to enter as well.

The French, now in the smoke, could barely see as they pressed forward until they spotted a silhouette coming right at them. Before they could react, five men screamed as they were knocked down following the sound of two shotgun blasts and a rifle shot. Richter switched to his Reichsrevolver and took down four more, then finished off the last soldier with a knife to his side. Before slugging him in his face.

As the smoke dispersed, another French squad held their ground trying to see what on earth was happening in there. The last sight they saw appearing from the smoke was Richter loading his grenade launcher and firing it. A single grenade wiped out the entire squad. Richter rushed over to the last two Breton-Pretot as he loaded his drilling shotgun. He cleared out the first tractor with his shotgun, with one casualty falling off the side; then he climbed up top and finished off the last crew on the next tractor with his revolver.

The French First Lieutenant and platoon sergeant, unhappy at the sight they witnessed, ordered the whole platoon into a full-scale charge with Chauchats laying down fire and as well as other self-loading rifle teams firing as they moved.

Richter retreated to the foxhole as bullets starts flying around him; the sound of the French shouting and cursing behind his back. Lothar got on the phone while firing his LMG.

"Thunder, new fire mission. Grid follows 2-4-8, danger close."

"You got it Titan. Get to cover. Laying down the thunder!"

"Get in here, you idiot!" Lothar shouted at Richter.

Richter jumped in the nick of time as fiery explosions detonated behind him. They duck and cover while the artillery continued to fire on their position. When the artillery strike ceased, they saw a familiar sight. Bodies were littered all over the place leaving a grisly scene. Two out of the three Boirault machines, model 1's, were also hit in the bombardment, leaving Richter to destroy the last one with his grenade launcher. It exploded into a ball of flames and then fell apart. The two stood there with their hearts racing and breathing heavily, then Lothar asked.

"So, is that what a Trench Trooper can do? I'm impressed."

"I was trained for something like this. I won't lie, that was intense. I'm just surprised it worked out so well. Is it over?"

"Nein, this was just the first wave, there was supposed to be another right after."

Suddenly another thunderous barrage of artillery was heard and ordnance peppered the entire area. Lothar and Richter took cover. Again, Lothar gets on the line to Thunder.

"Thunder, prepare for fire mission! Thunder... THUNDER!" Lothar grabbed the wire and started pulling it, only to find out it has been cut by artillery.

Meanwhile back at the German trench line, Stefan is running through the trench network toward the HQ dugout, dodging artillery shells and kicking dirt everywhere. As he ran past the officers who were hiding under the table, Stefan grabbed the special telephone.

"Operator put me on the line to Hermes immediately. This is urgent! Exception phrase G.P."

"Connecting you now, Geist," and a click is heard.

"This is Geist Platoon member PFC. Stefan, ID number 442."

"This Hermes, what's the situation Geist?"

"Hermes, Hermes, Titan squad has engaged the enemy force! Right now, they are holding but are severely outgunned and outnumbered. Where the hell are the other squads?!"

"Geist, the other squads have left and are on the way. The good news is that this is the only area that is currently under attack. There were no reports of any military buildup in the other sectors. We cannot confirm at this time of ETA, but we can safely assume they'll arrive in an hour or two."

"They'll be dead in thirty! Is there anything to spare?" Stefan queried with frustration.

"I'm sorry Geist, there is nothing else we can spare at this...Hold on. I have just been informed that 1Lt. Hoffmann of the Prussian Blue Tails is available for support."

"Tell that sarcastic jerk to spread his wings and fly as fast as a European Swallow, NOW!"

"He is on the way! Sit tight."

Back in no-man's land, the artillery continued to hammer the area for fifteen minutes, and the artillery eventually ceased after firing its last shells that were apparently smoke rounds. The smoke covered the area blocking the field of view from the foxhole. Lothar reloaded both his LMG and the Ladera. Richter reloaded his weapons as well. They slowly moved through the smoke only to be shocked by what they saw. Five armored Boirault Model 1's, with two machine guns on each side, ten Filtz armored tractors, and an entire company of French soldiers. The infantrymen came armed with Rossignol ENT B-1 self-loading rifles and B-2 Machine rifles, three Chauchat machine gun teams, the rest arrayed with Label M1886 bolt action rifles, Berthier bolt action, and portable shields.

"Oh Mein Gott (My God)! What's the new plan, Corporal?" Richter asked shakily.

Before Lothar could answer they were forced to quickly take cover as machine gun teams and riflemen opened fired.

"Verdammt (Damn it), I thought the Tsar tank was bad, but this is worse. Ok, ok, we are going have to continue maintaining our priority on the armored vehicles, but what about the infantry? I've burned through half of our ammo cache. If we have to retreat, how would the boys in the trenches fare against this incursion? Verdammt (Damn it) think, Ludvig, think, what would Maxis do?!" Lothar processes.

"LOTHAR! What's the plan?" screamed Richter, as he fired the rifle part of his drilling shotgun, still under fire.

"Uh, hell. Richter maintain security and prevent any Frenchie's from getting too close to us. I have French armor to hunt down."

"What if we get overrun?!" Richter asked.

"Then we fall back."

Richter didn't say anything after that response but hopped onto the machine gun and began firing.

Lothar aimed down at the first Boirault he sees. One of the machine's side MGs begins firing at his direction, but Lothar quickly snaps at it and fires the Ladera.

The bullet makes an impact on the landship but to no effect, he fires again. This time the thing stopped and started smoking from the inside before it blew up. He focused his fire on the next Boirault machine, and then the next. Lothar also targeted the Filtz armor tractors stopping them in their tracks with two or three shots in their front engine. Lothar managed to take out three armored Model 1's and four Filtz.

At one point a French soldier managed to sneak up behind them and went after Lothar. The Frenchmen yelled as he kicked him in his back and was about to bayonet him before a sudden boom and a hole appeared on his chest. He fell down bleeding in their foxhole. Lothar looked and saw Richter holding his shotgun with one arm and firing the machine gun with the other all while repeating this phrase "Count to four, target sighted (*deep breath*), count to four, targets down (*exhale*)."

Richter tried his best to keep Gallus company back but failed to see that one Boirault machine was coming up on their flank. Richter managed to pull Lothar out of the way as the thing crushed through their holdout. Richter destroyed the thing with his grenade launcher.

"Verdammt (Damn it), the Ladera gun is destroyed and there are still six Filtz and two Boirault machines left," Lothar said in frustration.

"There is also the fact that their entire Company is about to be on top of us," Richter added.

"Verdammt (Damn it), we have no choice but to fall back. Find another holdout position and hopefully delay them a little longer with whatever we got," Lothar said as he grabbed his LMG from Richter.

They vacated the area by moving downhill, as the sound of the French giving their war cry as they moved up hill with the remaining Boiruatl Machines and Filtz armor tractors. Lothar and Richter took position in a shell and fortified it as quickly as possible. A trench whistle is heard and over the horizon two of the Boirault machine appeared along with six Filtz tractors, moving down as they fired their MGs with a horde of French infantry coming behind.

"This might be the end. I don't have enough ammo for them all," Richter said nervously.

"I know," Lothar said, as he set up the bipod.

Then suddenly the sound of machine guns is heard from above. A LFG Roland C.II flew over, followed by three prototype Fokker Eindecker planes all with painted blue tails. They strafed into the French company with a hail of bullets as they swooped by. In the pilot seat was 1Lt. Hoffmann and his observer/gunner 2Lt. Schroder, who was firing his tail gun at the French troops below.

"Glad we weren't late to the party! Time to see what this new model can do," said 1Lt. Hoffmann.

"Go easy on the plane. She's has only been recently introduced to Imperial Flying Corps," said 2Lt. Schroder.

"Worry not, my friend. Just get ready with those bombs! I see armored targets moving along. I'll slow down some, don't hesitate or miss!"

"On it!"

The planes turned around and slowed their speed. They flew over the French armored vehicles and Schroder dropped bombs on each target while the Eindeckers strafed the infantry. The last Boirault Machines were destroyed and the Filtz armored tractors broke formation; the infantry's morale shattered. Lothar and Richter took the opportunity to launch their counterattack and went after the last Filtz armored tractors to escape.

Richter fired his grenade launched at one, disabling the wheel at the rear, before loading another round and destroying it completely. Lothar climbed up on another one, forced open the hatch, and threw a kugel grenade in, then jumped off before the whole thing exploded. The last five were hunted down by Hoffmann's plane as he passed by each one followed by an explosion. In the end, all the French vehicles were disabled or destroyed, and the infantry retreated back to their trenches.

Lothar looked around and observed the destruction now lay around him. A total mess would be one way to describe it. Lothar walked over to one of the destroyed tractors and saw a strange symbol on the side of it.

"What is with the chicken? No wait, I recognize that bird. It's Frances' national animal, the Gallic Rooster," Lothar thinks while analyzing.

The symbol showed the Gallic Rooster in what looked to be an aggressive stance. Above its head are three golden French lilies and behind the rooster were two French battleaxes in crossed blade position. The symbol had a French color in background behind the symbol.

Richter walked by Lothar, saluting the planes flying overhead before they disappeared into the clouds. It started to rain lightly as thunder rumbled in the background.

"We did it! I can't believe it we did! Look at them run. We stopped them!" Richter cheerfully exclaimed.

"Well, now we know what their unit symbol looks like. But why do I feel like I shouldn't let my guard down? It's over and yet I feel shoulder tensed..." Lothar turned over in his thoughts.

Around the corner from the destroyed Filtz tractor, a French officer appeared with his saber and revolver. He charged at Richter with his saber raised. Lothar noticed it and yelled, "Kid, lookout!" Just in the nick of time Richter managed to block the attack with his shotgun, chipping off the wooden part. Before he could react, in a split second the officer pistol whipped him, followed by a slash across his side. Richter fell face first.

"Richter, NOOO!" Lothar shouted as he tried to shoot his LMG but hears a clicking sound. He then tried to grab his pistol but was immediately shot in his right forearm before he reached the holster. Annoyed by this, he dropped the LMG, pulled out his trench shovel and charged. Instead, the French officer shot his left arm forcing him to drop the shovel. Then he shot him in his legs bringing Lothar to his knees. The officer walked over and kicked him to the ground, then plunged his saber into Lothar's left shoulder. Lothar screamed in pain and struggled to get the blade out of him but not before getting pistol whipped by the officer. The officer lowered himself to a squat and spoke.

"Don't try to struggle. It will only get worse," as he turned the blade a little. Lothar tried not to scream out in pain.

"I guess you know who I am. If not, I will tell you. I am Captain DuBois of the Special Hazard Division. Do you understand me, Jerry?" said Cpt. Dubois

"Je te comprends fils de pute (I understand, you son of a bitch)," Lothar responded in French.

"Hahaha, your accent is good German. Très bon (very good)." Cpt. Dubois stood back up and reloaded his revolver slowly, then began to talk.

"Operation Miracle Spear was supposed to be the very breakthrough the people of France have been waiting for. I had everything planned, everything! I was hoping your people would not show up, but instead you did," he growled. "Tout gâché (you ruined everything)," said Cpt. Dubois as he pushed the shell out from his revolver.

Lothar tried to think of something to do but could not. The pressure from the blade on his shoulder and the bullet wounds prevented him from coming up with constructive thoughts. The only thing he could do was listen while he slowly bled.

"It does not matter anymore. There will always be more men willing to sacrifice for the Third Republic, even if we must force them to do so. It is a shame really for you, Allemand (German). Had you been born in France before the war, I think you and our poster child 'Le Bête (The Beast)' would have been a dynamic duo and best of friends. Such a unique individual, but instead, you lie here in front of me about to be dead so..." He closed the hatch of his revolver. "Tout derniers mots (any last words)?"

As Lothar stared down into barrel his life flashes before his eyes.

"Check mate. In the end I tried everything to prevent this, but I failed. My new charge laying there dead and I'm about to be executed by a sadistic French officer. I tried to follow Friedrich's example but look what that led me to..."

Learn to take responsibility for your action and try to take an example from Sergeant Maxis as well, try to be like him at least...

Nein, my brutish Lothar...

You call that a plan...

No longer a brute but a thinker or better yet a strategist...

Such a unique individual...

Lothar flashes back to his childhood when he sees himself at the age of nine picking grapes with his mother in the vineyard.

Listen Ludvig, we love you and your brothers all the same for each of you are unique in your own way, never forget that. Don't ever change who you are, for you will lose your character and your heart while trying to become someone else. You are strong, gentle, and funny...my little mighty Lothar, Lothar's mother said, as the memory begins to fade away and last word left in his mind was "unique".

"Mutter (mother)," was the last word Lothar uttered. This puzzled Cpt. Dubois for a moment.

"Mère (Mother)? You poor sap, already seeing things? Do not worry. You will be seeing her very soon."

Cpt. Dubois took aim and cocked the hammer back. Then suddenly, a bullet rips through his hand, the revolver dropping to the ground.

Shocked, Lothar wondered, "*Where the hell did that bullet come from?*" It was Richter, barely standing. He fired the rifle part of the drilling shotgun.

"I'm not done with you yet, du BASTARD (you BASTARD)!" Richter raised his voice to get Dubois's attention.

Cpt. Dubois quickly yanked the saber out of Lothar's shoulder and charged at Richter with great speed, the saber raised. Just when he was about to slash him, Richter flipped the switch to shotgun and fired the left barrel at Dubois's hand, annihilating it and the saber in the process.

Cpt. Dubois gripped his right wrist, eyes wide, and let out a hellish scream of pain for his missing hand. Richter placed the shotgun barrel under the captain's jaw and pulled the trigger. A thunderous boom is heard and Dubois' head was obliterated, leaving nothing but bone fragments, visceral, and gore.

"How's that for a close shave?" remarked Richter, before dropping his shotgun and falling to the ground. Dubois's body hit the ground at the same time.

"*In the end, I guess I did find the niche I was searching for. I was too thick-headed to see it right in front of me. Being my true self as the strong man and a thinker. It doesn't matter now I'm already at the point of fading* out. *Thanks, mom, for reminding me...I'm sorry. Farewell Maxis...my parents...my brothers...and goodbye to...Mein fraulein blühend (My blossoming) Hannah,*" Lothar thoughts overcome him as he starts to slowly close his eyes. as the rain starts to die down.

"*Now I lay me down to sleep, I pray the lord my soul...to keep...*" Lothar's vision fades as he closes his eyes and rests for the final time.

But immediately he was interrupted by Richter's cough, as he slowly ot on all fours, still gripping his side. He looked up to see Lothar still somewhat awake and began moving toward him through the mud.

"Corporal...*Coughs*...Lothar! Lothar!" Richter raised his voice to get his friend's attention. Reaching him, he pulled out bandages from his pack started performing first aid on Lothar, trying desperately to stop the bleeding.

"Oh no, I'm not losing another friend not today or tomorrow," said Richter as he applied bandages over the stab wounds. Lothar faded in and out only to see Richter working hard to patch him regardless of the condition he was in.

"Hey, I see someone," said a K.W.S. soldier.

"Hey! Over here we need a...*cough*...sanitäter (Medic)!" Richter motioned and shouted.

"Mein Gott (My God), what a mess...Titan squad. An exceptionally good mess at best. Perseus and Ares squad secure the area and make sure it's clear," the squad leader ordered. There were ten solders surrounding the area with a squad leader guarding the duo.

"Where hell are those Trench surgeons at?" yelled the other squad leader.

"They are bringing the stretchers now," said one of K.W.S. soldier.

The Trench Surgeons rushed in with their stretchers at the ready. They placed them on the ground and moved Lothar onto one, then Richter on the other.

"You're going to be alright, my friend. Come on, schnell (faster)! Just stay with us, ok?" said the Trench surgeon, as he tried keep Lothar awake. His voice became distorted as Lothar falls unconscious.

CHAPTER 16

LOTHAR'S TRIUMPH

The next day...

He woke up in the medical room breathing heavily. He found himself shirtless but covered in bandages on both his legs, arms, and his shoulder. The lump on his face was sore when he touched it. Across from him, Major Reinhard was reading a newspaper as he smoked his cigar. The Major looked up and saw the Corporal awake.

"Ah, now, now don't try to get up. The doctor and nurses spent hours fixing you up so don't ruin their hard work," directs Major Reinhard.

"S-Sir, where am I?" Lothar asked, looking around.

"In an army field hospital, near Sedan. You were pretty banged up. Surprised the two of you managed to even survive.'

"Richter...where's the kid? Is he alright?!"

"Don't worry Corporal, he is stitched up and resting. It's a miracle he was wearing a thick leather vest underneath when he got slashed. Otherwise, he would have died on the spot. He said it was his 'lucky vest' as he puts it."

"Oh, thank Gott. Forgive me for asking Sir, but why are you here?"

"I'm glad you asked. It's about your mission, son. What you encountered and stopped! We weren't expecting an attack so soon after their Champagne offensive officially ended. The Commander placed a bet something might happen...he was right. The file that the Geist Platoon provided only gave a fraction of who we were dealing with besides names of course. From what Panacea, Perseus, and Ares reported you halted their advance and left a trail of destruction in your wake. They were horrified by the scenery while I thought it was impressive. Agent Stefan, Quartermaster Hugo Heinrich, and Cpt. Schmitz reported how you managed to be very resourceful from using diversionary attack to using the box telephone in the middle of no – man's land to guide the artillery. Not to mention you put the private's skills to great use on the field," the Major finished.

"He was very proficient with that shotgun."

"Indeed, it was bit risky to allow such a weapon, but the Commander cares about results. They will certainly be happy to know that. However, let's keep it secret from the Kaiser. Otherwise he may not be happy with the idea," Major Reinhard gave a nod and a wink.

"Understood."

"On to another matter. The aftermath in Sector Duff. We sent a cleanup crew to collect the wreckage for studies, but there was nothing there. This Hasardeux Division or S.H.D. was very thorough and didn't even leave a rifle behind. I guess they're following same rules as us, when comes to being nonexistent, huh?" Major Reinhard blows small plume of smoke.

"Do you think they will be a threat, Major?"

"No, I haven't received any reports of heavily armed Poliu running amok in the Western Front on the back of an armored tractor. I doubt they will show their faces again since you saw to it to make an example of them. I believe that covers everything, I'll take my leave and let you rest. We have big plans for this year and we need you fully recovered. I must say you certainly have learned your lesson."

"Sir, before you go, can tell what it takes to be a leader?"

"*Sigh*. Alright. It all starts with confidence," Major Reinhard began as he sat down.

A day earlier...

Standing on a hill was French officer who wore a Van Dyke goatee. He watched from afar with binoculars to take in the devastation of Operation Miracle Spear strewn about in no-man's land. Another French officer appeared behind him and spoke.

"I am here as requested, Ltc. Molitor."

"Stand by me, Major Fontaine," said Ltc. Molitor in deep voice.

"Oui monsieur (Yes, Sir)." Fontaine walked right beside him.

"Take look and tell me what you see," said Ltc .Molitor, handing the binoculars to Fontaine.

"I see the destruction of Gallus Company's attack. No doubt those bastards Boche were ready for us and stopped what would have been our assaut parfait (perfect assault)."

"Non(no), it was not the Imperial German Army that halted our attack. I saw what happened, Major. The assault failed because of the will of two Soldats (Soldiers) and their perseverance."

"I do not follow, monsieur."

"Napoleon once said, 'Victory belongs to the most persevering,' and that is what those two showed, for they are not regular German soldats (soldiers). They are K.W.S.'s finest that were fighting a force of two hundred men. Then came the planes that halted the assault completely."

"Impossible! I never heard such ridiculous thing...uh, apologies monsieur."

"'Impossible is a word to be found only in the dictionary of fools.' That is another quote from Bonaparte. We are still new as an organization though there is no room for incompetence and arrogance. Cpt. Dubois displayed such things as he ignored my order to cease the operation. Now he is dead along with our troops," Molitor said with disappointment.

"Dubois was étrange (strange) type but nothing short of a sadist on how he treats our troops and the POWs. I was ready to court-martial him before the assault."

"Anyway, we need to clean this mess up before the Germans or K.W.S. come to collect. Do what is necessary to get everything out; use smoke or tear gas if they become a bother. Today never happened and we were never here," Molitor finished.

"Oui, monsieur it will be done. Anyone asks, we deny everything, for we are the secret weapon of France!" Major Fontaine expressed proudly.

"Toujours prêt (Always ready), Major." Molitor turns to see Fontaine saluting, he returns the salute and the Major went on his way. Molitor takes off his cap to look at it. At the front of the cap was the symbol of the Hazardous Division.

"Jorgensen, Mon vieil ami (My old Friend), let the games begin. We shall see once and for all who can play the war game, better," Molitor said as he put his cap back on and strode away.

CHAPTER 17

BEWARE OF THE GALLIC ROOSTER?

April 20ᵗʰ, 1915, Ragnarök base, Belgium

Major Reinhard was in his office filing reports, filling out requests, and organizing his resources with a small pile of paperwork that surrounded him. He heard a knock on the door.

"Enter!" He harkened. The door opened, but the moment he looked up he saw Commander Jorgensen standing there. He snapped to attention and saluted but is met with, "As you were, Gunther," from Jorgensen.

"My, there is more propaganda, recruitment, and war bond posters than you can shake a stick at in your new office. I am glad to see there is a spot for unser lieber Kaiser (our dear Emperor) and the unit flag behind you," said Commander Jorgensen, as he admired the set of posters and frames on the office walls.

"I think supporting your country is the best show of patriotism. Blind patriotism will lead to denial of one's actions and that of your country. I thought it would add a little wisdom. Care for a drink, Sir?" Major Reinhard asked as he opened the hidden mini bar in the globe.

"Not today, I'm afraid. I'm here to hand in your new orders. Also, to inform you that you will be heading the Offensive that will take place in two days. Take a look," Commander Jorgensen said, placing the file on the desk. Reinhard picked it up and thumbed through it.

"Operation Gruner Tag (Green Day) and Gas? I didn't think our forces would go to that extent, Sir?"

"They will. The generals are growing restless with the stalemate continuing and so they are about to launch another offensive against the British using poison gas for the first time. The French started using tear gas earlier in the war," the Commander said as he took a seat in front of Reinhard.

"Yes, but tear gas isn't exactly deadly..."

"It is if you don't get treated, and even more deadly to those who have breathing problems; they can choke to death. Regardless of what we may think, you and I are to follow orders."

"Then how will our troops deal with this new weapon?" Reinhard asked.

"Worry not. I took the liberty to have Director Albrecht get in touch with certain individuals already and have them produce the first protection gear straight off the drawing boards, the gas mask. More about that is in the file I handed you. I didn't just come here to personally deliver a set of orders and plans that a regular enlist-ed man could have done. I think I might want to take that drink after all," Commander Jorgensen says as his face became serious. "It's about the French unit that Corporal Lothar encountered."

Reinhard removed the bottle and glasses from the mini bar and set them up, then starts poured. He hand-ed the commander the small shot and the two cheered as they both drank.

"When I read the report and the captured letter, I wasn't surprised when I read the name Molitor on it or about the existence of a French Elite unit. I should have made a bet that it would happen only because a certain major said so," Jorgensen started. scratching his chin as he pretended to ponder.

"It's debatable if they are 'elite' and I knew better than to bet against you since you seem be on target when certain events take place," Reinhard retorted.

"I wasn't born with the ability to see the future, it's just plain foresight and also knowledge of the past, so that way I don't repeat the same mistakes of oth-ers, Major."

"Anyway, I think it's time that you elaborate about this Molitor character." Reinhard poured another shot.

"Well, it is the same as it was for Vorshevsky as it is for Gaultier Jean Molitor. He comes from a line of offi-cers who serve in the military dating all the way back to the waning days of the Kingdom of France before the French revolution. He is cautious as a cat but cunning when he knows his plan is going to work. Like Vladimir,

247

Molitor and I got along great during our time in China since he and another officer saved me and the rest of my unit during the failed Seymore Expedition. We tended to get into debates, but they were calm. Even in a game of chess, we ended in a draw. He and I share the common thoughts and care for our own troops," Jorgensen explained, downing his shot.

"Another friend, yet another enemy, Sir."

"Too right, but Ltc. Molitor is not to be underestimated. He may be cautious, but he is a tactical genius when it comes to being unconventional but, so are we. Though the actions of last month's attacks were a bit odd, we must anticipate his next move; the same for Vorshevsky."

"If he is that much of threat then why did they put a rooster as their symbol for his division?"

"It wasn't just a rooster, it's the Gallic Rooster! And if he is using the national animal of France as his symbol then he means business as those creatures are quite fearsome when upset. You know old logic, if two male roosters are together they will fight to the death," Jorgensen cried, fist to the table before setting the glass down.

"I'll keep that in mind when I deploy troops on the southern and northern parts of the Western Front. I find it ridiculous that we just found another organization from the French and now I await what the British might have in store for us at Ypres. I'm already receiving odd reports and photos from the Blue Tails recon missions."

"Then I trust you know what to do. As for me, I must return to Valhalla base. I thought I would do something different by visiting the new base. It still baffles me that you named it Ragnarök," Jorgensen said with a grin as he got up.

"Because Sir, it will be Ragnarök for the Triple Entente!" Major Reinhard said proudly, giving a farewell salute.

"Indeed, Major." Jorgensen saluted in return.

CHAPTER 18

"ADVANCE, WE DARE!"

April 22, 1915, a train station somewhere in Belgium

"A lot has changed in the past month. I tried my best to write it down in my journal if I have the time. For starters, Lothar figured out what happened during my time in Przemyśl Fortress, just by looking at my tatter uniform. If I recall his exact words were "Thats a familiar sight I've seen before, let me guess you saw her, didn't you?" before he started laughing and made fun of me. I guess its retribution for teasing him about Hannah, oh well. Though his time in Champagne was far more interesting, he ended up badly wounded. At one time I grew tired of us getting hurt during our assignments, so I enrolled with the KWS Trench Surgeon Korp for combat medic training at E.I.T.C. These men are battle harden medics who will do anything to keep their patients safe even destroying the enemy if they have to. It took two weeks for me to complete the class, relearning the human body again, but at least I have the knowledge of how treat wounds effectively, more than just applying bandages especially for self-healing. As a graduation present, they gave me medic bag that has a red cross at the top and at the bottom and has printed "Trench Surgeon" in cursive," Maxis continued in his journal.

"Hey Maxis, come on. The train is ready for boarding," Lothar shouted as he went inside.

Maxis stopped writing and rushed toward the train. The passenger car was filled with other soldiers. There Maxis spotted Lothar waving him down from his seat. He walked over and sat down across from Lothar.

"Any longer, someone would have taken your spot," said Lothar.

"Heh, you don't say."

Maxis continues to write in his journal as the train whistle blows and begins moving.

"It's funny how we stand out completely from the crowd, they wear the new M1915 feldgrau while we still wear the same old uniform but completely different. We still have the red piping in our uniform along with our Battalions patch on our sleeves. If anyone asks about our uniform, we respond with either civilian or labor Corp to conceal our battalion's existence. Right now, we're being sent back into the Western Front, for Operation: Grüner Tag (Green day) at Ypres. We don't know the details, but Commander Jorgensen said Major Reinhard would explain the mission when we get there." Maxis finished writing and put his journal into his rucksack.

"What do you think we'll be doing in Ypres?" Lothar wondered.

"Beats me, but from the sound of the operation name something big is about to happen, Lothar."

"You think we might initiate an offensive in that area?"

"Most likely. My guess is that it would probably be called the Second Battle of Ypres though I'm not certain on the title if this is a success or not," Maxis commented with uncertainty.

"Well, whatever the case is with the two us back together, we can do anything," Lothar voiced with confidence.

They left at eleven in the morning for Belgium. The ride was nonstop until they would arrived by two in the afternoon and disembarked. Their transport was already waiting for them at the station. Other soldiers were in the back of the truck waiting for the last passengers. Maxis and Lothar climbed into the back of the Daimler Marenfelde truck and sat themselves down. Inside soldiers were wearing unit patches on their sleeves though they were wearing different types of hats, piping on their uniforms and the patches.

"Well, it seems our last passengers have just arrived. Driver, we're all aboard. Get us moving," said the soldier at far end.

The truck came to life and off they went on the way to Ragnarök Base. There was complete silence for a moment inside the truck until one of the soldiers spoke.

"I believe names and introductions are in order since the two of you bear our Battalion's patch, I'll start first. I'm Private First-Class Fischer. Pleased meet you."

"Corporal Weber, at your service."

"Pvt. Kraus, greetings."

"Private Graf at your service, and this muscle head is Konig." Graf gently slugs his friend's shoulder.

"Pvt. Brandt and the two next to me are Pvt. Müller and Pvt. Kruger. Don't mind them. They're the strong silent and stern type," Brandt said while Müller and Kruger looked at him

"That leaves you two last. So, what are your names?" Fischer asked.

"I'm Corporal Lothar or also known as the Mighty Lothar!" Lothar said with pride, while Maxis put his hand to his own face.

"Never heard of you! Kidding, I'm joking. I heard about your recent exploits. It's an honor to meet you, tough guy," said Fischer.

"I'm Sgt. Maxis. Pleased to meet you all."

Everyone was silent for a moment as a look of surprise crossed their faces.

"Oh great. We have damned glory hound," Brandt said with discontent.

"Shut it, Brandt! So, wait...you're THE Sgt. Maxis?...The hero of Liege, Conqueror of Brussels, the Black Wolf of..."

"Finish that last part and I will dislocate your shoulder, Private," Maxis barked with anger in his tone. Kraus immediately shut up, covering his mouth as to not utter another word, leaving everyone shock.

"Well, it seems the Sergeant here is a bit touchy with that last one, eh boys," said Pvt. Graf.

"Maxis here resents all forms of nicknames or titles that are applied to him. So do be careful," Lothar assured everyone with a half-smile.

"Not every nickname. It's just that one I don't like, brings back bad memories," explained Maxis.

"Alright boys, you heard the Sergeant, mention the nickname again and he'll turn you into bratwurst or liverwurst and serve it to our Kaiser for dinner. Verstanden (understand)?" said Cpl. Weber as he checked pickelhaube that had the KWS logo.

"JA, Korporal WEBER!" Everyone but Lothar or Maxis responded before they started laughing.

"So, are we all here on the same mission or separate?" asked Pfc. Fischer.

"Whatever do you mean? My job is with the labor Corp, I so enjoy being near frontlines," Kraus said in a sarcastic manner.

"Screw all you. I'm with the civilian Corp. I enjoy pushing paperwork and get first dibs on the wine," Lothar said jokingly.

"Well, that nots fair you arsch (ass)," Maxis responded with a grin.

The childish banter continued until they arrived at their destination. The truck screeched to a halt after passing the security checkpoint, and then the driver announced.

"Alright men, we have arrived at Ragnarök Base. Take care and good luck. Now get off my truck!" he said with a smile.

"So very caring...that it rhymes," Fischer said.

Everyone departed from the truck and started walking. The base had a similar set up like Valhalla base but was smaller with more tents. The only difference was that it was bustling with activity with soldiers coming and going. The layout had a few wooden buildings with a tent city behind it. They started walking in the same direction toward the command tent, not saying a word to each other as if each one had a different role regarding going to the command tent. Maxis and Lothar were the first to enter the command tent to see Major Reinhard, along with other officers, looking at the war map on the table. There was the smell of burning cigarettes and fresh ink. Maxis and Lothar stood to attention and saluted, not realizing the group behind them did so also.

"Sir, reporting for duty!" they all said in unison.

The major saluted back with a small grin. Everyone began looking at each other with confusion.

"I see the sergeant managed get you all organized, good. Follow me to the briefing tent. There I will explain what your mission is," said Major Reinhard as he walked past them and out of the tent. The rest followed, bantering as they walked.

"The sergeant got us all organized? Come on now," said Müller, breaking his silence for the first time.

"He could be using his charm as the Black Wolf, probably had a technique to get us to do it," whispered Fischer as he joked.

"That's enough! All you keep it to yourself if the topic is not related to the mission at hand," Lothar said in a serious tone. Everyone immediately shut up, then Brandt whispered to Cpl. Weber.

"Weber, what's the deal? I thought you had seniority next to the sergeant," he whispered, annoyed.

"Not this time, in case you weren't paying attention to how Corporal Lothar walks, talks, and the look on his face. He is the definition of the right-hand man to the sergeant. He certainly has seen more action than me. That scar on his face tells a story, in other words he has grit. Besides he probably became Corporal before me," Weber whispered back. Brandt said nothing as he shook his head in disappointment.

"Here we are. Everyone get inside and take a seat. The mission briefing will begin shortly. Watch you step, it is a little dark in there," directed Major Reinhard, as he stood behind the podium and shuffled some paperwork.

Everyone took a seat and got comfortable, ready to hear what the mission will be. There was small chatter before the major said, "Ears Soldaten(Soldiers)," and the voices died down. A soldier next to the lantern slide projector prepared the thing for the briefing. He turned it on and the first thing on the screen was the title "Oben Geheimnis, Betrieb Grüner Tag" (Top Secret, Operation Green Day)."

"Männer (Men), we are about to take part in an audacious attack. The Imperial Army has prepared for an assault on Ypres. As the name suggests this will be the very first in which we will use chemical weapons, most notably chlorine gas on a large scale. You'll be going in before the army. Next slide, bitte(please)."

The slide changes to an image of battle positions, a picture of the gas canister, and noted where to assault on the enemy trench.

"Here you take position at the frontline trench here at the 'Prince's trench'. Our intelligence reports that French Colonial troops are currently holding the area here. Mostly likely territorial troops and French Algerians. Next slide."

The next image was bit odd, but Reinhard would explain.

"Of course, we won't let you just go into the gas without some form of protection. This image shows the experimental M1915 gas mask. This will help filter out the gas, helping you breathe better. Your equipment will be provided along with your kit, depending on your class and designation. You will move after the gas has been released."

"So, we wear these funny looking masks to scare the enemy, Sir?" Fischer asked jokingly.

"If the enemy is intimidated by your gas mask, then yes, it's necessary but would I recommend it, no. Only use it when the gas is present. Next slide."

The next slide showed aerial photos and areas marked out in red.

"After you breach the frontlines, you are to make your way to Kitchener woods. Air recon reported that there is a contingency of British troops, though we do not what they are doing there, but we can safely assume that they are acting as reserve unit for French Colonials. Wiping out this reserve group would be one less thing to worry about if they launched a counterattack. Next slide."

The last image shows the entire Ypres salient with more arrows, question marks, and enemy and friendly positions.

"If the enemy has proven to be difficult or their numbers larger, there is nothing wrong with a tactical withdrawal to rethink a new strategy. But if the situation is far worse, then a full retreat will be in order. Now, on to the squad. Your squad's name for duration of the operation is Grün squad. Sgt. Maxis will be squad leader, Cpl. Lothar will be second in command, and thirdly, Cpl. Weber. This concludes the briefing. Get your equipment, get sorted out, and report to your designated spot by 5 pm. Remember men, you are the very spear head of this assault. Any questions? Nein? Then get to it, and Sergeant, if your men are acting like fools, you know what to do," Reinhard faces Maxis and gives a nod.

"Yes Sir," Maxis salutes the Major.

"*It has been a while since I worked with a full squad, not since 1914. I hope these guys won't turn their backs on me should something go wrong,*" Maxis thought.

"I can't believe we are being led by a war hero. How exciting!" Kraus said quietly to Konig.

"I can see that but try to focus on the mission. We need you focused Kleiner Kerl (little guy) as much as its thrilling. Its best to show class even among the brave and famous," Konig said in a hardy tone.

"Why are we being led by somebody we don't even know? I find it ridiculous. Let alone that man's reputation," said Brandt being snarky.

"Lighten up Brandt. Consider this a new experience to get to know someone new or known. You are always questioning everything before you even think," said Fischer.

"Yeah, well I have my reasons and doubts. I don't trust him."

They made their way to the quartermaster's tent. There they saw a young soldier with glasses checking things off his clip board. He noticed a group all lined up waiting for him to finish.

"Oh dear. How long have you been standing there?" the soldier reacts, almost dropping his clip board

"About thirty hours," Fischer jokingly said.

"Usually, I expected to see Heinrich behind the table waiting to give us our gear," Maxis whispers to Lothar.

"Yeah, that's normally the case."

The young quartermaster noticed the conversation and intervened.

"Oh, you're talking about my mentor, but wait, I forgot to introduce myself. I'm Quartermaster Winter, Heinrich's protégé," informed Winter.

"His proto-what?" Lothar responds.

"Protégé. He told me he was inspired by a duo last month at Champagne and that he decided to take on an apprentice to follow in his footsteps. So, I'm here learning the ropes from handling the equipment to modifying and crafting special gear for the Battalions needs," Winter added in a shrilled voice.

"Inspired by a duo...is he referring to me and Richter during our time in Champagne?" Lothar wondered in his thoughts.

"That is good to know. I'm sure you will turn out great, just don't copy his eccentric personality," said Lothar.

"Whatever do you mean, good Sir?" Winter replied in a happy sarcastic tone.

"Oh Gott, it spread."

"Hate to break the chit chat but we are on the clock here...So you have our gear ready, Winter?" Maxis asked firmly.

"Of course, Sergeant. I already labeled all your packs along with your gear and weapons. Just hold for a moment bitte (please)," said Winter as he walked around the corner disappearing from sight. Squeaky wheels can be heard coming around the corner. Winter appears with a cart filled with military grade equipment nicely organized in a row. Each pack had a name tag attached to it with a name and class.

"Alright then everybody, time to get organized in an orderly fashion and wait till I call out your name, danke (thanks)," instructed Winter.

The whole squad quickly arranged into two rows with the NCOs standing to the side of the formation.

"Sgt. Maxis, Class: Weapons Specialist. Your equipment: Luger 1906 with telescopic sights, Bergman No.1 pistol, kugel grenades, armor piercing bullets and dynamite. Since you're the squad leader here are the necessities for the like; small map, compass, wristwatch, and a dark blue scarf."

"Why the blue scarf?" Maxis quizzed.

"Beats me, I just followed the equipment list I was given for Grün (Green) squad."

"Hmm, alright then." Maxis grabbed his equipment. The dark blue scarf felt very soft and flexible like silk and he wrapped it around his neck to the point of being able to conceal his lower face.

"Next is Cpl. Lothar, Class: Machine gun Specialist. Your gear: a modified Madsen machine with a wooden foregrip, bipod, and painted reflex sights, Mauser 1912/14 .45ACP, smoke grenades, flare gun, and experimental incendiary bullets."

Lothar was in total happiness but only showed a smile that was witnessed by Maxis.

"Cpl. Weber and Pvt. Müller, Class: Advance Riflemen. Your equipment is as follows: a Mauser C98 rifle(-self-loading), Bergman 1908 pistols, and four kugel grenades each. Also, you are the ammo bearers for the machine gunners, that means you carry the ammo and the extra weight."

"Wait a minute you expect us to use the rifle that blew Paul Mauser's eye out?! Are you nuts?" Weber spoke out.

"Relax Corporal, these rifles have been properly fixed by R&D so that doesn't happen, I even double checked it myself," Winter reassured back calmly. He continued. "Kraus and Fischer, Class: Trench Grenadiers. Your stuff is Gewehr 98s, one set of incendiary grenades, one set of experimental gas grenades, stick grenades, and five karabingranate M1914 rod grenades each, and blank ammunition."

"Konig and Brandt, Class: Machine gun specialists. Madsen LMGs, Walther model 6 pistols, and one cage for the homing pigeons with a built-in gas filter. Which one of you will carry it?"

"Don't look at me, I'm not carrying those rats with wings," said Brandt with an attitude.

"I'll do it then. Unlike you, I like the little birdies," said Konig in soft and sweet tone.

"Alright, just be careful with them. They are your only source of communication to Ragnarök Base."

"Pvt. Kruger, Class: Sniper. Gewehr 98 with a scope, Sauer & Sohn M1913 pistol, a set of traps in the rucksack, tools kit, and stick grenades."

"A hunter never leaves without his rifle," stated Kruger as he grabbed his kit.

"Finally, we have Graf, Class: Trench Trooper. An experimental Becker M1899 revolver shotgun, two Schwarzlose 1898 pistol, impact grenades, slug rounds, trench mace, and Mauser M1913 Ladera rifle," Quartermaster Winter finished.

"Very nice," remarked Graf as he took his gear.

"Now for the real tools: your gas masks and the bags that come with them. Put these on your belt now so you don't forget. Each bag has spare filter." Winter set the small canvas bags on the table. Everyone grabbed one and attached it to their belts.

"Alright boys, lock and load. We're moving out," ordered Maxis, walking out of the tent.

The squad loaded and readied their weapons and headed outside, following Maxis out of the tent. He looked at the map before tucking it in the wristwatch.

"Maxis, where does our next objective lie?" Lothar asked.

"Judging by the map, we just head down this road about two miles and we'll run into the reserves before entering the trenches. From there we will take positions at the jump off trench and wait until five o'clock."

"Then we wait ten minutes, right?"

"That's right, Lothar."

"Let's get to it then. I'm right behind you or we're all behind you, heh."

Maxis takes point, Lothar and the rest follows. They march in single file line on their way to the front lines. It was quite a journey to the frontlines until Kraus started humming a tune.

"What are you humming, Kraus?" Fischer wanted to know.

"Oh, I was humming about the Schutzenmarsch, from my time with them."

"Do you sometimes miss being with them, the Schutzen?"

"I used to, but not any more. This new position is better, pay is great, and we're being led by the Bla...uh, I mean someone famous," Kraus said with excitement.

"Heh, that's good to hear."

Maxis was able see the small encampment from afar as they neared their destination. He checked the time; it was four o'clock in the afternoon.

"Soldaten(Soldiers), eyes front!" Maxis orders with an affirmative tone. Everyone looks forward to listen to what he has to say.

"We are arriving at the front lines and we have an hour before our operation begins. Let me set a few conditions before we start. I want things done by the numbers, people, so that means no screw ups. Furthermore, we are following standard protocol. If I catch you doing something you're not supposed to, like poor treatment of civilians or POWs, expect me to be upon you like a devil, and if you commit something worse than that... expect corporal punishment of the highest degree. Do I make myself clear?"

"Ja, Feldwebel (Yes, Sergeant)!" everyone responded, except Brandt who muttered, "That's rich coming from a merciless killer."

They walked past the encampment with onlookers noticing the heavily armed and equipped German squad moving about. The squad entered the rear trench before slowly making their way to the fire trench. Everyone sits or stands in the cross-section spread three feet from each other.

Maxis headed to the observation trench, pulled out his binoculars from his bread bag and slowly crossed over the parapet to get a look at the opposition.

"Looks like several machine gun positions, no sign of snipers. Can see the Algerians currently in the trenches since I can spot their red hats among with a few sentries. Hopefully, the gas will clear them out or force them out, otherwise this will be an "interesting fight" even with the gas around us. Now then what else can I..." Maxis processed in his thoughts.

"Hey, Sarge."

Maxis quickly reacted by pulling out his pistol aimed at Pfc. Fischer.

"Woah, woah, friendly, friendly!" said Fischer.

"Verdammt (Damn it) Fischer, don't surprise me like that. Almost took a bullet."

"Entschuldigung, Feldwebel (Pardon me, Sergeant). I didn't think you were that jumpy."

"No, it's ok, forget that just happened. What do you need, Private?" Maxis asked as he looked through the binoculars.

"Just came here to see what's going on over here."

"I'm observing the enemy right now."

"Intriguing. What are we up against, Sarge?" Fischer carefully peered over the parapet.

"A few machine guns and a lot of colonial troops, but no sign of the territorial troops yet."

"Hopefully, this new weapon will clear them out, eh Sarge," Fischer commented as he leaned against the wall of the trench.

"What are you really here for, Private?" Maxis asked suspiciously.

"I came to see what our new sergeant was doing. Wanted to get to know the war hero himself, the man who put down the Tsar's giant tricycle, hero of Belgium, now back to finish the job," He intoned dramatically.

"I'm not a war hero, just a soldier doing his part for our empire, our people, our Kaiser, and our country."

"Well, that is what I think of you who stands in front me. As for Kraus, that's a different story since he is an utter fan of yours. Since the day I met him."

"You seem to be well acquainted with everyone before me and Lothar arrived."

"The thing is, I know most of them from previous assignments across the Western and Eastern Fronts."

"Would you be generous enough to share the short versions of their stories, Fischer?" Maxis asked, still viewing the French trench line.

"I would normally suggest getting to know them yourself, but I understand that's difficult right now. I'll gladly start with myself first. I was a Landser, originally part of a unit fighting in Mulhouse, Le Cateau, and so on during the start of war back in 1914. I got recruited for my acts of bravery and my better understanding of using rifle grenades and bombs. Then I was properly trained to the full extent as K.W.S. Trench Grenadier. I couldn't be any happier now that I can effectively inflict more damage on the enemy." Fischer looked at his covered pickelhaube, then at the K.W.S. emblem with its small symbol of a bomb with a burning fuse beneath.

"At least you're happy with your specialization; most important thing is keeping a soldier happy," said Maxis as he turned to Fischer.

"True that," agreed Fischer, sitting down with his rifle on his side.

"Now, about Kraus..." Maxis prompted.

"Oh, you want to get that over with, I see. Alright. Kraus is interesting to say the least. He was part of the Schützen, and basically he is trained to be sentry, holding down sectors if an attacked failed or being attacked. He was close to them like family before he got this job. That's why he wears their special cap with a brass cross on the front. He heard about your exploits during the

Schlieffen plan as the rumor started circulating before you vanished. Like me, he's good with grenades and recruited the same way I was. It's only now he finally got to meet his idol. He won't shut up about it even when you barked at him when he mentioned your special nickname. Also, he's Jewish, though he keeps it to himself, but I spotted the Star of David on him one time. The Ruskies are not big fans and the rest of the world has a sour eye for them as well," Fischer finished as he checked his rod grenade.

"I didn't mean to lash out at him. That nickname brings back memories of the worst part of the Schlieffen plan. The only people I allow to call me as such is Lothar since he likes to banter with it at the biergarten."

"I'm sure Kraus wasn't offended, probably got inspired in a weird way. Now as for the others. Konig is the friendly giant, or he was until Cpl. Lothar showed up beating him by height. He was a Landser like me and knew his machine guns very well. At one point he placed an MG08 on perfect ambush position providing cover for troops during the withdrawal to Aisne, and inflicted heavy casualties on the French who were pursuing. Müller, now he is a bit unique. Specializes in quiet sneak attacks, night raids, and one hell of a fighter. Wears his Feldmutze like the Corporal does but like a beret since he came from a unit in Württemberg."

"Sounds like what Lothar went through in Tannenberg but a different scenario," remarked Maxis.

"Now Cpl. Weber isn't the best NCO there is though he was a Pioniere (pioneer; combat engineer). Good rifleman, good man, great scrapper, but not a good leader; more like a dog waiting to be told what to do than thinking for himself, although he does follow orders to the letter. Just not the ones that he thinks are bad like being order commit war a crime. The only time I saw him do something worth talking about was when he punched Brandt in face for running his mouth," Fischer smiled as he thought back to that day.

"What's with Brandt anyway? Never met someone like him that has a chip on his shoulder."

"He's always been like that. I've gotten used to him but even at times I get sick of him. His story is not anything to be interested in. He is a machine gunner but has not done anything spectacular since he joined the Battalion. Some of us think he might have got in through 'connections,' probably to avoid the frontlines and hoping to get a desk job."

"Apparently that failed," said Maxis, still watching no man's land.

"Well, it's just speculation really. The bad attitude got him in trouble several times and yet he's not been evicted from the Battalion. Just be wary of him since he likes to question just about everything."

"Asking questions that shouldn't be asked will get him trouble regardless," said Maxis.

"He read a questionable book in his spare time," said Fischer, looking at his rifle.

"Like what?"

"He was reading the Communist Manifesto."

"The book by Marx?" Maxis reacts.

"Yeah. That may be why he started asking some troubling questions that got him in trouble. From loyalty to why we fight."

"Great, now I have to deal with a socialist," Maxis groaned.

"Anyway, the last two are far more positive than Brandt will ever be. Graf is the definition of a mad dog. He served under Cpt. Willy Rohr for a brief time which gave him recognition for his aggressive tactics thus he wears a visored-crusher cap. Last is Kruger, our sniper. He was an Alpine Jäger, so he knows his way around mountains; can set traps and is crack shot thus he always wears the alpine shako cap with no cover like you. That's about everyone on the roster. You don't have to explain yourself or Cpl. Lothar since all of us know your stories," Fischer finished.

"That's good because it's time to meet the others at the fire trench. Come along, Private First Class."

"Right behind you, Sarge."

Maxis put the binoculars away and walked toward the fire trench with Pfc. Fischer following right behind him. The squad was standing close to the parapet waiting for Maxis. The two take position alongside them. Soldiers were moving about hastily getting ready for what was to come. Some carried large canisters up the small ladder and then placed them on the in row in front of the trench. They were manned by soldiers wearing make-shift gas protection upon their faces. The wind slowly started to pick up and the men started shouting to the others to clear out and return to the trenches.

"Anyone who doesn't have any protection will either find some or stay clear of the gas. The weapon will be released shortly!" warned one the soldiers.

"Releasing the gas. Gas, gas, gas in Deckung (take cover)!" cried the gas operator.

"Alright men, equip the prototype masks now!" Maxis ordered the squad.

"You heard him, men! Equip the masks, now!" shouted Lothar as he pulled out the gas mask.

Everyone reached down and opened his canvas bag containing their gas masked. They donned the masks making themselves a sight to behold. The moment of action is upon them, and they are ready but tense. Even Kraus seemed a bit nervous as he slowly gripped his Star of David that was under his shirt close to his chest.

The gas operator turned the valves, and a green mist sprayed from the nozzles. The small mist grew larger and larger as it covered the field in chlorine gas.

"Hey, you think these so-called gas masks will actually protect us?" Kraus asked.

"Don't know, but hopefully they buy us some time to tread through the gas," said Graf as he readied his shotgun.

"Maxis, you look terrifying with that thing on," Lothar said jokingly, his words muffled.

"Yeah, well, let's hope this will scare the enemy into a full-scale retreat and end this war quickly shall we," Maxis replied with confidence.

"That's the spirit, Sergeant." Major Reinhard said, wearing his experimental M1915 gas mask along with an armed escort wearing theirs.

"Stay as you were men, for today I'm here to see you off as you will enter the storm. Some words of inspiration are in order," Major Reinhard prepared to speak.

"The pride of Germany follows you into the battle. You fight with your comrades by your side!"

Everyone screamed out "HURRA!" despite sounding muffled in their gas masks.

"You are Germany's elite! You are the K.W.S.!"

"HURRA!"

"Into battle, soldiers, into battle!" Major Reinhard finishes his speech.

"HURRAA!"

"Over the top, men! Over the top, Angriff (attack)!" shouted Maxis as he climbed over the parapet.

"Los, Los, Attacke (Move, move, attack)!" shouted Lothar.

CHAPTER 19

INFILTRATION ASSAULT

The entire squad climbed out and over the top of the trench following Maxis' lead. The artillery began firing a short barrage then cut off after the third blasts. They moved across no-man's land enveloped in the gas mist hovering on the ground. The team mimicked Sgt. Maxis' movements and pace. Kruger followed behind the squad to provide sniper support if necessary. Lothar and Graf moved to Maxis' side while Kraus and Fischer covered the flanks. Konig moved carefully since he was transporting the homing pigeons, avoiding large pockets of gas and Brandt was moved slowly and with much caution.

They each heard the clattering of their equipment, the breathing noise from their gas mask, and the greenish cloud that now surrounded them. The prototypes worked perfectly as intended as neither of them coughed or suffered the effects of the gas.

A bullet flew by Maxis' head and he immediately went prone and so did everyone else.

"Someone fired a shot, Kruger. Can you see him?" Maxis called out.

Kruger slowly got up and looks through the scope. He saw the enemy trench and spotted a colonial soldier coughing while still holding his rifle. The Algerian fired another shot, this time at Kruger, but misses. Kruger focused his shot and slowly squeezes the trigger...the rifle fires killing the Algerian soldier in one shot to the chest.

"We're clear for now," said Kruger in deep gruff voice.

"Alright, let's keep moving. Schnell!"

Maxis and the squad got up. They kept moving bit by bit a little further, until they had a visual of the French colonial's trench.

Maxis raised his hand in a fist in a way of saying "Hold position," and the squad halted their advance and crouched down. Then he pulled out his bayonet fixing it to the end of his rifle. Everyone who had a rifle fixed bayonets except Kruger; then they waited.

Without a second to waste Maxis began to sprinting toward the trench and the whole squad followed. When they were five feet in front of the trench everyone gave their war cry and jumped into the trench but that scream died out quickly.

They saw the trench completely deserted of soldiers with nothing but the dead and the suffering left behind. They died manning their battle position, every last one of them, still gripping their rifle and some were still wandering about, violently coughing and blinded by the gas. This was a horrid scene of soldiers slowly dying.

"Move slowly but keep your guard up; though they may not have much fight left in them," said Maxis as he moved through the cross-section.

"This...this is an unpleasant sight," said Lothar as he walked over the bodies carefully.

The ghastly scene was terrible indeed. The effectiveness of their weapons proved to be devastating to the unaware and unprotected of its deadly mist. Soon the soldiers that wandered about began to fall.

"Ugh, I think I'm going to hurl," said Graf.

"Just keep moving, Graf. Don't want you throw up in your gas mask," said Fischer.

Kraus offered a little prayer in Hebrew after stepping on a soldier by accident.

They made their way through the trench line quickly and carefully, past the first three lines before reaching the reserve and then out in the open where the gasses' presence was minimal. They kept moving toward Kitchener wood.

"Squad, hold fast. We should be in the clear from the gas, but just in case," said Maxis as he slowly takes off the gas mask and breathes deeply.

The whole squad was a bit nervous seeing their squad leader take the first breath without a mask, but were relieved to see him not suffocating.

"Alright, the air is clean. Masks off. Take a breather for now while I get our bearings, straight," said Maxis as he pulled out his map and compass.

He analyzed the map to see how far away their objective was located. Lothar went around checking on everyone to see if they were alright despite what they just witnessed. Konig checked on the pigeons.

"Hey how are the birds doing, Konig?" Lothar asked.

"*Sigh*. I did what I could keep them away from the gas. I was given ten but five are dead, two are wobbling, but three still look healthy enough to fly," Konig reported as he took out the dead pigeons.

"You think they can still fly?"

"Oh yeah definitely. These are homing pigeons; nothing will stop them from going back home. If we need a message sent fast, these guys will do the job, I hope."

"Good, I'll go to check with the Sergeant on what's our next move."

Konig nodded as Lothar walked away.

"Maxis" called Lothar.

"Lothar," Maxis responded still looking at the map.

"Goods news first. The squad is in good shape despite the horrid scenery. Bad news, I probably won't be able to sleep after what I just saw. So, what's our next move, Max?"

"Well, we are deep in enemy territory, that much is obvious; however, trying to make heads or tails where to go is difficult. On the map we should be between Langemark and Gravenstafel, but our objective is in Kitchener wood. Should we approach from the left, right, or go deep into the center? What would you suggest?"

"It wouldn't really matter; the element of surprise basically is be gone if those French colonials have already informed them of the attack while running away," Lothar spoke firmly.

275

"Yeah, you're right. Might as well face them head on at the center where there's more cover. I think the best move is to send Kruger to scout ahead so he can give us the numbers on what we're dealing with.'

"Knowing the enemy's strength should give us the edge. Let's hope he's up for the task."

"Then it's decided. Pvt. Kruger front and center!" Maxis ordered. Kruger double times it to Maxis, standing at attention as he arrived.

"Yes Sarge, you have a task for me?"

"Indeed, I do. I'm sending you to this area for recon. I need to know the enemy's strength but do so quietly and don't get caught. We'll be moving to this area soon. Can you do that?"

"Yes, Sergeant. I needed to stretch my legs anyway. I'll be back before you know it," Kruger finished and sprinted off, disappearing as he entered the brush.

"Wow, that was fast. Lothar, get the squad ready to move in five minutes we've got a long march ahead of us."

"You got it, Maxis," said Lothar as he walked away.

"Something is telling me this won't be an easy fight. Then again nothing is exactly easy ever since joining the Battalion, but it beats being stuck in a trench, that's for certain. Still, I wonder how these guys will act when the fighting start. They should be already battle hardened from what Fischer told me. Well, all except Brandt." Maxis thought to himself.

Five minutes passed and the Grün squad was on the move. Walking in a small wedge formation with Lothar at the front, there were two riflemen on his left and two grenadiers on right. The widest wedge from left to right are the LMGs and behind that wedge was Maxis. There was no sign of Kruger yet, so the squad remained on high alert expecting to meet the British at any moment. Two hours passed and still no sign of Kruger. This worried Maxis immensely.

"Verdammt, where's is he? Kruger should have been back by now...did I compromise ourselves by sending him out? Did I send him to his immediate death, surely that would be the case, however, I do not like sending people to their doom and..." Maxis' thoughts were interrupted at the sight of Brandt breaking formation by moving on ahead of the squad.

"Brandt! Where are you going? Get back in formation!" Maxis ordered gruffly. Brandt ignored Maxis.

"Private, I gave you an order!" he said again.

"What are you going do, glory hound? I'm going to go find the enemy myself. All you are doing is slowing me down," Brandt scoffed as he moved past Lothar.

"He gave you an order and you will FOLLOW IT!" Lothar yelled as he grabbed Brandt by the collar and threw him back into the formation. Brandt hit the ground hard dropping his weapon. He lifted his head, now covered in dirt and dust then spoke.

"Why you long horse son of...*oof*," he was cut off quickly as Lothar placed his boot on top of his head.

"First, if you think you can take me on then you are sorely mistaken. Second, you will respect your NCO and follow his orders. Third, if you break formation again or back talk the Sergeant, I will throw you at a tree next time! Got it?"

"Muffling noise!" Lothar crouched down and grabbed Brandt by the hair. "I said...DO I MAKE MYSELF CLEAR?!"

"Yes, for the love of God, yes!" Brandt cried out, holding the back of his head.

"Good. Now get back in formation," Lothar ordered Brandt as he got up.

Brandt walked back in formation all while muttering to himself of the humiliation he endured.

"I told him Lothar had grit. I told him," Weber muttered as he shook his head.

They kept marching for a bit until they reached the forest. It was quiet except for the birds chirping. Maxis sensed someone's gaze and quickly turned, rifle at the ready.

"Impressive reflexes, Sergeant, very impressive," observed Kruger as he walked out in the open from behind a tree.

"Verdammt (Damn it) ...*sigh*. How long were you just standing there?"

"Not long, Sgt. Maxis, not long. I spotted you on the way back so decided to play a little trick though I quickly realized that could turn out to be a bad idea. Too late I guess."

"You don't say," Maxis smirked.

"Anyway, I'm here to report my findings, Sarge."

"Spit it out."

"North of our position is a British encampment though something was way off about it. It wasn't some ordinary reserve camp; more like an active military base, a small one at best with lots of troops, too. They also have these odd vehicles; looks like they're getting prepared for something big, I know the best way to get there."

"Great job, Kruger. Lead the way."

Kruger took point with Grün squad following behind. They moved through the forest hastily until they came to a line of bushes in front of them, where Kruger signaled everyone to get down. The men low-crawled toward the bushes. Slowly coming into view through the thick leaves was the British encampment with tents. Maxis pulled out his binoculars to take a look with Lothar by his side.

"Lots of activity going on. These guys are fully equipped with everything from mills bombs, rifles, I think a few self-loading rifles, machine guns, and I can see the vehicles you were talking about Kruger. Hey Lothar, are these the same tractors you dealt with in Champagne?" Maxis asked.

"Nein, these are completely different. I've never seen these models before," Lothar replied.

"Hey Sarge, take look at that big tent with flag," Kruger said as he pointed.

Maxis adjusted his sights to the large tent at the center of the encampment. The red flag had a unique design. At the center was a lion's head looking toward you with its mouth open. On top of its head dawns the royal crown of England; behind the head were a pair of weapons, and an SMLE Mark III rifle crossed with

British saber. At the bottom of the flag were three letters, R.O.B. in yellow.

"R.O.B.? What's that supposed to mean?" Maxis asked.

"I don't know, sarge. Whatever it is, it's not good. Looks like they are getting prepared to mobilize," Kruger responded.

"Scheisse (Shit), do you think it could be another organization, Maxis?" Lothar asked with concern.

"I don't know who these guys are. They could be another unit or a small detachment from the main army. Lothar, when you dealt with the mysterious Hasardeux Division, how would you rate their combat effectiveness?"

"From what I experienced, not that great. They used regular infantry mixed with specially trained soldiers with experimental weapons, as a form of mixed fire power. These Brits, however, can be the same for all we know."

"Well, there's one way to find out, we can't sit here speculating. Lothar, get the machine guns into position, grenadiers set up, and the assault team ready for action."

"The assault team that would be Müller, Weber, Graf, and me included right?" Lothar asked.

"Yep, get Graf and his Ladera rifle set up. Once the firing begins, they will try to use those tractors."

"What are you going to do then, Maxis?"

"I'll infiltrate their base and make my way to their command tent. While I do that, I'll be planting explosives connected to this detonator along the way."

"Hmm, alright. Let's see if it works this time, unless that Russian hündin (bitch) shows up to ruin it," Lothar smirked.

"Very funny," Maxis said sarcastically.

"Wait, what Russian hündin?" Kruger asked.

"Not important. Alright, let's get started." Maxis slowly crawled out of the bush.

He made his approach by keeping it low and avoiding being spotted and traced the wire at the same time. Maxis took cover behind some crates as two British soldiers walked by. Calmly, he held his breathe as they walked past chatting to each other.

"Oi, heard about Doyle and his wife?" said the soldier in a thick cockney accent.

"Yeah, she stopped writing to him. Hold on mate, I just noticed something."

"Scheisse (Shit), did they notice...oh no this is not good..." Maxis thought and stood fast. His heart started pumping hard and as he slowly readied his rifle, he heard the footsteps get close. Then closer and closer until they stopped.

"Holy shite mate, we got blood sausages in these crates."

"Oh, how revolting! You eat those things?"

"Ah, bugger off! Let's just go."

They walked away as Maxis breathed a sigh of relief. He continued his journey going by the tents near the armory, where he found the first suitable spot for the first bomb placement. He set it up, connected the wire, and moved on. The next location was a supply wagon and the last site was on one of the armored tractors that were lined up in a row. After planting all the explosives, the command tent was in sight and a pathway to it was clear. Maxis moved around the corner only to run into yet another Brit standing guard but with his back toward Maxis.

The Brit began talking to himself in a low tone.

"Bloody hell, how much longer? I've been standing guard for twelve hours straight! When the hell is that relief going to arrive, eh? God, I could use a stiff drink and some sleep."

"I can help you with that..."

"Wha-*hmphed!*"

Maxis quicky covered the Brit's mouth while putting him, in a headlock. The Brit struggled and thrashed about for a moment before becoming limp.

"Finally, he's out cold. I'm going to have to hide him before someone finds him,." Maxis thinks, trying to decide what to do with the unconscious Brit that lay before him.

He checked the tent next to him to see if it's vacant. It was so Maxis moved the body in and leaves it there. Then he quickly rushed over to the command tent and used his bayonet to make a hole on the side of it enters right through. The inside was clear of any enemy presence. The interior of the command tent was nothing short of a lavish lifestyle of a British officer.

"Geez, I thought Colonel Vorshevsky's tent was a bit much, but this is downright the scale of a noble. Then again, the Officers of the British Army always like to be treated like lords regardless of where they are."

Maxis shuffled through the tent searching for anything worth of value such as intel, battle plans, or anything. One part of the tent was built to be an officer's quarters, complete with a statue with a small compartment to house wine or other types of alcoholic beverages. The other was the war room filled to the brim with paperwork and maps along with a board with the map of Ypres. He goes through everything to find something of worth but found nothing until he checked the desk and started opening drawers. Here, he found a letter addressed to the commander that was partially opened. Maxis opened it but before he read it checked his surroundings to make sure that all was still clear.

"To Brigadier Wellington, Commander of His Majesties Regiment of Britannia,

Commander Wellington, if you are receiving this letter then the time has come to initiate Operation Goliath. Based on what our interceptors have informed us a German attack on the Ypres salient is imminent. You should have received a shipment of the new prototype, the Lincoln No.1 Machine (armed with a turret) and fifteen Killen-Strait armored tractors to assist in the defense and counterattack on Ypres. More reinforcements are already on the way from back home, about three hundred professional troops, trained to use the self-loaders as a fine addition to your Regiment. The weapon listings should be with this letter. If the defense of Ypres is successful, then commence the counterattack and drive Jerry as far away as you can. Base Camp Elizabeth will be your launching point. For King and Country, thus your regiments motto, "Advance, we dare." Do your country proud, Commander. Time to see if the Regiment of Britannia is up to a real challenge as a military organization of the crown.

Sincerely,

British High Command."

Maxis looked at the second letter along with drawings of the Lincoln machine.

"Weapon listings for the (150 troops currently at base) and the 300 additional arriving soon.

Five Griffiths-Woodgate rifles (self-loading) Models 1892 and 1893

Thirty Thorneycroft rifles (Bullpup bolt-action rifle)

SMLE MK.1, MK.2, and MK.3 rifles

Five Howell Automatic rifle (SMLE conversion)

Ten Rexer rifles"

"Well, well that should be enough. Though the worst part is that a new special organization has been discovered. I get a feeling this is going to be a war both on the battlefield and in the shadows," Maxis thought as he quickly put the letters in his bread bag.

Suddenly there was chattering outside of the tent. Maxis saw a large trunk and quickly moved in to get inside for cover, leaving his rifle leaning on the side of the trunk. Inside he moved carefully; there was nothing but darkness. Maxis left a small slit to see oncoming visitors from his post in the tent.

Soon, a British officer enters. He wore a bushy mustache, a khaki uniform with medals upon his chest and a red cape over his left arm bearing the symbol of the Regiment of Britannia. The two officers that follow behind him both wore brownish-green fatigues with officer's caps. Maxis listened in on the conversation.

"Is everything been organized, 2Lt. McManus?" asked Commander Wellington.

"Aye, Sir the unit is ready for action just say the word." Said 2Lt. McManus in a Scottish accent.

"Good."

"1Lt.Wilson, what's the status of the reinforcement?"

"Last time, I checked they should be arriving in an hour at port, Sir," said 1Lt. Wilson.

"Excellent, gentlemen. The time is almost upon us for the big show. Thanks to our code breakers we are properly ready to face Jerry with a wrath of steel that will drive them back to Germany. Once we hear the news from the French colonials that the attack has begun, that's our cue to rollout with armored tractors and the prototype Lincoln No.1 Machine. We will show the world what a fully mechanized unit can do. In the name of the British Empire and King George V, we will succeed," Wellington said proudly, holding his fist in the air.

"I guess they don't know the attack has already started. What pity for them..."said Maxis in his thoughts as he listened.

"Brilliant speech, Sir!" said 1Lt.Wilson.

"I concur best I heard yet," said 2Lt. McManus.

"You're too kind, Lieutenants. I forgot to mention, 2Lt. McManus, that a full complement of Scotland's finest are also arriving at the port to join the R.O.B. ranks."

"Thank you, Sir! That fills me with pride that my countrymen will be joining us soon. We Highlanders will get the job done, quick and clean!"

"I also saved something special on my desk and... Wait a minute, where is it? Where the bloody hell is it?!" barked Commander Wellington, searching around his desk.

"Kacke (crap)! is he talking about the letters I just took?" Maxis thought.

"What is the matter, Sir? Did something go missing?" asked 1Lt. Wilson.

"Oi, should we alert the base, Sir?" asked 2Lt. McManus.

Commander Wellington looked around the tent. Maxis slowly tried to control his breathing as the commander approached close to the trunk. He slowly pulled out his Bergman No.1 pistol. Then suddenly the commander's face changed from worried to shocked as he approached the statue and lifts the upper torso to reveal a bottle of Brandy.

"calmly exhales *Are you serious*?" Maxis thinks as he calmly exhales.

"Here it is lads. The best brandy England has to offer. I won't lie to you men; I'm half tempted to get into it. But then, what would we have for victory?" Commander Wellington asked as he lifted the bottle.

"Tea?" asked 1Lt.Wilson.

"Good old-fashioned Scotch, Commander?" 2Lt. McManus added.

Wellington placed the bottle back into the statue.

"Anyway, we should be off to go collect our troops and then stop by HQ. Come along, men, let's be on our way and...Hold a damned minute. What is that?"

"Now what?" Worried Maxis.

Commander Wellington hurriedly approached toward the trunk which sent Maxis into a slight panic as he readied the pistol and aimed directly at Wellington as he approached. The commander stopped and slowly squatted down in front of the trunk. Maxis held his breathe again, his heart racing. As he started to slowly squeeze the trigger as he senses the Commander's gaze.

"What do we have here...Is this the Luger M1906 rifle?!"

Maxis quietly exhaled, took his finger off the trigger and thought,

"I really hate this guy."

"Did someone leave this as gift? If it is, a fine present for this rifle was patented in our very own country. A fine weapon, very fine," said Wellington as he picked up Maxis' rifle.

"I've never seen anything like it, Sir," Said 1Lt. Wilson.

"I agree. This rifle uses the toggle mechanism from the Luger pistol! It is ingenious, Sir," agreed 2Lt. McManus.

"Alright men, enough time wasting. Let's go."

Commander Wellington and the lieutenants exited, prompting Maxis to spring out of the trunk. He stretched a bit then grabbed his rifle, ready to go through the hole he created. But first he walked over to the statue and opened it to find the brandy still there.

"This is for making me have miniature heart attacks Arschloch (asshole). So here's one from me," Maxis said to himself as he confiscated the brandy and put it in his rucksack. Then he placed a kugel grenade and attached a string to the pin. He closed the statue gently and headed to his exit.

"Here is a little present from yours truly. This might be crude or harsh but I might as well cut the head off the snake before it bites someone. Now to get back to Lothar and the others."

Maxis opened the tear in the tent and saw the area now bustling with activity. Small squads appeared from left to right. He chose his moments to move carefully as a Killen-Strait Tractor passes by.

"Steady...steady...now!"

Maxis sprinted out of the tent and made his way behind the wagon. He took cover as a small group of soldiers appeared around the corner and waited until they disappeared from sight. Then he bolted around the wagon and made it back to the crates. There was one last hurdle left before the bushes, and after waiting a minute he makes a run for it...until a British soldier walks out of an open tent, yawning. Without hesitation Maxis whacked the soldier in the head with the stock of his rifle and the soldier immediately dropped to the ground unconscious.

"No time to hide the body," Maxis tells himself , then jumped into the bush surprising Lothar and Kruger who gave an immediate "woah".

"Wow, such speed, Sergeant," said Kruger with surprise.

"Took your sweet time, didn't you, huh?" Lothar said sarcastically.

"Oh, shut it," Maxis snapped back.

"Something is telling me you're not happy. Give it to me short."

"New organization apparently, called themselves the Regiment of Britannia, planned counterattack, left a present for their commander," Maxis finished as he gets into position with the detonator.

"Gott, hilf uns (God, help us), our job just got even harder, didn't it?" asked Lothar, sounding a bit down.

"Not if we do something about it. Don't forget, we burned down the Imperskiy Tayna Brigada camp and destroyed their Tsar tank. You also stopped the Hasardeux Divisions attempt at a breakthrough. Now with us back working together, and with a whole squad, we will tear these dummköpfe (fools) apart, no sweat," reminded Maxis, as he prepared the detonator.

"That was inspiring Maxis, and it helped. Sometimes I wonder why you're not an officer yet, just curious," Lothar remarked, now cheered up.

"We can discuss that later. For now, we've got a camp to raze to the ground. Lothar, do the honors."

"Ka-boom!" Lothar said calmly as he pressed down on the detonator.

There was a large explosion sounding across the entire encampment, incinerating everything in its path and leaving nothing but a trail of destruction. The British, confused by this, were unprepared for what followed next.

"OFFENES FEUER (OPEN FIRE)!" Maxis screamed out the order.

The line of bushes in the tree line was now lit with flashes of gunfire. The spent shells falling on top of one another made chiming noises as they piled on one by one. Grenades of all sorts were thrown into the camp. One by one the Brits fell; others tried to run for it, but instead were met with a sniper's bullet.

Fischer and Kraus loaded their rifle rod grenades with blanks, firing them at an angle like a mortar. Graf aimed the Ladera rifle at targets that were behind thick cover. The British soldiers scrambled to find cover amid the chaos. There were some making an attempt to climb inside one of the Killen-Strait tractors and start it up. The three-tread vehicle moved forward with its rotating machine gun turret firing at the tree line to suppress the attackers. Graf quickly shifted the Ladera rifle toward the tractor and fired at the turret. After two shots it stopped firing. Then he fired at the driver's side, stopping it in its tracks.

Ten minutes later and the battle still raged on. the R.O.B. entrenched themselves in their encampment and a small group of British troops and their CO (commanding officer) discussed finding a way to inform Wellington on the situation at hand.

"That's insane Sir!" said a British soldier to his superior.

"It's the only way to inform our commander. Now shut your pie hole and give me cover," said the CO as a rifle grenade exploded nearby.

"Alright men, covering fire!!"

The small squad fired their Rexer rifles and Howell automatic rifles into the tree line as the CO ran toward the tent across from them. He attached a note to the messenger pigeon then set it free before the whole tent blew up from the rifle rod grenade. The pigeon flew away from the madness and chaos that engulfed the area heading to its destination.

"Assault team, ready up. We are going in. It's time we finish this," directed Maxis.

"Finally, I wanted to get up close and personal anyway. Been itching for a fight all day," Fischer jokingly said as he loaded a new clip.

"Move out! Graf, hunt them down!" Maxis ordered.

The assault team consisted of Maxis, Lothar, Weber, Müller, and Graf, who was lagging as he had to leave the Ladera behind. They moved into the camp while the rest of the squad were still laying down fire. The assault team split up, with Maxis and Lothar taking the right flank, Müller and Weber going center, and Graf to the left.

Maxis and Lothar worked together in sync as they tore down the British with constant fire, covering each other when one had to reload or providing covering fire, an exemplary form of teamwork.

At one point a pair of British soldiers tried to do a surprise bayonet charge but were quickly countered as Maxis blocked the charge and with one hard kick in the knee, and impaled the Brit through the neck with his fixed bayonet and tossed him to the side. As for Lothar, he grabbed the rifle neck before the bayonet made contact and he yanked the soldier in then head-butted him before hitting him with the sharpened side of his shovel.

Müller and Weber moved down the center slowly but surely, trying to match the speed of the Maxis and Lothar. The way they performed was similar but different. One British soldier peered out the corner of a tent with his rifle aiming at Müller but Weber quickly prevented by plunging his bayonet into the R.O.B. soldier.

They encountered a machine gun emplacement and ducked for cover behind the crates. The two were completely suppressed as bullets whistle by above them, but Kruger saw their situation and took aim at the gunner. With one squeeze of the trigger he fired and the gunner slouched over his Vickers MG, dead. Another soldier then tried a charge at Müller but was quickly countered with a stab from Weber.

"Pay attention to your surroundings, Müller!" shouted Weber as he lifted the dead soldier with his bayonet and used him as a shield. Müller quickly moved in behind him. They slowly inched forward with Müller providing fire. The two cleared out the center of enemy troops.

Graf, however, ran like hell on the left flank. He went on a rampage with his shotgun catching the British by surprise as he fired buck shots up close with his revolver shotgun. Whenever he had to reload, he would imme- diately switch to his dual sidearms and unleash anoth- er volley of fire at the enemy. His adrenaline increased and he immediately utilized his trench mace and went completely berserk as he charged the unsuspecting pair of infantrymen. He struck the first one with a clean blow to the head, and as the other one swung his rifle toward him, Graf managed to knock the rifle upwards. It fired leaving ringing in his ears but didn't keep him from bashing the Brit's skull. Then Graf proceeded to the center where he met the others.

The remaining British soldiers withdrew behind large metal barricades at the end of the camp. The squad ceased fire and held position at the tree line observing the battle as it unfolded except for Kruger who waited patiently for any potential targets.

The barricades the R.O.B. soldiers hid behind were large mobile shields, two of them had large wheels, but the one in the center had none. The center one was a Ped rail with a thick plate that housed a machine gun in the center and two hinged side plates had four ri- fle ports on each side. The rifle ports on all of them opened and a mix of SMLE, Rexer, Griffiths Woodgate, and Howell rifles stuck out, and fired a volley of bullets continuously. The machine gun laid down suppressing fire causing the assault team to once again split up and take cover.

The squad at the tree line opened fire at the large shields, hitting them with bullets but to no avail. However, Fischer hopped on the Ladera rifle and although the first shot pushed him back a bit, he quickly recovered. He aimed at the shield on the left and fired, sending a British soldier flying out of his cover.

Maxis quickly loaded his rifle with armor piercing bullets and took aim at the machine gun, firing the entire clip into the center where the it was located. Fischer followed that with another shot from the Ladera. After the fifth round the MG stopped and soon the rest of rifles ceased firing. Maxis stood up, held his hand up and the shooting stopped.

Everything went eerily quiet as Maxis guardedly walked toward the shields; the rest of the assault team followed as well. He made a few hand gestures for Kruger to see...telling him to keep an eye on him. Before Maxis reached the corner of the large portable shield, a pair of hands stuck out which made him jump a bit. Coming out from the side was an injured British captain.

"Oi, we bloody surrender ya fucking bastards!" said the Captain with an Irish accent.

"The rest you better be unarmed if you are surrendering unless you like dying like the rest of your friends," shouted Maxis, keeping his rifle at the ready.

"Come on ya damn blokes, it's over! I'm not dying in a losing fight. Come now," said the Captain to his men.

"Damn you, Kelly! We could have held them off a little longer!" said a soldier.

"Quit stalling Sergeant Major Dawson. I made a promise to your wife to bring you back in one piece and not in a damned coffin. Now, get out here and lay down your arms!" ordered Cpt. Kelly.

"Fucking hell! Fine you bloody coward!" Sgm. Dawson retorted.

The rest of the remaining R.O.B. soldiers came out with their hands up. Some of them had a look of anger or fear on their faces while some were expressionless. Finally, the battle in the camp was over and Maxis led the group to the center of the camp where there was more space. Lothar counted how many there were in the group while the rest of the squad emerged from the bushes and made their way toward the center.

"Now then, let's have chat," said Maxis as he rested his rifle.

CHAPTER 20

CALM BEFORE THE COMING STORM

Meanwhile...

Commander Wellington and his two lieutenants were at the port meeting the troops while the battle at their base camp was still raging on. The three hundred new soldiers stood at attention as Commander Wellington inspected them; then he began to give a speech.

"Men, I'm the commander of this regiment. You will be serving Britain's best interest at heart for we will fight to the bitter end until victory is achieved for her."

"Yes Sir!" everybody responded.

"We will fight on the fields, we will fight in the shadows, and we will certainly fight where we are needed the most."

"Yes Sir!"

"For we are His Majesty's Regiment of Britannia. We do what is necessary to win this damned war, even if we must fight as dirty as the Germans. For what is our motto?"

"Advance, we dare!" the soldiers shouted loudly.

"Advance, we dare, indeed and 'For King and Country' lest we forget," Commander Wellington finished.

"Jolly good show, Sir! The men are now inspired," said 1Lt. Wilson.

"I agree. Finer words couldn't have been said," said 2Lt. McManus.

"I appreciate the feedback on the speech. Now since we met the troops, we will make haste for our HQ for..." Wellington was interrupted as soldier rushed over to him.

"Commander Wellington, Sir! It's urgent Sir!" said the soldier in a panic.

"Calm down, Private. What is the urgency?" said 1Lt. Wilson.

The Private reads the report to them.

"Sir, Base Camp Elizabeth is under attack by hostile forces. Enemy strength unknown. Taking severe casualties. Holding our own but do not know how much longer. Send support immediately," the Private finished.

"I can't believe this! We would have been informed of an attack commencing by now, how did they find us?" asked 1Lt. Wilson.

"Should we even send in the reinforcement? I mean they just got off the boat. What do you think, Sir? Sir?" asked 2Lt. McManus.

"They attacked us at our own base? Well, we will send our finest to take them on. Cpt. Atkinson, front and

297

center!" Commander Wellington ordered with aggravation in his voice.

"I'm here Sir. What are your orders?" said Cpt. Atkinson.

"Take the company and double time it to our base camp to the south. Be on guard for Jerry is attacking as we speak."

"Yes, with haste," said Cpt. Atkinson as he rushed to his horse and took command.

"Men, we march for our camp. Forward, March!"

The bugle boy sounded the order with his bugle. What came next was the sound of bagpipes playing from the highlanders at the back of the company, the company marching in synch with the bagpipes on their way to battle.

"Goodluck boys." said Commander Wellington as he walked into his private car, then drove away to their HQ.

Back at Base Camp Elizabeth...

The squad rested up while two men kept watch on the prisoners. Lothar approached Maxis with a head count. Maxis was sitting on a crate looking at the map taking small sips from his canteen.

"Maxis, I counted one officer, four salty NCOs, and ten regular enlisted men."

"Hmph, what about their losses?" Maxis asked sipping again from his canteen.

"Too many to count."

"Heh, I guess no one was counting except me. There were a hundred and fifty of them here but after the battle there are only fifteen of them left. We were very accurate with our shots since I haven't found any wounded since I helped Weber and Konig move the bodies. So, we nearly wiped out eighty-nine percent of the encampment," Maxis said calmly.

"Well, if this counts for something, there are only two surviving armored tractors that didn't get blown up or hit with the Ladera rifle. Anyway, should we start questioning the prisoners?"

"Let's start with the officers first, I'll come across as a nice guy but if he decides to act tough then I'll call you in. Sound like a plan?"

"Quite. I will wait for you to summon the Mighty Lothar if Tommy needs persuading," said Lothar in proudful tone.

Maxis laughed a little knowing Lothar was going to say that. He got off the crate and placed the canteen back on his belt, and toward the group of R.O.B. troops that were sitting on the ground.

"I'll have to play my cards carefully here if I'm going to get answers. Though this place is set up as a launching point for them from what the letter stated. A combined force of armored vehicles and infantry attacking at the same time? To make this worse they appear to be weaponized with rifles and machine guns that I'm not familiar with. Better make sure to grab those unknown weapons before we move on," Maxis pondered in his thoughts. He stopped in front of the group then called out.

"I'm looking for, uh...Cpt. Kelly,. I just need to have a word with you please."

The group started muttering to each other.

"Hey! Where is Kelly? Step up now or get some lead in the noggin," Brandt threatened, pointing his machine gun at them.

"Brandt! Stand down this instance, we are not threatening the prisoners," shouted Maxis.

"And why the hell not..." Brandt was cut off as Cpt. Kelly rose from the group.

"I'm here, quit your fighting," said Cpt. Kelly as he limped over to Maxis.

"You're hurt..." said Maxis.

"What do expect lad? We were fighting, things like this will always happen."

"True, but time to make amends. Hold still," Maxis grabbed a piece of strong wood and reached for his med kit. He began aiding the injured Captain.

"Grrr, why are you wasting your time with this damned Tommy? We are supposed to be fighting them not helping them. This would be a lot simpler you had just cut down the bastard like you normally do, Black Wolf of Mons!" Brandt yelled.

"Watch your tongue, Private!" Maxis barked back, still helping the captain.

"Fahr zur Hölle (Go to hell), Jackass. I'm done taking orders from you, first you come in all high mighty with your lap dog, then you're trying to act like some damned hero by helping the enemy but erasing what you've done in that village a year ago doesn't just disappear. We should have just executed them so we can be done with this mission and be done with upstarts like you who get away with literal murder," said Brandt as he loaded a magazine into his machine gun.

"There you go. You should be able to walk. Now if you excuse me," Maxis finished fixing up Cpt. Kelly then slowly got up and faced Brandt.

"Oh dear, I recognize that look, oooh, you are in trouble boyo. Here comes the disciplining." the captain said, as Maxis started walking toward Brandt.

"Oh, what are you going to do, Maxis? Are you going to hit me or shoot me? Cause if you are, I won't go down without a-" before Brandt could finish his sentence Maxis grabbed him and threw him to the ground so hard it stunned him for second.

"How dare you, you son of ..." Brandt was cut off again, this time with bayonet inches away from his throat. The others were ready to step in, but Lothar and Fischer blocked their path.

"Men, it's in your best interest to not intervene or there will be trouble. Just watch," said Lothar, in a calm manner.

"I'm with Corporal on this one, besides I've been waiting for this to happen. So...enjoy the show," said Fischer with a smirk.

Brandt breathed heavily out of fear as Maxis began to speak.

"What exactly do think killing unarmed soldiers will get us? Well? Because I think it would make us look bad committing such barbaric acts, lower our sense of honor to the point of monkeys with no brains. If the enemy discovers what we did here...if we did do such horrendous acts then the tabloids will have a field day with making us, our families, our Kaiser, and our Empire look like monsters! I find your lack of humanity and understanding disturbing. And just so we're clear what happened in the past was not me, for I know the truth of what happened, back in '14, so I suggest you be careful with who you address. Well, Pvt. Brandt, do I make myself clear or not!? You better answer now because my patience is wearing thin," Maxis finished with the bayonet inching closer to Brandt.

"I-I understand, please...don't kill me," Brandt said in a weak voice filled with fear.

"Pfft. What a lousy response, Private," Maxis sheathed his bayonet. Suddenly he heard the slow hand claps from Lothar and Fischer.

"What a way to discipline the troops, Sarge! I'm impressed, really," said Fischer.

"I have to say, I've never seen you do anything like that before. I give it a ten," said Lothar.

"Lothar and Fischer, keep an eye on him," Maxis calmly ordered. Lothar and Fischer nodded in response and walked over to Brandt who was now sitting upright, still in shock.

Maxis dusted himself off and headed back to the captain, who was in awe of what he just witnessed.

"My, my I can see why you're the leader of your group. It's not just a blue scarf, I tell ya. A real leader of a pack," said Cpt. Kelly.

"Sure, whatever you say. Now then, may we resume our talks?" Maxis asked nicely.

"Since you patched me up, I'll try, but I won't guarantee that I'll have all the answers."

"Whatever counts then, Cpt. Kelly. Now, what was the purpose of your unit's presence here, last I checked the Royal Army was operating on the other side of this salient?"

"The thing is..."

"Don't you dare tell them you damned Irishman! I would rather see you die than spill your guts to Fritz, you traitor! I won't let you betray the Regiment!" screamed Sgm. Dawson as he pulled out a Webley automatic pistol he had hidden and aimed at Cpt. Kelly. Maxis drew his sidearm and aimed at Dawson.

Suddenly someone fired a shot at Sgm. Dawson's hand, disarming him. Kruger whistled quickly as he lowered his rifle, the barrel still smoking. Müller rushed over, knocked Dawson down to the ground with the butt of his rifle and restrained him.

"Stay down, Tommy," said Müller as he pressed his knee on Dawson's back.

"*Sigh.* You were saying, Captain?" Maxis continued the conversation while holding his weapon.

"Okay, our reason was to assist the colonials in this sector. We had no idea that you broke through. The rest is history when your people came in and shot up the place. We were to get ready for a counterattack once we repelled the enemy with an armored assault like the world has never seen before. I heard one of the machines was a favorite of the Commander. That is about all I know."

"At least that answers about Operation Goliath though I should ask about how big R.O.B. really is."

"What about the Regiment of Britannia? How big is this organization?" Maxis asked.

"That I don't know, lad. I do believe that Sgm. Dawson may know since he works closely with the other officers and the commander himself. I'm afraid you have to go ask him even though he tried to shoot me," Cpt. Kelly said with his arms crossed.

"You don't say. I appreciate your cooperation Cpt. Kelly, now go rest," Maxis said as he walks toward Sgm. Dawson.

"Uh, please do not kill him. I did make a promise to his wife to keep him alive even if he is thick headed bastard," said Cpt. Kelly.

Maxis turned to the captain and replied.

"That is last thing I would do."

Maxis stood in front of the Sgm. Dawson who was still pinned by Müller. Maxis squatted down and began to speak.

"Sergeant Major Dawson...How are you feeling right now?"

"Piss off, Jerry!" said Dawson and spat at Maxis boots.

"Ok, that wasn't nice. What can you tell me about R.O.B.?"

"I'm not telling you shite, fritz! You will never get anything from me. I will never betray my country or my Commander. So go take a flying leap, you Bratwurst-eating fucking kraut!" Dawson finished as he struggled to get free.

"Wow...That is harshest thing I've ever heard. Though I've heard better," said Müller in a nonchalant tone.

"Well, I tried to be a nice guy, but you have forced my hand. LOTHAR!" Maxis called. Heavy footsteps can be heard as Lothar approaches. He stands next to Müller and Dawson.

"What can the Mighty Lothar do for you, Sergeant?" said Lothar. Müller chuckled a little.

"Müller, take your knee off of the prick," Maxis ordered.

"Oh, you're in for it now, Tommy. It was nice knowing ya, heh, heh." Müller got up and took a step back. Dawson jumped up quickly, fists ready.

"Lothar, bear hug," Maxis said with a serious look.

"Wait, bear wha – *oof!*" Lothar put his arms around Dawson and lifted him up in a tight squeeze facing Maxis.

"Bollock's man...put me down, NOW!" demanded Dawson.

"You should know Sergeant Major, that Cpl. Lothar is known for a lot of things. He is tallest in our group, the strongest, and kindest man you'll meet. However, he does not like people insulting his friends. His arms have the strength of ten lumberjacks, and he can put the squeeze like an Anaconda snake. You know snakes, do you?"

"Bloody hell...bastards crushing...me," Dawson started kicking and struggling even more.

"This can be over quickly if you just tell me what I need to know."

"Bugger off, kraut. I face worst gents at the pub. You plan to squeeze my top off go ahead and try," said Dawson as he tried to squirm his way out.

"Don't say I didn't warn you. I don't enjoy these kinds of things but if gets job done so be it. Lothar...greet him like friend."

"You got it." Lothar applied the pressure and the Sergeant Major slowly turned red.

"Is that all you got...Billy with no mates!"

"Okay, Lothar treat him like he's your best friend," Maxis ordered again.

Lothar applies even more pressure to Dawson than before.

"*Choking*...Fucking...*choking*...Germans...I'mnottelling." With that Sgm. Dawson slowly choked out from Lothar's bear hug, Fischer walked by Kraus who was enjoying the show while sitting a on a crate.

"Hey, Kraus?"

"Yeah, Fischer?"

"Don't you think this a little excessive, what the Sergeant is doing?"

"Not really. For me it's more like payback for the boys at Hill 60."

"What happen at Hill 60?" Fischer asked.

"They blew it up with mines from underground, obliterating everyone in the area. Nothing left."

"I see..."

Sgm. Dawson, still refusing to answer Maxis, continued to resist but with every breath he takes, the constraint suffocated him more.

"I'm starting to see a little purple on your face Sergeant Major. How long do you think you can keep this up?" Maxis asked as he looks at his pocket watch.

Dawson doesn't answer.

"Alright then, Lothar...treat him like a...long...lost...brother."

"OKAY! *Choking*, okay. I'll talk!" Dawson struggled to get words out.

"Let him go, Lothar."

Lothar dropped Dawson to the ground with a loud thud. He was coughing and breathing hard. Maxis squatted down once again.

"I suggest you start talking. And if you spit on my boot, there will literal hell to pay."

"*Cough*...What the hell you want to know?" Dawson asked.

"What I have been asking, the size of the Regiment of Britannia, Bases, and everything else that comes to mind."

"Alright, think about the British Empire for one whole minute, then you will get the idea."

"So, the regiment is widespread. That means you have bases around the world," said Maxis, scratching his own chin.

"That's right. And the French Division has them too in their territories. We are Britain's finest not only in England, but we also use our dominions however as we see fit since they're not part of the regiment."

"Oh yes, we met your finest...they're all over the place," Lothar interrupted.

"Heh, I wouldn't doubt that. If there was a job too big or too dangerous you would send your colonial troops to deal with that," Maxis said to Dawson.

"You catch on quick, Jerry. We knew about your organization from the start of the war. Even that Frenchie bastard Molitor warned us about you, and Wellington didn't bloody take him seriously."

"What can you tell me about Molitor?"

"How the bloody hell should I know? The man is mysterious and so is his division. That's all I can tell you. Should you want more then you are going to have to ask the Commander himself. But that won't matter because you'll end up dead anyway. Agh!"

"What do you mean?!" questioned Lothar as he stepped on Dawson with his hob nails beneath his boot.

"We got a company's worth of troops on their way as speak! It doesn't matter if you retreat, they will catch up to you and destroy you. After we finish you off, we'll break through your line and torch your entire nation to the ground!"

"Well, that confirms it all, then. The three hundred that are on their way and the size of the R.O.B. Seems my crude method worked."

There was silence for a moment until Maxis spoke.

"I'd like to see them to try. Other than that, it's all we need to know. Oh, before I go, you should check yourself. Make sure your lungs haven't been pierced by your ribs because I heard the real interrogators are real rough on prisoners. Especially when you meet the Geist Platoon." Maxis stood up and walked away slowly.

"Wha – what are you bloody saying?"

"I cannot take in an account what you just said to be true, so I'll leave it to the real professionals to verify what you told me when you return back to base."

"Wait, do you mean...I told you everything! I bloody told you everything, ya bloody boche!" Dawson yelled as he was escorted back to the group by Müller.

"Lothar, Fischer, Kruger, and Kraus, come with me. We're going for a walk," Maxis ordered and they gathered behind him.

"Sarge, were you serious about him getting roughed up back at base?" Fischer asked.

"Of course not, that a was bluff just to scare him. I played my cards right and ended up with a royal flush."

"Heh, I see what you did there," said Lothar.

The small group walked around the corner of the camp and saw a large object covered with a tarp. Maxis walked over to it and pulled the tarp off to reveal an interesting sight.

"Woah, look at the size of that box vehicle," said Kraus.

"This would be the Lincoln Machine No.1. By the size it, I'll assume it's meant to be some type of support troop transport. Judging from what the drawings showed."

"Let's look inside then. I want to look," said Kraus. He rushed, climbed on the side of the machine and opened the door, then headed inside with the others following. Everyone was surprised to see the interior of the machine.

"Well, this is very spacious," observed Kruger.

"You can say that again! I'm already thinking of putting a little fireplace here, bookshelf there, and a comfortable chair," Fischer jokingly said.

"Hey, this thing has a mounted gun! I'm checking it out. Wow, this thing has a Vickers machine gun," said Kraus as he climbed the small ladder and stepped on the platform.

"Does it rotate?" Maxis asked.

"Hold on...it does. It does rotate, amazing!" Kraus rotated it left to right.

"Perfect. We are taking it then along with the Killen-Straits tractors." Maxis stepped out of the vehicle.

"Oh boy, listen up! Maxis has a plan," said Lothar as he walked outside with the rest following. They gathered in front of the three-track armored tractor. Maxis began to speak.

"There is supposed to be a company coming here soon, probably within an hour. The plan is simple, most of the squad will use their vehicles to transport the POWs back to Ragnarök base while me, Lothar, Graf, and Kruger will stay behind to delay the enemy."

"Wait you're going stay behind, by yourselves? What nonsense is this? I thought we were supposed work together like a team?" questioned Kraus.

"Listen Kraus, me and Maxis have done this before. It's different since there is going to be four now. Just follow the plan through and everything will go smoothly...I hope," said Lothar.

"Verdammt (Damn it), then I'm going to miss the action!" Kraus said, disappointed.

"Anyway, in terms of delaying the enemy, it will go something like this. Lothar starts by digging a fox-hole near where we were positioned last, in front of the bushes, then you create a small mound for yourself and your Madsen. Fischer, get the MG and place it over at the foxhole. Kraus, tell Konig to send a message to Major Reinhard about the situation then tell the rest of the squad of the plan. Kruger, I need you to set traps, at least three lines worth, by the dirt trail."

"I did see a tent filled with ordnance, I think I can rig them and attach a trip wire," offered Kruger.

"Make it happen. Whatever works, do it. After you are done, go scout ahead for any sign of the Regiment of Britannia's reinforcements. Once you spot them return to the foxhole and take your position. We don't have a lot of time so I will do what I can to help so we can be ready for them. Move out!" Maxis ordered.

"Yes, Sergeant!" Each one responded loudly and proudly.

They dispersed and went to do their assigned tasks. Kraus spread the word to the rest of the squad and told Konig to send a pigeon. Konig sent one pigeon out with the message attached and watched it fly away as it disappeared from sight. Cpl. Weber assisted escorting the POWs to the Lincoln machine, and from there one officer and three NCOs and an enlisted man entered the machine. Müller was already inside and Cpl. Weber watched from the outside before entering himself. The rest of the enlisted men would walked beside it under watch. The squad managed to get everything done in a matter of minutes with no hiccups, and even figured out how to turn on and drive the machines.

"Maxis, everything is set, what's next?" Lothar asked.

"Now we go into the second phase of the plan. Sending parts of the squad away with the prisoners in the captured vehicles."

"So just to recap, we stand our ground here. Not just to delay the enemy but also chip away their ranks as well. Is that what our battle plan consists of, Maxis?"

"Right on the nose, Lothar. Not only are we buying our friends time, but diminishing enemy ranks will help the regular army that will be advancing through here eventually. Last thing we need is them getting repelled by a small contingent of British soldiers hiding in the woods. We'll withdraw from the area and regroup with the squad once we have done enough damage, or we just run out of ammo."

"That last part I believe. Oh, hey, you still got that label attached. Let me get that for you," said Lothar as he took the small paper name tag off and tossed it aside.

The two walked over with Graf joining in and watched the rest of the squad leave. Fischer was standing outside one of the Killen-Strait tractors and next to him was a box full of items.

"Sergeant Maxis, come to see us off? I have something the squad pitched in to donate to you and Lothar," said Fischer.

"What is it?" Maxis asked.

"Let me speak for the whole squad that we don't exactly like being sent away while you guys have all the fun. So, we agreed to lend you some of our equipment to give you an edge when the Brits show up. The grenadiers gave what's left of the rod grenades with some blank ammo. For Lothar, Konig gave his ammo box for your Madsen. That's basically it," Fischer finished, setting the box down.

"Thanks Fischer," said Lothar.

"You can thank me when you come back alive, all of you. We'll be waiting in Ragnarök Base. Bis später (See you later)," said Fischer as he climbed inside the armored tractor.

"All right! We are set. Start 'em up!" yelled Kraus.

The vehicles' engines roared to life. The Lincoln machine lurched forward with the prisoners walking on the side. Behind them were two Killen-strait tractors with their MG turrets trained on the prisoners. Though the vehicles did not move with great speed, they did negotiate the terrain well. Maxis and the others waved goodbye as the small convoy vanished into the forest.

"Let's get into position men," said Maxis.

The group walked over to the foxhole and dugouts. Maxis positioned himself on the heavy machine gun. By his side was Graf who loaded his slug rounds into the shotgun. Lothar got behind the mound he made for himself. Then they waited for Kruger to return to them.

"Maxis, I see Kruger and he is coming in fast," announced Lothar, as he watched Kruger running and hopping over some of his traps. Kruger jumped in the foxhole and gave his report.

"Sarge, the British are closing in! Almost three hundred of them moving on the dirt road."

"Alright, squad, do not fire until I give the go ahead. Kruger, take position. I have some words of inspiration to say."

"We're listening," said Lothar.

"Stand fast men. We are experienced soldiers and know no fear. Let's show Tommy how real soldier's fight. Stand fast! Immer mits Präzision (Always with precision)!" Maxis finished and everyone shouted, "HURRA!"

"If we survive and succeed, I have a bottle for us all, courtesy of the Regiment of Britannia," said Maxis as he points at his rucksack.

"HURRA!!!" Louder this time with excitement.

CHAPTER 21

BLOODY TRAP

The sound of bagpipes could be heard in the distance. The tune of "Scotland the Brave" grew louder and louder until the Regiment of Britannia came into view walking in formation. On the side of the formation is Cpt. Atkinson riding his horse and walking beside him was the bugle boy. Maxis pulled out his binoculars to take a closer look.

"Kruger, do you have a visual on the officer and the bugle boy?" he asked

"I have a visual. I also see the bagpipes near the back and the Scots marching with them."

"Kruger, here is a set of targets for you. Take out the officer then bugle boy. Cut the leadership and their way of communication."

"I see. Then they will be forced to charge into my traps. I laid out a lot of rigged artillery shells. HE type, and AP type are both scattered about with some special traps I made myself; a set of phosphorus and smoke shells on the second line, and last line is where gas shells are, in case we need to escape, the gas will cover our backs."

"Perfect, Kruger. Fire when ready. The rest of you wait until I give you the go."

The R.O.B. marched along steadily until a loud bang and a horse fell to its side dead. The bugle boy pulled out his horn but was immediately jerked back and collapsed to the ground dead. There was utter confusion in the formation and the bagpipes stopped playing. Maxis loaded a blank round into his rifle and put the rod grenade in the barrel.

"Shit man, where that shot come from?" shouted one R.O.B. soldier.

"Are we under attack? Bloody hell, are we?" said another.

One of the lieutenants took over and ordered, "Lads, defensive position. Don't run but keep your guard up. Do not charge unless I give the..." He was quickly interrupted by the explosion that instantly took out six of his men, to which a sergeant immediately yelled, "Move it boys! Jerry is greeting us. Let's give him a taste of British steel. GO!"

"Wait...*cough*...you damned fools this...*grunts*...a, trap!" gasped Cpt. Atkinson, trying to warn the troops all the while struggling to free himself from the dead horse. But it was too late. One of the Scottish Highlanders set off the first trap killing him instantly in the explosion. Everyone froze.

"Hold position! Krauts laid out traps, cheeky bastards!" said the Lieutenant.

"What do we do, Sir? We're sitting ducks and..." The Scottish Highlander was cut off, after being hit by a sniper's bullet.

"Damn it all, sound the attack! Advance, we dare! CHARGE!" screamed an officer as he pulled out his saber.

The bagpipes began playing loudly as the order to attack was heard and every soldier fixed their bayonets and moved forward, forgetting the fact the whole area had been set up with traps. They shouted their Regiment's motto and other war cries before getting snuffed out by shells detonating, then Maxis fired the remaining rod grenades. No one looked back to see their friends blown up or cut down, but they pressed on ever so into the ambush.

"AAAHHH, MY BLOODY LEG!" one soldier screamed bloody murder as his leg was caught in bear trap before getting shot.

Maxis witnessed this and asked, "Kruger, did you set up bear traps?"

Kruger responds with a wink and smile. Another soldier set off a snare that yanked him off the ground before the sound of a click from a grenade was heard before it detonated. The first wave was slowed down by the traps hidden everywhere.

"They are almost through the first line. They are starting to learn my pattern, Sarge," said Kruger as he fired his rifle.

"Trupp, Feuer eröffnen (Squad, open fire)," Maxis said calmly as he cocked the machine gun.

The squad unleashed a hail of bullets at the oncoming British soldiers. inflicting more harm on them as they ran for cover. Some dropped to the ground and low crawled. The R.O.B. returned fire though could not hit anything as they were badly being suppressed. Some of them performed the "Mad Minute," firing as fast as they could, hoping their bullets would hit. The other R.O.B. soldiers armed with their experimental rifles laid down repeating fire and those armed with M1909 LMG tried to find a suitable spot to set up.

The second battle at Base Camp Elizabeth was bloody and chaotic with bullet tracers flying around, screams of men dying, and the tents catching on fire, just pure madness.

"Remember Maxis, control burst, control burst," Lothar shouted to Maxis while firing.

"Sarge, they're closing on the second line, just say the word and we'll show 'em what a mad dog looks like," said Graf ,firing the slug out of his shotgun.

The British moved past the first line of traps before igniting one of the phosphorus shells which created a plume of smoke and fire. Maxis grabbed the gas grenades and threw them as hard as he could. The greenish gas poured out and some were caught in it and choked. Immediately everyone pulls out their makeshift respirators to counter effects of the gas.

Graf also helped by throwing the incendiary grenades to block off any attempts to flank. By most of the Regiment of Britannia's soldiers had simultaneously set off the phosphorus shells and smoke shells covered the whole area, resulting in many soldiers' boots catching on fire.

"Graf! Start hunting!" Maxis yelled, as he fired the machine gun.

"I'm on it!" Graf immediately jumped out of the foxhole and sprinted into the smoke, putting on his gas mask as he ran.

Graf surprised the R.O.B. soldiers that were inside the cloud of smoke with a shotgun blast to their torsos. Another Brit appeared from the left, thrusting his bayonet forward at Graf but was quickly countered by a hard hit on his head from the butt of the shotgun.

Graf went on a complete killing spree with his crude yet effective weapons. He used up the last of his shells before switching to his pistols and when ran out of ammo for his sidearms, switched to his trench mace and impact grenades. He bashed with his mace and the soldiers were obliterated on impact with the disk grenades.

"Maxis, I'm running low on ammo here. I got three mags." said Lothar before pulling his pistol, quickly outshooting an enemy soldier to their right.

"Same here. I've got two clips left for my rifle. We are about to get overrun," Kruger added, concerned. to the concern.

"I already ran out of ammo for the MG, but I hear you. We've done enough damage. Squad, fall back. Let's get out of here! I'll provide cover.," Maxis ordered as he started firing his Luger M1906.

"Graf! Stop playing with Tommy over there! We're falling back!" Kruger shouted.

Graf was holding a British soldier by his collar ready hit him with the trench mace. He let him go and said "You got lucky this time," then ran away. Maxis provided cover for Graf as he sprinted back when bullet grazed his left arm ripping the symbol off his sleeve.

"Graf!"

"I'm fine. Just a flesh wound."

"Then get moving!" Maxis responded.

The squad retreated into the forest, moving and shooting until they were out of sight, leaving the camp entirely. The British tried to give chase but were stopped by gas shells they had tripped. The British grenadiers started firing their rod grenades at the retreating Germans although they missed their targets. They gathered near the outskirts of the woods and watched.

"We did it men. We drove them back. We should pursue them into the forest and..."

"Oh, shut it, Sergeant. It was merely a Pyrrhic victory. The camp is back in our hands but at what cost? No one is doing anything! Get this camp checked out for more traps before anything else happens, NOW! The Commander will not be pleased with this," directed Cpt. Atkinson, now limping with a broken leg as he looked at the almost destroyed camp.

Maxis and the squad kept running until they reached the end of Kitchener woods. They stopped to catch their breath, but no one said a word. Maxis then proceeded to help treat Graf's wound before moving again. They continued with Kruger taking point.

Night slowly fell and one of them pulled a flashlight out to light the way, but only one source of light to minimize them from getting spotted. It was nine and there was still no sign of any German troops. Finally they spotted a string of lights moving along. Everyone held their positions and crouched down.

"Graf, check it out. See if they are friendlies," Maxis whispered.

Graf nodded and moved out. Everyone else kept their weapons at the ready even though they had limited ammo. Twenty minutes later, Graf returned.

"What's the info?" Maxis asked.

"Sarge, I'm happy to say we have found our advancing force which means the pathway should be clear. They also offered us a ride."

"Best news I've heard yet. Let's go."

They approached the main force and after a quick greeting, they boarded the wagon to return to Ragnarök base. After thirty minutes of total silence, they arrived at the base when the wagon came to a halt. At one of the tents Sitting outside was Fischer and Kraus playing cards. When they noticed the wagon stopping, they quickly got up and ran toward it.

"Well, well, what do we have here? I see the Mighty Lothar on the right, Jäger Kruger to the left; Graf, did you get wounded? That's surprising, and at last the war-hero squad-leader in the flesh," observed Fischer.

"It's great to see guys made it back. The whole place was placing bets," said Kraus.

"You were betting on our odds of survival, really?" said Graf, still holding his arm to cover the bandage.

"Don't worry about that. The best part is I won, Ha ha. More papiermarks (paper money) for me," boasted Fischer, cheerful and happy.

"Well, if this makes it better, I did liberate this fine brandy from the Commander of the Regiment of the Britannia," Maxis pulled the bottle from his rucksack.

"Oh, this is going to be a good night," said Fischer with excitement.

"Unless you plan to share that bottle to the person in charge of this base won't you, Sgt. Maxis?" interrupted Major Reinhard, as he walked in on their conversation.

Everyone stood to attention and quickly saluted the Major and he saluted back.

"Fine work men, very fine. Though I'm uncertain whether to call this a success, since we've yet to get to Ypres itself. Nonetheless you are back here in one piece. Sgt. Maxis, prepare your squad for debriefing tonight before you all go and celebrate. One of the prisoners you brought in was very talkative as if he was scared of something; I want to know why. The vehicles you brought in are already on their way back to Valhalla base for R&D to analyze. I'll send Commander Jorgensen your reports after the debrief. Now get to it."

"Yes Sir. Let's go, squad," instructed Maxis.

Fischer went to fetch the rest of the squad while Maxis and the others followed Major Reinhard. After the debrief, the squad gathered at the mess hall tent and celebrated, all except Brandt. Everyone who participated took three shots of the fine brandy. Major Reinhard took a glass with him as he walked out of the tent. He stared into the night sky with the stars twinkling, but in his thoughts, something bugged him.

"This will be most destructive war man has ever seen. The most troubling part is the discovery of another military organization sponsored by their government. That makes three now. I wonder if there is a fourth. I hope not. Although the Grün squad did perform well together with Maxis at the helm and Lothar by his side. Perhaps I should recommend to Augustus in the foreseeable future that we think about forming a Task Force," the major pondered and downed his brandy.

Meanwhile back at Base Camp Elizabeth...

Commander Wellington stood in front of the now devastated base camp, steaming mad and in shock. Trying to contemplate how such a thing could have happened to this place. 1Lt. Wilson walked up beside him.

"We did a head count, Sir, for the defenders and for the company we sent."

"How many for the defenders, Wilson?" Commander Wellington asked.

"For starters, it seems that the Germans have some respect for our dead. The men said they were found neatly placed in rows in a respectful manner with their arms crossed and fennings on their eyes. It surprised us when we found them like this. We counted a 135 killed in action, and 15 M.I.A (missing in action). We presumed they may have been captured."

"And what of our company that came through here?"

"Based on what Cpt. Atkinson reported before being sent off with the medics, they were 300 strong and after retaking the camp they had 195 left. Jerry dug in hard to inflict such a toll."

"My God...that's one third of the company killed in action. Did the Germans take any losses? What about them?" the Commander demanded to know.

"I'm sorry Sir, but none of their corpses were spotted among the dead. It seems whatever they did to avoid such casualties they did so strategically."

"Bastards...the lot of them. How can they possibly..." Before the commander finished his sentence, he heard a scream coming from the right. They turned to see one of their own on the ground with medics around him. They rushed over to see.

"What happen here?" demanded Commander Wellington.

"Sir, we found a survivor, we are trying to get this thing off him," explained the medic as he and the others tried to grip the bear trap.

"Sir...SIR! I need tell you what happened. Come close, I don't have a lot of time left." said the wounded R.O.B. soldier.

"Don't say that. We're going get you out and you'll be home before you know it," comforted the medic as he administered morphine.

Wellington went down on one knee to listen to what the soldier had to say.

"We walked in with the pride of Britain on our minds and families in our hearts, but our training didn't prepare us for this. After they shot the horse and it fell on the captain, the poor bugle boy, Mac, was supposed to signal us but he bit the bullet. Chaos erupted. Next thing you know, we charged in there expecting a good fight but instead we were met with a slaughterhouse, and we were the lambs. All I can remember was the explosions and the dying screams of our boys charging into the fray," said the soldier as his eyes started to glaze.

"Alright on three. One...Two...THREE! PULL!" The medics opened the jaws of the trap and others pulled the soldier out of it. They quickly started wrapping his leg with bandages.

"There were four of them, Sir. Four of them. Did I make my country proud, Sir?...if not tell Mary...I-I..."

"We're losing him! Stay with me, John, stay with me!"

"It's too late. I'm sorry, Sir. We did what we could," said the medic in a depressed tone.

Wellington stood up and removed off his hat for a moment then walked away from the scene with the 1Lt. Wilson following.

"Finish your report," said Wellington.

"All but two of the Killen-Strait Tractors were not destroyed, but they are still missing, including the Lincoln Machine No.1 Prototype as well."

"Not the prototype! This is too much to bear! I need a stiff drink."

"Yes Sir, I think I know the solution to that. Private, go to the commander's tent and retrieve something from the top torso of the statue," 1Lt.Wisons ordered.

"Yes, Sir. I'm on it," said the Private, running toward the commander's tent.

"Oi, Commander I think I found something. You might want to look," said 2Lt. McManus.

"What is it, McManus?" Wellington grabbed the two items from him and studies them. The first one was the K.W.S. emblem and in the other hand, he held a somewhat crumpled name tag that said "Maxis".

"The K.W.S. It was them. I should have listened to Molitor's warning about them. I was a fool for not realizing what was going on sooner. But the other name has me curious. Maxis...the last I heard that name was at...Mons. Dear God..."

"The Black Wolf of Mons!" Wellington said out loud, followed by a huge explosion from his tent. The Private violently thrown out of it.

"Man down! We need a Medic here!" shouted one of the soldiers, as he rushed over to the private.

"*You come to my camp, slaughter my people, steal my prototype, my vehicles, and my brandy. You'll rue this day, Maxis and you too, Jorgensen, my archrival and now nemesis. But never doubt, I will be coming after your prized pet...eventually. Bet on that Augustus!*"

"Wilson, tell the men to pack up what they can and load our fallen into the Fowler 5B Armored Road Locomotive for transport," ordered Wellington.

"Wait, are we going to leave after all the hard work they did to retake this place?" Wilson protested.

"It will be done, Sir." 2Lt . McManus responded.

"We have been dealt a serious blow by the enemy and Operation Goliath has failed before it even got off the ground. 1Lt. Wilson, send a letter to the Canadians directing them to form up quickly to counter the German advance. We need whatever forces we can muster. They can use this camp as their launching point if they wish."

"What about the Regiment, Sir? What are we going to do?" Wilson asked.

"We'll head back to our HQ in Amiens and rethink our strategy. For now, we will let the subjects of Britain and her colonials do the work for us. We will still provide support, just not on a large scale, sadly. Today's defeat never happened. No will know of that, for the R.O.B. was never here!"

"Very good Sir, I'll get everything under way," Wilson walked away.

"The Black Wolf of Mons has finally shown its face once again. You want a war in the shadows? Well, you got one KWS..." Wellington conveyed his thoughts while looking at the name and patch then walking away.

2 weeks later...

Ragnarök base was completely active with troops coming in and out of the base, either deploying on a mission or returning from one. Planes with painted tails flew overhead on their way for recon duty and long-range artillery performing fire missions. Commander Jorgensen arrived by truck with his bodyguards, parking in the motor pool. It was unusual for an officer of great importance to arrive here, but it was discreet for Jorgensen as he did not want to alarm the troops with a fancy motorcade. He exited out of the truck through the back with his bodyguards and made way through the base. He walked by and saw a medical tent filled with KWS soldiers, bandaged up but still breathing, some were bed ridden. Next to the tent was a cadre of caskets being loaded up on the truck.

Many KWS soldiers stopped and saluted the Commander as he passed by. He made it to the HQ building of Ragnarök base and entered, ignoring the receptionist at the front. The hallways were bustling as soldiers and officers walked purposefully with or without paperwork in their hands. The rooms were filled with chatter, phones were ringing, and telegraph stations were snapping away. Jorgensen made it to the stairs and walked up. Finally, he reached the office of Maj. Reinhard but before he enters, Commander Jorgensen turned and ordered his troops to stay outside.

He found Major Reinhard standing over some maps and photos along with some other officers. He looked up to see the commander and saluted; the others followed suit.

"Men, remember what we discussed. Dismissed!" Maj. Reinhard said affirmatively. Everyone exited the office and closed the door behind them, leaving the two alone.

"Guten tag, Kommandant (Good day, Commander). I assume you received my report and the intelligence?" Maj. Reinhard asked as he took a seat.

"I did Major. Also, I came here to check the status of the base for myself while it undergoes a major offensive. So, far you're doing great job," Jorgensen complimented as he took a seat.

"Thank you, Sir. Means a lot. You should know that Sgt. Maxis and Cpl. Lothar and the rest of Grün squad are performing excellently against the British and..."

"And the Regiment of Britannia," Jorgensen finished the Major's sentence.

"Ja, I guess it's time for me to ask if this is the last colleague from your time in China, Sir," Major Reinhard inquired, but got no response from the Commander as he got up from his chair and walked to the window. He looked out at the activity outside the HQ building before he finally answered.

"Yes, but I'm afraid I may need to correct on something on that topic," started Commander Jorgensen.

"Oh dear, I actually did something wrong," said Maj. Reinhard.

"Nein, just the part where you called Wellington my colleague. More like his archrival or 'frenemy' if that's the phrase. The man is the definition of a stereotype pompous Brit that you would hear in entertainment or stories. Has a temper if things don't go his way but is a strategic tactician. Like the rest of us though has yet to show his weakness, besides some of those serving under him. When I met him and Molitor in China, he had more pride than lion and fire and the devil himself. A bragger, but a thinker in some respects. Even when he blows like volcano, the only thing that would calm him would be his brandy."

"You mean being drunk, calms him?"

"Not exactly. When angered he simply takes one shot of it and calms down. I tested that theory back in China when he tried to brag about the Royal Navy and said some rather challenging things about the High Seas Fleet. But do not think less of him, he is still a competent officer and, just like Molitor, he does not like to send his men into pointless battles...that is until now."

"Well, in report, Grün squad did take his brandy as a trophy before they drank it all," said Reinhard.

"I can imagine him angry right about now. Anyway, now that makes three enemy commanders for the Triple Entente and only one of us for the Central Powers. We'll have to tread carefully with both enemies and where they operate, regardless of what they do, we'll be there to greet them or the other way around," Commander Jorgensen finished.

"Rightly so, Sir. Have you considered my request in my reports?"

"About keeping Grün together and forming a ' Task Force' as you called it?"

"Yes, Sir!" Maj. Reinhard anticipates an answer.

"I gave it some thought but I'll have to decline since this requires more thought put into it. I am not suggesting giving up but come up with something better than one group of our elites while we already have a Battalions worth."

"Of course, Sir. I will get right on that. But what of Grün squad?"

"You will have to disband them when the job here is done. Ltc. Steinmetz wants a small volunteer force for an assignment he is currently investigating with the rest of the platoon on Entente shipments. I know there is a fine line between soldiers and spies, but sometimes they have worked together to accomplish what needs to be done. Pick anyone from the Grün squad you feel comfortable with and leave the rest for their redeployments or to simply return home for rest after fighting two weeks here. That is all, Major. I'll be going now. Bis zum nächsten Mal mein Freund (Until next time my friend)." Jorgensen walked out and closed the door behind him.

Reinhard leaned back in his chair, defeated, but instead of moping, he got to work. He pulled out the combat records of certain groups and squads that were currently operating around Ragnarök base. Then the list of names for each squad.

"He's right, I shouldn't give up. I just need to do a little bit better. In terms of how to properly set it up and...to hell with it, I'll just send over the same copy but with more additions and more thought put into it. Now for the lucky four going to help Geist..." Reinhard thought as he looked over the names.

The Second Battle of Ypres was the first battle where a large-scale gas attack was organized and used to great effect. Weakening Entente lines had devastating effects and soon turned into yet another bloody battle where the British would withdraw just three miles closer to Ypres by the middle of May. Even so, both sides suffered for little, alas, this was a modern war.

With all four pieces were now set: the Kaiserliche Waffen Spezialisten Battalion (K.W.S.), the Imperskiy

Tayna Brigada (I.T.B.), the Division Spéciale Hasardeux (the Special Hazard Division or S.H.D.), and the Regiment of Britannia (R.O.B.). With these elite units now revealed, the real and bloody war in the shadows can begin.

CHAPTER 22

THE SHIP

"It is the most important to attract neutral shipping to our shores in the hope especially of embroiling the U.S. with Germany." –Winston Churchill

May 7th, 1915, somewhere in the Atlantic Ocean

In the corridors of U-boat 20, lighting was limited and the air was hot and humid. The smell of fumes and constant humming of the diesel engines running sounded a peculiar ocean noise that they all heard while the submarine was submerged.

"How did you let this happen to yourself? First, we got a special order from Major Reinhard regarding the Geist platoon on special assignment. Then we found ourselves sitting in a U-Boot that has horrid conditions similar to the trenches. I would take fighting the R.O.B, with the sarge than this or maybe waste that cute receptionist's time back at Valhalla base...yeah," Fisher thought as he leaned back, trying to make himself comfortable.

"Hey Fisch(fish)!" Graf calls out, as he wiped the sweat from his brow.

"For the last time Graf, stop calling me fish!" Fischer retorted as he sat up straight.

"I'll keep calling you that since this is my form of entertainment in this boring assignment. After all, you had to drag us to the middle of the damned Atlantic!"

"Come on Graf, it's not that bad. I mean it's a first for me to be inside a sub. Though I think definitely, now, I hate it," said Kraus as he tried to make himself comfortable against the metal walls of the sub.

"Yeah, Kraus, but think about it like this. While we waste away in this sub our buddies, including our newest, Maxis and Lothar, are out there fighting and achieving victory for the Battalion. We are missing out on the continuing story of the Black Wolf of Mons, Kraus." Graf said to Kraus whose eyes are wide open.

"Okay, this your fault, Fisch (Fish)," Kraus immediately turned against Fischer.

Fischer rolled his eyes as he returned to his thoughts. *"Our mission was supposed to be simple, they said. We are to investigate certain civilian shipping that may contain war contraband. So far nothing aside from a few merchant ships that were sunk before our arrival. We missed, however, a cruiser that alluded us by doing a zig-zag evasive course at top speed. I would like to reenact boarding an enemy vessel like old-timers would tell us about when we were children. So much for that. Now I have two of my own against me. What a world."*

"Hey guys, we got something. Quit picking on the Fisch and let's go!" Kruger strode in bearing the news with a smile. Annoyed, Fischer looked at him while the other two seemed happy as they got up; soon Fischer followed.

The crew inside shouted to one another as the procedure to surface commenced. A sudden shift could be felt outside as the U-boat broke the surface then steadied itself on the water's surface. The small hatch opened and out came four German soldiers as they climbed onto the top part of the sub, near the deck gun. Fischer, Graf, Kraus, and Kruger felt the breeze, the smell of the ocean, and sun bearing down on them.

Smiles were all around but that quickly changed when they spotted the ship. The U-boat's captain came climbing up and spoke.

"That's the ship we're looking for. It seems the captain hasn't heeded the Royal Navy nor our own Embassy's warning in America about avoiding war zones. Now before you four boarded my sub, I had already sunk a few merchant ships. This time is different because you four are going to board that ship! Find anything relating to the enemy contraband. If there is nothing, then we leave it alone but, if there is something illegal on board, then we give a warning, let everyone exit the ship, and then we sink it. Nothing can be simpler than that and..." The captain paused as the loud thumping of someone rushing up the sub's ladder.

"Captain!" a sailor interrupts, as he climbed up the ladder.

"What is it?" the captain asked.

"Sir, it's from the Ocean liner. They just sent a message to us via telegraph! It reads…" 'The captain wishes to speak with you. STOP. Come aboard in the starboard side. STOP. We will lower our speed. STOP.'"

After the sailor finished, the four K.W.S. soldiers wore looks of suspicion. The captain headed back inside the U-boat to give the order to come alongside the Ocean Liner.

"How did they spot us that quickly?" Kraus asked.

"Over there! Crow's nest, though I can see only one sailor at the top. No one else has spotted us, not even the civilians," Kruger answered Kraus.

"I still don't get why we should even be boarding. This type of job is more fitting for the Imperial Marines or Sailors," said Graf.

"True, Graf, but we got a job to do. Just keep that mad dog tight on the leash unless told otherwise. We wouldn't want the hund (dog) start biting people for no reason," said Fischer, joking with Graf.

"Ja, Ja, poke fun, why don't you? It's not my fault I'm itching for fight, Mr. Squad Leader who is only a Private First Class," Graf retorted, poking at Fischer's rank.

"At least I'm one grade ahead of you, brawns for brains," Fischer bantered with sarcasm.

The two were staring at each other, almost ready to duke it out before Kruger and Kraus separated them.

"I think we should focus on the matter at hand or… sea, rather than this. Right, Gentlemen?" said Kraus as he pulled Graf away.

"Yeah, I'm sure the sarge would do something like this. Also, we are approaching the boat now," said Kruger, gently pushing Fischer away.

The two looked away and both took a deep breath to cool off. The U-boat pulled up to the Ocean liner. The four could hear a small announcement from the ship.

"If you look to port or the left side of the ship, there should be whales about to surface." The thumping of footsteps of passengers all rushing to the port side could be heard while the sailors on the ship rushed over to drop the rope ladder starboard. The U-Boat captain emerged from the hatch once again.

"Listen up Soldaten (Soldiers), we're going to keep the sub at a safe distance while you four investigate. Be alert and stay alive. You never know when it comes to these Americans or Brits. We'll keep a watch through periscope. Good luck," said the Captain as he climbed down again and closed the hatch.

Everyone flips the safety off their pistols and checks their ammo. Kruger was armed with the Jäger M1914 pistol, Kraus had a Langenham Model FL M1914 pistol, Graf had two Becker & Hollander (B&H) Beholla M1915 pistols, and finally Fischer had the Mauser Nickle M1915 with .45 ACP ammo.

Fischer made sure the vest pocket camera he had hidden in his bread bag was secured before he started climbing up the ladder. The ladder moved a bit, but Graf kept it secured while everyone went up before going last. Fischer made it onto the deck, pistol drawn on the sailors who reacted with hands up. Kraus, Kruger and

Graf boarded quickly with their weapons at the ready. They checked their area.

"Deck clear. Alright men, lower your weapons, but stay alert," directed Fischer with firm tone. The sailors lowered their hands in relief as Fischer approached them and spoke.

"Either bring the captain to us or take us to him. I don't care, just as along we're not seen by your passengers," Fischer demanded.

"Yeah, make it snappy, heh," Graf added.

"Sure, sure, just follows us," a sailor responded. The second sailor led the way quickly, taking a different route away from the passengers watching the portside. After going through the corridors of the ship then up the steps to the bridge, they saw the captain of the ship himself with the view of the sea behind him.

"'Ello there, I believe you may have the wrong ship. We're just an Ocean Liner. Nothing else. I thought I might as well get to the point," said Captain Turner. Fischer and others looked at each other with more suspicion.

"Oh sure, we believe the word of the captain who just happened to call us up just to say that. Jokes aside, I'll be the one whether your statement holds true," Fischer informed him with a firm tone and his arms crossed.

"I'm telling you Germans the truth. Why must you insist I would be saying otherwise?" Captain Turner asked.

"Because I know how to play cards and I know a bluff when I hear it. We're searching the lower decks. If your words hold true, then an apology would be in order if not, then we'll make sure the passengers leave the ship," commented Fischer, not changing his expression or movement. The captain looked worried as he turned away from them.

"Jungs (Boys), let's check below where the cargo is. Sailor, take us to the lowest decks to the cargo holds," Fischer commanded, and the sailor obeyed out of fear.

"This is preposterous! You can't just..."

"Captain, if I recall, you invited us here to have a word and we just did that. You should have honored the German Embassy's warning before you left port. Also, you're in warring waters so..." Kraus shrugged his shoulder after interrupting the captain and stating the obvious.

The squad followed the sailor deep within the ship. The hallways and corridors were quiet except for the low hum of engines, the sound of sea outside, and the soft steps of the four K.W.S. soldiers following a nervous sailor.

When they were about to enter the lowest deck, Graf stopped for a moment noticing an interesting sight. In the hallway was a machine with bright red and white colors with a logo on the front. The squad not too far ahead and Graf approached the strange machine. It was sitting on a small table, a barrel cut in half professionally with a coin-based operating system on top that kept the latch closed tight. The front bore the name its creator, Geo S. Cobb.

"Coc-a...Cola? I heard about these! They're supposed to be very good and sweet. Oh yeah, a sweet, carbonated beverage. Hmm, it's only a...nickel or was it five...cents, whatever the Americans would call it. A bit much...but I wonder if it takes a mark?" As Graf thought of the idea, he

took out some spare change, found a coin and dropped it into the slot. Suddenly the click of the lock, and Graf grabbed hold of the latch and opened it. Inside were twelve glass bottles of Coca Cola beverages.

"Süss (Sweet)!" Graf excitedly said.

"GRAF! Where did you go?" Kraus called out, causing Graf to pause as he was about to reach in.

Back with Fischer's squad, they descended the steps until they reached a small area where there were signs pointing in different directions. One pointed toward the engine room and the other the cargo hold. The sailor dared not go any further as he pointed toward the large bullhead door and then exited up the steps.

Fischer doesn't say a word but he points out certain spots with his hand like and the squad responded immediately. Kruger and Kraus ready their pistols as they position themselves on both sides of the door while Fischer groans as he wonders where their fourth member is. The sound of rushing footsteps is heard coming down the steps and Fischer turns to see Graf, holding one of his B&H Beholla pistols on his right and a glass soda bottle on his left.

"Really? You lagged behind just for a beer?" Fischer asked as he stares at the bottle.

"It's not beer, Fisch. It's a soda pop!" Graf whispered as he took another drink of it while getting behind the bulkhead.

"Oh really?" Fischer said, swiping it from Graf and gulping down what was left, then handing it back to him. Everyone was in shock.

"Why you...never mind," Graf looked away and tossed the bottle aside.

"Well, that's surprising. I thought you would want to rip my head off for that. Good drink by the way," Fischer commented and burped loudly

"Yeah well...you know what? It doesn't matter, Fischer."

"Hiding something, Graf?" asked Kraus.

"Nein, let's open this. What should we expect?" Graf asked Fischer as he opened the door. Fischer walked by and answered.

"Oh, I shouldn't expect much. Probably nothing but luggage, some items of importance, or just finding an automobile with a young unmarried couple having much more fun than they should have. But I expect nothing less than a...Ach Scheiße (Oh Fuck)," Fischer paused after stepping through the door.

Twenty feet in front of him were small bands of soldiers doing small tasks around wooden crates with different markings. They spotted artillery pieces that were strapped down, and a few vehicles. Upon closer observation the soldiers wore a mix of uniforms. One wore dark blue attire with a sailor cap with the marking of the US Navy. Next to him, was another wearing an olive drab green uniform and on his hat had the pin of the USMC. Another soldier wore a khaki brown uniform with the Montana peak hat of the US Army.

"Hey careful with the shipment. Don't want those Brits to complain!" said the American soldier with a Brooklyn accent.

The most bothersome of all to Fischer was that they all had one thing in common. There was patch on their upper sleeves, yet he could not tell what it looked like. His heart started to race as he noticed that there was group of those men in front of him playing a game of cards.

"Hey, nobody is supposed to...be...here..." the American soldier spoke as he slowly paused and turned to see four unknown German soldiers at the door. The man across from him glanced up, surprised as well.. Another dropped his cigarette and his deck of cards. Quickly everyone else noticed them, their faces registering shock as the two parties stared at one another awkwardly.

"Uh...Guten Tag (Good day), Yanks?" Fischer uttered the words with uncertainty.

"We've been made, boys!" screamed a soldier with country western accent.

"Kill'em!" shouted another with a southern drawl.

Weapons flew into sight as they all revealed their pistols, bolt action rifles, shotguns, and even some self-loading rifles. As chaos erupted, Fischer shouted, "In Deckung gehen (Take cover)!" and fired his Mauser Nickle pistol, killing two soldiers in front, while the third American soldier knocked the table to its side and used it for cover.

Kruger, Kraus, and Graf rushed through the door, guns blazing as they took cover behind the stacked crates with Fischer. Bullets were flying as snaps and cracks were heard. The American soldiers ran for cover as well, after a few of them sustained wounds.

"I think you started a war with America, Fischer!" said Kraus, peaking out quickly to get a shot off from behind a crate.

"Nein! America started a war with us and we're going to end it here!" Fischer responded, firing another shot from cover before reloading.

"I think...we just discovered something; they don't want us to live and talk about it. Right now, I'm out of my element here. I'm a sniper, not a close quarter combatant," said Kruger, as he scored a headshot then ducking as wood chips started raining around from the crate.

"We'd better find some better weapons and soon!" said Kraus, as he moved to new cover.

The skirmish began to take its toll as more soldiers garnered casualties while the K.W.S. squad slowly burned through their pistol ammo. The Americans were in the same situation, their ranks slowly diminishing as they tried to treat their wounds with no medic.

"Keep firing on them, men!" screamed a U.S. Marine.

"Those sons of bitches don't want to die! Stubborn bastards!" a U.S. sailor called out, loading his Krag-Jorgensen rifle.

"What matters, boys, is that we defend the cargo! If they leave, we're sunk," shouted a U.S. Army soldier as he fired his Springfield M1903.

"Damn it all, it's time we show the Huns what America's teeth looks like! Get ready to rush'em and leave none to live!" an Army officer ordered. A few of them read-ied themselves as they waited for the signal. The officer blew the whistle and several charged in screaming with some of Marines shouting "Oorah!" as they moved.

"Here they come! Here comes the U.S. Military with donations!" said Fischer, as he readied his knife.

The moment the gun barrel stuck out, Fischer grabbed it and pulled in the soldier. He threw him to the wall of the large crate then thrust his knife into his throat then slashed it across. He snatched the Remington Model 8 self-loading rifle with an extended detachable magazine from the fallen soldier.

"I've never used a Selbstlader (self-loader) before; guess there's first for everything!" Fischer thought as he quickly loaded the rifle. The others saw what he did and immediately stood fast.

Kraus was second as he pulled out his Boot knife. The moment he saw a barrel peer from the edge of the crate, he quickly grabbed hold, lifted it up, and moved in, plunging his knife into the soldier's neck then pulling him out of sight of the others. Now armed with the Winchester M1907 SL with a ten round magazine and ammo, he loaded it but couldn't find the charging handle or bolt handle.

"Where is it...wait, is it at the end?" Kraus pushed down the plunger at the end of the rifle, cocking it, now ready for action. "Interesting rifle," breathed Kraus as he fired the rifle.

Graf got low and waited. The same fate would befall another unlucky soldier as he spotted the barrel across from the top, bayonet fixed. He too grabbed, pulled, then shot the soldier straight in the head, blood splattering all over him. The weapon he held was a Lee Navy bolt action rifle.

"Hey Kruger! I have a present for you!" Graf tossed the rifle to Kruger, then the ammo.

"That's more like it," He said with a devious smile then immediately started pulling impeccable shots as fast as he could.

Graf waited. This time he took a prybar from the floor. A Marine jumped over the crate and swung his shotgun around, but was met with a loud clang as the prybar knocked the shotgun to the ground. Then Graf fired with his pistol before finishing him off with one hack to the neck.

"Browning Auto 5 shotgun...very nice. And here's the ammo," Graf remarked, quickly taking the shotgun bandolier.

The attackers ceased their assault and went to find cover, continuing to lay down the fire. The squad stoped firing and gathered behind an automobile and crouched low.

"Okay, now we take a page out the Black Wolf of Mons strategy book," said Fischer as he reloaded.

"You mean do what we did with the R.O.B and at Ypres?" Graf questioned.

"Ja, except the part where you almost got killed by a Gurka," Kruger said, loading his rifle.

"At least we'll be on the offensive. I can't endure much more of this suppressing fire," complained Kraus as he rubbed his ear.

"We move when I throw these Mills bombs. Bereit (Ready)?" Fischer asked as he cocked his rifle. Everyone nodded, a stern look giving their answer. Fischer pulled the pin on the two Mills bombs and hurled them over the car.

"Shit, Grenade!" shouted an American soldier.

"Take cover!" yelled another.

The moment the grenades went off three rushed out of cover while Kruger stayed behind providing sniper support and aiming for the soldiers on the catwalk. The trio dodged through the crates, surprising every soldier they saw before pulling their triggers.

Graf unleashed his full fury using his shotgun, pistols, and prybar. Kraus coordinated with Fischer, clearing every corner in the little maze of boxes and crates, while Kruger already delt with the catwalk sharpshooters and climbed on top of the crates for higher advantage.

The front line quickly changed as the K.W.S. soldiers were now advancing like never before, forcing the combined U.S. forces to slowly fall back. One of the soldiers ran to the officer amidst the explosions, screams, and bullets hitting everything in sight.

"Doggone it! They're kicking our ass, Sir!" he said, as he ducked down behind a metal crate.

"I can see that, Private! This was supposed to be a simple mission!" As the Officer was speaking, he witnessed a small group of soldiers get cut down moments before a perfectly timed grenade wiped them all out and thrust them back violently.

"Son, it's time to abort this mission. Get over to the engine and place the explosives," the officer ordered, his voice somber.

"What? Sir, you can't be…"

"Now, Private!"

The soldier saluted and ran off while the officer holstered his revolver and dashed for the telegraph room. He made it, as more servicemen are getting mopped up by incoming K.W.S. Forces. He put on the headphones and started keying the message.

"Liberty to Washington, the sled is broken Stop

Repeat, the sled is broken Stop

Small enemy forces attacking Stop

Commencing Emergency Plan Rocket's Red glareeeeeeeee…"

The message was incomplete as the officer was face-down, dead and bleeding after getting shot in the head by Kruger. Fischer broke into the telegraph office and found the scene.

"Whoever he was transmitting to, I hope it wasn't a full message. Otherwise…"

"Verdammt (Damn), that cola was good!" Fischer burped as he rushed back outside and returned to the action.

"Them bastards, ripping us apart! Get the MGs going, men!" one sailor calls out as two soldiers rush in carrying Colt-Browning M1895 machine gun on a tripod. Another soldier jumped behind a Maxim M1904 MG on carriage mount.

"Get the potato digger set up and fill'em full of lead!" shouted a Marine.

The machine guns opened fire, forcing Kraus and Fischer to take cover behind another automobile. Graf moved on the flank while Kruger goes prone and takes aim. At the same time, Graf unloaded his shotgun on the MG crew while Kruger sniped at the HMG user.

"This is hopeless! RETREAT!"

"Let's get out of here boys!"

The American soldiers went into a full retreat. Several of them survived the ordeal as they ran through the metal bulk door on other side of the cargo hold and closed it behind them with a loud bang. Fischer, Kraus, and Graf checked the area while Kruger started to climb down.

"Alles klar (All clear). No sign of any threats," said Kraus as he knelt down for a breather.

"Should we pursue them? I'm still not done with them, after all that!" Graf expressed his frustration, his shotgun was still smoking from the barrel and his prybar dripping red.

"Leave them. We've got to check this place out. See why they were hellbent on protecting this place and wanting us dead. Search their bodies for intel. I'm going on a photography spree," directed Fischer as he pulled out his vest pocket camera. The squad split up and started looking. Fischer surveyed the area, taking photos of the bodies of fallen American soldiers, weapons, and even the cargo.

"Geeze, these Yankees fought hard. All for what exactly?" Graf asked as he used the prybar to open a crate labeled British .303.

"Doing something completely illegal like supplying the Triple Entente. So much for American neutrality!"

Kraus exclaimed, as he cut a piece of fabric off the dead American's uniform.

"Well, they could simply be protecting the cargo. Remember the U.S. is neutral and are making money off this war since they are the biggest industrialized nation in the Americas." said Kruger as looked at a Dodge scout car and the armored Model T trucks.

"Sorry to say this Kruger, but that statement became invalid when they shot at us and even admitted their intent," remarked Graf as he picked up a Winchester M1915 lever rifle.

While the three debated amongst themselves, Fischer was focused on photographing the aftermath. Corpses were strewn about the deck of the cargo hold, some missing limbs. He entered the telegraph room again. He walked over to the desk where the U.S. officer had died, his hand still on the telegraph key. Fischer opened a drawer and found a file.

"Hallo (Hello), what is this?" Fischer muttered to himself as he picked it up and opened it. The front had the stamp of the U.S. Military and the word "Confidential" stamped in red. He reads it out loud.

"By the approval of the Department of War and signed by the President. The creation of this unit has been approved and the request to send said unit to Europe on a training mission has been granted under the supervision of Brigadier General Lazlow and Commander Wellington of the Regiment Of Britannia (once he is informed upon arrival) as per the American Corporation Act of 1871.

The importance of this training mission is to have a better understanding of this new conflict raging in Europe and how to best be prepared for it. A contingency has been placed in case of an interception on the RMS Lusitania. Discretion is key to this success. Let no one know of our presence, for this is an order from the Department of War and the President. More details regarding the contingent of the troops, training, and expected training will follow"

Fischer was shocked by what he read and as he turned the pages, more details were revealed.

"These boys were trained how to use the weapons we used against them. This is bigger than we anticipated, he thought looking over the orders."

Fischer kept reading pages of the files but eventually remembered what his mission was, and quickly placed the files on the table. He took pictures of each page then stashed the file, along with the camera, in his bread bag and rucksack. Then he rejoined the other three who now just waiting and talking.

"So how many were there that we just faced?" Kraus asked as he looks at a dead serviceman.

"Forty. The remaining ten escaped when they knew the battle had been decided. I would know since I was on top of the stacked crates," said Kruger, cradling his rifle.

"That many? I didn't even notice," Said Graf as he accidently stepped on a hand.

"Yeah, I mean, I thought these guys would be better trained. Similar to a regular Tommy or us even," stated Kraus as he picked up a S&W .38 revolver.

"You're leaving too much to assumption. They would be trained, but that doesn't mean they know how to fight until they survive their first battle. Look at us for example, we came from Prussian military tradition and training that taught us to be disciplined and ready for the worst; then the K.W.S. battalion trained us even further. Even for someone like me who lived in Wurttemberg, despite that I was born in Brandenberg, I have learned a lot with the K.W.S." Kruger said as he rests his rifle.

"Same here. I was born there but moved to Saxony," added Kraus.

"Same, but lived in the Rhineland," Graf seconded.

"I'm saying is that these...boys were not ready for us. After I took care of the shooters on the catwalk and provided support, I witnessed the major difference. Kraus, you and Fischer were clearing and sweeping the corner and corridors as if you were in a trench with perfect coordination, covering each other's backs. Graf, even though I had to save your sorry butt multiple times, you still went all out like a real Verrückte Hund (Mad dog) more so than at the R.O.B. base camp or at Ypres, showing that 'Trench Trooper Training' at its full potential. If the Sarge or the Mighty Lothar, heh, were here, those two would be extremely impressed with how we performed." Everyone nodded in agreement with small grins while Kruger continued.

"While we had teamwork and our elite training, these poor saps didn't think, besides attacking and attacking with more gusto. No coordination when they bunched up behind cover. They may have fought hard, but they died hard. They were not ready for a fight in this new conflict nor against hardened Kaiserliche Elites (Imperial Elites)." Everyone felt proud of what Kruger had said but they were still baffled at the number of dead in one place as the smell of copper began to permeate the air.

"Hmph, so we stepped into the belly of the beast and came out on top. I'll remember," said Kraus with pride in his tone. Fischer walked out of the office and back to the group.

"Actually Kraus, what we stepped in is the total conspiracy involving the American eagle and their secret involvement in this war. Ltc. Steinmetz would want to hear about this and--" Fischer was interrupted.

Suddenly a large fiery explosion erupted from the walls of the ship's cargo hold, knocking everyone off their feet. Fischer hit the deck hard, then water started flowing like a waterfall. Kraus, Graf, and Kruger slowly got back on their feet.

CHAPTER 23

ABANDON SHIP

"Scheiße (Shit)! What the hell happened?!" Graf called out, as water rushed past his boots.

"Did our own U-Boat fire a torpedo before we even got off the ship?!" Kraus asked aloud before water splashed in his face.

"Worry about it later! Water is coming in fast! We need to leave, now!" Kruger frantically said. Graf rushed over to Fischer.

"Come on, get on your feet, spaßvoge (Joker), I got you buddy. Wir gehen jetzt (We're leaving now)!" Graf helped Fischer up.

"Follow me!" Kruger signaled with a wave as he led the way out of the cargo hold.

They went back through the entrance where they had come from, then up the steps. The ship started to creak and tilt to the starboard side. As the squad rushed through, they heard the sound of people panicking, screaming, and a bell ringing from above.. A sailor appeared in the hallway, stunned at the sight of German troops.

"Hey, what are-"

"Move it!" Kruger shoved the sailor aside.

The sound of metal creaking worsened and a steam pipe burst, causing rivets to fly as the boat leaned further to right. The squad stumbled a bit but kept moving.

"Which way!? Which way to the upper decks!?" Kraus cried out.

"Richtig, richtig (Right, right), now straight up," Kruger responded as they headed up the stairs.

The ship was now touching the water on the starboard side as sailors shouted "Get to the mustering stations!" as they ran by. The squad made it out to the port side. They quickly grabbed onto the railing and climbed over.

"Where the hell is that sub!? They didn't leave us?!" Graf cried out in anger.

"This isn't good. We'll have to jump!" said Kraus as he looked down.

"I can't! Not with the intel and camera on me. They will get destroyed if sea water touches them," Fischer declared with a worried look as he gripped the railing.

"Verdammt (Damn it)!" Kraus cried in defeat.

Along the port side of the ship the U-Boat emerged and the hatch quickly opened. The captain popped out with the grappling hook in hand and threw it hard, latching it onto the rails where the squad was now hanging.

"EILE(HURRY)! CLIMB DOWN!" the captain shouted.

Fischer went first. The squad held on to the hook as Kraus went second, then Kruger third. They all made it to the U-boat safely and Graf was ready to move, but a second explosion erupted, and the hook fell off the rail, back to the sub.

"Dive for it, Graf!" Fischer shouted out. Immediately Graf stood on the rails and performed a dive into the ocean. They heard a loud splash, but they lost sight of Graf. They looked frantically for their friend until he emerged out of the water, breathing hard.

"Danke Gott (Thank God) I learned to swim while skinny dipping in the Rhein River!" he said as he swam toward the boat where they helped him up. All were relieved.

"You better have good reason why you tried to sink us!" Graf barked at the captain, holding a tight grip on his uniform.

"The hell are you talking?! We didn't even launch the first tube!" he answered quickly.

"Hey, look!" Kraus called out, pointing.

The remaining American soldiers were seen diving off the sinking ship and at the same time a U.S. submarine emerged. It came and picked up the survivors, then submerged quickly and the first few rafts were deployed.

"Bastards...sunk their own ship. Not good...not good for us," said Graf as he watched the passengers jumping off the ship.

"Those poor souls did not even know what they got into," lamented Kraus, as he took off his hat and placed it on his chest.

"For now, let's get out of here. It's depressing enough seeing all those poor souls drowned," commented

Fischer as he walked away and climbed down into the sub.

The three others took their hats off in respect then headed down also as the U-boat submerged. Everyone was sitting down, contemplating what had transpired. No words were said except when Graf opened his pack and pulled out a bottle filled with soda.

"Hey, I hope this helps lighten the mood. I managed to take it all before the fight. Have some guys," Graf said and handed the first drink to Kruger then Kraus. They popped open the bottles with their knives and started drinking. Kraus drank his fill while he pulled out the piece of uniform fabric he had taken from the dead. On the front were the letters..."A.T.O.G."

"Hey Fisch, want one? I have ten more," Graf informed as he held the Coca-Cola bottle.

"Sure, just save one for when we get home," Fischer said, as he grabbed the soda pop.

A week later in the interview room at the Geist Platoon HQ building in Valhalla base Fischer sat while Ltc. Steinmetz and another Geist agent sat directly across from him with pen and paper and glass of soda beverage on ice.

"That's your report? I see. Hmm, we're going have to accept the responsibilities as a cover despite what really happened. No doubt you are upset like your friends are. Though I do thank you for this rather...addictive gift your squad gave me," said Ltc. Steinmetz crassly.

"Of course, Sir, and I'm not exactly upset that we're forced to accept the blame. This is what we signed on for and nobody will know the truth of what happened. So...what's our next mission?" Fischer inquired with a friendly smile.

Historically speaking, the RMS Lusitania did get sunk by a German U-boat, U-20. Ship personnel ignored the warnings and was cruising carelessly slow. As a result, 128 (or 124 or 114, depending on the source), Americans died, and from the two thousand passengers, eleven hundred ninety-eight perished. However, the ship's captain, Cpt. Turner, did survive the ordeal. This shocked the people of America even though the German Embassy in New York had given an official warning about sailing through a warzone. Regardless, anger amongst the American people raged, but President Wilson kept America neutral for the time being. The German government did send an apology, still the American people were angered by the event despite forgetting that a major war was going on.

The event regarding Lusitania can be best described as conflicted. In times of war, the warring nations do what they can to warn other neutral nations' citizens when they are embarking on a trip through contested waters. Information is provided so that those who are willing to take the risk may do so, even if it means costing them their lives in the cold waters of the Atlantic. However, others would have alternative motives, whether it is something political or a false excuse to have a reason to go to war. Perhaps with money or reason to discriminate against a certain group of people, a country would consider it a thorn in their side; possibly through anti-sentiment or discrimination. War is an unforgiving and hellish business and as the old saying goes, "Truth becomes the first casualty of war."

CHAPTER 24

FORTEZZA DI MONTAGNA

May 22, 1915, Trentino near the Italian Alps

"A lot of things have happened in the past two weeks. Our celebration during Operation Grüner tag was cut short when we heard our forces were countered by the Canadians. Without a feeling of a buzz, we geared up and went back into the field in the middle of the night where we met them...the result was a significant development. Throughout the night we fought with gusto to provide our forces with time to regroup and reposition themselves while we were in the thick of it. We made the Canadians pay for every inch of ground in ten pints of blood or un-til we burned through our ammo and had to retreat. The squad performed very well during that instant action. The next day was different for us. We met the Canadians again but, this time attacking them at St. Julien. We performed the same tactic, marching with our prototype gas masks on. However, the enemy wasn't expecting us in the gas, the

results were quite favorable with the combined might of the imperial army behind us; we managed to drive them back causing them serious damage.

The 25th of April would bring something new for us as we faced the Crown's colonial troops...the Indians and Gurkhas; they marched into the conflict with their nations pride on their shoulders and their turbans on top of their heads (Indians). They were easy targets for Kruger and the other rifle men. The battle was peculiar for me because they came charging at us while holding yellow flags to tell their artillery spotters their exact positions and not to shoot. We held the line steady even as our snipers and artillery had a field day. I and the assault team moved into the fray and ended up in a very bloody melee with them.

They fought aggressively while we tried to match them with our sharpened skills and even sharper bayonets. Even Graf's Trench trooper training gave him a run for his money and damn nearly got him killed, if it wasn't for Lothar who saved him from getting stabbed. I swear, I saw Lothar literally kill that one with one blow to the temple while wearing brass knuckles for the first time. Seeing death floating above our heads, I made the call to tactically withdraw either with our artillery or when the British started hitting our positions with shells providing cover for us. We remained in the area until the squad was pulled out...in the end getting nothing more than scrapes, bruises, and bullet grazes or two. We were disbanded much to the dismay of Major Reinhard though our combat readiness was higher than any other squad operating in the area. They were all sent away on different assignments afterwards.

In my honest opinion, I really enjoyed my time with them, aside from getting used to Brandt or having to discipline him when he tried or said anything. Me and Lothar were shipped back to Valhalla Base for some rest before our next assignment, but the next thing we knew we were back at the E.I.T.C. building training and learning the basics of a Mountaineer or alpine trooper. It was tough but we made it through thus being sent to our new base in Trentino, Austria-Hungary; the base's name was Heimdall Base. Ironic really, because it was located on a tall flat mountain top overlooking the borders. On a last note, still held on to the blue scarf, it's become rather...fitting."

"Hey, Maxis. Commander Jorgensen is coming to give us our mission," Lothar shoved and whispered.

"Oh, right." Maxis responded as he put his journal away in his rucksack. Commander Jorgensen strode into the room with an officer following behind him. The room dimmed and a projector turned on revealing a blank white screen.

"It's good to see you boys again. Welcome to Heimdall Base, our overwatch in the mountains. Next to me is the commanding officer of this base, Major Weiss. Private, start the briefing," said Commander Jorgensen, as an image and a title appeared on the screen.

"Gentlemen, you will commence Operation Vesuvius. Geist platoon agents came back with damning intel. We learned that Italy will declare war on Austria-Hungary soon. Italy took notice of the Habsburg failures of the past few months and has convinced our old Triple Alliance friend to think they can switch sides and fight for the Triple Entente. Despite the Italians' effort to offer a resolution for the Habsburgs to relinquish some territory, but not that the Austrian hierarchy would be smart enough to say "yes", which leads us to this. Next slide."

An image of the mountain range is shown though with black smoke appearing over one of the mountains.

"A recon plane detachment from the Blue Tails has reported strange occurrences in the Italian Alps. After a flyby they noticed smoke emerging from the horizon. At first, they thought it could be nothing, until they came in for a closer look and saw this. Next slide."

The image revealed a tall mountain peak, but something was different indeed.

"Last I checked, mountains don't have a fortress and mountain guns on the side of them. There was also smoke coming out of pipes as if there was a factory or something built inside, not to mention a wide dirt road leading to what appears to be an entrance to the mountain. The last thing they reported was that they saw a window panel near the top. Perhaps someone's office, and that matters. Next slide."

The next slide showed a map of the pathways in the area.

"I'll leave the explanation of your objectives to Major Weiss. I need to go back to Valhalla. Goodluck on your mission men, lebewohl (farewell)," bid Commander Jorgensen as he exited the briefing room.

"Thank you, Commander. Men, if this place is a factory or a new type of fortress then the mission is the same, destroy it. You'll be deployed to this area here near the Italian border and from there you will link up with one of our alpine troopers, Pvt. Jonas Steiner. He will lead you through a secret passage. There you will traverse high and low through the Alps until you reach your current objective. Infiltrate the enemy base, collect intel, and destroy it. Since they will declare war on Austria-Hungary and not with us, you must remain incognito to the enemy. Thus, your winter coats will not have any German markings. The duration should take about a day. We know of both of your reputations and we hope you'll live up to them. Any questions?" asked Major Weiss with a Bavarian accent as he walked in front of the screen.

"What about my pickelhaube wouldn't that raise suspicion?" Maxis asked.

"Nein, the Austro-Hungarians have a similar helmet design like ours. The Italians will be none the wiser."

"Will the mess hall be serving any fine Italian cuisine?" quipped Lothar.

"How is that related to your mission, Corporal?" The Major looked at Lothar with annoyance.

"Excuse the corporal here, Major. He hasn't been eating anything but rations during E.I.T.C. training for weeks," Maxis interjected respectfully.

"Hmph...anyway go to the quartermaster to retrieve your climbing gear and report to the truck when you are ready to embark on your mission. Dismissed!" Major Weiss finished.

Maxis and Lothar got up, saluted, and walked toward the door. They entered the hallway, but before they continued any further Maxis stopped Lothar for a moment.

"Fine Italian cuisine, really?"

"Come on, Maxis. I've been eating those rations for weeks now. I couldn't help myself but to ask. Cut me some slack," Lothar said, looking down.

"*Sigh*...I understand what you mean. Tell you what, if we finish this mission quickly, I'll bet we can find an Italian restaurant in Selzen," Maxis said with a cheery look.

"Don't get my hopes up, Max."

"No really. I read on the bulletin board in Valhalla base there was one opening in Selzen."

"You're sure? Alright then, I'll suffer a little longer on these canned rations." Lothar raised his head.

"That's the spirit," said Maxis and patted Lothar's back.

The duo moved on until they reached the door. They opened it only to be met with a cold strong wind blowing in their faces. Around them was a familiar sight but much different background. The base was filled with lodges, tents, and metal huts. Soldiers were putting up more tents while others hauled in military equipment by horse drawn wagons and trucks. There was a platoon of K.W.S. soldiers marching in formation that passed by the HQ building, then another came by, double-timing it and singing a cadence with Feldwebel (Sergeant) moving beside them. The cadence was strongly lead by the Feldwebel fast and steady and each time he finished a verse, a strong "Hurra!" was shouted from the platoon.

"We are marching into battle and give a..."

"HURRA"

"We march in front of the Kaiser and give a..."

"HURRA!"

"We fight for our homeland (taps 3x) ...we're going into combat (taps 3x) ...Marching pass the Mädchen (girls) and give a..."

"HURRA!"

"We're the K.W.S. Battalion and we shout out..."

"HURRA!"

"The Commander stands and watches, while we give a..."

"HURRA!"

"Princess Victoria, the Colonel of the Hussar, she stands there, and she praises while we give a..."

"HURRA!"

"We march till the wars end (taps 3x) ...We march till it's over (taps 3x)."

The platoon marched away, their cadence sounding more distant. Another cold breeze blows in.

"Brrrr, why on earth did they place the new base on top of a flat mountain? The cold wind is too much, downright dreadful," complained Lothar, sounding annoyed.

"It's funny really, even though we are used to the winters in Germany, we have trouble adapting to this new environment. It is very different than fighting in the woods or the trenches. The only challenge here is conquering the high cliffs of Italy. And the mountain sickness," pondered Maxis in his thoughts.

They continued toward the quartermaster's tent, passing by rows of armored cars, artillery, machine guns, and even another platoon of soldiers performing P.T. (Physical Training). The base was quite busy preparing for the call to action as they waited for Italy's declaration of war.

The two managed to find the quartermaster after searching around the encampment. Maxis and Lothar entered and found none other than Hugo Heinrich sitting at his desk reading a book. He immediately jumped to his feet after noticing the duo standing there in front of him.

"Well, if it isn't the eccentric gun enthusiast Quartermaster Heinrich who honors us with his presences," said Lothar with sarcasm, then bowed.

"Quite the honorary title you gave me Corporal, though I doubt you are here for small talk or flattery. Nein, you are here for your weapons and gear since you have a mission, ja?" asked Heinrich with a smile, pointing toward his wares.

"You are on the ball; we'll have the usuals including some hiking gear as well," said Maxis.

"Well, good. It's been a while Sergeant, not since that whole Russian tricycle tank event or whatever you called it. I see you kept the blue scarf that you were given by my protégé. It suits you. Nice chit-chat. Now let's get down to business, shall we?" said Heinrich as he walked around the corner of a stack of crates. He returned while wheeling a cart with two crates on it.

"Alright, one crate for Cpl. Lothar. It contains a Luger P08 carbine, your standard infantry gear, hiking gear, scabbard knife, balaclava mask to keep your face warm, stick grenades, and a special package I'm not at liberty to say because it's a surprise and new to the list. Here is a Gaede stalhelm (frontal head armor). They recently approved its use for the Battalion which means added protection. Oh, before I forget, here is your winter coat since you're shivering like a skeleton."

"Thanks, Heinrich," Lothar said, relieved as he took the coat and his gear.

"Here's yours as well, Sergeant. I do have a spare wrap that you can take...I'll put it in your crate. Speaking of which, here is your loadout. A Mauser C96 scoped carbine with a cone hammer, also easy to dissemble, one sawback bayonet and scabbard knife, standard infantry gear, bandolier, three Kugel(ball) grenades, and a special package as well, along with several modified time charges shaped like jam cans and some hiking gear. The time charge is well-packed and with enough fire power to destroy a hill, so be careful with. It will start ringing when the timer is set and the fuse is lit," Heinrich finished.

"Noted. So why are we using pistol-based weapons?" Maxis asked.

"Because Sergeant, you will be tracking through the mountains and will be climbing. It's necessary to carry light. Plus, the two of you are resourceful, I've seen it before. I'm sure you will be okay."

Maxis nodded in agreement. They put on their gear and loaded their weapons. After gearing up, they thanked Heinrich and headed out of the tent, on their way to the truck. They boarded the truck and knocked twice on the back part to signal the driver. The engine came to life and off they went. None of them spoke a word to each other as they mentally prepared themselves for the mission. Lothar broke the silence.

"Hey Maxis, something's been bugging me," Lothar started as he checked gear.

"What's the matter?"

"We'll be fighting the Italians, but they used to be our ally before the war. Now they are going to war against us, or I mean, the Hapsburgs. Why?"

"Well, I think I have a simple answer to that. For starters, we were originally a defensive pact until the Habsburg's decided to go to war. The rest is history. The second is land. Since everyone wants more, even the democratic nations can't hide their contempt for it. Just look at England and France. Last, is the parliament in Italy. They think they can take on the Habsburgs due to their recent military failures and the Entente offered something they couldn't refuse. That got all the pro-Entente supporters fired up, added in with a bit anti-Austrian sentiment. Thus, here we are. Did that help?"

"*Sigh.* I still can't believe we are fighting them. It hurts a little because most of my mother's business came from Italy. They always bought her wine before the war for their restaurants and parties," said Lothar with sad tone.

"Well, from what I can speculate, they will probably end up with the short end of the stick since the Entente are trying to make a million promises to nations just to drag them into war against us. I understand how you feel though. I have nothing against the Italians, but this is war."

"Yeah..." Lothar checked his weapon again before they arrived at their destination.

The truck came to a halt and the driver honked the horn. The two exited through the back and hopped off. There in front of them is a soldier sitting on a rock wearing a brown fur coat with his grey mountaineer uniform underneath, grey pants, and an Austro-Hungarian army grey feldkappa (field cap). At his side was his weapon, a Steyr–Mannlicher M.95 Gewehr carbine with a scope. His face was partially covered, the only visible part were his blue eyes. He looked up with a serious gaze for moment, sizing up the German soldiers that stood before him. He stood up from his rock.

"Are you two the saps that will be entering the mountain path of kings?" asked Steiner, in a low tone with an Austrian accent.

"Saps?! Oh, I'll show you..."

"Hold Corporal, let me handle this. Are you the fool who will lead us through the path of kings?"

"That I am. I'm Pvt. Jonas Steiner, K.W.S. Bergsteiger und Scharfschütze Korp (Mountaineer and Sharpshooter Corp). Sgt. Maxis, I presume, and you must be Cpl. Lothar," Steiner said and rested his rifle on his shoulder.

"Yep, that's us. Though what was with the word play? They didn't brief us on code phrases," said Maxis, arms crossed.

"There wasn't any. I made it up to see which one of you would catch on. The mountain path of kings is what I named it after going through it. It is treacherous and only the experienced can traverse it. Not to mention that there are Italian Alpine patrols as well. So, are you ready to begin our mission and hike these mountains?"

"Ready!" Maxis and Lothar both said.

"Alright, I'll recite the basics. Watch your step. Be sure to take deep breaths for the air will become thinner as we go up. We'll take breaks as we increase altitude, that's it. I must assume they covered everything else in your training. I'll lead the way and keep a look out for snipers or patrols. Let's not waste any time, so don't lag behind." Steiner finished as he started marching.

The group moved onto the path. Their journey at first was long and easy until they reached a dead end; then Steiner began climbing quickly. Maxis and Lothar followed using their climbing gear. The weight of their equipment weighed on them as gravity took its effect.

Using their upper body strength as they climbed and eventually reached a cliffside after thirty minutes. Maxis and Lothar felt their bodies ache and their hearts pounded and their hands felt sore. They rested for a moment then pressed forward on the path as this was just the beginning.

They traversed the mountains, following pathways and climbing up and a routine started to develop. Once in a while they took cover from an Italian patrol that was also traversing the mountains but with much ease, for they were the Alpini.

No words were said during the journey to save their breath as the air got thinner. When they got to higher ground their ears would pop. Without even realizing it, they scaled the mountains from a thousand to almost three thousand meters. It took them five hours to get halfway through the mountains when they ran in to an obstacle, a wall of ice that covered the slope.

"Hmm, it seems this ice hasn't melted yet even though we're close to summer. We're going to climb it since there is no other alternative...unless you want to take a longer route," suggested Steiner, feeling the ice.

"Better take our chances now. We must stay on schedule right, Maxis?" Lothar turns to Maxis.

"Right. We need get to our objective before tomorrow, otherwise we'll be encountering more Alpini."

"Then it's settled; I'll check the ice. Wait for my go." Steiner pulled out his ice axe and began climbing onto the ice.

"Alright, the ice is good. Follow me.," Steiner said as he reached the ledge.

Maxis and Lothar pulled out their ice axes and started to climb. As they progressed, they heard the sound of a plane. The two didn't move a muscle as it flew overhead.

"Hold...hold...ok, keep moving," said Maxis as he continued to climb.

They made it to a ledge and rested a bit. They squatted near the ledge a view of the whole Italian Alps in front of them, a magnificent sight to behold. Lothar pulled a piece of candy from his pocket, a lollipop. Maxis noticed.

"Heh, how long have you been hiding that?" Maxis asked.

"I was actually saving this till the mission was over, but right now my sweet tooth is calling me," said Lothar as he unwrapped it, then pulled down his balaclava.

As Lothar was about to take the first lick a strong wind gusted and swept the lollipop out of his hand. Maxis started to laugh and Steiner gave a small chuckle before lighting a cigarette. They squatted there for a few minutes until Maxis realized the sun was almost setting.

"Ok, break's over. We need to get over the cliffside before the sun sets," said Maxis.

"Right, then. Just a little ways more until we reach the cliffside. From there we should be on easy street on our walk down toward the tree line," said Steiner, as he tossed the cigarette and readied his ice axe.

They all got up slowly and shifted along the edge carefully, trying not to look down. Steiner swung his ice axe on the ice and began climbing while the others followed his lead. He made it to the ledge with a little more space then walked over to analyze their surroundings. Maxis and Lothar made it and they saw Steiner kneeling near a drop-off looking down surveying the area.

"There is a drop-off here, but we can make a leap from here and be one step closer to getting past this mountain and onto the lower ground."

"Let's do this." said Lothar.

"Alright. I'll lay down the rope and tie it to my hip; you'll do same."

Everyone laid down the ropes they carried and tied the ends together. When they finished, Steiner took a deep breath, ran toward the edge, then leapt across, making contact by digging the ice axe into the ice. It drag slightly before stopping. He grabbed a spike from his person and stuck it in the ice, then pulled out a small hammer and started hammering. He climbed up then repeated the practice. By the time he reached the cliff-side he had already put the last spike down at the top. He fastened his rope to it.

"Okay. Everything should be secured. Now it's your turn," Steiner shouted out.

"We hear you. Lothar, is your rope fastened tight?" Maxis asked.

"As tight as it can ever be. We go on the count of Drei (three)?"

Maxis nodded and the two started to count.

"Ein (One)...Zwei (Two)...DREI (Three)!" The two ran and leaped off the cliff connecting their ice axe to the ice. Suddenly Maxis slipped and didn't connect his on the right side. He quickly slid down with his left axe still in the ice.

"Not to worry the spikes will cease my decent...he thought to himself."

One of the spikes pops off the side and Maxis panicked slightly and quickly began making attempts to get his ice axe to pierce the ice. Then another spike popped off, worsening the situation.

"Scheisse, Scheisse, Scheisse!!" Maxis grimaced, in a panic.

"Hold on! Don't let go!" screamed Lothar, as he lowered himself down quickly. Steiner held on to the rope tightly.

Maxis was hanging onto a small slope, his ice axe still holding. He made a few more attempts to get his right axe embedded into the ice, but in a matter of seconds, he was hanging by one arm.

He held on for dear life, his heart pumping, gripping tightly, breathing heavy and staying still although wind blew slightly. The ice axe slowly whittled the ice then gave way. Suddenly an arm reached out toward him. Lothar grabbed him by the forearm as he held the rope, and he tightened his grip, still breathing heavily. Lothar looked down at Maxis

"Hey Friedrich...*breathing heavily*...Hows it hanging, Heh?" said Lothar trying to lighten the situation. His face still wore a worried expression.

"Almost fell to my death. Can you boost me up?"

"Okay...I'll try to throw you up. Try to connect with ice this time!" said Lothar, readying himself.

"Ragghhh!" Lothar grunts as he threw Maxis back onto the ice wall. This time his axe successfully connects to the ice.

Steadier now, Maxis started climbing again with Lothar following behind. Steiner acted as an anchor to help them out. When Maxis reached the top, Steiner lent a hand and immediately helped him up. Maxis felt total relief the moment he stepped on solid ground, though his legs were trembling and his breathing remained heavy.

"You got lucky Sergeant; may I suggest not to try your luck again?" Steiner quipped sarcastically, looking down at Maxis.

"I'll put it under advisement, and thanks."

"I need help, too," Lothar grunted as he appeared over the edge.

Steiner and Maxis rushed over to assist Lothar and pulled him up. Once over the ledge, Lothar quickly hugged the ground, a feeling of relief taking over.

"Oh man...they made it look easy in the film and pictures. Did I ever tell you that I resent climbing?"

"You just did, Kamerad (Friend)," Steiner replied.

"That was little too close for comfort. Take a breather, Lothar," instructed Maxis.

CHAPTER 25

MARCHING THROUGH THE MOUNTAINS

They rested for a moment then marched on to the tree line. As the sun set, the trio entered the woods, darkness blanketing all around.

"We have to minimize our position, one light source only." Maxis pulled out his flashlight as Steiner lead the way, Lothar watching their backs as they walk. Only the rustle of the wind blowing and sound of their footsteps crunching the snow could be heard.

"Hey, what can you tell us about yourself? You know just to pass the time," Maxis asked, holding the light steady.

"I'm soldier, just like you" Steiner responded in his usual low tone.

"Every soldier has a story," Lothar interjects as he checked their surroundings.

"If you insist. As you know I'm an Austro-Hungarian soldier."

"Yeah, the feldkappa was a bit of a dead giveaway," said Maxis.

"Yes...my mother was Italian and my father an Austrian. She was born in the Alps and my father in Carpathians, see the connection? Trekking through treacherous hill, valleys, and mountains is in our blood. I can speak to the mountains and the mountains speak to me, figuratively speaking. I was with the Kaiser Jäger when I joined the K.u.K before the war. Me and all my friends were in the same unit; all the boys from the same village. When we were deployed into Serbia, we marched with our heads up high. That is until the setbacks happened." Steiner passed by a couple of trees.

"Setbacks?" Maxis asked.

"You, at least, would know the mistakes that were made in Serbia, Sergeant."

"You mean the incompetency of the Habsburg military."

"I was trying to be diplomatic, but yes. Setback after setback, we're forcefully evicted out of Serbia, and with each battle I lost more of my friends, leaving me the only survivor of our village. After that I slowly started to change from being cheerful and naïve to silent and dead serious. To new recruits and other experienced soldiers, I was known as the "Veteran" or the "old guy". Old, barely even entering my twenties." He stopped for a moment to look down a hill then proceeded carefully.

"It sounds like something similar happened to someone I know but, he was traumatized by it," Lothar commented as Steiner continued.

"The last straw came in early 1915 when we were deployed to the Carpathians. There it happened."

"What?" Lothar asked as he kicked a small pebble.

"Hotzendorf. He launches three winter offensives into the Carpathians to drive the Russians out and hopefully relieve a Fortress in the process. But it failed spectacularly; we received even more casualties, both in combat and to the cold due to the lack of winter gear. I had to kill a chamois (mountain goat) and skin it for its fur just to survive," Steiner said as he rubbed his fur coat.

"That still doesn't explain how you joined up with our battalion," said Maxis as he walked over a log.

"I spotted a squad of German troops armed with weapons I hadn't seen before. My commanding officer told me to ignore them and even said, 'You never saw them!' That really raised my curiosity. I tracked them down though I kept my distance until they stopped to rest. I was laying on top of small cliff when I was suddenly flipped onto my back and had a revolver aimed toward my face. It was a K.W.S. Scharfschütze (Sharpshooter) who was providing overwatch for his squad. After a few questions and answers, he admitted that he was impressed with my ability to trek through the harsh terrains just to follow them." Steiner paused as he crossed a dirt road quickly; the others did the same.

"His exact words were 'I like your style. How would feel if you were offered the opportunity of life a time?' I was tired of taking orders from my incompetent superiors so my only response to him was 'Where can I join?'. The next day I received a letter and my transfer orders, and the day after that I was in Germany going through intensive training," Steiner finished.

"Very intriguing Steiner, even soldiers through- out the Central Powers have certain skills that would get you recruited into the battalion," said Maxis as he looked up to see the sky glittering with stars.

"It breaks my heart though that I must fight and kill in the place my mother once called home," Steiner said with a saddened tone.

They exited the woods into the valley after three hours. The group took a break when dawn was break- ing over the horizon. With light finally illuminating the valley, they were able to see their rocky surroundings.

"Hey Maxis, do you know what this place reminds me of?" Lothar asked.

"Westerwald?" Maxis responded.

"Yep, almost looks like it without these mountainous rocks in the way. Do you remember when we marched like this during basic before Kurtz started training us? We all sang songs to pass the time."

"I remember the whole company sang 'Schwarzbraun ist die Haselnuss (Black Brown is the Hazelnut)' until we reached the...you're going to sing it, aren't you?" said Maxis with a grin.

"You know me too well. Care to join in?"

"Sure. Why not? As along we stay in rhythm."

"Terrific," Lothar said with a little excitement as he cleared his throat and started with a beat. Maxis and Lothar began singing the marching song together. It was an old folklore song which was a favorite to German soldiers everywhere. The two sang as they marched.

"Are they seriously singing a marching song? Sigh. This is why I usually work alone. Gott (God) they sound terrible!" Steiner thought as they sang.

The singing paused for a moment.

"Steiner, how about you chip in?" Lothar asked.

"Nein, I'm okay staying silent."

"Come on, now. At least you can sing only the chorus part," prompted Maxis.

Steiner thought for a moment, then groaning, "Fine, just the chorus!"

"Excellent! Now where were we?" Lothar said.

Maxis and Lothar picked up where they left off now with Steiner as chorus, singing as they marched along.. In between Maxis and Lothar would laugh change up the lyrics, making Steiner laugh a little.

Steiner sensed what he hadn't felt for a long time and that was joy. That sudden change in him made him feel comfortable for the moment and so he sang along cheerfully with his brothers-in-arms...his new friends. That is, until a bullet swooshed their heads, by creating a loud snap.

"SNIPER! Get to cover, now!" Steiner shouted as another round flew by, hitting the dirt.

Maxis and Lothar took cover behind a bolder on the left and Steiner one on the right; then a bullet hit the side splintering the rock and pegging Lothar's right arm.

"Ouch! That stings!" said Lothar.

"Stay in cover! Keep your face away from the edge of the rock. If he hits the rock and your face is near it, you'll go blind from the fragments!" Steiner shouted as another shot hit the rock near him.

Everyone guardedly stayed put. Steiner put his hat on the end of his rifle as bait and lifted it out into the open. It was struck in seconds and flew off as a loud bang was heard from a distance.

"Scheisse, he definitely knows where we are, but I know where the shot came. We're going to have to draw his fire so I can take the shot," Steiner directed, as he picked up his hat.

"I'll draw his fire then, just be ready take him out. I'll run to the next cover" volunteered Maxis.

"Are you sure, Sergeant? This Alpini has a good aim."

"Then show me you can do better than him, Private!" Steiner nodded.

"Bereit (ready)? Now!" Steiner shouted.

Maxis darted out into the open as a bullet whistled by his head. Steiner peered out from cover and quickly took aim. Time itself slowed down as Steiner concentrated his focus at the silhouette crouching on the opposite cliffside. He took a deep breath and slowly squeezed the trigger.

"Got you now."

Steiner pulled the trigger and the reverberation was heard as the bullet traveled across the valley, immediately killing the sniper. as he fell backward, his hat flying.

"He's down. We're okay for now, Sergeant Maxis."

"Good aim, Steiner. See, I knew you were better than him," complimented Maxis with a smile.

"I guess you are right, but no time to celebrate. The patrols would have heard those shot. We need to keep moving. We're almost there. It should not be far now."

"Then let's hurry it up. Let's go!" Maxis ordered.

They double-time it through the valley with Steiner taking point. The three-man squad kept their wits about while on the move, ready to encounter another sniper or a patrol. Steiner stopped, motioning Maxis and Lothar to stay low. Maxis moved up carefully.

"Something afoot?" Maxis whispered.

"Ja, I can hear voices, coming from around that corner."

"Let's take a look then, Steiner."

"After you, sarge."

Maxis and Steiner moved up cautiously to the corner and looked around to see two Italian soldiers chatting, their backs toward the duo.

"How do you want to play this out?" Steiner whispered.

"We take them out quietly."

"Understood."

The two pulled out their blades; Maxis with his bayonet and Steiner with his hunting knife. Maxis gestured to the one on the left motioning a slit throat movement and Steiner nodded. They could hear the Italians talking again.

"Hey, did you heard those shots?"

"Eh, it's probably Antonio, shooting birds out of boredom."

"I understand how he feels. This task is boring."

Maxis leapt first and covered the soldier's mouth, muffling him as he attacked him. Steiner kicked the other soldier's leg then grabbed hold of his chin before slitting his throat. Seconds later, the soldier's struggling body goes limp. Maxis and Steiner quietly laid the bodies out on the ground.

"Riposa in pace, soldato (Rest in peace, soldier)." said Steiner, giving a small prayer.

Maxis wiped his blade clean before sheathing it then gave the signal to move out. Lothar emerged from behind the corner and the group was on the move again. Soon the soldiers arrived at their destination. Steiner slowed down and went prone; Maxis and Lothar followed suit. They low-crawled to the edge of the cliff and located a small pathway to the far right. Maxis pulled out his binoculars and Steiner looked through his scope. Lothar moved up beside them.

"Did we make it? Where on earth is this mountain fort or er, factory at, huh?"

"Right in front of us." Maxis handed him the binoculars and pointed.

Lothar looked and immediately was in awe of what he saw. In front of them was the mountain, a large and tall ominous rock. Around the middle were four Fortress guns pointing in every direction, as well as some caves with cloth covering the entrances. Below was the checkpoint area, replete with an Italian guard on duty and a few more patrolling the area. On other parts of the mountain there were tall chimneys where the smoke was coming out.

"Mein Gott (My God) …I thought it would be smaller. How are we going to disable *that*?" Lothar stammered.

"Well, Lothar, the better thing to ask who is going to answer that question," Maxis responded.

"You could try asking whoever is in charge. I'd start with that," Steiner suggested, as he continued looking through his scope.

"Okay, but how are we going to get in? Any clues, Maxis?" Lothar asked.

"I spotted another entrance closer, but it's guarded by soldiers wearing…wait…I see three guards, but what's with bicorn hats?" Maxis sounded puzzled.

"Bicorn hats? Where?" Steiner asked. Maxis pointed toward the entrance. Steiner took another look through his scope.

"Oh boy, it's the Carabinieri," Steiner said, sounding concerned.

"What?" Lothar asked.

"Carabinieri. They are an elite force for the Kingdom of Italy. If they are here, then something important must be going on in there for them to be stationed here."

"Elite or not, they are in the way. I'm sure we can take them but we need to do so quietly and…" Maxis was cut off by loud artillery firing from the Mountain Fortress, followed by an announcement through the loudspeaker in Italian.

"Steiner, what is he saying and what are they doing?" Maxis asked.

"Weapons testing. They're firing the fortress guns," Steiner answered.

"Firing the fortress guns, eh? I have an idea. Steiner, me and Lothar are going down there, but when we get into position, then the moment they fire the big guns again we'll take out two and you get the last one."

"Hmm, that might work. The noise would block out my shots," said Steiner.

"Perfect. Let's go, Lothar."

"Right behind you, Max."

Maxis descended the path leaving Steiner to set up. The two slowly moved without being noticed behind the three guards as they stood guarding the entrance. Maxis pulled out his knife from his boot and Lothar pulled out his shovel.

"Is he really going to kill him with a shovel? They are an interesting bunch to say the least," Steiner thought as he focused his sight. The loudspeaker sounded off.

"Attention. Attention. Firing will commence in three, two, one."

Steiner readied himself and took a deep breath and focused on the guy at the center. The Fortress gun with a loud bang and at same time Steiner pulled the trigger dropping the Carabinier with one shot. Maxis performed a stealth kill while Lothar used the edge of his shovel and struck the Carabinier in the back of the neck.

All three guards were taken out in one swift motion and Maxis gave a thumbs up as he wiped his blade.

Steiner responded back with a thumbs up as well, keeping an eye out. Lothar walked toward the heavy doors and opened them and the two moved into lair of the Mountain Fortress.

"Goodluck Sgt. Maxis and Cpl. Lothar. I shall wait for your return...hopefully, ." Steiner thought as he shuffled behind a bush.

CHAPTER 26

HALL OF THE MOUNTAIN FORTRESS

There was a low incline as they moved through the tunnel. They kept going until they reached a flight of stairs, in front of them at the top was a catwalk. They slowly moved onto it and below them was a sight that left them flabbergasted.

Down below was an array of armored cars, ammo crates, supplies and more. There were soldiers and civilians walking about, and in one corner an assembly line for infantry equipment and yet another building bullets and artillery shells.

"Maxis, you're seeing what I'm seeing, right?" Lothar asked as he looked over the catwalk.

"Yeah, this place is massive. They must have hollowed out the entire mountain to fit all this in. Not only as a factory, but also a base too. The perfect Fortress for any army. Now I'm wondering how many stories this place has. Mankind never ceases to amaze," he remarked, his eyes fixated on the machinery and conveyor belt.

"Let's keep moving before you start drooling Maxis, although this certainly is wonderous sight. Too bad it has to go."

"Yeah, sure."

Maxis and Lothar moved across the catwalk before quickly ducking back in the corner as an Italian officer walked across the hallway. He was holding a clipboard and when the wall telephone began to ring, and he quickly answered it.

"Hey, he's about to talk to someone. Go in and listen, I'll cover you." said Maxis as he readied his C96 sporting carbine.

"On it." Lothar closed in, quietly listening in on the conversation.

"Saluti (Hello)? Oh, Commander Molitor. How are you?"

"Wait a minute, did he say Commander Molitor?" Lothar now has his interest piqued.

"Everything is settled, Sir. We are still expecting more workers, but production is in progress...Yes, Sir."

"*Come on, keep talking...*"

"Thanks to the contribution of your government and your Hasardeux Division, the Kingdom of Italy now has an active organization under your wing, Sir."

"*Small Italian organization sponsored by the Hasardeux Division. Hmm, I wonder what their name is?*"

"La legioni d'Italia (The Legions of Italy), is at your service and command."

"*Of course...*" Lothar rolled his eyes as he continued to listen.

"Yes Sir, the Pavesi Tolotti weapon is almost finished. Production on all equipment is going steadily. When it is in place, we will be ready to act against the Hapsburgs. The troops are ready in their barracks and the new recruits have just moved in; which concludes my report, Sir."

"*Pavesi Tolotti? Whatever it is, that thing gets destroyed with the rest of this mountain.*"

"The commander of this base is not present for the moment, but I will inform his second in command, Cpt. Romano. He should be at the top floor."

"*That's all I need to hear...*" Lothar sneaks up on the Italian then gets his attention.

"Hey, ravioli!"

"In cui si (Where)? *oof.*" Lothar delivered one good right hook, sending the soldier flying and already unconscious. The telephone was left hanging.

"Hello? Hello? What's happened?"

Lothar picked up the phone and spoke.

"Mauvais numéro, Croissant (Wrong number, Croissant)," he said in a deep and intimidating voice as he hung up the phone.

"Damn, now I'm hungry," Lothar muttered as he walked back to Maxis, who was watching the whole thing.

"What's the word from our sleepy friend?" Maxis asked, staring at the unconscious officer.

"The entire mountain is not only a factory, but also a military base for a small-time organization sponsored by Commander Molitor of the S.H.D. and the French Government," Lothar reported sarcastically.

"The Hasardeux Division? How would you know this?" Maxis asked.

"The Italians that run this base call themselves La legioni d'Italia or the Legions of Italy. Not only that, but some type of weapon called "Pavesi Tolotti," whatever that is, is near completion.

"It won't matter since we're going blow this place to kingdom come, somehow," Maxis said, as he checked the corner.

"The commander of the Legioni isn't here but his second command is. He is at the top of the mountain in his office," Lothar pointed upward.

"Then let's go have nice chat with him. We'll use the elevator."

They double-timed it to a nearby elevator and pressed the button. The doors opened, they entered, and pressed the button for the first floor. The elevator closes its door, and a ding is heard as it jolts and begins to move up.

"Hey Maxis, may I have a word? Something's been bugging me."

"What's on your mind, Lothar."

"I just been thinking about Steiner's story and the tragedies that followed him. It reminds me of my charge who was assigned to me back in Champagne and what he went through that traumatized him. Maxis, we have had a fair share of action before and after joining K.W.S. in this war, but how long do you think it will

390

be before we get affected or change like the others?" Lothar asked with concern in his voice.

"It depends, really. I already went through a change in Belgium, and after the death of our mentor, Sgt. Kurtz, then seeing how everyone turned on me before Jorgensen gave me a chance and got me out."

"Yeah, I remember Sgt. Kurtz. He was the one that got us properly trained and conditioned, before the war and then...*Poof*...he gets killed in action. I'm try-ing to remember some of his wisdom, but without the yelling part."

"Lothar, remember we all go through a change, but it depends on the strength of your resolve and an iron will. Look, as long we live, the heart of this battalion will never be broken; we will never be broken. I don't how long this war will last, but verdammt (damn it) we'll finish it together as brothers in arms," Maxis raised his fist as he finished.

"That was a bit of inspiration, but promise me this, Friedrich. Try not to die. It's already difficult enough trying to work alone, without someone who can think faster than me. One more thing...Before the year goes out you'll tell me what happened in Belgium, right? What happened to Kurtz?"

"Deal. Though I can say the same to you about not dying since you almost bit the big one with four bullets and a stab wound by a sadistic Frenchie," said Maxis with a smirk.

"Heh, when you put it like that, I feel pathetic about what happened. I was fortunate that Richter came and saved me, but yeah, I'll try to stay alive though danger seems have an interest in me after Tannenberg; but, it can be said for you when that Russian Hündin (Bitch) is around."

"Strong words."

"She grazed my face, Maxis. Anyway, I'll try to be careful."

"Good. Besides, Hannah probably would kill me if anything happened to her Mighty Teddybär (Teddy bear)."

"Wait, her Mighty wha-" Lothar was cut off as the elevator opens.

They stepped out with their weapons at the ready, checking their corners. The coast was clear and the hallway appeared empty; nothing but doors and ceiling lights. They moved carefully down the hallway until they stumbled upon as door that read, "Comandante della legione (Commander of the Legion)".

"Here it is," said Maxis, pointing at the golden letters on the door.

Maxis stood on one side of the door and Lothar on the other. Lothar knocked on the door then waited for a response. He tried again, but nothing. Maxis opened the door that was surprisingly left unlocked. They entered and checked the office. The room was empty.

"The room is clear; no sign of him. Now what?" said Lothar lowering his pistol carbine.

"We can...wait, do you hear that?" Maxis whispered as he listened closely to the wall.

"Hear what?"

"Footsteps. Someone's coming. Quick hide!" Maxis hid behind the desk while Lothar stayed close to wall near the door.

"Lothar, when I give you the signal, grab him, okay?" Maxis whispered.

Lothar nodded as the door slowly opened slowly, almost making contact with Lothar's face. In came an Italian officer who sipped from his coffee mug while reading a file. He closed the door after entering and walked toward the desk where Maxis was hiding. Maxis slowly stuck out his hand for Lothar to see, then gave the signal.

Lothar sprung into action apprehended the Italian officer in a full nelson as he dropped his file and mug. Maxis leapt out and managed to catch the mug before it hit the ground.

"Second in command, Cpt. Romano, I presume?" Lothar asked in an Austrian accent, keeping a tight grip.

"Who the hell are you? Identify yourself!" barked Cpt. Romano.

"Nothing to concern yourself with. We just want a couple of questions answered." said Maxis, also in a Austrian accent as he walked in front.

"Bastard, I'm not telling you anything. Habsburg dog!" Cpt. Romano reacted furiously.

"Good, he doesn't know we're German. I need to figure something out to get him to budge but, what?" Maxis thought for a second then looked at the window.

"I have an idea how to make you talk. Follow me," Maxis said, motioning with his hand.

They walked to the window and Maxis opened it and a gush of cold air blew in.

"Get him over the sill and keep a good grip on him because he is going to panic."

"Oh, this going to be interesting," said Lothar as he dragged Cpt. Romano over to the window..

He put Cpt. Romano headfirst out the window while holding on to the collar of his shirt and his belt. Romano started to struggle in a panic as he looked down and gave off a weak scream.

"How do I destroy this from the inside?" Maxis asked bluntly.

"You are crazy. Crazy son of a whore!" Romano panics.

"Okay then." Maxis looked at Lothar and nodded.

Lothar let go of his shirt collar and slowly lowered him down until he was held only by his ankles. He screamed but was drowned out by the howling winds as they picked up.

"I tried to communicate with you, but you left me no choice. You know, I'm curious about Galileo's theory of gravity. He dropped two items off the Leaning Tower of Pisa. I'm wondering how fast your body will go if you were dropped off a mountain!" said Maxis, the captain screaming.

"OK, OK! I'll talk you, psychopath!" Romano screamed.

"Now we're making progress. Lothar pull him up." Maxis ordered.

"On it. My hands were getting tired, anyhow."

Lothar pulled the officer back in and set him on a chair. He was shaking from the experience and from the cold wind. Maxis walked over and grabbed the mug of coffee, still warm.

"Here, drink up so you can stop shivering," said Maxis as he handed him the mug of coffee.

Romano grasped the mug firmly, still trembling. He drank the whole thing in one gulp. When he was done, he set it aside and looked up to Maxis.

"What do you want to know?" he asked.

"I'll ask it again. How do I destroy this entire facility? Don't even try to lie."

Cpt. Romano gave off a laugh.

"You are joking, right? You are destroying Fortezza di Montagna (Mountain Fortress) and getting away with it. Please! What you are going to do is end up dead! This place is the greatest achievement the world has ever seen."

"Sure, it's a great achievement but you're using it as factory and producing war material. It's part of your war effort which is why we are here."

"I still think you are pazzo (crazy) Austro-Hungarian. But if death is your calling, then so be it. You would have to go to the last floor of the Mountain, there you should be able to find our generator room and gas room that connects throughout the whole Fortress. It doesn't matter now, General Cordona has his troops ready to strike the Hapsburg Empire and as for you, like I said before, you will fall before you even reach it, for we are the Legioni d...*oof...*" Lothar punched him across his face, knocking him out cold.

"I was getting tired of his tone. Sorry if acted without permission," said Lothar.

"It's fine. I needed to know where to strike, and the files he just dropped will be an added plus for Heimdall Base to analyze regarding the Legioni and their connection to the Hasardeux Division. Grab everything you can and let's get going. We have a Mountain Fortress to destroy."

Maxis and Lothar grabbed anything useful before heading out of the second in command's office, then headed back to the elevator.

"I'm still a bit concerned about this elevator, Maxis. Feels like it might snap at any moment," Lothar spoke, sounding a bit concerned after pressing the button.

The elevator descended, dinging at each level until it finally stopped, then the doors opened.

"Lothar, you worry too much. We'll be just fine..." Maxis paused and froze in his tracks barely exiting the elevator.

In front of them were Italian soldiers putting on their uniforms, equipment, even body armor and other forms of protection in the Barracks.

"Lothar, did you press the right button for the ground floor?" Maxis whispered.

"Oh, Mist (crap)," answered Lothar as he looked at the panel and saw the glowing number five.

One of the Italian soldiers looked at the elevator, surprised to see to unknown soldiers standing there. The stare-down was bit awkward for Maxis and Lothar until they gave an innocent wave.

The Italian soldier waved back before yelling "Intrusi (Intruder)!" Maxis and Lothar both fired their weapons, taking him down along with three more soldiers. Everyone in the barracks pulled out their weapons of all sorts; including bolt action rifles and Cei Riggotti self-loading rifles. The pair took cover behind the elevator walls which gave some cover as the Italians unleashed a flurry of bullets into the elevator.

"Lothar, press a button now!" Maxis shouted, suppressed by gunfire.

Lothar quickly tried to reach the panel without getting shot. He managed to press the number one button and before the doors closed he pulled the pin on two of his grenades and tossed them into the barracks.

"This how we say 'hello', Legioni (Legions)!" he said as he tossed the stick grenades.

Without a second to waste the doors slowly closed as the bullets made tinging sounds as they hit the metal wall, then a loud boom came after. The elevator began its descent.

"Just for the record, that was horribly my mistake, Maxis."

"You don't say. Well, they know we're here, which will make things a bit difficult," surmised Maxis as he reloaded his weapon.

"Come on, Maxis, these are Italians. We can handle a bunch of pasta eating..." Suddenly the elevator cable snapped. "What was thaaaaaaa???"

The elevator was now falling fast as the pair tried to hold on to something. There was a loud bang as they hit ground level. Dust was in the air, the lights flickering. Maxis came to and got up very slowly.

"The bastards cut the line in an attempt to kill us. What were you saying about the Italians Lothar, heh? Lothar? Lothar!?" Maxis called out.

"I'm up, I'm up. I told you I was weary of elevators. Man, that hurts, glad I was wearing the new helmet. Otherwise, I would have receive a bad concussion."

"Come on Lothar, we need to keep moving." Maxis walked over to the elevator door.

He groaned, "Verdammt (Damn it). It's stuck."

"Let me try, Maxis. *Grunt*...There we go, after you."

Lothar successfully opened the elevator door and motioned Maxis to go through first. Leaving the destroyed elevator, they made it to the final floor.

They moved through the rocky hallway until they heard the sound of humming generators, pumping noises, all getting louder as they got closer. In front of them was a large door. They opened it and saw the generator room with several engineers and one guard. Maxis fired the first shot, dropping the guard instantly and Lothar fired a few rounds in the air to scare the engineers.

"Generator room is clear. Let's set these charges," Maxis said as he put down his rucksack and rifled through it and pulled out the canned-shape charges. He placed them around the room, some close to gas lines.

"Lothar, time check."

"In fifteen seconds, it will be nine o'clock in the morning." Lothar checked his watch.

"Alright, setting the charge now. We have thirty minutes before this place turns into Mt. Vesuvius." Maxis put his rucksack on.

"Maxis, what about the factory workers? Are we going to leave them here to die? Shouldn't we raise an alarm?"

"Scheisse, I don't see any, Lothar. Maybe we can try..." Maxis was interrupted by the communication tube from above.

"Attention, Attention! Enemy infiltrators are inside the base. All non-essential staff evacuate now! All soldiers to arms!" said the announcer.

"Well, there's our answer, set the charge!" said Lothar.

"Alright, charges set, let's go!" Maxis finished the last charge and lit the fuse. The bombs were spread apart and connected. The main bomb started dinging at a slow rate which would increase as timer ran out.

They moved out, taking turns leading and relying on their instincts to find their way out. The one thing that would stay on their minds was constant dinging coming through the communication tubes throughout the base from the generator room.

Maxis and Lothar would come across the catwalk again only to see the workers below all evacuating and Italians troops moving through the large doors at the main entrance.

"Lothar, time?" Maxis asked.

"Twenty minutes. We're making good time."

"Good. I think we're almost there. We just need to and...Hold fast!" Maxis suddenly whispered.

The two froze in place as large group of Italian troops ran from the left hall toward the right, boots clattering. Maxis held his breath as he watched them move. They almost got off Scott free; that is until one of soldiers stopped abruptly and turned to look down the hall. Maxis and Lothar gripped their weapons tightly. The soldier pointed his finger the moment he saw them.

"Nemico avvistato (Enemy spotted)!!!" yelled the soldier.

Everyone stopped and looked where he was pointing at. Maxis and Lothar opened fire on the group then took a slight detour into the hallway next to them.

"I'm reloading! Cover me!" Lothar shouted to Maxis as he pulled out another pistol magazine for his P08 carbine.

"Providing cover!"

They kept moving as bullets hit the walls and doors of the hallway. Maxis spotted two metal doors and immediately led Lothar to it.

"Quick in here. Into the armory, now!" said Maxis as they ducked inside.

They closed the door tightly and flipped the lock. There they waited as the yelling and shouting of the Italians was still heard as soldiers ran past the metal door. Then everything went silent.

"What just happened?" Lothar whispered.

"I don't know. We have to wait and see. Hopefully, not for too long."

Suddenly they hear rifles being loaded and cocked. Then a man started to speak through a portable megaphone.

"This is Cpt. Colombo! We know you are in there! Come out with your hands up!"

"I think they know we're in here, Maxis," said Lothar in a low tone.

"Austro-Hungarian soldiers, we have captured one your amicos (friends). If you do not come out, your friend will die!"

Maxis and Lothar looked at each other with a surprised look.

"Steiner, captured?" Lothar sounded shocked.

"Impossible. He was well concealed when we left him," Maxis said, sounding suspicious.

"What's the new plan?"

"Lothar, there's a metal slit on the door. Open it slightly and see what we're dealing with," Maxis directed and pointed at the slit.

"On it." Lothar opened the window slit just a little and looked through the crack.

"What do you see?" Maxis asked.

"A lot of angry Italians. Riflemen armed with Carcano M91s, M1870 Italian Vetterlia, some Cei Rigotti self-loaders, one Fiat–Revelli Modello 1914 MG, and one weird small gun with two mags sticking upwards on a bipod," Lothar finished as he slowly closed the metal slit.

"Any sign of Steiner, Lothar?"

"Nope. That was a total lie in an attempt to draw us out."

"Well, let's make them pay for it, Lothar."

"I'm listening." Lothar bent down a little to listen.

"The time has come to see what's inside Heinrich's special package. Set it up!"

The two put their packs down and pulled out the wrapped packages. Lothar was surprised when he opened it.

"What the...it's armor! I've never seen this type before," said Lothar as he picked it up.

"Hey, there is a letter that came with it." Maxis pointed at an envelope that fell out of the body armor.

Lothar reached for the envelope. On the front it said, "To the Daring Two." He opened it and read aloud while Maxis examined the package.

"To the Daring Two,

If you are reading this letter, then it means you got yourself into trouble with a particular group of Entente soldiers that are giving you a hard time. Thus, I have given you this set of armor that came from R&D. The armor you will be wearing is Schutzweste armor along with a pair of protective visors for the Corporal. This has been refined from captured British armor that pilots and soldiers who wore it and it has undergone major improvements. In other words, we replaced the old metal with stronger and lighter ones that should be enough to stop shrapnel, pistol rounds, and even high caliber rounds. For Sergeant Maxis, I've prepared a special set of attachments for his pickelhaube since he likes to drag danger to himself, though I can't blame him for his need of attention, ha. The first piece is frontal armor that connects to sides of his pickelhaube, and the other is chainmail that covers the whole helm and has a small metal wall to cover the frontal lobe of the helm. I hope this set of protection serves you well, boys. Best of luck.

Yours truly,

K.W.S. Quartermaster Heinrich.

P.S. Try to leave feedback on the armor because R&D is hell bent on feedback."

"That's Heinrich for ya, just full of surprises. Is he sure this armor will protect us?" questioned Lothar as he put on the visors and the Schutzweste armor.

"It'll buy us some time, but we need to break through and fast. Ready up!" said Maxis as he applied the front piece on his pickelhaube, then the chainmail. When he put it on, he felt the weight on his head, and he could see through the metal shield through the two eye slits.

"All suited up, Maxis. I'm commandeering this Perino M1908 machine gun for the time being. This thing is no different from the Hotchkiss LMG; it takes strip mags except I have to stack them. Also, some additional protections," said Lothar, putting on the arm, shoulder, and shin armor taken from the stockpile

"Same here, but I'm taking this Cei Rigotti with the extended mag. It's already loaded with fifty rounds, so we'll burn though their ammo. Heh, a long time ago you once said, 'I look scary with the gas mask on.' Well take look at yourself in the mirror now," Maxis said as he applied an Italian bayonet to the rifle then put the armor on his limbs.

"Pfft, you look like a knight from out of time, Maxis," Lothar retorted, then snorted.

After donning the armor they placed their coats into their rucksacks and tornister. With Lothar's Gaede helmet, visors, and body armor, and with Maxis' added protection to his pickelhaube, and body armor and extras, the two looked like knights of old, but with guns.

"Quite right, my friend. Now for plan B. In courtesy of the Italy joining the Triple Entente, we are using this magnetic limpet charge to make an exit," Maxis announced as he picked up the charge.

On the other side of the metal door. Cpt. Colombo grew irritated and impatient from hearing the constant chatter coming from the armory. He picked up the megaphone and spoke.

"I've grown tired of you trying to make decision! Surrender now and we may give you some mercy!" declared the Captain.

"Well, that is not encouraging. Are you setting that thing up, Maxis?" Lothar asked.

With a loud bang Maxis slammed the magnetic charge on the door, and turned the windup key to arm it.

"You have five seconds to reply!" The captain bellowed, beginning the countdown.

"Five!"

"Get to cover Lothar and get ready," said Maxis.

"Four!"

"Heh, I'm ready to get this pasta party started," Lothar responded, sounding excited.

"Three!"

The pair readied their weapons as the magnetic bomb ticked away.

"Two!"

"ONE!"

"Zero, Penne!" said Maxis.

The explosion blew open the metal doors and propelled them forward, crushing the first few soldiers unlucky enough to be in the way, then knocked the rest off their feet. The hall was blanketed with smoke and dust. The soldiers, including Cpt. Colombo climbed back to their feet and started chattering.

"Che diavolo (what the hell)?!" said one soldier, incredulously.

"Did they blow themselves up?"

"I do not know."

"Silence! Damn bastards. Get ready men! Fire on my uhhhh..." Cpt. Colombo stood there in fear and shock as he saw Lothar walk out, fully armored and armed to teeth with Maxis behind him.

"Arrivederci (Goodbye)! Maxis shouted, giving them a sendoff.

"Fear The Lothar!" Lothar opened fire on the Italians as they tried to take aim and others fled; but it did not matter, for they all were cut down.

Maxis moved beside him and fired a volley into the retreating soldiers, killing Cpt. Colombo. They moved up quickly however there was no chance for them to regroup or find a suitable defensive position. The Italians had attempted to fight back only for their bullets to bounce off the armor.

"My God! The Hapsburgs sent knights! Pull back, pull back!" an Italian soldier cried out as he and the others started to fall back.

"Lothar, time!?" Maxis asked and kept firing.

"We have fifteen minutes, Maxis."

"Keep up the pressure, we are breaking through!"

The daring two unleashed hell on to the enemy as they advanced. The Italians that managed to escape the wrath of the armored soldiers set up barricades at parts of the hallway; others ended up leaving the facility to live and fight another day.

Lothar led the way back toward where they came through when they encountered more resistance. Two Italian soldiers were setting up the machine gun aiming down the hallway. They listened to chaos unfolding. At the same time the announcer came on the speaker repeating the same message but sounding more panicked than ever.

"Hurry Mario! Get that machine gun ready! They are coming!"

"There! The machine gun is ready!"

The soldiers opened machine gun fire the moment they saw Maxis and Lothar walk around the corner. But Maxis quickly opened a metal door that was close to him for cover, and Lothar jumped behind a crate.

"Scheisse, Fiat-Revelli got me pinned," said Lothar, under heavy fire.

"I rather not test the armor against a machine gun, festhalten (hold on)." Maxis reached for his kugel grenades and pulled the pinned on one of them. He threw it hard toward the MG.

"Granata!" a soldier screamed out.

The grenade exploded, killing the machine gunners and blowing up the ammo box that was there, creating fireworks with bullets flying all over the place.

"MG down! Good throw, Maxis!" Lothar gave a thumbs up.

"Let's keep moving, Mighty Lothar!"

They peered out from their cover and pressed on further but encountered more resistance.

"Maxis, I see marksmen taking positions at the far end of the hallway. Take them out before they try to aim for my weak spots!"

"Yeah, I see them!"

Maxis aimed, then fired at marksmen. A bullet struck Lothar, but it was deflected by the armor.

At one point during their advance a soldier was hiding in a corner waiting for them to pass by as they laid down fire on to his comrades. He fixed his bayonet and the moment the two were in sight he blindly charged in, thrusting his bayonet while screaming. The soldier heard the sound of metal-on-metal rings and opened his eyes to see that he had completely missed his mark. Lothar turned his gaze toward the soldier, still wearing the balaclava, Gaede helmet, and visors as he stared down at the Italian soldier. Maxis peered at him from Lothar's side.

"Heh, Mi scusi (excuse me) ...."

Lothar grabbed the man by the shoulder and butted heads with him.

"Nice try," said Lothar and proceeded reloading his machine gun while Maxis covered him.

They were nearing the exit. In their wake they left nothing but a mess of fallen Italians who had perished in their defense. They mopped up every soldier that tried to stand in their way.

One Italian soldier mimicked Lothar's walking fire maneuver by holding his own Villar Perosa with his ammo bearer by his side. When they encountered the armored troops, they fired the Villar Perosa with its high rate of fire, filling the entire hallway with bullets. One of the rounds hit Maxis in the arm.

"Ouch, that stings!" Maxis reacted.

The moment the firing ceased, Maxis quickly took aim and fired a shot, putting a hole in the gunner's head. Lothar quickly dispatched the ammo bearer before he could reach for his pistol.

Near the entrance there were two soldiers still arming the explosives. They lined up the explosives around the walls, almost to the rocky ceiling.

"Hurry, Bernardi! We can't let those dogs get out that easily!" said the demolition trooper.

"I'm almost done here..."

"Too late! They're here...aah!"

Bullets were flying everywhere in the hallway and the demolition team was cut down, leaving Bernardi mortally wounded on the ground. His body was riddled with bullets, but he looked up, eyes full of pain. Maxis and Lothar walked past him talking but he could not understand due to the constant dinging of the bomb growing steadily louder.

"I see the exit. We're almost there, Maxis!" said Lothar.

"I wouldn't celebrate yet, Lothar," Maxis responded.

Bernardi looked at the detonator as his vision slowly started to blur. He crawled toward it as the pain increased, his wounds bleeding profusely and leaving a blood trail behind him. He crawled past his fallen friends as he reached the detonator.

"O la vittoria (We either win) ..."

Lothar turned around to see the Italian soldier gripping the detonator. He quickly took aim only to hear that dreadful clicking.

"Oh, kacke (Crap), Maxis! The soldier!"

Maxis spun around to see and also took aim but...

"Stop him!" Lothar yelled.

"O tutti accoppati (or we all die)." He pushed the detonator.

CHAPTER 27

AN ERUPTION IN THE ALPS

The humongous explosion destroyed sections of the hallway bringing the rocky ceiling down and spreading fire all over the walls, ceiling and floor. Moments later, Lothar regained consciousness pushed the rubble off him. He glanced down at himself and surveyed his armor, now covered in shrapnel, visors broken, balaclava nearly burned off and his Gaede helmet dented.

"Damned fool. He sacrificed himself in vain...in an attempt to kill us, Maxis. Maxis? Oh, scheisse! Hold I'm coming!" Lothar rushed over after ripping his equipment off.

Lothar removed the pickelhaube attachments then the Schutzweste armor as it dangled with its straps destroyed. Maxis slowly came around, feeling dizzy and unable to see much since there was a piece of shrapnel lodged into his frontal face armor, protecting him as its last act.

"Our armor is shredded but it certainly served its purpose, Maxis."

"How much time we have left?" Maxis coughed as he took off the chain mail of his pickelhaube.

Lothar checked his watch, now cracked.

"Verdammt (Damn it), it's broken!"

Maxis pulled out his pocket watch and replied, "One minute."

"Then let's not waste any time. Come on, up you go!" Lothar helped Maxis up.

They started running up the incline toward the exit, but the bomb was at its final moments. The ringing went faster and grew louder as it echoed throughout the mountain, no longer faint in the speaking tubes. Then the loudspeaker came to life with an important announcement.

"Attention, Attention! A bomb has been discovered in the generator room and is about to explode! Evacuate all personnel immed..." The warning was cut short due and a muffled boom was followed by deep rumble.

"Scheisse, we're too late. RUN! Ditch the guns! We need to book it, NOW!" shouted Maxis. Both men dropped the Italian weapons and made a mad dash up the incline.

Suddenly the bomb went off causing a chain reaction throughout the whole mountain base; pipes were shooting bolts and spouting fire and steam.. Explosions were heard as the quaking of the ground continued. Maxis and Lothar kept running, though they grew tired and their legs felt weak, but they were almost there.

Suddenly a pipe fell on top of Maxis, pinning him down. He tried to move it, but when he put his hand seared when he touched it and he groaned in pain. Trying to tough it out through the pain, he gave it another try but failed. Maxis was running low on energy. The heat of the hallway started to rise as everything turned to a fiery orange illuminating the hallway.

"Verdammt (Damn it), I can't move it! Come on Friedrich, PUSH! Damn it all, I'm too weak, too tired but I can't give up! COME ON!!!" Maxis cried out.

Once more, Maxis gave it a try but failed. The smoke blinded his vision and the temperature rose as the flames grew more intense. Suddenly he spotted a figure through the smoke. Lothar emerged with a piece of cloth torn from the winter coat that he was no longer wearing.

"Hey! Already breaking your promise?" said Lothar sarcastically as he wrapped the cloth on both his hands.

"On Drei(three) ready? Ein, zwei, DREI!" Lothar grunts as he picked up the steam pipe, his hands covered but still feeling heat. He threw the scorching pipe aside.

"There! Come on, my friend, take my hand! I need you alive!" Lothar shouted and grabbed Maxis, lifting him back to his feet. They sprinted with everything they had as the fire behind them started rumbling toward them.

"KEEP MOVING, MAXIS! WE'RE ALMOST THERE!"

The fire was closing in and they felt its heat touching their backs, rocks falling from above. The explosions worsened as the final countdown was neared its end. Maxis and Lothar made it to the entrance and leapt forward; the explosion gave them a much need boost and they flew out of the entrance.

They landed face first but immediately looked back to see that the mountain itself was exploding left and right. It gave off the loudest explosion, so violent and ear shattering that it was like the eruption of Krakatoa in 1883. The mountain peak was now gone and in its place was a large smoke cloud billowing out from it which could be easily mistaken for a volcano.

Maxis and Lothar watched the thing unfold. The sight left them speechless as they realized that they had destroyed the Fortezza di Montagna. Overwhelmed, Maxis laid his head on the ground, trying to regain his strength.

"I–I can't believe it, Maxis. We did it! I can't believe it! We destroyed a mountain! We destroyed a..." Lothar abruptly paused his celebration.

After hearing the rifles being cocked, Lothar slowly turned around and Maxis lifted his head and saw four Italian Carabinieri, three Alpini soldiers, and Cpt. Romano who was aiming his Glisenti Model 1910 pistol directly at him.

"Ricordati di me, fottuti bastardi (Remember me, you fucking bastards)!" barked Romano with great anger. He continued, "Oh, I forgot you don't understand me. No matter, you will end up dead anyway." Romano raised his hand and the squad behind him aimed their rifles toward the pair who were still on the ground.

"You know, I'm starting to think you are not Austro-Hungarians since they couldn't pull an operation like this without losing half an army. No...you are Germans, the type that are efficient at their jobs. Breaks my heart to see our former ally and friend fighting against us," Romano said sympathetically.

"I've got to keep this guy talking. I know in those hills and cliff sides that Steiner is waiting for the right moment," Maxis thought as he sat up.

"Let me handle this, Lothar. Oh, that's rich coming from someone like you," Maxis said mockingly.

"Watch it, boy. We pulled out of the Triple Alliance because the moment the Habsburgs started invading Serbia it became clear that we weren't getting compensated under Article Seven, so we declare neutrality. The French and the British were our source for food and supplies. The higher-ups wanted more land, and we want to put ourselves on the world stage with the other great powers. We gave the Austrians several chances to give us what we wanted, but it is now too late."

"Pfft. What did you expect by asking the Austrian-Hungarians? You just entered into the deadliest war ever created and you think the Entente will honor their word with you?" asked Maxis, as he raises his eyebrow.

"What would you know, boy?"

"Enough to understand ridicule and petty political squabbles that is the Kingdom of Italy, France, Britain and the rest of the Entente Alliance. Tell me, how exactly were you going to win this war? I would like to know before you kill us," Maxis said in a challenging tone.

"For a young soldier, you are well educated to the point where you might as well be a scholar, politician, or even officer. It's a shame really, but since you ask, I will honor your last request since I will grant you a quick death as a favor for not dropping me off the side of the Fortress."

Cpt. Romano started elaborating on Italy's war plan toward Austria-Hungary. Maxis did not listen, however, for he was looking for any sign of Steiner among the rocks, the bushes, or even the trees. Suddenly he saw a glint coming from the rocky hills. Maxis gently elbowed Lothar and discreetly pointed toward the sniper's glint.

"Did you see that?" Maxis whispered.

"Yeah, it's Steiner."

"I've got the three on my left," Maxis tilted his head toward his left.

"Two on my right," Lothar responded.

"Hey! Why are you two whispering? Pfft, doesn't matter anyway. You destroyed the Fortezza di Montagna, destroyed the momentum that General Cordonna would have had for his offensive, made a fool of me, and spit on the honor of the Legioni d'Italia. Soldati! Pronto al mio segnale (Soldiers! Ready on my signal)," said Cpt. Romano as he aimed his pistol.

"Nine and three o'clock," said Maxis, clenching his fist.

"What? What do you mean? Rrrng, open...!"

Cpt. Romano didn't finish saying the order as a bullet ripped through his chest, blood spraying everywhere. Before the soldiers had time to react, Maxis and Lothar each pulled out their weapons and quickly dispatched the soldiers on both sides.

As for the four Carabinieri in the center, the sound of Steiner's rifle could be heard after the first shot.

Four more bullets were fired, killing the Carabinieris with headshots. After five seconds the entire execution squad, including second in command Cpt. Romano, were dead. Maxis raised his hand before clenching his fist signaled Steiner.

"You owe me one though, that was a close call. Glad you guys made it out of there, otherwise I would have lost my two new friends." Steiner thinks this as he got up. He made his way toward the exhausted Germans, holding his rifle in a rest position.

"Good shot, man. I thought you would just run off back to base," said Lothar.

"Hmph, I was thinking of that, but my good conscious told me to stay, and nothing more."

"Good conscious or not you came at the right time and at the right place," commended Maxis. Steiner nodded in agreement.

"So, how are we going to get back, Maxis?" asked Lothar.

"Well, we must assume that Italy has already declared war. Which means there is no need to stay out any longer, though, I don't know if we can trek through the path to the right." Maxis looked at Steiner, expecting an answer.

Steiner didn't say anything but instead he motioned them to follow him outside of the entrance of the destroyed fortress. He stopped and pointed at an abandoned car with a machine gun mounted at the back. Steiner walked over to it then explained.

"This is the Dodge M30 scout car with a mounted gun on the back. This thing can go faster than any automobile we have in our arsenal. Perfect for our return to Heimdall Base, quick and clean. I know the roads well so I'm driving," Steiner finished, getting in the M30 scout.

"I'm sold. Let's get out of here!" said Lothar as he walked to the M30 Dodge scout car. Maxis hopped in the front next to Steiner and Lothar climbed on the back.

"Well, a Fiat-Revelli M1914 Machine gun with four boxes of ammo. Nice." Lothar loaded the ammo into the gun but when he looked up, he was horrified by what he had just seen.

"Maxis...we have situation!"

"What?" Maxis asked, resting on the seat.

"The fortress guns...they're rotating!" Lothar pointed.

Maxis looked back and that the fortress guns which weren't destroyed in the blast were now rotating toward their position.

"Steiner get this thing moving before..."

They heard a loud bang on the metal door and a slight metal bulge appeared on the metal. Steiner quickly turned the keys and started the engine. It roared but then died out. He tried again. The loud bang continued as if something was trying to get out.

"Steiner, what's taking so long? Those guns are almost aimed toward us!" Lothar said in a panic.

"I'm trying! Something must be...grrr!" Steiner groaned out of sheer frustration and kicked the car. It immediately comes to life.

The moment they drove off the fortress guns fired, letting off a thunderous boom as the dual shells flew, striking the location where the car once was. At the same time the metal doors burst opened, and a giant machine rolled out in hot pursuit of the M30 scout. As they drove down the dirt road, Maxis noticed the metal monstrosity gaining on them.

"What the hell is that?!" Maxis asked frantically.

"Oh Gott, that must be the Pavesi Tolotti coming in!" Lothar quickly fired his machine gun at it.

"That thing has tough armor. Steiner, try to lose that thing!" Maxis ordered.

Steiner shifted gears and the car moved faster. He then made a turn into a tunnel then out again, but the Pavesi Tolotti tank was still on their tail. Ahead was a curve where they slowed down to make the sharp turn, however, the Pavesi Tolotti managed to get close enough that the vertical wire cutters were shredding the back of their car and sparks started flying.

Lothar tried to aim at the tires, only to realize they were not tires at all, but instead a special type of wheel that was not inflated. Steiner managed to make another turn, breaking off the Pavesi Tolotti's shredding of the Dodge. The crew inside the armored vehicle manned the guns at the top where the two machine guns were located. They readied the MGs and began firing at the M30. The car zig-zagged to avoid the armored vehicles attack.

"This needs to end! Steiner, get us close to that Tolotti and stay on it. Lothar, suppress those guns! Also, you got a grenade?"

Lothar tossed Maxis a stick grenade before opening fire on the turrets. Steiner slowed down until he was directly on the side of the Pavesi Tolotti. Maxis jumped on clenched the sides and then pulled himself up. He took out his Mauser carbine and shoved the barrel into the machine gun port, gripping the machine gun. He unloaded several rounds into the port and the machine gun went silent. The gunner on the turret noticed and rotated its gun toward Maxis before firing. Maxis pulled the pin and shoved the grenade through the gun port.

Meanwhile, Steiner tried to get behind the armored vehicle but was warned there was another machine gun at the rear of it. They held their original position, then Maxis jumped back onto the car and told Steiner to "Floor it!" and M30 scout sped off again. The Pavesi Tolotti driver was ready to continue the chase until an explosion blew up one of the turrets, sending the vehicle swerving off the road.

During the ride the sound of constant artillery, machine guns, and rifle fire echoed throughout the Alps and valleys. They made it back to Heimdall Base in one piece, not only with the M30 scout, but also enemy intel and a job well done. As they entered the base, they spotted Major Weisse standing there and looking at his watch. The whole base was active with K.W.S. Alpine troops coming in and out, the artillery providing fire missions, planes taking off to provide recon, and armored cars rolled in waiting for tasks. The war in the mountains had finally arrived.

Steiner drove up in front of Major Weisse, Maxis and Lothar disembark. They saluted to the Major and returned their salute.

"Well, I'd say you arrived on schedule. I was expecting that your mission might take a day or two more, but it seems you've completed it, and you brought me a new car for the base! Terrific, exemplary work, well done, men," Major Weiss said as he looked at the Dodge.

"Sir, we also have obtained enemy intel from the Mountain Fortress," informed Maxis.

"So, it was fortress, huh? Very well. I'll get that decipher and send it back to Valhalla base. In the meantime, Sgt. Maxis and Cpl. Lothar, debrief in five minutes. Steiner, how were they?"

Steiner pulled down his covering and answered, "They're...tolerable, Sir."

"See that...tolerable. That means you made a good impression on him since he is a bit of the strong silent type, and a loner."

"I've noticed," said Maxis, grinning.

"Uh Sir, I have to report back to the quartermaster to give feedback on the equipment that R&D recently given us," said Lothar.

"Fine, be on your way then. Just report back to the mission room for debrief. That is all." Maj. Weisse walked away.

Lothar walked off to see Heinrich and Maxis was about to head off to the mission room.

"Hey, Sergeant," called Steiner.

"Yeah?" Maxis turned.

"If you ever need a sniper or an expert mountaineer, you know who to send. I like working with you guys, made the mission a little less 'stressful' for better or worse. Anyway, I'm going to take this Dodge to the motor pool, so the base can find a use for it. Catch you on the battlefield," Steiner gave a two-finger salute.

"Take care, Steiner. Hope to work with you again."

Steiner nodded, then drove away.

"This war has a lot of interesting characters. Though I love to see the look on Jorgensen's face when he hears this," Maxis pondered as he walked away.

Meanwhile in Paris, France at the Hasardeux Divisions Main HQ a couple days later...

Commander Molitor was at his desk signing off some paperwork when Maj. Fontaine barged right into his office with a soldier following him.

"Commandant Molitor, Commandant Molitor!" Fontaine stopped in the middle of the large office.

"I'm right here in front of you, Major. Quit shouting. What is an Italian soldier doing here?" Molitor said as he kept writing.

"Apologies, Sir. I come with grave news and with me to report that is 1Lt. Amato."

"Okay, Major. Tell me what happened."

"The Mountain Fortress that was to act as home base for the La legioni d'Italia has been destroyed."

"Quoi (what)!" Molitor stood up, his eyes now focused on Fontaine.

"I'm afraid it's true, Monsieur. 1Lt. Amato will explain the rest. Lieutenant?" Major Fontaine motioned the Lieutenant to step forward. He saluted Molitor.

"Tell me what happened, soldier," Molitor directed, with is hand behind his back.

"Commander Santoro was away on a meeting, leaving Second-in-command Romano in charge. I was with Cpt. Colombo when we heard reports of gunfire at the barracks. We rounded up our men and sounded the alarm. Habsburg infiltrators got inside our base and…"

"Wait, wait! Did you say Habsburgs infiltrated your base?"

"Yes. We thought we had them cornered in the armory with fifty plus men until they blew off the doors. Then they started slaughtering everyone with our own weapons even though we were fully armored. Cpt. Colombo was killed, but I managed to survive by playing dead." The First lieutenant looked down in shame.

"Hmm, something tells me these aren't typical Austro-Hungarians soldiers," Molitor commented as he sipped his coffee.

"We tried to fight and hold them off, but they broke through our defenses. We managed to evacuate the facility with eight cohorts, but regrettably left two behind. The rest of the legion went to their defensive positions because we thought there were more Habsburgs on the way."

"I'm sorry. I'm not familiar with the term 'cohort'. Is it something Santoro is using?" Molitor asked with puzzled look.

"It was Commander Santoro's idea to use old Roman military terms; a cohort is equivalent to a battalion which ranged from three hundred to a thousand troops, Sir."

"Now what were the loses?"

"Right now, we believe we lost six hundred. But rescue efforts are underway and so far, we've managed to free the fortress gunners from being barred from the rubble, but as for the rest I've yet to hear back."

Molitor's eyebrows raised after hearing that revelation but remained stern.

"What was enemy strength during the attack?" Molitor took another sip of his coffee.

"Two, Sir."

Molitor spit out his coffee, the sputtered. "T-two! Wait...what?! Were you able to properly identify the infiltrators? I have a very strong feeling you fought something far worse than Habsburgs." Molitor took out his handkerchief to clean up the mess.

"Well I...um...they were wearing armor, Sir. One had a spiked helmet and I don't know about the other."

Molitor sat back for a moment to think.

"Two soldiers took down an entire base...two soldiers stopped Cpt. Dubois' attack...and four soldiers wiped out Wellington's base camp. I'm sensing a pattern here."

"Did the enemy soldiers say anything?" Molitor asked.

"There was a time that I did catch their names. I think it was Maxis and...Lothar.

"Maxis and Lothar. That name Maxis rings a bell for I heard Commander Wellington muttering it to himself once during our meeting. Lothar, however, I don't seem to recognize it. Wait a minute...'Mauvais numéro, Croissant.' I remember now, he was the one on the phone who called me a croissant."

"Commander Molitor, we still have the upper hand to deal a direct blow to the Austrians and..."

Molitor raised his hand to silence the First Lieutenant.

"Italy had a chance to do so a month ago, but now the Russians are pulling back slowly from Galicia and the Austrians have entrench themselves in the Alps with more reinforcements. So, as for Cordona's grand plan to launch a quick assault through the mountains, instead they are going to get bogged in and will probably be stuck there. No thanks to K.W.S.

"K.W.S.? I've never heard of them, Sir."

"As you shouldn't. Dismissed!" Molitor ordered. The soldier exited the room quickly. Molitor rubbed his temples then looked to Major Fontaine.

"Major, fetch me the list of the most dangerous and infamous soldiers of the Central Powers, please."

"Oui, Monsieur (Yes, Sir)," said Fontaine as he walked away. A moment later, he returned with a file an inch thick, and placed it on the commander's desk. Molitor flipped through the pages.

"Commander, what are you looking?" Maj. Fontaine queried.

"Searching for two names, based on intelligence gathered by us, the British, and Russians. There!" Molitor reacts as he points at the name. Fontaine looked at the file as well.

"Sgt. Friedrich Wilhelm Maxis, known by many names. Der Wolf, Black Wolf, and the Black Wolf of Mons by the Belgians and the English. Even the R.O.B. are familiar with him as they dread hearing his name...

even Wellington. The Tayna Brigade know him as the Infamous Sergeant. Hmm, quite the reputation. It said he disappeared in November last year. Only to reappear as recent as of last month." Molitor flipped through the pages again.

"If he is such a menace then why hasn't anyone tried to stop him, Molitor?"

"Because the answer is simple, like a wolf he strikes fast and fierce then leaves before more dogs of war join the fight. He is an enigma, a phantom, the demonstrations, and characteristics of a hunter or...le tombeur de femmes (Wolf). Let's see...Lothar, Lothar...ah bon (good) it's here as well." Molitor found the file. Maj. Fontaine read aloud.

"Cpl. Ludvig Hansel Lothar...Known for brute strength, tough, and well known for his actions in Tannenberg. Known to his allies as the Juggernaut of Tannenberg and the Hero of the Masurian Lakes, that's it. Disappeared in early November 1914 as well," Fontaine paused.

"And has reappeared during our assault in Champagne and no doubt in Italy also," said Molitor.

"This man sounds almost like our newest yet troublesome member, Le Bête (The Beast). Though complete opposites of the coin, Commander."

"Oui, for now we just must keep an eye on these two. Something tells me they are about to become a headache for the Triple Entente, especially with the K.W.S. Battalion behind them and with Jorgensen at the helm. Put out a notice for our forces to be alert for these two and to maintain vigilance for K.W.S. movement." Molitor closed the file.

"Oui, monsieur. It will be done," Maj. Fontaine responded firmly and exited the room.

In May of 1915, Italy had officially joined the war on the side of the Entente. With promises of more land and territories, the Italians would enter the conflict with high hopes of a quick victory against the Austro-Hungarians. Instead, they found themselves in the costliest conflict in human history and the war in the mountains would begin yet another front.

CHAPTER 28

THE SANDHAI RAIDERS

June 5, 1915, Gallipoli, Ottoman Empire (Turkey)

In Gallipoli, Entente forces launched an assault on June 4th to take the high ridge of Achi Baba and the village of Krithia which commanded most of the peninsula. This was yet another attempt to take the first of the objectives at the beginning of the landings in April.

As the battle raged on between the British and the Ottomans, a rather large unit consisted of two full squads of R.O.B. and S.H.D. (Special Hazard Division) troops and a full platoon of Australian riflemen, New Zealand riflemen, and a small band of Maori troops as sharpshooters. It was still early in morning and the sun had yet to peak over the horizon.

The R.O.B. and S.H.D. managed to break their way through the Ottoman line, utilizing their advanced

427

weaponry (Howell rifles, a Lewis gun, Rossignol ENT B-1 &B-2s, Chauchat, grenades, and Hotchkiss LMGs) and experimental infiltration tactics with the platoon in tow. While British forces struggled for dominance, the Turks fought relentlessly for defense of their home and the infiltration unit made way for the village of Krithia in the ensuing chaos.

"Come on, lads. We're almost there," said the R.O.B. officer.

"Come on, come on, my friends. Keep marching," said S.H.D. officer as they trekked up the hill.

"Oi, what's with the poms sending us in with these strange fellows?" said an Aussie soldier.

"It doesn't matter mate. They, I mean we, managed to break through the Turks defense. I see the end in sight. We can finally take this town without the damn poms or the new troops pissing away out momentum," said another.

"I still can't believe we made it this far, snuck past the bastards. Surely this is the end of this bloody campaign and the hellish trench warfare. Enough of us Kiwis and Aussies combined have perished in this struggle for a rocky coast," said another NZ (New Zealander) soldier.

The two squads stopped as the squad leaders raised their hands in a fist. The platoon halted and everyone readied their weapons, checked their ammo, or reloaded their rifles. They heard the sound of loud marching as the two squads spread out; their weapons trained at the moving column of Turkish soldiers. The Maori sharpshooters shifted into position and the platoon did the same.

"Engage the enemy, lads!" the R.O.B. officer ordered. The squad leaders gave the signal to open fire and the Turkish column received a hail storm of bullets.

"Enemy ambush! Return fire...– *ack!*" The Ottoman officer is cut down along with his unit as they tried to fight back. The R.O.B. and S.H.D. pressed forward even though the platoon kept firing.

R.O.B. squad leader raises his hand and shouts, "Cease fire, lads!". The platoon was amazed at the speed and accuracy of these two squads with their odd weapons and complete aggressiveness toward the fearsome Turks.

"This sure beats the devil out using Enfield rifles, if you ask me, laddie. Just a wee bit, don't you know?" said R.O.B. soldier with Scottish accent.

"Sir, we've got some wounded Turks over here. Ideas?" asked an R.O.B. with Irish accent.

The officers looked at each other then back to the troops and responded with "No witnesses." Followed by gun fire. The platoon was in shock.

"The commonwealth troops won't understand, men. If we are to succeed, it is them who did the deed of capturing an essential objective. As our commander once said, "Goes the victor the writing of history" and as our motto suggests, "Advance, we dare" and so we do. Keep that in mind men," The R.O.B. officer reminded his squad as they gathered.

"Monsieur, we are closing on Krithia," said the S.H.D. officer as he pointed toward the village ahead.

"Good, then. Let's make haste, men. Time to claim the prize our empire has been denied for these last months. Onwards!"

They moved toward Krithia at a steady pace through the darkened fields; the rustle sand and dirt echoed in their march. There was barely any resistance to their approach but the sound of artillery could be heard in the distance. They passed many fortifications the Turks had built in preparation in case of a breakthrough, along with some ancient ruins.

The squads checked their surroundings as they entered the village. The buildings were slightly damaged from shells that went too far from their intended targets but most of the urban area was still in good condition as the squad passed through although the bath house had a minor hole in its roof. In the far distance, the squad could see the faint lights of their ships and dreadnoughts as barrels from their large cannons flashed before thundering boom could be heard.

"Spread out! Frenchie, take your men and secure the bath house. The platoon will hold the courtyard. This will be a momentous day for Britain and the Triple Entente. Once we hold Krithia, Gallipoli will be ours!"

The rest of the R.O.B. and S.H.D. cheered, while the platoon did not as they kept their wits about them. Suddenly everyone became quiet as someone appeared out of the shadows.

"I'm afraid I can't let you do that, Tommy," spoke a German officer in a khaki uniform wearing a pith helmet. He brandished his saber and a Walther Model 4 pistol.

A few soldiers of both the R.O.B. and S.H.D. chuckled a little except for the two officers. They immediately pulled out their pistols and aimed at the German officer; quickly the two squads followed their lead.

"You're a long way from home, Jerry. Especially for a K.W.S. officer of all things," said a R.O.B. officer, spotting the K.W.S. patch on the German's uniform.

"Hmm, I never did formally introduce myself. Well, as you know, my name is not Jerry. I'm Captain..."

"Sod off, Jerry!" an R.O.B. soldier shouted.

"You'd better surrender or die, German," barked an S.H.D. trooper. As the troops cursed at him, the platoon watching from the courtyard was confused. Nonetheless, they too had their rifles at the ready.

"What exactly are you going to do? We have the full might of His Majesty's army right here and there is only one of you K.W.S. Battalion bastards," taunted the R.O.B. officer.

"Monsieur, we're better off just getting rid of him and saving ourselves the trouble," said the S.H.D. officer. The two nodded in agreement.

The German officer chuckled. "You think I came here all alone? Well, let me make this quick for you. I'm Captain Dresden and I did not come alone. For I have brought with me..."

At once the loud sound of footsteps could be heard all around the buildings and in the alleyways. Suddenly, leaping off the rooftop, came a dark figure that was il-luminated by the sun's breaking light.

"Raiders!" Captain Dresden said as the figure landed on the first soldier, impaling him with dual blades, an Ottoman kilij and Yatagan Sword.

The soldier was wearing an all-white Ottoman uni-form and white kaffiyeh. The Ottoman soldier act-ed fast and he withdrew the Kilij sword then threw it at the nearest R.O.B. soldier, striking him deep with-in his chest. Then taking out a C96 stocked pistol and his Yatagan Sword, he attacked the British and French troops. He slashed the first then spun around then shot the the second before switching to his C96 handgun.

Cpt. Dresden fired and wounded the two officers then joined the Turk in coordination. The R.O.B. and S.H.D. couldn't back away but instead engaged in the melee with their rifles and knives as they charged toward the pair with a loud war cry.

"Come lads! They need our help. Let's get the bas-tards!" an Aussie shouted.

The platoon snapped out of their shock and immedi-ately rushed in to help when the wooden panels on the windows in the buildings opened. What followed was intense fire from the windows as German, Hapsburg, and Ottoman soldiers, all wearing the K.W.S. patch on them, fired with Mondragon M1908 self-loaders, Madsen machine guns, and a MG08.

The platoon was cut down with a few fighters return-ing fire toward the buildings, however, the fire was in-tense forcing several of them to retreat for cover. The

Moari sharpshooters had a hard time trying to pick off their targets; every time they spotted the shooters, straight away the K.W.S. soldier would relocate.

The two squads remained engaged in the melee, taking severe damage as their numbers dwindled. The Ottoman soldier tore through their ranks with precision shots, while Dresden kept up his assault. Soon the rest of the raiders emerged from their hiding place and struck down the remaining platoon members. Appeared from the rooftops, the alleyways, and the courtyard, the raiders in the courtyard charged in with bayonets fixed, screaming like mad men.

"Damn it all, mates. Time to fall back! To hell with this," lamented the Australian soldier. They made a mad dash back to where they came from. Cpt. Dresden raised his hand and immediately the K.W.S. soldiers ceased fire.

"Captain, should we purse them?"

"Nein soldat (soldier), let them go. If they are lucky enough to make it back to their trench lines with the British, so be it. Men, we have driven them back. Cpl. Yusuf Al-Khali, satisfied with your little show of skills, are you?" Cpt. Dresden asked. The Ottoman soldier removed his Kiji sword from the corpse, then turned to answer.

"I will be satisfied when the imperialist beast is kicked off our shores, to answer your question..." Yusuf twirled his swords, blood flying off before sheathing them. "Evet, kaptan (Yes, captain). I am satisfied," Yusuf finished with a smile.

"Good! Sergeant Willy, take your men and scout out the outer perimeter. Cpl. Berger, send a runner and inform Colonel Kemal of the recent development. The rest of you gather the wounded enemy and patch them up so we can transport them back to HQ and get them a real doctor. Los Sandhai (Go Sandsharks)!" Cpt. Dresden ordered. Everyone scrambled with their given tasks.

In the aftermath of the battle, they searched and checked the bodies. If they were dead, they put them to the side, respectfully and for the living they would perform first aid. They transported them to a truck, then loaded them onto a train bound to the K.W.S. Sandhai Raider HQ. The soldiers that survived the ordeal, especially those who managed to survive Yusuf's sword dance, were treated carefully by Trench Surgeons as some of them were in critical condition. Yusuf muttered a little prayer for his foes, as he wandered past the corpses.

"*Cough...Cough.* Damn...savage!" choked an R.O.B. soldier lying on the ground.

"What did you just say?" Yusuf turned with a look of anger.

"Damn Savage! Bloody Ottoman savages the lot of you!" the soldier cursed while coughing up blood.

"Maybe I should do you a favor and end your pagan bad mouthing, wounded British Lion! Ahirette huzur bulursun (You will find peace in the hereafter)," Yusuf offered and unsheathed his swords.

"Yusuf, hayır (no)! I said take them alive not cut them alive!" Cpt. Dresden barked.

434

"But Cpt. Dresden, this infidel decided to insult the honor of my country, my people, and the Sultan! I was granting him a merciful death."

"The answer is no, Corporal. Let the Trench Surgeons treat him."

"Evet, Efendim (Yes, Sir)," Yusuf responded as he sheathed his weapons. He looked at the British soldier one more time.

"You have been spared by the German eagle, but the grey wolf will always be around to end your miserable existence. Believe that, English!" Yusuf spit on the ground before walking away as two K.W.S. soldiers move in with the stretcher.

The objectives of the Third Battle of Krithia had been more realistic than the previous attempts, but it ended in failure; all the same with only small gains for the British. However, that changed when the Ottomans launched a counter attacked so effective to the point of almost breaking the British forces and would stem the attack. The Triple Entente withdrew from the Gallipoli Peninsula in January 1916, after eight months of heavy fighting and torturous trench warfare. It was a military disaster for the British that helped strengthen and unite the Ottomans instead of demoralizing or weakening them.

CHAPTER 29

THERE WAS THUNDER
IN ARTOIS

June 15, 1915, Artois, France

Maxis sat on his bunk in the underground barracks writing his journal while the rain and artillery was heard from outside. The ground would shake every time a shell hit near the trench knocking items over but for Maxis it was more of an annoyance.

"A couple of interesting things happened after the mission in the Italian Alps. For starters, we stayed for another week to provide support as much as we could before being redeployed to our new assignment, which I'm not at the liberty to say since it is classified. Plus the Geist platoon has been keeping a close eye on me and my journal. Before we were sent to Artois, I heard we launched a combined offensive with the Austro-Hungarians, helping them push the Russians back, which also means K.W.S. had been busy

but so was the Tayna Brigade. I have heard rumors that the "Huntress" or what Lothar likes to call her sometimes, either that or hundin (bitch,) has been making strides against our forces and K.W.S.

I heard another rumor that one K.W.S. squad got completely wiped out by her, which normally is rare, since we try to keep casualties to a minimum, however, a wipe-out was a bit shocking to us. The circumstance is that we are marching on the Russians...hard into their territory...so Tayna is getting serious, with Col. Vorshevsky calling the shots and unleashing more prototype weapons against us and worst...Arina is at the far front of it all. The only good news is that we recently liberated Przemyśl Fortress, though a bit late. It would have been nice to work with Colonel Josef and Cpl. Zell had they joined the K.W.S.

It's been a while since we worked with a whole squad, specifically the now disbanded Grün squad, I wonder how they're doing right now? I do hope they survive this conflict since Italy joined the Entente and the war is getting bigger every month. Speaking of surviving, I still owe Lothar one for saving me when that pipe fell on me. The harsh lesson is that when you have someone tall and very strong like Lothar around, and someone fast and efficient yet strategically deadly like me, we certainly are a force to be reckoned with...although Lothar has been thinking and planning more effectively, but not fast as I am. Steiner was an interesting character, quiet and deadly with a rifle. He certainly helped a lot in our operation in the mountains. If there was a unit or squad to be formed, I would want him *onboard since him and Kruger would be a deadly combination and likely the best of friends."*

Maxis closed his journal and reached for his footlocker but before he put it away, he took one last glance at the scorch marks on the edges of the journal. The ground shook and dirt fell from the ceiling.

"I almost lost you in Italy, but this time you are staying here," Maxis said to himself.

After putting the journal away, he grabbed his kit, rucksack, two Kugel stick grenades (M1913/15 Poppenberg), and a flare gun. Then he put a small bandolier for flare shells around his right arm, the Bittner pistol, and a Mondragon 1908 self-loading rifle with a painted reflex sight. He walked up the stairs and out the door.

The sky was overcast as rain continued to fall lightly; the artillery fired on a regular continuous schedule. Maxis walked through the cross-sections of the trench lines until he made it to another dugout and walked inside to find Lothar sitting on the crate wearing his Gaede helmet and his new feldgrau colored scarf around his neck. He was analyzing his new rifle that had been issued to him. He looked up to see Maxis descending the stairs.

"Oh, hey Maxis," greeted Lothar.

"Guten Nachmittag (Good afternoon), Lothar. I see that you're still working on your new rifle."

"sigh This thing is a pain," Lothar signed. "The Madsen M1896 (self-loading) rifle is interesting but I can't seem to get this last screw in...I keep dropping it!" Lothar struggled to put the last piece in its place.

"Here let me help," Maxis walked over and Lothar handed him the rifle.

"It's a bit odd that Lothar is using a self-loading rifle though without proper training. Then again, we are in the middle of another French offensive which means weapon shortages. The only reason he chose this model is because he's familiar with the company's work. Even if he's an MG specialist that doesn't normally play with self-loading rifles. He should have taken advanced riflemen class," Maxis thought as he put the last screw in its hole, then grabbed the screwdriver. After tightening it, he cocked the rifle and pulled the trigger only to hear a click.

"There."

"Pfft, like I said, a pain," Lothar retorted.

"Welcome to my world. At least you can use magazines while I'm stuck with stripper clips for this thing. Anyway, did you survey the area like I ask?" Maxis asked.

"Yep, took a lift in the observation balloon and managed to doodle a small map for our infiltration tonight," said Lothar, loading bullets into his Mauser "Zigzag" revolver.

"Good. That means you're taking point on this one."

"I can't wait. I'll be sure not to guide us through a machine gun nest," Lothar said with a bit of sarcasm and a smile.

"Ok, now I'm worried."

Lothar laughed a bit before speaking.

"Heh, I managed to get in contact with...oh, before I forget. Here are your wire cutters. I have mine already."

Lothar tossed the pair of heavy-duty wire cutters to Maxis. He caught it and attached it to his belt.

"Hey, I forgot to ask. Do you have that special barrel extension you received from R&D?" Lothar asked as he got up.

"Oh, yeah. I forgot about it. Hold on," Maxis reached into his pocket and pulled out a black barrel.

"This is an exact working replica of the Maxim Silencer, but R&D made some improvements to this device."

"Did you manage to test it out yet?"

"Not yet, though I'm about to find out. Come on," Maxis put the silencer in his pocket and walked out of the dugout. Lothar holstered his revolver, grabbed his rifle, along with four stick grenades, three kugel ball grenades, handheld flares, tornister, and a compact trench knife with a knuckle duster.

They both walked outside of the dugout and made their way to the jump-off trench. When they arrived, Maxis put the silencer on to his pistol. It was specially threaded for such, and fired a few shots to their amazement. They heard very little besides the shells hitting the wooden board. After the test fire, they sat down in the jump-off trench and waited for night fall.

"Hey Maxis, do you mind recapping the mission to me again; that Lieutenant was a bit too short with us during our briefing. Hate to admit it, but Reinhard did a better presentation than his stand in," said Lothar as he held his rifle close.

"Certainly. We are about to commence Operation: Donnerschlag (Thunder strike). Air recon spotted the

Regiment of Britannia setting up base camp in the Artois region. Since the French are in the middle of their offensive it seems the Regiment of Britannia is willing to lend support to the battered French. From what our phone interceptors, you know, those field phones of the earth return variety, and photos from air recon have provided, base camp King George is serving as a launching point for their little shock operation that will be coming soon."

"Little? The number of armored cars, big guns, and anti-air that was in the photo says otherwise!" Lothar interrupted.

"You're telling me! Anyway, our objective is to infiltrate through no man's land, pass the French trench lines undetected, then do nine kilometer (five mile) march through the countryside, and find the base camp. Once we locate it, we need to clear out the pom-pom guns and anyone else, then mark the target zones such as ammo depots, command center, barracks, and artillery. The Prussian Blue Tails will be flying in at noon which will give us enough time to clear out any resistance. They will be flying with a new prototype, a modified Siemens-Schuckert Gleiter (Flying Torpedo or Flying Bomb) that is radio controlled!" Maxis explained with excitement.

"Radio controlled!? Boy, I would like to see that baby fly!"

"R&D took an existing prototype and gave it more add-ons. It seems there is nothing lab boys, military inventors, and intellectuals cannot do when they work together. It's almost frightening," Maxis said with sincerity.

"The longer this war keeps going, we are going to see more wonderous and yet bizarre or even terrifying weapons of war on the battlefields, either from us or from Triple Entente. That is the same thing you told me once after that incident in Bochnia," Lothar slowly peered over the parapet.

"Too right."

"So, when do we start our infiltration, Max?"

"At midnight. We are going in to do our job and get out. We're supposed to meet at the rear trench line with Geist agents when we finish our mission. Hopefully, they don't forget our things," Maxis shifted and made himself comfortable while maintaining watch.

They sat there and waited, all while keeping a look-out toward no man's land. As day turned to night, it was now time to begin the operation. Maxis pulled out his black cover for his pickelhaube and puts it on then pulled up his blue scarf over his nose. Lothar grabbed some dirt to coat his new Gaede helmet and pulled his feldgrau scarf over his nose.

He went first, Maxis following right behind him as they went over the top. The two crouched down, then sprinted across the desolate landscape passing through the mud, shell holes, and puddles, some as big as miniature lakes. They moved quickly and carefully.

The area was under cover of complete darkness, for the only source of light was flashes from the artillery impacting the ground or illuminating the sky with tracers; the leftover fire was still burning off dead trees, wagons, and destroyed buildings.

Time and time again they came across the fallen, the stench of death fresh in the air and sound of flies buzzing about; either that or the coppery odor of fresh blood. In a bright flash, the rotting corpses could be seen, badly decomposed or near a skeletal state. The sights were all too familiar for the daring two, but still they pressed on. Lothar immediately dropped to the ground; Maxis did the same.

"Stay down, we've got incoming! Trench raiders. Just act like a corpse," Lothar whispered. They heard distant voices coming toward them; the sound grew louder.

"Keep moving, men," whispered one French soldier as he passed by.

"We're gonna take the Germans by surprise!" whispered another French soldier.

"Keep quiet!"

The trench raiding team moved past Maxis and Lothar, paying them no mind. The French did their best not to trip over the bodies, except for one. A French soldier bumped into Lothar and Lothar held his breath, his heart racing.

"Merde (Shit)! A corpse. What waste," complained the soldier, sounding annoyed.

The soldier walked over Lothar but then immediately fell, tripping over another body. The other soldiers try to contain their laughs.

"Damn it! They are like cats who are always in the way!" The Frenchmen kicked Maxis' side out of frustration.

Maxis tried not to let out peep after getting kicked; the pain was present but was quickly replaced with anger.

"Ok, now I'm mad!" Maxis thought.

After the trench raiding party passed, Lothar turned to Maxis.

"Maxis, what's the game plan?" he asked.

"One grenade!" replied Maxis as he turned over on his back and pulled out kugel stick grenade. He pulled the pin, counted to three ,then threw it hard as he could; it twirled in the air. The grenade struck the back of the Frenchmen's head and he jerked around.

"My god! What just hit me?...Grenade!" the Frenchmen shouted as the grenade exploded taking out five others along with him.

The remaining ten were confused and in a panic; now are making too much noise. This attracted the German sentry's attention who then fired a flare into the sky, lighting the whole area. Maxis and Lothar kept their eyes closed, blocking the flare's blinding light.

The gunners of the MG08s opened fire on the trench raiders, ripping them to shreds; even the riflemen joined in. The raiders died in mere seconds. After the flare died out and the screams of Frenchmen ceased, they moved on.

"Geez, I'll remember not to get you mad," said Lothar.

"Let's just keep moving," said Maxis.

They slowly got up, now covered in mud as they proceeded a little bit further to the French trench line. Lothar stopped the moment his rifle rattles the barbwire. He quickly quieted the rattle.

"Hey, we made it. Get over here, so we can cut it together, Maxis."

Maxis moved slowly, dropped prone, and then pulled out the wire cutters.

"Alright, we'll cut the wire when the artillery hits. That will conceal the noise. Wait for the impact," instructed Maxis.

"Got it."

They waited until they could hear the whistle of an incoming shell before making an impact. Maxis and Lothar cut the first layer of barb wire before stopping. Another whistle was coming, and the result was the same...they cut through. They continued the process through the first, second, and third rolls of barbed wire as they slowly crawled under.

While they were cutting the second wire, Maxis failed to notice the corpse hanging from the barbed wire above them. Shortly after cutting through, the corpse fell on top of Maxis literally making him gasp as the flash of the artillery impact revealed the badly decomposed corpse of a German soldier's face, riddled with maggots, missing an eyeball, and his jaw wide open. Maxis gingerly laid the rotting corpse aside.

After cutting through the third roll of wire, they holstered their wire cutters and crawled forward. Ten feet in front of them was the trench line. The faint lantern lights could be seen and there was small pile of sandbags in the middle, with a small opening and sticking above that was a periscope. Maxis moved closer to Lothar and spoke quietly.

"French sentry. You flank right, I got left. Move silently, no need to draw attention."

Lothar crawled slowly and carefully to the right as Maxis moved to the left. The sentry was standing still looking through the small opening in the sandbags but he was slowly dosing off and struggling to stay awake. The sentry started to mutter to himself as Lothar crawled near him.

"I must stay awake. The Germans could be anywhere. Oh man, I'm so tired. I'm glad I'm not in the meat grinder unlike the others," mumbled the French sentry, keeping himself awake.

Lothar grabbed the sentry by the head, keeping his mouth shut as he muffled him. He held the sentry's neck until he passed out. As the body went limp, Lothar gently lowered him down to the ground then jumped into the trench and made some adjustments to make it look like he was sleeping.

"Rest soldier, for you deserve it," said Lothar, as the soldier was sound asleep.

"You knocked him out without making a sound or killing him. Impressive," said Maxis as he jumped into the trench carefully. He pulled out his Bittner pistol.

"*The only thing that I didn't tell Lothar is that these silencers are sensitive to heat if fired too much. Though that shouldn't be a problem if I was using a machine gun, but I must display restraint and only fire as a last a resort, if there are no other alternatives,.*" Maxis thought as he attached the silencer then pulled out the blade from the inside of his boot.

Maxis moved forward but with Lothar still taking point. The trench line was less active as the French were seen sitting in a row sleeping and snoring, now accustomed to the sound of constant artillery. Some slept with their rifles while others had their pistols.

Not even one soldier was awake, even the officer was resting comfortably in his chair while everyone else was on the ground. Maxis and Lothar moved about carefully over the soldiers so as not to alert them. They were almost past the first trench line when Lothar accidentally tripped over a soldier's boot. The French soldier moved slightly and groaned.

"Uh, it's already my turn?" stammered the French soldier, stretching. Lothar acted fast and he pulled down his scarf and spoke.

"No, soldier. Sorry, it's not time yet. Go back to sleep."

"Oh, okay," he responded, and without even opening his eyes went back to sleep. Maxis lowered his pistol, breathed a sigh of relief, and immediately gave Lothar a thumbs up.

They moved past the first trench and as they entered the second, continued navigating through the network. Lothar passed a wooden door and paid it no mind until the door swung wide open behind him. A French soldier stepped out of the built-in out-house.

"Ugh, no more onion on bread and..." Before he finished his sentence, Maxis sprung into action and plunged his blade into the soldier's neck, then pressed the silenced pistol into his chest and fired three rounds.

He caught the body and quickly put him back into the stall in a sitting position, then closed the door. Maxis reloaded his Bittner and placed another en-bloc clip into the pistol.

"*He died as he lived...in the shitter,*" Maxis thought jokingly.

After traversing the second trench line, narrowly avoiding patrols by either knocking them out or silencing them permanently, they tried to find creative ways to hide the bodies. Eventually they reached the rear trench line. Lothar moved across it just before he heard someone singing, coming from the path on the left.

Lothar signaled Maxis to hold position. Maxis had his knife and pistol at the ready. A French soldier walked by singing a song most dear and patriotic to his heart and mind. Upon hearing that song, Lothar was immediately aggravated by it and quickly interjected with "J'aime mes oignons dans un ragoût!" before delivering a right hook to the man's face. The punch sent the Frenchman flying and he hit the ground hard. Maxis moved in quickly and dragged the unconscious soldier away from sight and placed him in a corner where no one would notice him. He then turned to Lothar and whispered.

"Lothar, what the hell was that for? What was he singing that made you do that?" Maxis quietly demanded.

"Well, Maxis, he was singing 'The song of the onion'."

"Song of the onion? Never mind. What did you say?"

"For starters he was talking about loving to fry the onion in oil, and I said, 'I love my onions in a stew' before knocking him out."

Maxis rubbed his hand on his fore head and took a deep breath.

"Just move."

"Ja, Feldwebel (Yes, Sergeant)," Lothar replied.

They moved through the rear trench line. As they reached the end, they heard the noise of trucks, artillery fire, and men shouting behind a set of ragged cloth sheets hanging at the exit.

"What's going on out there? Quick, let's check it out," said Lothar, moving closer behind the cloth, Maxis right beside him.

Lothar moved the cloth slightly with his rifle and observed major activity in the rear of the trench. There were French infantry arriving by wagon, truck, and on foot. There were armored cars parked in rows, and artillery trucks were rolling in.

"Verdammt (Damn)! It's a circus out here. I can still see our exit point where the light ends. How are we going to do this, Maxis?"

Maxis moved the cloth again and took another glance then turned to Lothar.

"Ok, do you see where the armored cars are parked. We'll rush over when no one's looking, past the artillery truck, duck underneath the armored cars, make our way to those crates, and finally into the tall grass, covered by the night."

"Too much for me to memorize. Can you take it from here?" Lothar asked, relinquishing his lead to Maxis.

"Very well. We'll move on my mark. Move fast and try keep up, got it?"

Lothar nodded and they waited as a truck rolled past them.

"Steady...steady...Los(go)!" Maxis whispered as he bolted out toward the artillery truck with Lothar fast behind. They hid behind the artillery truck as a group of French soldiers' jogged by with their Sergeant shouting "Bouge, bouge (Move, move)! We are needed at the armory."

"Wait for it...Los (Go)!" Maxis said. He and Lothar rushed forward toward the armored cars and quickly went prone with Lothar shifting on his side because of his tornister.

They crawled underneath, then Maxis directed, "Position halten (hold position)!" as a truck pulled up to park right where they were about to exit. The front of the truck was facing toward the armored cars and the occupants disembarked from both sides of the vehicle. As their boots hit the ground Maxis grasped his pistol and watched them walk away.

"Alright, we're in the clear for now. Let's keep moving. Crawl under the truck, hurry!" Maxis whispered as he crawled forward.

They moved through the mud under the truck which slowed them down. When they reached the end of the line of trucks, they got up quickly and moved toward the crates. Hiding behind the crates as a Frenchmen walked by, they waited until another artillery truck approached. Then Maxis and Lothar moved to the other side of the truck to avoid detection before moving toward the tall grass under the cover of darkness. Maxis stopped suddenly, as they were nearing the artillery position.

"Don't move! We've got a lookout on the tower. Cover me, I going to take the shot, otherwise he'll spot us for sure." Maxis took aim with his rifle and waited for the artillery to fire.

"Heard, providing cover," said Lothar, checking their surroundings.

The artillery fired with thunderous booms and Maxis immediately fired his shot at the watchman who jerked back before falling dead.

"Alright we're in the clear. Move out," Maxis said.

They moved into the tall grass, hidden from sight. The infiltration is a success and the rest of their journey clear as they push through the tall grass, and able to move faster than normal. At last the sound of artillery fire became ever more distant, but what lies ahead in their mission remains to be seen.

CHAPTER 30

ADVANCE TO THE R.O.B. BASE

They stopped to take a breather. Lothar looked up at the now clear sky, the stars now twinkling bright like diamonds. Maxis sat down and opened the bolt in his rifle to load one shell then unscrewed the silencer from his Bittner pistol. He put the silencer in his pocket while Lothar sat there still watching the stars.

"It's quite remarkable that our infiltration was successful. We are one of the few squads in K.W.S. to pull off such a feat, while the Geist Platoon can do it in their sleep; though I can't say the same for the Ententes, specifically the Regiment of Britannia or the Hasardeux Division. For weeks they tried to infiltrate our lines and come into the occupied lands that we are holding, but their squads wouldn't get far as they were intercepted rather quickly by Geist Platoon or a K.W.S. squad. The end result would be three things...an all-out firefight, surrendering, or retreat, which they would end up with casualties regardless,

as more K.W.S. squads and even the Prussian Blue Tails would join in on the hunt whether it's behind the lines or on the frontlines; that is until they reach their home base and the hunt is called off," Maxis thought as he began loading another en-bloc clip into his Bittner and continued his thoughts while cleaning the dirt off his weapons.

"The Tayna Brigade however is a different topic. With people like Arina on their side it's a bit troubling since they already know we cracked their codes and still we cannot anticipate their movement. Time and time again when we tried to infiltrate their territory it seemed like a game of cat and mouse, with her as wolf instead of a cat. Some of our squads returned, either driven off or badly wounded after leaving the domain of the Bear or being hunted by a she-wolf." Maxis holstered his weapon and turns to Lothar and asked.

"Hey, you mentioned earlier about how you managed to get in contact with someone. Who was it?" Maxis quizzed Lothar.

"Oh yeah...I managed to get in contact with Fischer. I sent a letter to him a long time ago. I haven't heard anything since, until a couple of days ago when I received a letter from him."

"What did the letter contain?"

"From what I can remember, that the censors had not blacked out...Fischer, Graf, Kruger, and Kraus all were busy with 'special' missions that they're not allowed to say, which was obvious. Weber, Muller, Konig, and of course Brandt, were sent to the Eastern

Front to join the two new K.W.S. bases that were established. They've been doing fine, besides defying the odds stacked against them and nearly getting obliterated by the combined might of the Triple Entente. Other than that, it's business as usual. Fischer wrote that he speaks for all that they kind of missed having you as their squad leader, well, all except Brandt, of course," Lothar finished as he stood up.

"Touching."

"Well, you set an example for them, Maxis. And the same can be said for me as well," Lothar said.

"Indeed."

"Now, I think I've had enough looking at the stars for the night. Shall we proceed to our objective?" Lothar asked.

"What? Don't want to wait for Hailey's Comet?" Maxis replied sarcastically.

"Ha, good one, but no, I'm more interested in seeing that prototype fly actually."

"Then marsch soldat (march soldier)! We have a long walk ahead," Maxis said firmly.

Lothar pulled out his flashlight and led the way. They marched across the countryside with the stars above and the path being only illuminated with one source of light as they walked. It was silent except for the sound of their footsteps crushing the grass.

By six o'clock the sun finally started to appear on the horizon and birds began chirping, Maxis took off the black cover off his pickelhaube and stuffed it in his rucksack. The area looked normal, untouched by the war, and the French countryside was a magnificent sight to behold. They came to a dirt road and everything changed when Maxis heard music and a car engine on the road in the distance.

"Incoming! Get down!" Maxis ordered frantically.

They both hit the deck as the sound of the music and noise of the engine grew louder. Driving by was a truck carrying a squad of British soldiers who were listening to their record player that they had taken with them on the ride. The tires kicked up dust in the air leaving a trail as they drove by Maxis and Lothar who were perfectly concealed in the tall grass.

"Alles klar (all clear)," said Maxis as he emerged from the tall grass.

"Well, that was close. Good ear, Maxis," Lothar got up, dusting himself off.

"Thanks. Judging by the direction that truck went we seem to be heading in the right direction, thanks to them."

"Hmph, never thought we would be thanking Tommy for leading us back to their base...oh well." Lothar said with a grin.

The two proceeded further on toward the Regiment of Britannia's base. After marching a full nine kilometers (five miles) they started to see smoke trails in the distance.

Maxis moved ahead with Lothar right behind him, both with their weapons at the ready. Needing to check out what was ahead, they low-crawled up a hill to get a good vantage point. Maxis pulled out his binoculars and Lothar reached for his spy glass.

"Hmm...they're making a base in an abandoned small village using some of the houses and buildings as their barracks. There's also Rolls Royce armored cars, Landchester armored cars, and AEC B-type London passenger bus, turned armored trucks, though without the second deck above," observed Maxis.

"I can see where their ammo depot is located and a few tents. Ok, I have spotted the three QF2pdr MKII and two Lanzia QF3pdr mobile pom-pom guns parked on the other end of the base," said Lothar as he looked closely with his spy glass.

"Das gut (That's good). Our first target finally spotted. Now let's see what the troops are and...oh no."

"Oh, no? What do you mean?" Lothar hurriedly asked.

"Lothar, take a look at that group of soldiers taking smoke break. There against the wall of the white building with flowers on the left."

Lothar focused where Maxis described the location.

"Do you see them?"

"Nein, what am I looking for? All I see is couple of Scottish Highlanders and a couple of Indian troops taking a break."

"And not to mention the Gurkhas," said Maxis.

"Gurkhas?! Here?! How-How can you be certain?"

"Look at the Kukri that they carry on their uniforms."

"Verdammt (Damn it), I hate fighting these guys. They almost killed Graf during the Second Battle of Ypres. We've got to be careful. They are seriously nuts when comes to combat especially in close quarter."

"Noted, Corporal. Let's keep surveying and see what they have in store, and I can see Fijian soldiers as well and they are carrying...Totokia clubs. Hold on, what the hell is that?" Maxis pointed toward the end of the base. Lothar looked once more with his spy glass.

"What, oh...yep, that's a rail gun and those train tracks weren't there before in the photos which means they just recently built them."

"Can you identify the make and model, Lothar?"

"That is a British Ordnance BL 12-inch Mk IX rail gun. If it's here that means the Regiment of Britannia really are going to try to punch a hole in the frontlines along with their armored units. Though, good luck with the mud."

"Come on. Let's go in for a closer look, shall we?" said Maxis, getting up and putting away the binoculars.

"Lead the way," Lothar agreed as he did the same and put his spy glass away.

They moved in carefully toward one of the houses without being detected. Lothar squatted down with hands together to give Maxis a boost. As he stepped on Lothar's hands he was thrusted upward and reached the roof's edge. Maxis then reached down as Lothar jumped up and grabbed his arm. It took all his strength to pull Lothar up, then they crawled to the peak of the rooftop.

"Alright, here is the battle plan. Judging by the amount of troop movement we saw, there must be at least a platoon's worth here. I'll throw my last grenade at the oil barrels they have stacked at the corner. The massive explosion that will cause confusion, enough for us to spring into action and cut them down quickly."

"Got it. Let's do this."

CHAPTER 31

FIREFIGHT IN THE BASE CAMP

Meanwhile in the command tent in Base Camp King George...

1Lt. Wilson was on the phone in the command tent while the troops carried out their business of performing regular tasks around base.

"Yes Sir, everything is prepped for the upcoming shock operation. The rail gun is loaded and ready to unleash Britain's might on Jerry. The colonials are also ready for action; the Gurkhas thirst for combat, Fijians are itching for scraping, Highlanders have checked their rifle countless time, the Indian troops making sure their bayonets and blades are extra sharp, and our small detachment of Britannia's finest are ready for war. Sir. No, Sir. I haven't seen the extra reinforcement. They've not yet arrived, but when they do, we'll get things started, Commander Wellington. I'll be sure to keep an eye out for Griffin squadron in the skies when we get under way.

Thank you, Sir. I'll return to HQ when the commanding officer for this unit arrives. Goodbye," 1Lt. Wilson put the phone down and headed outside of the command tent and into the center of the base.

"Alright, you miserable lumps and colonials gather round!" 1Lt. Wilson ordered. The platoon gathered round at the center of the village near the well and awaited what the lieutenant had to say.

"Our operation will begin soon as more reinforcements arrive. We will stay put until then."

Everyone groaned at the news and immediately started commenting.

"Come on now, we've been standing around for too long," complained a Gurkha soldier.

"I agree. We should be in the fight by now," added an Indian soldier.

"What's taking those blokes so long?" a Highlander added third.

"'Advance, we dare' is our motto not 'sit and stare', Sir!" said an R.O.B. soldier.

1Lt.Wilson responded to the impatient soldiers.

"I know, I know. Calm yourselves, ya bloody wankers. You are eager for battle and want to end this war, but we can't just go in without additional support. The French may be present even though they're too busy with their own offensive. It doesn't hurt to be a bit cautious after the wipeout of Base Camp Elizabeth where many of our brothers-in-arms perished at the hands of Jerry's elite and one of their most savage soldiers the Black Wolf of..." Before he could finish that sentence, a kugel stick grenade hit the metal oil barrels creating a loud bang.

Everyoneturnedaroundtosee,onlytobemetbyamassive explosion that incinerated several soldiers who were close to it. The tremendously loud explosion shook everyone to their core, and the large fire that followed spread slowly consuming the nearby tents. Many men died from the explosion and others were rolling on the ground still on fire.

What came next was hellfire from the rooftop as bullets sprayed the area. Maxis quickly took down the gun crews on the stationary QF2 pom-pom guns then Lothar fired the first rounds taking down ten soldiers while everyone quickly ran for cover.

"It's them! It's K.W.S.! To action stations! Battle station! Repel the bastards! We cannot let them interfere with our operation!" said 1Lt.Wilson, as he ran behind a building before being stopped by an R.O.B. soldier.

"Wait a moment...where the hell are you going, Sir?! Shouldn't you be helping guide the troops?"

"Are you mad?! They'll go for the officers first, if you haven't realized that. Now unhand me and fight!" 1Lt. Wilson shouted as a bullet whistled by.

Maxis and Lothar laid continuous fire from the rooftop, shell casings rolling off the edge. The combatants at the base returned fire though they could not hit anything due to the confusion, chaos, and being suppressed.

"It's a bit odd that these guys don't seem to be armed with their usual prototype weapons or self-loaders, just SMLE rifles. Looks like we have the high ground and the upper hand," Maxis thought, still firing.

Lothar kept firing his Madsen 1896 self-loading rifle at the British, killing, wounding, and occasionally missing one before reloading quickly. He threw his grenades at soldiers who had entrenched themselves behind cover. Each grenade thrown destroyed any form of cover and sent some R.O.B. soldiers flying through the air with limbs missing. Others tried to find new cover only to get cut down in the open. The two German soldiers made sure none of Brits tried to make a run for the Vickers machine guns or the pom-pom guns.

The battle ensued until the Highlanders managed to regroup and fired all together, utilizing the "mad minute" that quickly forced the Germans to take cover. This in turn allowed some of the Indian troops to rush over to the BL 12-inch gun that sat there dormant.

The squad of ten together with several Gurkhas reached the rail gun. The Highlanders fired their last shots before reloading, eventually taking fire again and taking casualties. The Indian troops cranked the gun toward the house where Maxis and Lothar were. The two were occupied with R.O.B. who were now pressing the advance toward the house; slowly the rail gun had moved into position, facing right at them.

"Hölle (hell), these guys are starting to move on us and...oh scheisse(shit)! We need to get off the roof!" said Lothar, pointing at the rail gun which was almost ready to fire.

"MOVE!" Maxis yelled and the two moved quickly to get off the roof while bullets whistled and snapped around them.

"Fire!" shouted one the Indian soldiers.

The rail gun fired with such force that it kicked the dust off the ground and the sound was deafening for operators, their ears ringing. The shells struck fast at the house and just in the nick of time as Maxis and Lothar jumped off the building as it blew up from the impact from the 12-inch gun.

The explosion sent them flying in the air. When they hit the ground Maxis felt pieces of wood and small amounts of shrapnel on his uniform. He looked at Lothar and saw a piece of metal lodged in his tornister.

The R.O.B. soldiers took the opportunity to deploy smoke grenades to the daring duo's position, creating a large plum. Maxis got up quickly even though he was a bit shaky and his leg trembling. He helped Lothar up and they grabbed their rifles and went back-to-back. Maxis quickly attached his bayonet to his rifle.

"Oh Gott (God), what is the deal with us getting blown up? It's bad enough I have a headache," said Lothar, regaining his composure and rubbing his temple.

"Worry about that later. For now I think they're getting ready to charge us."

They can see shadowy figures running left and right but did not fire. Suddenly a Gurkha appeared on Maxis' flank. He struck his kukri on Maxis' head but it became stuck on the leather of the pickelhaube.

"Hands off the pickelhaube!" said Maxis not wasting a second as he plunged his bayonet into the man's neck and heard him croak.

Another Gurkha appeared through the smoke with his kukri raised in the air, but Maxis quickly fired two shots through the impaled soldier and hit the other square in the chest.

Lothar spotted two Indian soldiers charging fast at them with bayonets. He fired the first shot at the one in the back killing him instantly. He blocked the others charging with his rifle, threw him to the ground then finished him off with his revolver.

Maxis continued firing four more shots at more in-coming R.O.B soldiers who were charging into the smoke. They kept firing at anything emerging through the smoke until Maxis' Mondragon suddenly jammed after firing the fifth shot.

"Damn rifle..." Maxis switched to his Bittner pistol and took the bayonet off the rifle.

A couple of Fijians charged toward them with their Totokias raised. "Behind us!" Maxis shouted as he blocked the sharp pointed club with his bayonet then fired the Bittner into the chest. The second Fijian almost struck Maxis but was countered by Lothar's shovel who pushed him back before finishing him with his zig-zag revolver.

"Maxis! The smoke is clearing. We'd better start mov-ing!" said Lothar, as he loaded another mag into the rifle.

"I hear you. Fnd the first cover you see! I'll provide cover and follow!"

"Got it!" Maxis picked up an SMLE and his remaining ammo before taking Kugel ball grenades from Lothar.

The moment the smoke cleared Lothar sprinted ahead while Maxis provided covering fire, mimicking the

"Mad Minute" with the SMLE rifle as he moved. Lothar jumped behind a sandbag emplacement and Maxis followed in. One of the R.O.B.'s sergeants rose from cover.

"That's it, lads, we got Jerry on the run! Let's sweep them away like the mosquitoes they are. Onwards!" shouted the Sergeant.

The short speech inspired what remained of the platoon as they revealed themselves from cover and fire and moved toward the sandbag emplacement then slowly advanced. They unleashed a continuous volley of bullets while some screamed "For King and Country!" or "Fight for the Empire! Fight for your lives!" as they moved. Meanwhile Maxis and Lothar remained behind the sandbag.

"Maxis, I can't do anything with them laying down the fire!" Lothar shouted as sand lands on top of him.

"I'm thinking, I'm thinking! Ah, verdammt (damn it)!" Maxis sounded frustrated as a bullet snapped above him.

Maxis hit his elbow on piece of metal but instead of reacting in pain, it was replaced with an idea as he looked upon what he just hit.

"Lothar, I think I found our solution! Quick help me set it up! Fast, I have an idea."

"Whatever you're going to do, do it fast. I can put this together no problem!" said Lothar as he began to work.

The remaining twenty soldiers pressed the advance still firing until they saw a rifle emerge from the sandbag emplacement. A white cloth waved from its end.

"Cease fire!" shouted one of the soldiers.

The firing stopped and the could hear the sound of them reloading their rifles. Maxis stood up slowly holding the makeshift flag.

"Stay on guard everyone," said an R.O.B. soldier, as the Sergeant stepped forward.

"Surrendering already, I see? About bloody time!"

"Yes, I'm surrendering. We're out of ammo and... hope," said Maxis putting on a disgruntled face.

"Well, well, well...the Germans finally can't stand British might, eh. Heh, what are your conditions, if I may ask, and I'll see if they're...acceptable," the sergeant said as everyone began to laugh.

"Keep going Maxis, they are buying it. Keep talking, I need a little bit more time," Lothar whispered as put in the screws.

"I can offer an abundance of information regarding the K.W.S. Battalion. So much, that I can even tell you what commander Jorgensen does in his spare time," Maxis said, placing his foot on the sandbag.

A small "Ooh" is heard among the soldiers until one said, "Shut your gobs, ya blimey bastards!"

"Alright, is that all? What about you or your friend?" the sergeant asked.

"Oh, my friend is already crying through the socket of this defeat. As for me, in exchange for vital information, I politely request proper treatment at whatever installation you send me and my friend. I expect better living conditions than what you are already providing for my captured brothers. Also cheese and crackers, wine, and a collection of books to read,"

466

Maxis said as his face twitched a little as he tried not to smile.

"Wow, you're good at making up blödsinn (nonsense). Though I wonder, how will they respond?" Lothar whispered.

The R.O.B. sergeant thought for a minute before speaking.

"Hmm...I would have to consult the acting commander of this base with this, but he ran off to do... important things."

"Yeah, like running!" the soldier jokingly said followed by laughter.

"Shut it! Since he is not here to hear your offer and request, I will make the decision for him."

"What will that be?" Maxis asked.

"No."

"No? I'm offering a treasure trove of intel and you are saying no?"

"Well, let me be frank with you. You are Sgt. Maxis, right? The Black Wolf of Mons?"

Maxis remained silent, hiding his clenched fist as his expression changed.

"Oh no, he did not just say that. I better hurry," Lothar thought.

"What's it to you?" Maxis rudely asked.

"A lot of things. For starters, Commander Wellington put a bounty on you for anyone in the Regiment to claim. £500 for Sgt. Maxis, Alive or Dead. Our Russian ally in the east told us they put out a capture order for you by a lovely lass but, after the hell you put my men through,

I think it's better for all of us that you die here. It's a safer course of action. Shame really, for a German you were very polite and not the brooding brute like they said in the war posters. Guess you can't believe everything the government says. Men, get ready to fire!" the Sergeant finished as he signaled the troops and aimed his rifle.

Lothar nudged Maxis' foot, indicating he was ready with some grenades in hand. Maxis then dropped the rifle that carried the white cloth.

"What a pity that you rejected my offer. However, you will not be collecting that reward for you have forfeited your lives," Maxis said calmly as he pulled up his blue scarf slowly.

The entire group began to laugh at Maxis, so much it seemed they had forgotten who they were dealing with.

"Oi, get a load of this! Kraut thinks he's intimidating! Ha, what a riot! Downright pathetic!" mocked an R.O.B. soldier.

"Now, Lothar!" Maxis shouted as the sound of a grenade's click is heard.

From behind the sandbags three kugel ball grenades are thrown high in the air distracting the British and Colonial soldiers. At the same time Lothar pushed up the Vickers machine gun, now locked and loaded.

Maxis manned the gun while Lothar peered over his cover gripping his Madsen M1896 rifle. But the moment the R.O.B Sergeant noticed what was going on, it was too late. Maxis and Lothar opened fire on him the remaining twenty that stood before them.

wiping them out in seconds as some tried to break for cover but failed. A few tried to return fire only to be cut down.

"Hold fire! I think we got them all," said Maxis, as he exhaled and immediately sat down beside the machine gun, pulling down his blue scarf.

"Man, that was exhausting," said Lothar. He too sat down, breathing hard and pulling down his scarf.

"I shouldn't be surprised that my rifle decided to jam in the middle of the battle. I was about ready to throw it to the side and just stick with a British rifle."

"Maxis, I would strongly advise against doing that," Lothar commented, looking over at Maxis.

"Why?"

"In the letter that Fischer sent, he stated to avoid losing any special or prototype weapons that either Heinrich, his protégé Winter, or any Quartermaster has issued to us. He said that in one mission, Graf lost a special combination gun that was issued to him, and Heinrich was ready to ring his neck. Just something you should know," Lothar said as he pulled out his canteen.

"Noted." Maxis grabbed his canteen to take a sip before getting up.

"Come on. There's still one left."

"Are you serious? I thought we wiped them all out."

"Not everyone, Lothar. Also, what's the time?"

"It's five minutes to eleven."

"We're on schedule," Maxis said as he walked and pulled out his Bittner pistol. Lothar loaded a new magazine into his rifle and cocked it.

They moved through the now partially destroyed village where some of the tents were still burning, while others were just nothing but charcoal. The buildings themselves were not in the best shape and bullets holes could be seen in the walls, doors and windows along with some now deceased R.O.B. combatants slumped against the wall. One soldier was hanging out the window, still bleeding.

Everywhere else was littered with the destroyed platoon that had been comprised of regular British troops, Indian soldiers, Fijians, and Gurkhas. All had perished in this bloody battle for Base Camp King George, a camp that now bore the scars of war. Maxis stopped for a second to analyze the body of a fallen soldier's upper shoulder.

"Hmm, it seems they've copied our idea of putting their unit emblems on their uniforms. By the look of it, they seem to have managed to put the Regiment of Britannia's symbol lion head and its little decoration on their patch for easy identification," Maxis pulled out his knife and cut the patch off the soldier's uniform.

"What are you doing?" Lothar asked.

"Taking something back for the higher ups to use, so Battalion can now memorize and identify the enemy a little easier. Anyway, let's keep moving," Maxis put the piece of fabric in his pocket and moved on. They walked around the corner of the storage house where there were a couple of pickle barrels.

"Uh, there's nothing but just barrels of..."

"Shh," Maxis interrupted.

He squatted down and pointed his pistol at the barrel where the pickle brine was seeping out of it and leaving a trail. Lothar quickly understood when he saw it then nodded in agreement. Maxis got up and signaled Lothar to be ready.

"Do it!" Maxis ordered.

Lothar kicked the barrel over and brine, pickles, and 1Lt. Wilson tumbled out. Maxis picked up the First Lieutenant by the scruff of his neck and threw him to the wall then used his forearm to pin the First Lieutenant's neck, tightly controlling him.

"We're going to have a little chat ratte (rat)! If I were you, I start talking, NOW!" Maxis ordered fiercely.

1Lt. Wilson was quivering with fear like a cornered animal.

"Honestly, I didn't think an officer would turn tails and hide in a pickle barrel," said Lothar, containing his chuckles.

"Oh, you think I was going to stick around and let the bloody Black Wolf of Mons kill me?" Wilson responded with panic in his voice. Maxis pressed his forearm against Wilson's neck.

"Why is there a price put on my head, huh?! You'd better answer quick 'cause my patience is running thin!" Maxis angrily demanded.

"I thought it would be obvious for the Black Wolf of..."

Maxis pulled and aimed his Bittner at Wilson; all while a small growl can be heard.

"Ok, ok, don't shoot, please! After the attack on Base Camp Elizabeth and the discovery of your little name tag on the ground, Commander Wellington immediately put a kill/capture order on you. He considers this retribution for the defeat at Mons and Base Camp Elizabeth," Wilson said in a terrified tone.

"Verdammt (Damn it)," Lothar mumbled.

"But why me? I've never met the man," Maxis said.

"It doesn't matter whether you met him or not. You have a reputation."

Maxis stood there thinking, keeping a tight grip on his pistol and maintaining the pressure on Wilson.

"That's all I know...please let me go. Please, for the love of God, don't kill me. Please Black Wolf! I don't want to die!" Wilson began sobbing.

"Go," Maxis said as he let the First Lieutenant go. He dropped to the ground, surprised.

"Go."

"Wha – what, you're actually letting me go?"

"I do not kill unarmed soldiers, let alone cowards. I was never that person back then or now, so I suggest you run along. Go! Beat it!"

Wilson quickly jumped up and started to jog away from the base.

"Faster!"

"I'm going as fast as I..."

Maxis fired his pistol in the air and the First Lieutenant started sprinting as Maxis watched; Lothar standing there chuckling.

"Heh, I didn't think officers could run like..." before he could finish his statement Maxis smacked him on the back of the head.

"Ouch! What the hell was that for?"

"Lothar...what exactly did you do with that name tag that was stuck on my gear back at Ypres?" Maxis asked as he crossed his arms but still holding his pistol.

"Oh, I crumpled it up and tossed it."

"Say that again, but slowly, Lothar."

"I crumpled it up and...oh scheisse (shit). I didn't realize it sooner."

"Lothar, you have just given them info about me from a piece of paper and now I have a target on my head," Maxis said as he holsters his pistol.

"Well, you have a target on your head in Russia as well, but at least it's a capture order," Lothar said as he shrugged his shoulders.

"That can easily change, Lothar."

"Oh...right."

"*Sigh*...Just deploy the flares and I'll gather intel before firing my...oh, you've got to be kidding me!" Maxis pointed to the sky.

"What?...Oh."

They both looked upward and saw an air wing of British planes flying. There was one squadron of Vickers F.B.5 fighters, one squadron of Martinsyde G.100 fighter bombers; leading the air wing was one squadron of Avro 504 fighter bombers. They all bore the Bullseye of the R.F.C. (Royal flying Corp), but next to it was the head of the Griffin. The Regiment of Britannia's "Griffin Squadron" had arrived.

CLEARING THE SKIES

"Quick, get on the pom-pom! They're probably here to provide support for their Regiment. We need to clip them out of the sky before the Blue Tails arrive!" Maxis ordered. The two rushed over to the anti-air guns.

"You remember how to use these, Maxis?" Lothar asked as he loaded the weapon.

"Yeah, it's like a machine gun only bigger."

"Almost. Same rules apply. Avoid overheating them and if they do overheat, it'll take few seconds to cool down."

"Alright, let's get started!" Maxis cocked the pom-pom gun.

Maxis and Lothar rotated the guns toward the sky ready to face the onslaught of planes. They waited until the air wing was near their position; the sound of engines growing louder and louder as they approached.

"Open fire!" yelled Maxis.

They fired the pom-poms at the planes, taking down five before they dispersed. This took Griffin squadron by surprise as they were not expecting anti-air fire from an R.O.B. base. The F.B.5 fighter front gunner pulled out his binoculars and looked, only to see the entire base decimated, and the only occupants were two German soldiers firing on them. The gunner turned to the pilot and yelled.

"Pilot, those aren't our boys down there. Jerry has taken the base and they're using our own weapons against us."

"What?! Are you serious?!" The pilot gave a shocked expression before changing to anger. He then signaled the other planes to tell them of the situation instructing them to form up.

The squadron of the F.B.5 fighters formed up and then immediately dove toward the pom-pom guns with their front gunners opening fire. The second squadron of Avro 504 fighter bombers would come next, followed by the Martinsyde G.100 squadron.

Maxis and Lothar turned their guns toward the incoming fighters, now under fire. They pulled the trigger and fired into the strafing F.B.5s, clipping another six before they broke off.

The second wave was fast approaching as the Avro 504 fighter bombers went into attack speed as they fired the machine gun. Maxis and Lothar fired at the incoming planes. Some of the Avros quickly dodged the fire while others came crashing down. Maxis noticed a little door opening at the bottom of the plane and sees shining objects being dropping.

"Move! They're dropping darts!" Maxis shouted, getting out of the way and taking cover behind the crates.

Lothar moved without question. The sound of the darts making impact could be heard, some bouncing off the pom-pom guns while others were sticking upright in the dirt. After the Avros flew by, Maxis noticed a dart that has pierced the crate.

"Taking you with me," said Maxis, as he pulled the dart from the crate and stuffed it in his bread bag. Before he could return to the pom-pom, a pair of Martinsyde G.100s flew past the anti-air guns dropping their bombs on top of them. The two Vickers QF2 were destroyed, leaving only one.

Maxis signaled Lothar to follow and they double-timed it to the last pom-pom gun. Maxis positioned himself behind the trigger while Lothar loaded the ammo.

"Gun ready!" Lothar shouted.

Maxis fired, taking down three Martinsyde G.100s that were coming for another bombing run. The ground to air battle continued, then Lothar checked his watch after Maxis shot down five Avro 504s.

"We've got five minutes before they arrive, and it looks like we've got more company coming in from the north," Lothar pointed north.

Appearing over the horizon were the reinforcements for Base Camp King George. The AEC B-Type bus, (this time with a second deck), drove along side with a small squadron of motorcycles with side cars, regular motorcycles, two Rolls Royce armored cars, and a Landchester armored car.

"Yeah, I see. I also spotted the Blue Tails coming in from our south," said Maxis as he nodded toward the small formation of AEG C.II planes emerging from the clouds.

"Scheisse (Shit), we're out of time! I'm going to mark the target zones, but I'm going to need cover, Maxis!"

"You got it! LOS (GO), Lothar!" Maxis shouted.

Lothar pulled out the handheld flares and sprinted to the areas he needed to mark, while Maxis kept firing the pom-pom at incoming fighters who were now focused on Lothar.

He made it to the ammo depot, ignited the flare then threw it. Maxis kept firing at the fighters as they tried to strafe Lothar until one of the F.B.5's got on Maxis' blindside and fired at him hitting the ammo box.

The ammo box exploded and he shielded himself from the metal fragments, now hearing that familiar ringing in his ears. Lothar marked the final target zone of the two Lanzia QF3pdr mobile pom-pom guns, while Maxis picked himself up and pulled out the flare gun from his bread bag.

He took one shell from the bandolier around his upper arm and loaded his weapon. A F.B.5 fighter was firing on his position again. Irritated by this, Maxis aimed the flare gun toward the oncoming pusher aircraft and fired. The front gunner dodged the shot and instead it hit the pilot, setting his jacket on fire and causing him to lose control of the plane; they came to crashing into the house in front of Maxis. He reloaded and fired another round, this time toward the sky.

"That went better than expected," Maxis thought as he went to Lothar to regroup.

Meanwhile in the cockpit of the AEG C.II ...

1Lt. Hoffmann and his observer/gunner 2Lt. Schroder were taking notice of the action unfolding in front of them when they spotted the blue flare.

"Well, it seems our little K.W.S. elites decided to start the party without us," 1Lt. Hoffman said sarcastically.

"We're not equipped to engage with those plane hunters, Hoffmann!" said Schroder, concerned.

"I know. However, we still need to deliver the payload and see how this new weapon works. That's why the commander of the Blue Tails ordered the War Hawks to deal with them."

Emerging from their three o'clock (right) was a single Fokker E.II monoplane with its black and red painted body, German crosses, and most important of all a painted blue tail.

The pilot of the monoplane looked toward Hoffmann and pointed toward the action. Hoffmann nodded and gave them the signal to engage. The pilot responded with a thumbs up. The Fokker E.II moved ahead as an entire squadron of Fokker E.IIs appeared in the clouds bearing the same color pattern and moving in at full speed.

"God bless Ltc. Mückenberger and the Warhawks," said Hoffmann.

Back on the ground...

Maxis and Lothar were moving to cover trying to avoid the oncoming fire from the fighters and avoiding getting bombed by the fighter bombers, all while firing back at the planes.

"Maxis, I see a motorcycle we can use to get out of here."

"Then run for it now before those bastards make another pass!" he said as the two sprint to the bike.

At the same time, the R.O.B. convoy stops a mile away from the camp with the armored cars and motorcycles moving to the sides of the buses. The troops riding on the second deck were chatting among themselves when one of them pointed at the battle. The commanding officer moved to the top side to get a good view of the situation. He grabbed his binoculars and saw the two Germans running toward the motorcycle while being fire upon by Griffin squadron.

"What are your orders, Sir?" asked one R.O.B. soldier.

"Men, our base is under attack and Griffin squadron requires our support. Half you, get in there and retake our base from those damned Krauts; the other half stay behind to provide support. Captain Wiltshire, lead the charge!" said the R.O.B Major.

"Yes, Sir! Men of the crown with me!" the captain shouted to his men. The R.O.B troops exited out of the buses at once and formed in front of the vehicles.

The captain stepped forward and pulled out his saber and yelled "fix bayonets" before blowing his whistle. They moved and shouted their war cries as they charged toward the base camp.

Meanwhile back at the base...

Maxis and Lothar made it to the motorcycle, Lothar behind the handlebars and Maxis in the side car. Lothar tried to start up the engine.

"Oh, come on really!" said Lothar in frustration as he tried again to start the bike.

"Hurry up! Those planes could come right at us at any moment!" Maxis said as kept firing his pistol.

"I'm trying! These damned British motorcycles won't turn on. I got it!" Lothar revs up the bike.

"Too late! Incomin!." Maxis shouted as three Avro 504s came right toward them.

All of sudden machine gun fire comes from behind the duo, sending the planes crashing in a ball of flames. The two look to see three Fokker E.II's fly past them.

"That was the Blue Tails?" Maxis asked.

"I think so..." said Lothar, bullets snapping around his head. "Okay, we are going!" Lothar throttled the bike and off they went, exiting the base. As they left, the Regiment of Britannia was now entering the area. The R.O.B. soldiers started firing at them.

Overhead, the battle in the sky was intense and the Prussian Blue Tail's Warhawks were slowly gaining dominance. One by one British planes were falling to the ground. At approximately twelve o'clock the skies were cleared as the small squadron of AEG C.II planes moved in while towing the Siemen-Schuckert Gleiter.

"Schroder, get the modified Siemen-Schuckert Gleiter ready!" ordered Hoffmann.

"On it." Schroder flipped the switch and turned on the small propeller on the Gleiter and established connection to it.

"Testing ailerons. Right side good, left side good, tail wing nominal," Schroder reported as he looked back.

"We are approaching the target zone. Detach tether!" Hoffmann shouted.

"Detaching tether now!" Schroder cut the line, and the Gleiter starts to fly on its own even though it slightly wobbled. He turned back to the dials and guided it below the plane where he can see through the floor panel. The AEG C.II did the same to their Gleiters but controlling them via wireless.

"Alright, bombs away!"

"Bombs away," Schroder repeated after Hoffmann. He guided the flying bomb toward one of the marked zones via the wireless connection, directing it to its intended target.

Back on the ground...

Maxis and Lothar were riding away when Lothar suddenly stopped the motorcycle and looked back at the base.

"Lothar, what are you doing?!"

"Hold fast, Maxis. I want to see this," said Lothar as he looked at the many gliding torpedoes descending from the sky.

Back at base camp King George. An R.O.B. soldier noticed the gliding objects fast approaching.

"What the bloody hell is that?" he demanded.

Wiltshire looked up to see the flying torpedoes approaching and a look of terror formed on his face.

"MOVE! GET THE HELL OUT OF HERE BEFORE IT'S..." He was cut off as a huge explosion erupted in the base camp and then another detonated.

The explosion was loud and thunderous, and fire filled the sky as dirt flew through the air as a result.

Everyone felt the force and vibrations from the impact of Siemen-Schuckert Gleiter, but never expected how powerful the ordnance might be. The entire village and the Regiment of Britannia base was now nonexistent, nothing but a crater.

"YEAH! WOOHOO! That's outrageous, man! What a spectacular show of force! Ha ha!" Lothar cheered.

"Wow, that packs a punch, indeed." Maxis said, looking with awe.

"Hoo, that made my day. Alright, let's go home."

As they drove off the squadron leader flew by, close to Hoffmann's plane. The pilot pointed toward the motorcycle and Hoffmann responded with a signal indicating "protect them" and "lead them".

The pilots nod as Hoffmann gave the ok sign; the squadron leader descended, signaling his squadron what to do.

"Hoffmann, what's the verdict on the Gleiters?" Schroder asked.

"I can safely say that we will be using this new weapon on our planes, zeppelins, and hopefully, the new bombers that will be coming soon. Returning to base!"

"I hear that!" Schroder said with a smile.

The squadron and their armed escort flew off into the clouds disappearing from sight.

On the ground, the commanding officer watched in horror at the complete annihilation of Base Camp King George along with Cpt. Wiltshire and half of the company. Nothing but smoke, fire, and total devastation. He looked through his binoculars again to see a motorcycle with a sidecar driving away in the distance.

"Send the armored cars and motor bikes after those two! NOW!" order the commanding officer, his anger rising.

The two Roll Royces, Landchester, two solo bikes, and two motorcyclist armed with Vickers machine guns in their sidecars drove after the two Germans.

The two were admiring the countryside, riding and taking in the breeze and Maxis processing in his thoughts while he reloaded his pistol.

"Great, just great...not only the British will be gunning for me now, but I also have to watch my step if I'm operating in the Eastern Front. "The lovely lass"? Could they be referring to Arina? If so, then I really have to be careful which means no more close calls, though that tends to happen regardless. It's interesting that they seem to formulate a communication with each other even though they have different agendas despite being a part of the Triple Entente," Maxis pondered.

"Hey what are you thinking?" Lothar asked.

"It's...nothing."

"Come on now. I know that tone when I hear it. Just tell me."

"It's this whole thing about the price on my head here and in Russia. Them knowing me and the nickname that I resent so much, I thought I had left it behind," Maxis spoke, resting on the edge of the side car.

"Maxis, you're going to have tell me sooner or later where you obtained that nickname. You've been acting on edge when someone even mentions it. Well, except me, but that's because I heard from some drunk soldier who thinks he knows. That was right before you showed him what floating stars look like with one punch to the head," Lothar recalled as he made a left turn.

"I don't react toward you because you don't press the matter. But how about this? If we make it to the end of this year or get in a life/death situation, then I'll tell you, Lothar. Deal?"

"What? You added another condition to agree to on top of the whole surviving this terrible war we're in?" Lothar asked.

"Well then, at least till the end of the year or close to it."

"You just like keeping people waiting, don't you? Fine. It's a deal then."

They clasped their lower forearms Viking style and shook on it. A bullet whistled by and Maxis looked behind them.

"We've got company! Tommies to the rear. Just out run them. Los, los (Go, go)!" shouted Maxis as he pulled out his pistol once again.

Lothar turned the motorcycle to the left and into a heavily wooded area, but the motorcyclist follows them in. Maxis continued firing but could not directly hit his mark as Lothar kept swerving the bike to avoid trees, logs, and bushes as they rode. One of the solo rider's managed to get next to them on the left side and pulled out a Webley automatic pistol, aiming at Lothar's head. He fired a round, but it was deflected off his Gaede helmet leaving a mark.

Maxis grabbed the large piece of shrapnel that was still stuck on Lothar's tornister and threw it into the spokes of the enemy motorcycle, causing the bike to flip and throwing the screaming soldier to the dirt.

"Good thinking," said Lothar.

"We're not out of the woods yet!" Another motorcycle rolled up from behind.

"Keep it steady, Lothar!" Maxis took aim and fired at the gas tank. The bike went up in flames as the rider jumped into the bushes.

A motorcycle with a sidecar started gaining on them with the machine gunner firing. Lothar made an immediate left turn, almost tipping the motorcycle tipping, but Maxis countered it by leaning in the opposite direction. The R.O.B. rider performed the same maneuver but failed to time it correctly causing him to fall. The last motorcycle took an alternate route and managed to pull up to Lothar's right side.

"Oh no, we're not doing this again!" said Lothar, pulling out his "Zigzag" revolver and aiming it at the rider before the gunner could swing the machine gun.

Lothar fired a shot into the rider's head, killing him instantly. The R.O.B. slumped over and the gunner tried to take control of the handlebar before they hit a random tree and sent the gunner flying.

"Hopefully that's the last of them," said Maxis as he holstered his pistol.

They exited the forest and returned to the dirt road. Immediately they again came under fire from the armored cars that were also on the road.

Lothar tried to outrun them, but it was no use since their machine guns were trained on them. Bullets whistled and snapped around them, even hitting the bike itself, but they kept their heads down.

"Verdammt (damn it), I can't shake them!" Lothar exclaimed.

Suddenly there was a barrage of machine gun fire from above causing the gunners on the armored cars to cease fire as they started rotating to see where the attack came from.

In a matter of seconds, five Fokker E. IIs flew past the armored cars then came around again. One of them flew over a Rolls Royce armored car and blew it up by dropping a bomb from the side of the plane by hand. Another plane flew over the other Rolls Royce armored car, but the bomb landed two feet to the right causing the car to spin before toppling over.

The crew of the toppled vehicle left through the back door and made a run for the hill, leaving the Landchester armored car alone. The driver turned it around and tried to retreat before being bombed by the Warhawks. Maxis watched the whole thing and let out a sigh of relief as their pursuers were no more.

"Maxis, have I ever told how much I appreciate the Prussian Blue Tails? Because that's two times that they have saved my hide, and a first for you," said Lothar.

"Heh, you think?"

The squadron leader flew by their motorcycle about twenty feet from their right and waved to get their attention. Maxis and Lothar waved back but noticed the squadron leader was trying to tell them something via hand signals. He waved hand while pointing in a circle before pointing toward himself.

"Maxis, do you know what he is saying?" Lothar asked.

"I think he's saying regroup...on me."

The squadron leader pointed at himself again then pointed forward. He then pointed at Maxis and then again pointed forward.

"Hmm...I think he's saying, 'where I go, you go.'" I think he knows an alternate path for returning to our lines and wants us to follow them," said Maxis.

"Okay, then."

Maxis gave a thumbs up, and the squadron leader nodded with a smile. The other Fokker E. IIs joined their squadron leader in formation and maintained a normal speed while Lothar followed them.

The travel back was rather quick since they were on proper transportation. The last obstacle they must overcome in order to complete their mission was getting past the French. By three in the afternoon the distant sound of artillery fire could be heard and the sight of smoke was seen on the horizon.

The squadron went left, and Lothar followed where they could see opening in the trench line. It was a gap between the trenches where the road leads and was protected by a small guard unit and barricades. The squadron moved ahead and opened fire at the barricade scaring the guards off. They dropped their last bombs destroying the barricade in the process, however, it alerted the French in the area. It did not matter as Lothar stepped on the gas. The moment they passed through several French soldiers looked over the trench to see what the commotion was, but didn't notice anything.

They rode through no man's land following the Warhawks until they flew ahead. The motorcycle eventually broke down after running through the mud.

They disembarked and marched the rest of the way back to the German Trenches. The sentry spotted them as they approached and notified his NCO. A small squad of German riflemen were sent out to escort Maxis and Lothar back quickly.

"What on earth were you two doing out there?" the NCO asked very sternly. Maxis and Lothar didn't say a word as they walked past him.

"We are too tired and exhausted to even give our excuse on why we were out there. Then again, it's no one's business to know what we were doing there in the first place," Maxis thought to himself.

"Hey, I was talking to you, Soldaten (soldiers)!"

The NCO followed them, this time with his guards. When they reached the rear line there were three Opel halbgepanzerter Wagen light armored cars. The NCO and his guards were stopped by several soldiers wearing their army issued trench coats and field caps.

"What is the meaning of this!?" said the NCO.

"Soldat, stay calm. You're interfering on a military matter that is above your paygrade. Return to your post," said the soldier.

The NCO looks at the upper sleeve of the soldier's trench coat and saw the symbol of an eagle with decorations around and below was a little ghost symbol.

"Thank Gott, for the Geist platoon, eh," said Lothar.

"You can say that again."

A Geist Platoon agent walks up to them.

"Cpl. Lothar and Sgt. Goody-Goody, long time no see," said Stefan with cheerful attitude.

"Hey, Stefan," said Lothar.

"Private," said Maxis sternly.

Stefan walked toward the door of the armored car but before opening it he said, "Major Reinhard is waiting for you inside along with a special guest."

"Who's the guest?" asked Lothar.

"Now, I wouldn't ruin the surprise." A smile appeared on Stefan's face as he opened the door.

Maxis goes in first and took a seat. Lothar came in after and turned to left and saw Major Reinhard. Sitting next to him was Crown Prince Wilhelm.

"Sirs!" Lothar stood up straight giving a sharp salute, but at the same time accidently ripped the canvas roof of the armored car with his head. Maxis tried to hold back his laughter, covering his mouth so not to reveal a smile. Crown Prince Wilhelm gave a small chuckle and smiled.

"No need for formalities, Corporal. Please take seat and relax, I can see you are tired," said Major Reinhard with his hand to his face in embarrassment.

"Yes, Sir. Sorry, Sir," said Lothar as he took off his Gaede helmet and sat down. The armored cars started their engines and drove away.

"Gentlemen, allow me to introduce you to Crown Prince Wilhelm, Commander of the 5th Army. Before I explain why he is here, first things first. I must congratulate you two on another job well done. Not only have the Prussian Blue Tails reported on the success of the new weapon, they also took some considerable photographs before and after. I can also tell you fought really hard seeing the destruction which occurred before the deployment of the flying torpedoes," Major Reinhard showed the photos of the battle at Base Camp before and after the airstrike along with a photo of the large fiery explosion.

"It's similar to what your old squad mates have done in this photo during a full-scale French assault before they were redeployed elsewhere," Reinhard said, then showed another photograph. The photo showed a trench line. Outside of the trench were bodies of French soldiers, some hanging on the barbed wire, others near the edge of the trench. Inside the cross-section were more bodies, including some Germans, but mostly French soldiers who were scattered all over the place.

At the center of it all were eight K.W.S. soldiers. The left side of the trench showed Fischer leaning against the wall smoking, Graf holding his bloody mace, Kraus holding a French officer's hat, and Kruger aiming his rifle over the parapet. On the right Weber was sitting, König was holding a French Chauchat LMG, Müller was sleeping, and Brandt was sitting down looking disgruntled. There were bullet casings all over the place, their bayonets and uniforms bloody, and their weapons smoking. At the corner of the trench was a regular German soldier who had a look that mixed of shock and horror at the scenery.

"Anyway, besides the photographs, I still need a debrief so I can send in a report back home. Now, as to why the Crown Prince is here. I think it's better that he speak for himself.

"Soldaten (Soldiers), I come to you today with a special award given to your battalion. The Kaiserliche Waffen Spezialisten have performed beyond expectation, for that I grant this Totenkopf (Death's head) badge, not only to the battalion, but for you two to bear for your gallantry, bravery, and your march into the fires of hell in this war of modern times. Congratulation men, you are an exemplary model to all our allies in the Central Powers across the world." Crown Prince Wilhelm handed the Totenkopf badge to Maxis and Lothar then shook their hands.

"There is still one more thing left to give, but as I recall, it's for the Sergeant," said Reinhard as he looked to the crown prince.

"Oh, yes. Thank you for reminding me, Major," Crown Prince Wilhelm spoke as he revealed a small purple bag with a golden crown symbol.

"Sgt. Maxis, you have quite the reputation in your unit, along with your friend of course. I also know about the nickname you go by, though I heard that you resent it. I may be the next in line to the throne, but I'm also a gentleman, and for that I must ask you before presenting this. May I have your permission to say your given title as I address you?" the Crown Prince asked with a solemn look about him.

"Of course, Sir. Anything for the House of Hohenzollern," Maxis said respectfully.

"Excellent. Sgt. Maxis, the Black Wolf of Mons, the hero of Belgium, now sits before me. On the recommendation from your commander of the Battalion, I present this to you." Wilhelm presented an ornamental front plate that is usually attached to the front of a pickelhaube, but this one was different.

"This was made specifically for your Pickelhelm. The spread-winged eagle remains the same but, in the center, is a Totenkopf. I was informed that you refuse to wear the covering on your Pickelhelm in battle, leaving yourself exposed, but still you come out victorious. Take heed we did not make this for just anyone, for there is no purpose if you go into battle wearing this and then cover it. Now wear your badge with pride and continue making your Vaterland (Fatherland) proud." Wilhelm handed the metal plate to Maxis and again gave him a firm handshake. The armored car stopped gently.

"Well, here is my stop. I bid you farewell and good luck. It was nice to meet the Black Wolf that I've heard so much about," Crown Prince Wilhelm bid, as he gave a salute to them before leaving the car and closing the door. The armored car moved forward again.

"Now that's over. After you debrief, you'll be heading back to Valhalla Base for some rest before redeployment. We have a lot of plans going on in the east and I'm putting in a recommendation to the commander for you two to go over there," Reinhard finished as he lit his cigar.

Maxis and Lothar give a firm "Yes, Sir!" before they slumped back into their seats and enjoyed the ride to the train station.

"Oh, Sir, before I forget. Here." Maxis handed him the dart that he picked up during the battle and the R.O.B. patch. The Major took it and analyzed it.

"I'm not surprised they would use a weapon like this. Silent and deadly. I'll be sure to also show the patch to the commander. Good job bringing this, Sergeant, especially since now we can properly identify them," said Reinhard, letting out another plume of smoke.

CHAPTER 33

BEARING THE BAD NEWS

Meanwhile, in the Office of Commander Wellington at the R.O.B. HQ in Amiens...

Wellington was at his desk filling out paperwork, a glass of brandy on his desk, and smoking a pipe when he heard a knock on the door.

"Come in," said Wellington.

The door opened and 1Lt. Wilson walked in.

"First Lieutenant Wilson, it is good to see you. What do you have to report? Uh, the bloody hell is that wretched smell and...?" Commander Wellington looked up to see 1 Lt. Wilson's uniform slightly tattered and smelling foul.

"That would be the pickle brine...Sir." 1Lt.Wison responded nervously.

"What happened?" Wellington asked.

"There has been an incident at Base Camp King George..."

"Go on," Wellington prompted, getting up slowly.

"It's been destroyed, Sir"

Wellington slowly removed the pipe from his mouth and put it down, as his hand began shaking. A stern look appeared on his face as he slowly turned red.

Wilson continued to explain from beginning to end the recent events from the attack on the base to its destruction along with half a R.O.B. company and Griffin Squadron's defeat in the skies.

"So...they used a flying bomb of sorts that annihilated the base while dominating the skies. It sounds almost ridiculous, Lieutenant, close the door all the way shut," Wellington ordered.

"Yes, Sir."

As the door closed, muffled shouting could be heard.

"How the bloody hell did you let this happen? You hid in a damned pickle barrel! So many lives lost at the hands of K.W.S. and worst of all, the Black Wolf of Mons was in the middle of all this! And he's still walking the earth!?" said Wellington, slowly going into a rage, slamming his fist on the desk then walking to his chair.

During his meltdown, throughout the five-story building the sound of Commander Wellington's yelling could be heard almost clearly and the military staff and civilians trembled with fear at the explosive reaming out that their commander was delivering.

2Lt.McManus walked into the building holding some documents and went to the front desk.

"Pardon me, ma'am, is the commander in today?" 2Lt. McManus asked calmly.

Before she could answer, a muffled "Raahhh" echoed in their hearing, followed by glass shattering as a chair hit the ground outside. Everyone but McManus turned to look as the crowd panicked at the scene.

"Never mind, I got my answer. Thank you, kindly madam," McManus said as he walked into the elevator and pushed a button.

McManus opened the doors walked out of the elevator. Down the hall, he saw Wilson, who waved when he noticed McManus approaching.

"Before you say anything, lad, let me hand this in," said McManus as he walked into the commander's office. He saw the commander cleaning shards of glass before he turned to McManus.

"Here's the full report for the destroyed base and combat reports from Griffin squadron. I'll also be sure to call in the craftsman to replace the window and the quartermaster to give you a new chair, Sir." McManus said, putting the documents on the desk.

"Thank you, McManus. You're dismissed," said Wellington, placing the shards in the trash.

2Lt. McManus saluted before quickly leaving the room and met with Wilson.

"Alright lad, come on. Let's get your uniform cleaned up. I'm sure that nice lass down the street would be happy to clean it. After that we go straight to the officers club to get it out of your system boy-o," he said as he put his on Wilson's shoulder.

"A stout would be nice or a glass of water like you usually drink," said Wilson in a low tone.

CHAPTER 33 • BEARING THE BAD NEWS

"Atta boy. Let's get going while you tell your version of what happened at the base camp," said McManus as they entered the elevator.

The Second Battle of Artois ended on June 18, 1915, with the battle lasting six weeks. The French Army suffered tremendous loss of life, over one hundred thousand casualties with very few gains in their campaign.

Historical Context: The Totenkopf badge was an award that dates to the Kingdom of Prussia during the Napoleonic wars, mostly to a famous cavalry unit and it stayed in use until the Great War. The award was given to troops who displayed gallantry and bravery during dangerous times in war and was considered a great honor. The German Empire would continue giving out this award until the end of the Great War.

CHAPTER 34

ARGONNE

June 26, 1915

Over at the decimated parts of the Argonne Forest, in the trench, Cpl. Weber, Pvt. Konig, Pvt. Müller, and Pvt. Brandt waited as rain poured down, along with lightning and the boom of thunder. The other soldiers were preparing themselves and loading their bolt action rifles. An officer stood and stared at his watch, holding his whistle.

"Alright, remember the plan. We go in while providing support to the Crown Prince's forces. Once we get through the French defense, locate and eliminate their HQ dugout. If we can't take the sector, then we'll cause mass confusions for the enemy," said Weber as he flipped the safety off his Mauser C98 self-loader.

"What if we run into the R.O.B. or the Hasardeux Division?" Müller asked as he shook the water off his C98.

"Then we deal with them like any other foe, my silent friend. With extreme prejudice!" Konig answered hardily, rainwater dripping off his Gaede helmet.

"I don't understand why we are fighting in this sector. We're much better than supporting some noble's planned assault. We'll end up dead like the rest that went before us," Brandt said in a resentful tone. Everyone looked at him with a disapprovingly.

"Watch your tone, Brandt. Our orders didn't come from the Crown Prince, it was from Major Reinhard," Weber retorted toward Brandt. Müller moved in close to Brandt and spoke.

"And for your information, the assault was planned by the Crown Prince and General Knobelsdorf."

"I have something to tell you as well, Brandt," continued Konig.

"What's that?"

"Just shut up."

"Pfft!" Brandt blew off everyone's comments.

"Hush, all of you. Looks like it's time," said Weber, as he pointed at the officer who was climbing out of the trench, then crouched down.

The officer shouted, "Get ready, men," and the troops fixed bayonets and waited near or on the fire step.

"It's time. Konig, I need you to lay down cover fire once we reach the enemy trench. Müller, keep those flares on you tight because we'll receive support from two planes from the Prussian Blue Tails, so be ready to throw them. Brandt, just do your job and provide covering fire when we're in the middle of no man's land. If in any case the mission backfires, I'll fire the flare gun to signal our guns to open up on the whole sector. Get ready!" Weber finished.

The squad checked their weapons. Müller, with his modified Mondragon rifle with a thirty-round magazine, Konig with his Madsen, and Brandt armed with a captured Hotchkiss M1909 Benét-Mercié LMG. There was a large artillery barrage that lasted for a few seconds.

"Vorwärts Männer (Forward men)!" he shouted then blew the trench whistle. The soldiers gave out their war cry as they went over the top and charged. Weber's squad followed, staying together. Konig fired his Madsen while the squad advanced.

The thumping sound of their boots was heard and with mud splashing all over the place, they passed over the smoking craters and shell holes in no man's land as they charged at a steady speed. They barely made half a mile before bullets started flying past them and French machine guns opened fired.

"Get down!" Weber shouted as he quickly went prone in the mud.

The rest of the squad took cover as rows of German soldiers fell, screaming in pain or gasping while the rest pressed forward. Soon, French artillery fired into the sector killing more men, bogging them down.

"Brandt, covering fire now! Suppress that MG!" Weber ordered as he fired his rifle.

"God, you sound like that damned Sergeant!" Brandt said with insolence as he fired the LMG.

"Come on guys, let's move!" Weber ordered again.

The squad low-crawled through the mud halfway to the French trench line with cover fire from Brandt; then they stopping and started crawling. The intense fire was now above them while more German troops perished in the line of fire, screaming in pain or yelling while charging toward the trench.

"Squad, provide covering fire! Brandt and Konig, pump out some more lead!" Weber yelled.

The squad provided supporting fire for the advancing troops, all except Brandt, who was covering his head as the intense fire was getting to him.

"This is a nightmare! I told this would happen, I told you!" Brandt freaked out.

"Shut it Brandt! Here comes our fly boys!" Weber shouted as he looked to the sky.

Two German planes with painted blue tails entered the air space. An Otto C.I pusher base biplane and the Otto C.II regular biplane came into view, both with their gunners at the front. Gunners wielded the MG14 as well as some bombs; the same for the Otto C.II.

"Defense is too strong! Retreat!" a German officer cried out.

Already the assault was halted and the majority of the German troops began to retreat and regroup. However, that left the squad alone in no man's land along with a few other soldiers who didn't fallback.

"Now, soldiers! Counterattack them as they retreat! For France!" shouted a French officer as he stood atop of the trench waving his saber and pistol. A chorus of war cries erupted as men wearing horizon blue uniforms went over the top, their faces grimaced as ready for war.

"Müller! Throw a flare, NOW! Konig and Brandt, watch the flanks!" Weber frantically ordered.

Müller reached into his bread bag and pulled out a flare then quickly ignited it. He threw it hard toward the center of the field at the advancing French troops.

Konig and Brandt covered the flanks and opened fired at the advancing French troops. Weber fired at the front with Müller soon joining him. They cut down French troops all around while the flare glowed bright, emitting smoke.

The French attacked in mass, not spreading apart. Despite their losses, they were pressing on, failing to notice the German squad firing from prone position or the flare that they were passing. They kept passing the squad as they advanced toward the German trenches.

The planes noticed the flare and got into an attack formation with one behind the other. As the rumbling of the engines was heard, they swooped in with the gunners firing their machine guns at the advancing French, killing dozens. The flare fizzled out, but the French continued their advance until Müller threw another.

A second time around the Otto C.I went in first, flying by, gunning down the enemy. Then came the Otto C II. By now the German machine guns at the trench line were already firing. The French were forced to retreat to their trench while the Germans had yet to contemplate what happened to their counterattack. A German soldier rose up and shouted out.

"Come on! This is our chance to...*aack!*" The soldier was cut down by French machine guns as they opened fired again and artillery.

"Squad! Grenades, now!" Weber ordered. Everyone took out their stick grenades and threw them at the MG nest, blowing it up. Müller readied another flare and threw it toward the trench.

The Otto C.II flew in as the pilot slowed the plane down. Once he was passing over a large group of French soldiers who were in their trench, he pulled the lever, and the small compartment opened. The aerial darts fell out and struck their targets and several soldiers screamed in pain as they fell to the ground.

"Los geht's (Let's go)!" said Weber as he and the rest of the squad moved in. They jumped into the trench with Weber and Müller checking the cross-section before the rest jumped in.

"Mein Gott (My God)! Such cruelty. First gas and now this?" Brandt said in shock as he observed the French dead all around him with darts protruding from their uniforms.

"Can it, Brandt. The French were the ones who used them on us and even the Brits started using them. So, this is cosmic payback. Sweep the Trench! I want that HQ dugout found." Weber gave out the command.

"You're starting to sound like the sarge, Webs," said Müller with a smirk, and with Konig giving a thumbs up.

"Compliment taken, now move!"

The squad moved through the first trench line with Weber taking point and Müller behind him. The two MG specialists watched the rear. German troops would slowly join them in the trench though in a smaller number while the rest had yet to realize their comrade's success.

The planes flew around like hawks, taking small opportunities to harass the French. The French troops stayed in their dugouts or tried to shoot the planes before being met with bullets from the K.W.S. squad or the planes. Eventually the planes had to withdraw to refuel back at base.

The squad entered the second trench line. There they engaged in a small skirmish with the remaining French troops and officers before they were cut down like the rest with volley of intense fire.

"Trench clear!" shouted Konig.

"Alright, let's find that HQ dugout. Toss grenades before you go in but be mindful of medical facilities," said Weber as he pointed at a dugout with red cross symbol. The squad began to search, throwing grenades in and blowing out any stragglers.

"Found it!" Konig shouted out to the rest as he tossed a grenade toward HQ. The explosions cause the cloth to fly out.

He moved in afterward. Inside the HQ dugout was a mess with paperwork scattered all over but the phone lines and telegraph remained intact. A French Officer popped up from behind an overturned table, revolver in hand and fired at Konig's head. The bullet bounced off the Gaede helmet he was wearing. Konig returned fire, killing the officer.

"Now it's clear. Good thing I wear this mighty helm," said Konig as he tapped his Gaede helmet as the rest of the squad came in.

"Gute Arbeit (Good work). Now collect any intelligence or documents essential to our plans," directed Weber.

The squad looked around until Konig noticed low volume chatter on the telephone line that was left hanging. He picked it up and listened while the squad gathered folders, orders, photographs, and maps.

"That's all of it, Webs. Come on, Zweifler (Complainer). We need to ensure our exit is clear," said Müller as he headed outside, followed by Brandt.

"Konig, set the charge." Weber's order was ignored as Konig was listening to the phone. "Konig!" he said again.

"Weber, I can hear the French talking. They are sending in reinforcements! The Spécial Hasardeux Division are sending their best!" Konig reported with a worried tone.

"That's why we have to go! Now plant the charge!" Weber shouted.

Konig set his tornister down and pulled out a can shape bomb. He set it on the floor and lit the fuse. The bomb bell started ringing loudly.

"Verdammt (Damn it)! Why do these things make such noise?" Weber asked a rhetorical question.

Outside, Müller and Brandt watched the cross-section of the trench. Unaware what was going on inside, they saw a few German troops moving about. The two heard the ringing inside as Konig and Weber leave the HQ dugout. Suddenly, the sound of rapid gun fire erupted from afar and Müller turned to look at Weber.

"Webs, that gun fire...they sound like..."

"Selbstladers (Self-loaders)! We need to hold here until the bomb finishes counting down. We can't let the S.H.D. make it inside to defuse the thing. Squad, hold down this position!" Weber ordered. Everyone quickly reloaded their weapons and stood fast.

"We're all doom," Brandt muttered.

A German soldier ran up to them in panic.

"The French are wielding machine guns and... AAAAH!" The soldier is shot in the back multiple times.

A squad of heavily armed French soldiers armed with Chauchat-Sutter CS M1913 LMGs and Halle rifles. On the other side of the cross-section, Brandt witnesses a group of German troops charging across, but they were met with a wave of flames, incinerating them.

Appearing on the top of the trench and moving across it were French soldiers with makeshift gas masks and goggles wielding a Schilt n° 3 Lance Flamme (Flamethrower). They were accompanied by a rifle squad armed with Label rifles. Brandt was outright horrified. The French all turned and saw the K.W.S. squad and heard the incessant ringing.

"It's the S.H.D.!" Konig shouted.

"K.W.S.! K.W.S.! Take them out!" said the S.H.D. soldier rapidly.

Both sides took cover. Immediately gun fire erupted in the cross-section and bullets whistled and snapped all around.

"Don't let them destroy the HQ dugout!" shouted the French flame trooper as he shot his flame thrower. The fire traveled across the cross-section fo the trench but barely hit its targets. The bomb warning rings louder and louder until it sounds continually.

"We need move out of the blast range! Brandt, toss a smoke grenade!" Weber ordered and Brandt obeys and throws it toward the LMG and self-loading riflemen. Weber turned around and fired a shot at the flame trooper. The flame trooper unleashed flames again but a bullet struck the gas tank causing an explosion and thus cleared the way.

"Come on. Let's go!" Weber led the way while Konig fired from the hip, covering their escape.

The S.H.D. squad moved in through the smoke when the bomb's timer hit zero. The explosion destroyed the HQ dugout and partially wiped out the S.H.D. squad, and created a large crater in the French trench line.

Weber and company ran through the trenches, making turns, trying to make their way back to no man's land. The remaining German troops fell back shouting "Französische verstärkung (French reinforcement)!" as rifle fire was heard all around. They arrived at the first trench line.

"Up the ladder, I'll cover you," said Weber.

Weber watched the rear while the squad carefully climbed. Everyone made it up and started moving back to their own trench line. Weber readied to climb up when he heard a commotion down at the cross-section of the trench. He saw a German soldier with his hand raised as he walked back.

"I don't have a gun, can't you see? I surrender!" the German soldier begged. Weber took his rifle and aimed then he spotted a hand holding a revolver sticking out of the corner. Immediately he was shot in the head and Weber's heart sank as the young soldier fell on his back, dead. Suddenly the sound of loud footsteps could be heard.

Appearing from around the corner was a French soldier. He wore the Horizon blue uniform, sleeves rolled partially revealing his buffed forearms, and chest armor with an inscription that said "fidèle jusqu'au bout, Toujours prêt (faithful to the end, always ready)". His face was covered in a yellow scarf and his eyes were completely protected by goggles with a leather cover around them. The armor on his shoulders went down to the elbow, and a French skull cap with a stocking cap underneath covered his head. He also wore webbing with ammo pouches and a pistol holster, and was armored on both legs. He looked down and fired three more rounds at the dead soldier. Weber took aim and pulled the trigger. But he only heard a *click*.

" Mist (crap), don't tell me it jammed?!" he muttered to himself, looking at his rifle.

When he looked up, the armored soldier was staring at him through his cold tinted goggles. The feeling of terror and fear started to rise and Weber felt the strands of his hair stand on end. The soldier moved slowly toward him and he pulled out a long trench club. Weber pulled out his Walther Model 6 and fired, but the bullets bounced off the armor and the armored soldier laughed and began to sing slowly.

"Frère...Jacques...Frère...Jacques...Dormez vous?"

As he sang the nursey rhyme, the soldier knocked over an ammo box then whacked a lantern as he approached, causing a small fire. Weber holstered the pistol and climbed the ladder. The sound of footsteps grew louder as he went over the parapet and ran, and as he looked back he saw the soldier was gaining on him.

Weber ran like hell across no man's land and could hear loud thumping before the sound of puddles splashing. He pulled out the flare pistol while he ran but then he felt a sharp blunt strike on his back knocking him flat on his face into the mud.

He quickly turned on his back to see the armored soldier standing a couple feet away...laughing as more French appeared behind him in the far distance. His trench club was doused in red blood and dripping.

"Now you are going to die," he threatened in a menacing tone.

Weber aimed the flare pistol at him and the armored soldier laughed until Weber aimed at the sky and fired the flare. The round glowed bright through the burning smoke, then a thunderous noise erupted.

"Hmph, Intelligent Allemand (Smart German)," the armored soldier said as he looked up.

Weber got up and ran again. When he looked back, he could see the armored soldier returning to his trench in a calm manner while all other French and S.H.D. soldiers ran back in a panic, shouting out to one another as the whistle of incoming shells resounded over the entire sector.

Weber made it to the trench and dove in, the bombardment now behind him. Breathing hard, the pain in his back grew worse. He put his hand to feel the wound only to realize the wound trailed down his back, like a claw slash from a wild beast.

"Webs! You made it. Mein Gott (My God), what happened to you?" asked Müller as he looked at the wound.

"I think I just faced one of the S.H.D.'s best...a real monster," Weber said, sounding very exhausted.

"We need to get you to the medic or Trench Surgeon. Come on, we'll tell it to the Major later. One more thing." Müller said and helped Weber up then escorted him to the medical tent.

"What?" Weber asked in an exhausted tone.

"You finally actually started acting like a leader. The Sergeant would be impressed," Müller said with a smirk.

"Really? I guess learning from the best is beneficial," Weber remarked as they entered the medical dugout.

Next day...

Weber and the others were back in the Ragnarök base. Inside debrief tent they filled out their forms. Soft footsteps were heard and they look up as Major Reinhard entered the scene. They all put their forms down and stood to attention, giving a quick salute. The Major saluted back and spoke.

"As you were, troops," he started. Everyone sat back down and paid attention to the major as he lit a cigar. He smoked for a second then let out puff of smoke that filled the room with the pungent smell of cigar.

"The Crown Prince was impressed by your actions in the Argonne. What you did will certainly keep the S.H.D. and the French confused for a while. We have plans that are in motion in the East and soon I may have to call upon you along with your Kameraden (comrades). As much would like to put your bunch back together like at Ypres with Sergeant Maxis..."

"Pfft..." Brandt scoffed.

"Corporal! Discipline your troops!" Major Reinhard yelled with thunder. Straightaway Weber and even Konig slug Brandt in the stomach.

"As I was saying, just be prepared for redeployment when the time comes. Dismissed!" Reinhard strode out of the tent.

The attack in the Argonne on June 26th by Crown Prince Wilhelm lasted for a week. The fighting was intense, but the French held the line. Afterwards the attack was called off, however, in the Eastern front the Germans were not being held back as they plowed through the Russian lines quickly and with stunning results. What happened next sent shock waves to the Triple Entente Alliance.

What challenges await Maxis, Lothar, and their comrades in the Eastern Front in this Great War? What significant events lie ahead of them in the home of the Imperial Russian Bear? One thing is certain, they will not be spending their time during the war inside a ... Trench.

To be continued...